I0736983

The Rain Drops

Boniface Ossai

The Rain Drops

Boniface Ossai

Paperback Edition First Published in the United Kingdom in 2018 by aSys Publishing

Second Edition published in the United Kingdon in 2023 by aSys Publishing

Copyright © Boniface Ossai

Boniface Ossai has asserted his rights under 'the Copyright Designs and Patents Act 1988' to be identified as the author of this work.

All rights reserved.

No part of this book may be reproduced or transmitted in any form or by any means, electronic, mechanical, photocopying, recording, or otherwise, without prior written permission from the Author.

Disclaimer

This is a work of fiction. Names, characters, businesses, places, events and incidents are either the products of the author's imagination or used in a fictitious manner. Any resemblance to actual persons, living or dead, or actual events is purely coincidental.

ISBN: 978-1-913438-69-2

This book is dedicated in loving memory of my brother Felix Ossai. Felix will be deeply missed by the whole family.

This book wouldn't have been a success without the effort of my wife Nkem, who worked tirelessly to ensure the success of this book, not to forget my children Ikechukwu and Ifeanyichukwu.

Finally, a big thanks to my friend Mark Campbell for his immense contribution towards the success of this book.

CHAPTER

ONE

The suicide note

It was a pretty humid morning, and the street was quiet as neighbours peeped through their windows, watching with a bated breath as LAPD officers hurtled one after another into the home of Harry Crow.

The Los Angeles Police Department is investigating the death of Harry Crow, and at the moment, the police didn't suspect any foul play in Harry's death as they await his autopsy result to determine how to proceed with the investigation. However, the scene of the incident was preserved, and two days later, the autopsy result showed Harry Crow died from the ingestion of ricin. The autopsy result automatically meant the LAPD officers are looking at a possible murder investigation. While this investigation morphed into a homicide investigation at its budding stage, the LAPD had to pass this case onto the FBI, particularly now that they're dealing with a possible homicide because that's the FBI's jurisdiction.

Eddy Taylor, the head of the FBI unit in Los Angles received a phone call and was briefed about the investigation. Lieutenant

Busco informed Eddy Taylor that Harry's body was discovered by a friend with whom he was planning a holiday together. His friend said Harry wasn't picking up his phone, so he decided to check on him but by the time he got to his door and knocked, Harry didn't open the door either. He then dialled Harry's phone and realised he could hear the phone ringing from inside Harry's house. He first thought Harry was playing hide and seek with him, but then decided to peep through the window, that was when he saw Harry's body on the floor of his kitchen and then called the police. Lieutenant Busco briefed Eddy Taylor on the work done so far on this case. He then narrated how they traced Harry's last movements to the Cornish bar, and said the crime scene was preserved and the evidence collected so far, will be handed over and signed for, to maintain the chain of evidence. Immediately after the phone call, Eddy Taylor called his officers, Agent Donald Whitley and Agent Pauline Fisher, and asked them to visit the crime scene, take over the scene and preserve the scene. He asked them to take a forensic team to the scene.

The officers investigating Harry's death tried to follow his last movements before his death. While watching the CCTV in the bar he visited, the night before his death. FBI detectives saw a lady making light flirtatious passes at Harry, they saw Hanna run her hands through Harry's shoulder as she smiled all through. Unfortunately, Hanna is Fraser's fiancée, and Fraser was fuming inside yet canned his anger as he watched his fiancée from afar messing about with this younger man.

Moments later Harry stood up from his seat and walked to the bar for his second glass of gin and tonic, but this time he'll need to meet Fraser at the bar to attend to him. Harry got to the bar, and waited for a while to be attended to by Fraser who seems to have largely ignored him. It's obvious that Fraser's gritty integrity is unwittingly his character flaw, and he isn't overly fond of young men messing about with another man's woman. There was a sudden bust-up between them, as they went into a tirade in a manner that voices were inadvertently raised, and even though they tried keeping their voices as low as possible so as not to attract attention, they still created a scene. Funnily, this was the second night of Hanna's flirtation with Harry, and it was as if Fraser had been waiting for Harry, at least this time he will give Harry his comeuppance for messing with another man's woman.

Harry is a young man never known to be someone who would fly of the handle easily, because he doesn't give in to temper. He knows how to stand his ground when he needs to be assertive, particularly when he thinks he has done no wrong, because in this case Harry didn't reciprocate Hanna's flirtation.

So, he seems to have given Fraser a dressing down for asking him to turn his attention somewhere else. CCTV captured how Fraser served Harry his gin and tonic, but the way Fraser went about it was like he obscured the glass of drink he served to Harry from the CCTV within the bar, this raised suspicion and made Fraser a person of interest. However, Agent Donald is still trying to work out whether Fraser's action was deliberate or mere serendipity. Despite the light tiff between this two, instead of rabbiting on over being picked on innocently by Fraser, Harry paid for his drink and walked away, yet he remained pissed by Fraser's harsh rebuke.

Hanna remained seated opposite where Harry was sitting, her gaze was fixed on Harry as he walked to the bar for a second glass of drink. The smile on her face was permanent not minding her observation of what looks like a tiff between her man and Harry.

Harry was quite upset as he walked away from the bar towards his seat, and didn't know when he bumped into another customer who seemed to have had plenty to drink and now smelling like a brewery. A tiny fraction of Harry's drink splashed on the curtain inside the bar, the peaceable customer apologised to Harry and offered to get another glass of drink, but Harry asked him to forget about it, and then returned to his seat. While Hanna eagerly waited for Harry to return to his seat, this time Harry turned around and chatted with the customer on the other table and left Hanna alone, knowing what's at stake. This disagreement between Fraser and Harry the night before his death captured on camera makes Frasier a possible suspect with a motive for murder, and Fraser was immediately arrested for interrogation.

Fraser denied deliberately obscuring Harry's drink from the CCTV, and was shocked to hear of Harry's death. However, he smiled at the news but said he had no hand in his death, and at least, the silly boy will leave his fiancée alone.

Agent Donald walked out of the interrogation room, and joined Eddy and Agent Pauline who are watching the interrogation.

"This is Harry's killer, he'd motive, he'd opportunity, and he killed him," said Agent Pauline.

"He was shocked to hear of Harry's death, if he has a hand in it, he wouldn't have been surprised," said Agent Donald.

"After Harry's encounter with Fraser, he went home, and didn't have any direct contact with anyone. "Where then did he ingest the ricin?" asked Eddy.

Agent Donald then stopped and said he really didn't think Fraser committed the act because people don't just go about with ricin with the intention of killing someone who might flirt with their fiancée, an act they'd no idea will occur. Agent Pauline perceived Fraser as a man who loves keeping his powder dry, and insisted that Hanna flirted with Harry for two days in a row, and this puts him in Fraser's cross hairs, and as such Fraser remains their prime suspect in this case, until he provides a strong alibi that exonerates him.

While the detectives were racking their brains on how to proceed, Agent Donald suddenly said the drink that was supposedly poisoned by Fraser that made him a suspect in Harry's death had some of it in the curtain after Harry bumped into a customer and his drink splashed on the curtain, and that curtain holds the clue in this investigation. The FBI immediately carried out forensic testing of the content of the curtain and funny enough there wasn't any poison in the drink Fraser served Harry, meaning Fraser is free and had no hand in Harry's death.

The detectives then turned their attention somewhere else and began a thorough search of Harry's apartment for a second time, and this time they decided it's time to crack open a safe they found in Harry's house, because they couldn't find the key to this safe. Fortunately for the detectives they stumbled into a suicide note left behind by Harry, alongside his laptop in the safe.

Donald Whitley isn't just any other detective who's an early riser and first to appear in a crime scene, Donald is more than that, call it providence, or call him the man who knows. The truth is, he's blessed with a good investigative mindset, a perfect sixth sense and understands the intricacies associated with the job of a detective.

Agent Donald and Agent Pauline Fisher are assessing the scene of the supposed suicide committed by Harry Crow in Los Angeles, and as they carefully pick apart every piece of item in the victim's house.

"Donald, this is a simple case of suicide," said Agent Pauline.

"Why do you draw your conclusions so easily, don't you know investigating a supposed suicide is a complex process?" asked Agent Donald.

Agent Donald insists that people leave suicide note in visible places where people can see them and read, so as to get the message the victim is trying to pass across. "Where is the key to the safe? We have undertaken a thorough search of his house and we can't find the key, which implies that someone else locked the safe and took the key to the safe with them," said Agent Donald.

Agent Donald is quick witted but he needed to brainstorm with Pauline as he ponders over the too many questions posed by this crime scene. He then proceeded to ask Pauline, how possible is it that someone will drink a lethal poison, then write a suicide note and lock it up with their laptop in the safe, and then throw the key away. Its either the key is on him or someone else was involved in his death. "May be Harry made his death to be some kind of puzzle for us to solve, people have all sort of crazy ideas as their dying wish," replied Agent Pauline.

Though, Pauline seems to have drawn her conclusion but that isn't the case with Donald who seems to have more questions than the answer provided by this crime scene, and he isn't giving up until every piece of evidence is picked apart and questions answered. He then picked up Harry's phone and said these phone conversations between Harry and his friends show that Harry can't wait to travel to Miami on holiday with his friends, next week, and people don't just kill themselves before a dream holiday. Funnily, Pauline's mind is made up and this crime-scene has said it all. "It's what it is, Donald," said Agent Pauline. Donald is plagued by his hunch that kept him bound and hesitant into toeing Pauline's line. This carefully orchestrated murder totally disillusioned Pauline, and she has drawn her conclusion already.

"Take a deep breath, Pauline, suicide is what the killer wants you to think. That's if at all, there is a killer," said Agent Donald. "Then what do you think, Donald?" asked Agent Pauline.

"I can't say if it's suicide, until I exhaust all possibilities that make this a murder case," said Agent Donald.

Agent Donald isn't overly accepting of the crime scene from a cursory look, his experience of crime scene investigation is that he'll never always acquiesce everything the crime scene tells him, because the scene might be staged, and he understands too well that the dead speak and leave clues that might help solve their murder. More so, some clues are hidden away in plain sight and requires just a pair of good eyes, and while for others, you might have to dig deeper.

"From what we have here, there's a suicide note in the victim's handwriting showing he killed himself, he browsed the internet, and his debit card was used to pay for the ricin he drank and nothing was stolen to indicate the presence of a third party," said Agent Pauline.

"What if, someone forced him to use his card to pay for the ricin, forced him at gun point to write the note and forced him as well to drink the deadly potion?" asked Agent Donald.

"But suicide is still an option even though we're not ruling out the possibility of murder. Isn't it?" insists Agent Pauline.

"Yeah, of course, you're right," said Agent Donald. As they continue to rummage through the victim's apartment, Pauline suddenly stopped and was motionless for a while, then took a deep breath, and ended her silence with a big sigh.

"Donald, why do people commit suicide?" asked Pauline.

"I don't know, but the world is so beautiful that you wish to behold its beauty one more time, and one more time, and one more time," said Agent Donald.

"When people make death the only option, why can't they reconsider their choices even at the point of committing suicide?" asked Agent Pauline.

"I once have a friend who womanises a lot, but for one reason or the other, he wanted to commit suicide and while he was on top of the Pen bridge in Oklahoma wanting to dive into the river, he came to a point of reckoning. He saw a pretty lady walk past and he'd a second thought, like, if I die now who'll be there to tell a pretty lady like this, you look beautiful?" said Agent Donald. There was a momentary silence between the pair after Donald's story, as the detectives continued accessing the crime scene and twenty minutes later, Pauline stopped again and fixed her gaze on Donald. "Did he still do it?" asked Agent Pauline. "Who?" asked Agent Donald. "Your friend, of course," said Agent Pauline.

"Of course he didn't, he now lives in Los Angeles where he'll have the opportunity of appreciating the beautiful handworks of God," said Agent Donald.

"Women?" she asked. Donald then smiled, with this cheeky grin all over his face.

"Yes, women," said Agent Donald with a smile.

A week later and while in the open office reviewing the suicide, Agent Fidel Lane, who's one of the detectives in the unit brought the FBI pathologist report on Harry Crow. "Donald, the pathologist report is out," said Agent Lane.

"What did it say or rather let me have a look?" said Agent Donald.

"Autopsy reveals redness of the lips and dilation of the pupils. Cause of death is the ingestion of ricin. There are no bruises or whatever to indicate struggle, self-defence and even murder," said Agent Lane. Agent Pauline interjected immediately Agent lane finished reading out the autopsy report, at least she's right and Donald is wrong this time.

"I told Donald exactly the same thing at the scene of the crime," said Agent Pauline.

Donald's subtle response to Pauline's claim is that the pathologist report isn't the FBI's conclusion and the case is still open. A young man planning a dream holiday with friends can't commit suicide just a week before the planned trip, he insists.

"Maybe the young man had issues, or what do you think?" asked Agent Lane. The pathologist report didn't reveal any trauma, blood clots from blunt force, and now Agent Donald is left in the dark but his hunch tells him to investigate further even though Pauline thinks he's grasping at straws, yet he continues to ponder.

"Pauline, give us a rundown of the victim's profile. I think, focusing on the victim is the best way forward," said Agent Donald.

"Harry Crow was twenty-three, the only child of James Crow who divorced Harry's mother when Harry was seventeen. James Crow made his fortune after the bitter divorce to Harry's mum," said Agent Pauline.

"What about Harry's mum?" asked Agent Lane.

"Harry's mum moved to the suburb of Los Angeles where she found herself a boyfriend, she lives closer to nature, enjoying clean air and a stress-free life, something she placed no value on because it costs her nothing, but meant a lot to others. But she has been plagued by the nagging thought that she's living in penury since she's not in the heart of the city," said Agent Donald.

"Oh Donald, that's insightful," Pauline chuckled.

"Ahh, never mind, that's been my way of analysis," said Agent Donald.

"You know I like it, that's why I love being in your team, because there's lots to learn," said Agent Pauline.

"Pauline, tell us about Harry's dad, does Harry have any life insurance?" asked Agent Donald.

"Harry's dad died last year and Harry inherited his father's entire fortune, which he wasn't willing to share with his mum and he has a life insurance," said Agent Pauline.

"Which means if Harry dies, his mum will inherit his fortune," said Agent Donald. "Of course, yes!" said Agent Pauline.

Harry's unwillingness to share his inheritance with his mum might mean a subtle animosity towards her son, and that now puts her as someone with a possible motive, even where there isn't anything linking her to her son's apparent suicide.

"Then, we have a lead," said Agent Donald.

"But Harry bought the ricin himself using his laptop, and wrote the note himself," said Agent Lane.

Agent Donald had to work the case backward, shifting his focus away from the day of Harry's death, he then focused on two weeks earlier, which is the day of the purchase of the ricin and couple of days before.

"That's just one lead, please review the CCTV camera in the front of Harry's house for some specific days, that day of his death and the day or days before the purchase of the ricin," said Agent Donald.

"But the CCTV camera was already reviewed and showed that nobody visited Harry on the day of his death," replied Agent Pauline. Agent Donald explained further that he has just decided to expand the review of the CCTV to uncover any possible foul play surrounding this death.

"Possibly they came in from the back garden which the CCTV camera didn't pick up," said Agent Donald.

"You're beginning to steer this case away from suicide," said Agent Lane. "I can't tell if this is a murder case, but if this is a murder case, then we'll be looking for two people. One will be a relation and the other will be someone not too familiar to Harry," said Agent Donald. "Why these two people?" asked Agent Lane.

"Buying the ricin online with Harry's bank card using his laptop is something a family member who comes in pretence to visiting can do using Harry's debit card without him knowing. But forcing him to drink a deadly potion is a brazen act that requires an unfamiliar face to do, to make Harry write a suicide note and drink a death potion," said Agent Donald.

"Ok, we now have an idea of what we're looking for," said Agent Lane.

But while he was busy at work, Natasha called Donald's phone. "Hello honey," said Natasha. Donald saw the phone call from his wife and walked some steps away.

"Honey, how're you?" asked Agent Donald.

"I'm fine, but are you free to talk?" asked Natasha.

"I'm in the middle of something but you can go on with what you want to say," said Agent Donald.

"I just got a call from Jonathan's school," said Natasha.

"I thought you wanted to tell me how much you love me, and can't do without me," Agent Donald said jocularly.

"Don't worry, I'll tell you about that later but for now, it's about Jonathan," said Natasha.

"What about him? Please tell me," asked Agent Donald.

"Jonathan was involved in a fight and the head teacher called to have a word with either of us," said Natasha. This couple are known for their jocular banter each time they're on phone to each other, and even when it's an urgent matter, they still squeeze some jokes between.

"It must be that the head teacher wants to apologise on behalf of another parent, because my son doesn't fight," said Agent Donald.

"You're right; the head teacher said the boy attacked Jonathan first," said Natasha.

"I taught him never to fight unless he's attacked, we'll see her tomorrow," said Agent Donald.

Donald ended the phone call and returned to work as his colleagues were reviewing Harry Crow's profile. Pressure from the big guns in government means there is more to this case, and Donald is working round the clock to work this case to get it resolved as soon as possible.

The next morning, Donald and Natasha were in Jonathan's school, and having a word with the head teacher who invited them for a meeting a day before.

"I suppose you've seen the scratch on your son's wrist," said the head teacher.

"I saw it and was mortified, and I asked myself why a child should do such a thing to his school mate," said Natasha.

"I invited you to let you know of the action the school has taken concerning this, and to as well promise you we'll do our best to make sure it doesn't repeat itself," promised the head teacher.

"Head teacher, please do, because I've instructed my son never to fight unless he's being attacked and he has to save himself," said Agent Donald.

"The parents of the pupil were invited yesterday and I've explained the possible actions of the school to them if this repeats itself," said the head teacher.

"Thank you for handling the situation maturely and neatly," said Agent Donald.

Donald Whitley rushed to the office after his meeting with Jonathan's head teacher. He immediately continued reviewing the Harry Crow's case from where he left it.

"Agent Lane where are we on the CCTV review of Harry's premises?" asked Agent Donald.

"Take a look at this," said Agent Lane. Donald walked closer, joining Agent lane and Agent Pauline to watch the CCTV footage.

"Harry's mum visited Harry the day of the purchase of the ricin and never left until two days after the purchase," said Agent Lane. Agent Donald requested a further CCTV review to see if there was any parcel delivery before Harry's mum left his son's place.

Agent Donald proceeded to suggest that if aside from Harry's mum, no other person visited him, then they're close to affirming that Harry didn't purchase the ricin himself but his mum did.

"And the day of the purchase was two weeks before Harry's death," said Agent Pauline. As far as his colleagues are concerned, it's overkill to categorically say that Harry's mum is behind Harry's death.

"It's possible she used his card to make the purchase without Harry knowing, waited to receive the ricin and then took it away with her," said Agent Donald.

"Then I suppose, it's possible they came with it on the day of Harry's death," said Agent Lane. It's now imperative for Donald to tie these tit bits together to help narrow this investigation down to a few possible suspects.

Donald then requested the review of the CCTV footage around the suburb where Harry's mum lives to see if she left her home on the day of Harry's death. If she did, who did she leave with and what train they boarded and what direction they went.

"Let me make that request immediately," said Agent lane. While they were at it, Eddie Taylor the head of the unit walked into the conversation. This death is particularly of interest to the big guns in the White house, and even some in Capitol Hill wants to know what happened to Harry Crow.

"Donald, where are we on the Harry Crow's case, is it confirmed to be suicide?" asked Eddie Taylor.

"We can't tell for sure, but that's what the possible killer wanted us to believe. But the whole thing has taken a new twist; let's see if it leads somewhere," replied Agent Donald. Eddie Taylor became curious with the new turn of events, and said he wants to know where this rabbit hole leads. "Oh, then fill me in," said Eddie Taylor.

"Harry's mum visited him on the day of the purchase of the ricin which he possibly killed himself with. We're thinking she may have used his card to make the purchase without Harry knowing and waited until it was delivered to her before leaving," said Agent Donald.

"Harry's mum DNA was found on the handle of the back door to Harry's back garden," said Agent Pauline.

Eddy Taylor then suggested they now need to confirm if she was in town on the day Harry died, since the CCTV in the front of Harry's house didn't pick her up. "We're already doing that," replied Agent Donald.

Eddy turned to leave but stopped and asked Donald to keep him in the know of everything about this case, because the Head of the Criminal Division of Main Justice is interested in this case.

"Why has this case attracted so much interest?" asked Agent Pauline.

"Harry's father is the nephew of the Attorney General," said Eddie Taylor. "You mean, Johnny Crow? Now, I get it," said Agent Pauline.

"Now that you all know, let's find the killer if there is one," said Eddie Taylor. Eddie left them and walked into his office, but immediately Eddie Taylor entered his office, he received a phone call from the Strategic Information and Operation Centre of the FBI headquarters.

"Eddie, how are you?" asked Sarah Black.

"I'm fine, Sarah, I know you're calling me for update on Harry Crow's case," replied Eddie Taylor.

"Of course, yes, if not, why should I be the first person to call you today?" asked Sarah Black.

Eddie laughed and continued his conversation. "Sarah, what make you think you're the first person to call me today?" asked Eddie Taylor.

"Even if I'm not, I said so to let you know how serious the situation is," said Sarah Black.

"I've just been briefed by my unit that it's possible we're dealing with a murder case," said Eddie Taylor.

"Oh, that's good; Johnny Crow has been insisting the boy isn't suicidal by nature," said Sarah Black.

"But the Attorney General should let us do our job, so we don't draw premature conclusions," Eddie Taylor protested.

"You're sounding like this because you aren't in my shoes, as the head of criminal division of main justice I'm always the first to take the heat," said Sarah Black.

"Don't worry, Sarah, we're already narrowing the investigation down to a few individuals and as such we're close to drawing a conclusion," said Eddie Taylor.

"I've always given you support from the top because your units is among the few that has always made me proud of my job," said Sara Black.

"Thank you Sarah, I'll get back to you as soon as I tie loose ends and narrow this investigation down on someone," said Eddie Taylor.

By evening of same day, Donald and Natasha went into a retail supermarket for shopping, and as they strolled down the aisle of the supermarket. "Honey, I'm done, let's proceed to the check-out," said Natasha.

"Ok, but shopping with you is always an interesting experience, because you use it to remind me of how much a pint of milk cost," Agent Donald said jocularly.

As they stayed in the queue waiting to make payment, Natasha realised her shopping is incomplete. "Honey I forgot to pick mouth wash, remain in the queue, and let me rush to the shelves and get some," said Natasha.

The moment his wife left, he noticed the woman in front of him was about to lose her money as it was about to fall off from her pocket. "Excuse me," said Agent Donald.

The lady turned around "What's it?" she asked. Donald pointed to the lady's pocket. "Your money is about to fall out," he said. "Oh, thank you, but I'm not up for your cat and mouse game," replied the lady. Donald was just worried sick that this fellow customer is about to lose her money, but she seem to be giving him the short end of the stick as a thank you.

"I just saved you from losing your money, a thank you will suffice, and what's the cat and mouse game you're talking about?" asked Agent Donald.

"You showed me my money as a way of initiating a conversation, and the next thing, you'll want to ask me out," said the lady. Donald didn't hesitate to point the lady to his wife who's walking towards him. "But that's my wife over there, and I'm not interested in what you're thinking," said Agent Donald.

"I saw your wife, you might want to have a quickie before she comes back and I don't want your cat and mouse game," the lady retorted.

"What's it with you about cat and mouse, why do people always think a cat chasing a mouse is a game? It isn't, because the cat is chasing the mouse to kill the mouse and minutes later the mouse will be resting in the belly of the cat," said Agent Donald.

Natasha joined the queue and inquired from her husband what the matter was "Honey, what's it?" asked Natasha.

"She said I want to have a quickie the moment you stepped out," Agent Donald said and smiled ingeniously.

"It's true, and you don't have to trust him. You can't trust men!" she retorted. Natasha laughed, after her momentary laughter and the hysteria that followed, she dissuaded the lady of her concern. "The last thing in my mind, is to worry about my husband, he isn't that kind of man," said Natasha.

Moments later, they left the store and continued their conversation about the lady's accusation, as Donald wasn't quite convinced that he deserved the middle finger for his neighbourliness. Funnily, Donald's curiosity is his character flaw, and this lady just exploited this flaw to spook him. As they leave the store Donald revisited the encounter and began putting the conversation back into perspective, saying, not everyone will tell you thank you, even when you just saved them from a burning fire.

"Maybe the men in her life are usually unfaithful and that might have informed her perception, which might explain why her opinion about men was skewed in that manner," suggested Natasha. Donald thinks otherwise, as he insists that he shouldn't bear the cost of the spill-over from this stuffy lady's failed romance, and reminding Natasha that the lady is a piece of work carrying baggage of ingratitude around.

Agent Donald buttressed further on the difficulties associated with lending a helping hand to the wrong person, saying no matter how hard you try, they may blame you for not coming to their rescue on time, even when you aren't the fireman and not responsible for their safety.

"These are perspectives developed over time," said Natasha.

"Half full or half empty, it depends on how they see things; many see the bad side more than the good side," said Agent Donald.

Two days later, the CCTV footage of Harry's mum's movement on the day of his death is now available for review and analysis.

"Donald, from this CCTV footage, Harry's mum and her boy-friend travelled together on the day Harry died," said Agent Lane.

"Where did they travel to? We need to know, to help us draw an inference," asked Agent Donald.

"They alighted at the train station close to where Harry lived," said Agent Lane.

With a possibility of a break in the investigation, following new revelations, Agent Donald breathes a sigh of relief and said this case that's presumed to be suicide is largely turning into a murder case.

Donald has a ravenous appetite for truth and justice, and inter-estingly he knows where to find it and how to find it because he's willing to go the whole hog to get it. Hunch alone doesn't do the trick, narrowing the evidence to someone does. Each case has its own merit, and the approach is dependent on the circumstance.

"Donald, you've applied your wizardry to successfully work this case away from suicide and succinctly into murder," said Agent Pauline.

"It's time we bring Harry's mum in for questioning," said Agent Donald. "Is it her alone or we're bringing her boyfriend in as well?" asked Agent Lane. "We're bringing both of them in," said Agent Donald.

Eddie Taylor walked into central office and joined the conversation, and asked who they're bringing in, and what their investigation uncovered.

"Harry's mum was around his house on the day of his death," said Agent Donald.

Eddie Taylor got interested and listened keenly as his detectives gave a rundown on Harry's mum.

"Ok, fill me in on this," said Eddie Taylor.

Donald played back the CCTV clip showing that Harry's mum visited him on the day of the purchase of the ricin, and she's also captured on camera with her boyfriend alighting from the train in the train station closest to where Harry lived on the day Harry died.

"Oh good, but the defence can poke holes in Gina's DNA on the door handle of Harry's back garden, this is a lady who visits her son once in a while, we should expect her DNA to be anywhere in her son's house. Except we can prove the date the DNA was left there, the District Attorney won't prosecute based on this evidence. Bring them in so she can fill in the blank spaces that need to be filled in, as far as this case is concerned," said Eddie Taylor.

"Ok, I think we should get going," said Agent Donald.

"Donald, go with Pauline; and let Agent Lane stay behind in case something comes calling," said Eddie Taylor.

Moments later, Donald and Pauline left for the suburbs with some LAPD officers to bring in Harry's mum and her boyfriend. As they entered the car to leave, Pauline got a call from her husband, Bruce Fisher.

"Ooh, thank God. Babe, where are you?" asked Bruce.

"I'm on my way to the suburbs and I believe you're on your way back to Los Angeles," replied Agent Pauline.

Bruce Fisher muttered as he continued to express his frustration. "Darling, I'm just tired," he retorted.

"What are you tired of? You said you will be coming back today," said Agent Pauline.

"Yes, actually I was on my way but my car broke down, and now I'm stuck," he muttered again.

"I advised you to go by air but you insisted that you love to drive, and you love to drive cross-country, just get a mechanic to fix your car and continue," said Agent Pauline.

This trip has sadly become a life stretch, and sometimes the uncanny truth about adventures is its ability to precipitate into a sting in the tail. This experience isn't enough to leave a scar in Bruce after all, adventure is his thing.

"That's what the issue is, because I just can't find a mechanic," Bruce retorted.

"What do you mean you can't find a mechanic, there are mechanics everywhere in the United States, where are you?" asked Agent Pauline.

"I'm in the state of Arizona, in the town of Nothing and I've been looking around for help but found none," said Bruce.

Pauline now has a better understanding of Bruce's predicament, his trouble isn't just a function of not knowing what to do, but it's a function of the location in which her husband finds himself. Bruce was worried sick that his ill-thought-out trip will cause a gut-wrenching experience he may never forget, unless help comes his way fast.

"Oh my God, what are you doing in the town of Nothing, every-one in the United States knows you'll find nothing in Nothing," Pauline retorted.

"It isn't me, it's the car, and that's where my car chooses to break down," replied Bruce.

"Go to the next town and get a mechanic or place a call for one, they'll come and help you out," said Agent Pauline.

"A towing van is already on its way," Bruce assured his wife.

With help on the way, Pauline can now heave a sigh of relief. "Oh, that'll be better, and I'll call you later to know the situation," said Agent Pauline.

Agent Donald was sitting beside Pauline as her husband vents his frustration while her conversation with her husband lasted, and the frustration in Pauline's face call for attention. "What's it, Pauline?" asked Agent Donald.

"It's my husband," she said.

"What about him?" asked Agent Donald.

"He's in Nothing, looking for a mechanic," replied Agent Pauline.

"Ooh," Donald chuckles. He won't find a mechanic in Nothing, everyone knows there is nothing in the town of Nothing," he retorted.

Not long after their conversation, the car moved as they set off for the suburbs, Pauline turned to Donald while the car was in motion.

"I like your investigative mind set, you're intuitive, and I wish I am like you," said Agent Pauline.

"You're good in your own way, and I've equally learnt a lot from you as well," said Agent Donald. Pauline is stoical and isn't a person who engages in corrupt flattery, but she is always keen to know what's in Donald's head, particularly how thinks. She likes working with him, the way he thinks things through is quite amazing and fascinates her, and Donald has a good quiescence of humour.

"You see, the human mind is likened to an ocean, and just as there are fishes in the ocean, so also are there thoughts in the human mind. The kinds of fishes you find in a particular ocean are different from the ones in another, so also the kind of thoughts in a person's mind are different from the thoughts in another," said Agent Donald.

Marvelled at Agent Donald's metaphoric analogy of the human heart, which is central in solving crimes, but speaking in veiled terms seem not to be doing the magic enough, Pauline wants clarity and not literary illusions.

"I want you to go a bit further," said Agent Pauline.

Agent Donald then proceeded to say that we all have this duality in us that we carry around with us. A little good, and a little of evil is in all of us. The proportion of these variables in us is what make difference, and makes a person good or bad.

"Just as certain fishes don't survive in the wrong water body, bad thought hardly survive in the mind of a good person, and good thoughts hardly survive in the mind of the bad person. These opposing thoughts don't last because of conflict between the person and the thought," said Agent Donald.

"But there are certain fishes that are common to both water bodies, and so are thoughts common to both hearts," Agent Pauline said as she probed further.

Donald elucidated by shedding more light to his view, and said there is a bit good of good and bad in everyone, just that as there are certain thoughts that are common in both minds, people tend to be good to those who like them and prejudiced against those who hate them. He also proceeded to say that good people sometimes show love to a bad person that's nice to them, and the reverse is the case. "You find these tendencies in both good and bad people," said Agent Donald.

"Hmm, so that's the variable that's constant?" asked Agent Pauline. Agent Donald Nods his head in response to Pauline's question.

"Yeah," said Agent Donald.

Minutes later they arrive at the house where Harry's mum and her boyfriend live. Agent Donald pressed the bell and a minute later the door was opened by Gina Beckley.

"Gina Beckley?" asked Agent Donald.

"Yes, who are you?" asked Gina Beckley.

"I'm agent Donald from the FBI," he said.

While Gina was by the door with the detectives her boyfriend, Tony Shaw, spoke from inside the house from behind her. "Honey, who is it?" asked Tony Shaw.

"The FBI and the police," she said. Tony Shaw walked to the door. "What do they want?" he asked.

"I suppose you're Tony Shaw, her boyfriend?" said Agent Donald. "Yes, I'm Tony Shaw and I'm her boyfriend, is anything the matter?" asked Tony Shaw.

"Gina Beckley, you're under arrest for the murder of Harry Crow," said Agent Donald.

"What! You're arresting me for the murder of my own son, while I'm still mourning his death?" she exclaimed.

Agent Pauline put the couple in handcuffs and immediately read their rights to them. "Whatever you say or do will be used against you in the court of law and you've the right to an attorney".

"What have I done, and why're you arresting me?" Tony Shaw protested.

An hour after they were brought in for questioning, Gina Beckley was now being interrogated by Agent Donald in the interrogation room, while other detectives observed.

Agent Donald joined Gina Beckley who's already seated in the interrogation room "Sorry about your loss, but we need to do this," said Agent Donald, as he sat opposite her.

Gina Beckley clears her throat. "Thank you," she said.

"Where were you on the day of April 12th?" asked Agent Donald.

"I was in Harry's place," she replied.

"When did you come to Harry's place and when did you leave?" asked Agent Donald. Gina Beckley quickly assumed the position of the victim, as she insists the FBI is chasing an illusory suspect, and she's now using her emotion to weep up dormant sentiments.

"I visited Harry on the 12th of April, and left his place on the 14th of April.

Since the death of Harry's dad, you never stayed more than a day each time you visited your son, but this time you spent three days, why?" asked Agent Donald.

"Yeah, you're right, but this time I felt like spending more time with my son," said Gina Beckley.

"Did you make the purchase of ricin using Harry's debit card?" asked Agent Donald. "Ricin! That's what he used to kill himself, wasn't it?" she asked.

"Yeah, but how did you know that was what he used to commit suicide since you've not received a report from the pathologist confirming that was what killed Harry?" asked Agent Donald. Gina is a smart woman, quick on her feet and hardly on the back foot, interestingly, outsmarting agent Donald will be quite a tall order. She's now grasping on straw and might start falling apart as agent Donald breaks her resolve to play the catch me if you can.

"He wrote it in the suicide note; it's there for everyone to see," she said.

"Ok, but you made the purchase of the ricin he used to kill himself?" asked Agent Donald.

"Of course, not! I'm his mum, what do you take me for, a monster?" asked Gina Berkeley.

"But it was purchased on the day you visited your son, and to be precise, the purchase was made while you were in his house," said Agent Donald.

"You know how these kids are, he must have made the purchase without me knowing," she said. "If Harry actually made the purchase, he wouldn't delete the link from his browser," said Agent Donald. The kitchen is now hot for Gina, and her resolve to be evasive is unavoidably beginning to thaw as Agent Donald decides to play her game with her. She was red-faced, following the sustained badgering by the detectives, the evidence before her was overwhelming and it didn't take long before she crumbled.

The detectives find this case of immense interest, particularly when the mum of the victim is the prime suspect. Their thoughts about Gina are that she's ugly and cold at heart, and that isn't enough to compensate for her good looks.

"Maybe somebody else did," said Gina Beckley.

"From what we know, no one visited Harry during the three days you were with him, and why would Harry call the bank to complain his account was debited the same twenty two dollars used to purchase the ricin if he knew about the purchase?" asked Agent Donald.

"Did he?" asked Gina Beckley.

"Yes, he did, so you made the purchase three hours after you arrived your son's house," said Agent Donald.

"Actually, Harry was busy that day so he asked me to help him make the purchase, but I never knew what he wanted to do with it," she said.

"And you never cared to ask?" asked Agent Donald.

"I tried to ask him, but he refused to talk about it, so I'd to let him be," said Gina Beckley.

"Your seized laptop revealed you browsed the website of the seller of the ricin even before visiting Harry to make the purchase," said Agent Donald.

"I stumbled into the website in error," Gina Beckley replied ingenuously, even though her eyes say otherwise. With her eye flickering like a troubled light bulb, the guilt of her action was obvious even as she tried assiduously to conceal her emotion. Agent Donald sustained the pressure in his bid to get what actually transpired. "Where were you on the day Harry died?" Agent Donald queried further.

"I was with my boyfriend and we came to town," she said.

"You came in with your boyfriend through the back garden to avoid the camera, I suppose," said Agent Donald.

Agent Donald reiterated to her that she should get a lawyer because it's obvious she's neck deep in this.

"Are you accusing me of the murder of my son?" asked Gina Beckley. Gina didn't see the need for a lawyer, she protested as any other accused person would normally do, but that didn't stop Agent Donald from giving her the stinker that riled her.

"Yes, you visited him two weeks earlier, used his debit card to buy the ricin. You waited for it to be delivered to you before leaving his place then came back with your boyfriend who threatened him with a weapon and made him drink the ricin to make it look like he bought the ricin and committed suicide with it. You did this just because of his inheritance from his dad and his life insurance money," said Agent Donald.

This stinker riled Gina Beckley and got her screaming on top of her lungs. "It's a lie, I didn't do it," she protested.

"Gina Beckley, you'll need an attorney because I'm charging you with the murder of Harry Crow," said Agent Donald.

Gina Beckley was returned to the cell after being charged, and immediately Donald left the interrogation room and joined his colleague watching the interrogation. "Donald, she did it; this is now a murder case," said Eddie Taylor.

"She admitted buying the ricin because you tricked her into believing Harry called the bank to complain about the deduction from his account," said Agent Pauline. After getting the facts out of Gina Beckley who's still protesting her arrest, it's time to corroborate her story with her boyfriend in the interrogation room.

"Get her accomplice; bring him into the interrogation room," said Eddie Taylor.

Thirty minutes later, Tony Shaw was brought into the interrogation room by one of the detectives and Agent Donald joined him minutes later.

"Tony Shaw, I want you to know that Gina Beckley, your girlfriend, has told us everything about the murder of her son, Harry Crow," said Agent Donald.

"What did she say I did?" asked Tony Shaw.

"She told us how she bought the ricin her son drank and how you threatened him with a weapon to make him write a suicide note, and then drink the ricin to make it look like suicide. That this whole thing is all your idea," said Agent Donald.

Tony's disposition changed immediately from the hard man to a man whose vulnerability was laid bare, he inadvertently became agitated and now felt betrayed. Sadly, Tony is now the Judas goat, an accessory to murder, and his first instinct is now to try extricating himself from this whole saga, particularly now that he's been thrown under the bus by his accomplice.

"Why did she make it look like it's my idea? It's not about me, it's all her idea. I tried to talk her out of it, but she refused. She insisted on getting Harry out of the way, since he refused to share his wealth with her," said Tony Shaw.

"Then tell us all you know about it," said Agent Donald.

"She went to her son's place, waited for him to use the bathroom, and quickly used his debit card to make the purchase and then delete the link immediately to make it look like he bought the ricin himself. Two weeks later we went in through the back garden to avoid the camera, he opened the door to let us in. When we went in, I pointed the gun at him and Gina to make it look like I'm very mad at them, then I threatened him and told him to write the suicide note and drink ricin," said Tony Shaw.

"You'll need an attorney. Tony Shaw, I'm charging you with the murder of Harry Crow," said Agent Donald.

"It's not me; it's her. Gina, tell them it's all your idea," Tony Shaw screamed in protest as he was returned to his cell.

Mystery is Agent Donald's strong suit, he eats it like breakfast and all he does is give suspects the run-around and leaves them second-guessing until they unravel on their own without any threat or coercion.

"They both did it, at least this is sorted; thank you all for job well done. Ooh, one more thing, I want you to bring in the seller of the poison," said Eddie Taylor.

"You mean the seller of the ricin?" asked Agent Donald.

"Yes, we can trace the seller's location from the seller's website," said Eddie Taylor.

Agent Donald immediately asked their IT person to use the IP address of the seller of the ricin to fish out his location, and it didn't take long, the detectives are on their way to bring him in. Not long after the team of detectives went to get the seller of ricin, Eddie Taylor calls Sarah Black to update her on the Harry Crow's case.

"Hello Sarah," said Eddie Taylor.

"How're you Eddie, and how did your investigation go?" asked Sarah Black.

"Yeah, I asked for a little time to narrow the investigation down to a few individuals and we've done that," said Eddie Taylor.

Sarah heaved a sigh of relief; at least the big guns in the White House breathing down her neck will give her some breathing space.

"What did you find?" asked Sarah Black.

"The boy's mum, Gina Beckley was behind his murder," said Eddie Taylor.

"Good Jesus! Are you sure you did a good job?" asked Sarah Black. Sarah was miffed and befuddled by the result of the investigation, it's like her head was spinning and needs someone to help keep her head still. Though, Sarah has been around the block for a while and knows that this isn't some kind of childish drive-by hit job, and parent's involvement in their children's murder is rare, but isn't unheard of.

"Yes, her boyfriend has already confessed everything and she has already confessed in part," said Eddie Taylor. "Why did she do such a thing, and what does she want?" asked Sarah Black.

"We think she did it because of his life insurance money and his inheritance from his dad," said Eddie Taylor.

"I need the complete update of this investigation on my desk by the day after tomorrow," Sarah Black ordered.

"Ok, you'll have it," replied Eddie Taylor.

"When are you charging her and her accomplice?" asked Sarah Black. "We're doing that immediately," Eddie promised. "Ok, good, let me update the Attorney General," said Sarah Black.

Immediately after speaking to Eddie Taylor, Sarah Black put a call across to the Attorney General to update him on his nephew son's case.

"Hello Johnny, I guess you were expecting my phone call?" asked Sarah Black.

"Of course, Sarah, I've been looking forward to your phone call, any update on my nephew's son?" asked Johnny Crow.

"Yes, and that's why I'm calling," said Sarah Black.

"Now I know why you sounded so confident on the other side of the phone the moment you said, 'hello Johnny,'" Johnny Crow said Jocularly. Sarah Black laughed as Johnny Crow mimicked her on the phone.

"One universal truth about success is that everyone loves to succeed," she said.

"Now that you've succeeded, give me the update," replied Johnny Crow. "Gina Beckley and her boyfriend were behind the murder of her son," said Sarah Black. The last thing Johnny Crow expects to hear is that Gina is behind her son's murder. He knew Gina to be very soft spoken person who radiates gentility, and softness. He's overly fond of Gina and her late son, her soft spoken nature seem to have veiled the devil inside her, yet he seem not believe his hearing.

"Gina! No, that can't be, but how can Gina do such a thing? And she claimed to love her son so much," He exclaimed.

"Johnny, when money is involved the definition of love becomes more complex," replied Sarah. "Why would she do a thing like that?" asked Johnny Crow.

"Because of his insurance money, you'll get the details of the investigation later," Sarah promised. "Ok, then when are you charging them?" asked Johnny Crow.

"We're charging them immediately, the investigation is completed and there isn't any need for delay," she said.

"Ok, thank you," said Johnny Crow.

The detectives are all set and ready as they stood at the door to bust the seller of the ricin, who's operating an illegal business.

Agent Donald knocks the door. "Solomon Young?" he asked. "Yes, I'm Solomon Young, is there a problem?" asked Solomon. "You're under arrest for the sale of a banned substance," said Agent Donald.

"What's it you're talking about? I'm not selling any banned substance," said Solomon.

"Donald, leave him with the cops, let's search his house for evidence," said Agent Pauline.

Funnily, the detectives searched the home of Solomon Young and found nothing, but convinced that he has a garage where he stashes things away. They obtained a warrant to search his garage as well, and luckily, the team found the ricin where it was kept away. Hours later, Solomon Young was brought into the interrogation room, and Agent Donald joined him.

"Do you know the sale of ricin is prohibited?" asked Agent Donald. "Yes, I know, but I don't sell ricin," replied Solomon.

"Are you denying it because you think you've hidden your products where the cops can't find them?" asked Agent Donald. Solomon Young thought his stash was securely hidden away from the prying eyes of the detectives. He was glad when the search of his apartment yielded no result, but he eventually lost his mojo when the search extended to his garage and the ricin uncovered. Despite being found out, he continued playing the tough nut with the detectives, even though he was there when the detectives found his stash.

"I didn't hide anything and I don't know what you're talking about," said Solomon.

Agent Donald showed him a photograph of where he stashed away the ricin, and then placed the bottle of ricin on the table.

"Look at this picture, that's where you hid the products you sell online and you're there when we found them, so you don't have to continue denying it," said Agent Donald.

Solomon Young's defiant posture began to thaw now that his business is now unravelling, and he's now showing signs of admission of guilt, and his facial disposition now tells nothing but guilt.

"It's not mine, it's for a friend," said Solomon.

"But you said you'd no idea of ricin anywhere in your property," said Agent Donald.

"I said so because it isn't mine," said Solomon.

"The website for the sale is on your laptop, the payment from buyers goes into your account and you say it isn't yours, well then, who owns it?" asked Agent Donald.

"Actually, I'm the owner, but I didn't know it's a banned substance," said Solomon.

"But at first you told me categorically you're aware it's a banned substance," said Agent Donald.

"I just said so, I'm sorry," said Solomon. It's too late to apologise after playing a tough nut to crack, Solomon's composure began falling apart as all attempt to obfuscate his dealings on ricin failed.

"There's nothing to be sorry about, your product has just been used to commit murder. I'm charging you with the sale of a banned substance," said Agent Donald.

Five months later, the jury found Gina Beckley and Tony Shaw guilty of murder. Gina Beckley was sentenced to life imprisonment without the possibility of parole, while Tony Shaw was sentenced to forty-five years imprisonment. Solomon Young was sentenced to eight years imprisonment.

CHAPTER

TWO

The Transfer

The Federal Bureau of Investigation reacts to a court decision to discharge and acquit a murder suspect.

Sarah Black, the head of criminal division of main justice at the strategic information and operation centre of the FBI headquarters was not happy with Andy Grey, the head of the FBI unit in New York City. She'd to put a phone call across to Andy to express her displeasure after a hue and cry of New Yorkers, following a known criminal being discharged and acquitted by the court.

"Hello Andy," said Sarah Black.

"Good morning, Sarah," said Andy Grey.

"You seem to know why I'm calling you this early morning," Sarah retorted.

"No I don't, please fill me in," he said.

She admonished Andy, urging him to stop being funny, and asked if he thinks she will keep quiet over the decision of the court to let a murderer back on the streets simply because his unit couldn't put the right evidence together for a successful prosecution of a murderer.

It was actually a summer of discontent with the hue and cry that followed almost immediately as most New Yorkers expressed disbelief that another murder suspect has been returned to their streets.

Sarah isn't screaming blue murder, she's spiting fire, not just because the FBI department in New York engaged in skulduggery, rather this failure would mean the chicken might come home to roost, and it most likely will, if nothing is done to improve the manner of their investigation. Andy Grey pleaded with Sarah, and said he knew his unit didn't do a good job and agreed he knew Sarah would call to express her disappointment, but then said he never expected she'll call this early.

The failure of this unit is now an open book to FBI headquarters, and now Sarah is nothing but all thunder and fury. "Is there a better time to express my disappointment? Answer me, Andy!" Sarah exclaimed.

"No, there isn't. Though, I've thought of holding a serious conversation with members of my unit," said Andy Grey. "As the head of the criminal justice, I fail when any unit fails in their responsibility, and Americans are watching because they knew the truth as well," Sarah Black retorted. Sarah have to take responsibility for the failure of any FBI unit that falls short, and the Senate might come calling on her to answer for the failures of the detectives. Andy silently rambled in a soliloquy as he held onto the phone, and brainstorming within himself the way out of this mess, yet tried making light of his troubles.

"I consider this failure as taking the proverbial custard pie straight in the face," said Andy Grey.

"I'm not up for platitudes, Andy. Just do your job and give me results," said Sarah Black.

"Sarah, I'll say every failure of my unit is my failure as well, and I take full responsibility," replied Andy Grey.

Sarah reminded him she really liked his work in the past and said she felt that he deserved being the unit head that he is, but if the job is too much for him then she'll bring in someone to head his unit.

Sarah Black isn't the kind of head of criminal justice that accommodates failure, particularly one that's glaring to all Americans. And if the American people can't tolerate having murderers meant to be put away parading the street of the United States, then Sarah Black isn't having it either.

"Sarah, it hasn't gotten to that, just give me an opportunity to turn the fortunes of my unit around for good," said Andy Grey.

"The senate might invite me to explain the failings in my division because they knew that criminals that were meant to be put away are returning to our streets," said Sarah Black.

Andy had to plead with Sarah to give him some time, even though time is a luxury Sarah can't afford at this time, yet Andy pleaded for more time, promising to get things back on track.

"Ok, now you know I've a particular interest in your unit and I'll be watching from afar," she signalled.

Later that morning, after his tough phone conversation with Sarah Black, Andy Grey walked into the central office carrying a burden of furious internal dialogue within him.

"Agent Solana and Agent Barry, I want you in my office, now," said Andy Grey.

Agent Barry stood up immediately.

"Solana, Andy wants to see us in his office," said Agent Barry.

"Has he gone back to his office?" asked Agent Solana.

"Yes, let's go, he said we should see him now," said Agent Barry.

Agent Solana stood up and walked side by side with Barry. "My hunch tells me, something is wrong with that tone from Andy," said Agent Solana. As they walked side by side to Andy's office, Barry decides to make a casual remark to lighten Solana's mood and funnily, she isn't up for his jokes. This really isn't the right time for such a self-sabotaging joke, and Barry might get burnt if his casual joke spills over into Andy's office.

"Your make up is a bit lighter today," said Agent Barry.

"Is that a complement or an observation?" Agent Solana asked with a stern look.

They entered Andy's office and stood right opposite him, funnily Andy wasn't in any mood to babysit his staff after being told off by the head of criminal justice.

"Barry, how long have you been in this unit?" asked Andy Grey.

"Andy, I've been in this unit for six years," replied Agent Barry.

"What about you, Solana?" asked Andy Grey.

"I've been in this unit for eight years," she replied.

"You've been here for six years, and you eight years, yet both of you couldn't build evidence to successfully prosecute a murder case, and this unit is now the topic at the strategic information and operation centre of the FBI headquarters," said Andy Grey.

"Andy, we did our best, the evidence we gathered was all the possible evidence available in the case," said Agent Barry.

"You built desperate and unsubstantiated claims into your evidence that was why they failed," Andy retorted.

"They weren't desperate, I make my claims based on what I think and feel about a case," said Agent Barry.

This isn't some kind of thinly veiled insult, his boss is pushing him to be as good as he can conceivably be, because it will do him no good faffing around, shoulders high, and priding himself as a mischief maker.

Andy turned the heat on Barry accusing him that the way he parades himself as a good detective is in sharp contrast to the abysmal quality of his work, saying detectives don't charge criminals based on hunch alone. He proceeded to accuse Barry of employing archaic investigative mentality that isn't evidence-based, but more of perception and what side of the bed Barry wakes up from.

"Then I don't know what else to say, Andy," replied Agent Barry.

Andy Grey then turned his attention to Agent Solana who led the investigation of the failed case.

"Solana, what do you have to say about this?" asked Andy Grey.

Solana on the other hand, showed contrition as opposed excusing her failure. She had a lot of personal stuff going on in her life, and immediately accepted that their best wasn't good enough and apologised unreservedly for the poor quality of her work. She then proceeded to remind Andy Grey she once told him she would love to get a transfer to Los Angeles, because her mum needed her, and that will help reduce the tendency of working with divided attention.

"If I must confess, I'll say I'm disappointed at the two of you, because the head of criminal justice just called me to express her anger," said Andy.

Andy now fixed his gaze on Agent Barry, who stood opposite him, and looking for a cheap excuse for his failures. "Andy, maybe the guy didn't commit the murder," said Agent Barry. Shocked to hear how quickly Barry retracts his statement after building unsubstantiated claims into the evidence, Andy went ballistic. Agent Barry realised his pinballing from one excuse to another didn't go down well, and he quickly went softly, softly, just to let this storm pass.

"What are you saying, Barry? You and I know very well that Dennis McGuiness was responsible for the murder of Janet Fox. But for your poor evidence, we've just let a murderer back into the street," said Andy.

Agent Solana apologised for a second time for the collapse of this case because she led that investigation. She took full responsibility for the failure of the case because of the loopholes in the evidence presented. Yet, reminded her boss who can also testify that her performance has always been exceptional before she asked for this transfer. If Andy can understand Solana's failures, his ruminative thought seem to have gotten the best of him and he's still rattled with Barry's inability to build a good case, and decides to lash out at Barry for putting him in the spotlight for the wrong reasons. This time Barry can't play the little boy that cries wolf.

"Barry, I'm disappointed at you, why can't you build evidence that makes a good case? Solana, I'll communicate your transfer request to the head of criminal division of main justice," said Andy.

Andy Grey can't wait to return to his boss's good books and days later, he gave Sarah Black a call to discuss Agent Solana's transfer because the distraction resulting from her mum's ill health is beginning to impact on her performance.

"Hello Andy, how're you doing?" asked Sarah.

"I'm fine. Sarah, I'll need a favour from you," said Andy.

The head of criminal justice doesn't compensate failures with favours, especially for a unit that's performing badly, and haemorrhaging in terms of reputation, yet Andy Grey had to press on for favours from his boss if he must fix the setbacks in his unit.

"Do you need a favour from me to fix that? I know you want to ask for more resources, but your unit shouldn't be a drain," Sarah insists. She isn't ready to splash more money around for old rope, and this leaves much to be desired from this FBI unit that hasn't earned its keep.

Andy interjected and said he isn't asking for any form of resources from her boss because so far he isn't running an office with an anaemic purse, "all I'm asking is for Solana to be transferred to Los Angeles," said Andy.

The head of criminal justice expected the head of this unit to get his act together, but not to implode into chaos and didn't hesitate to let Andy know that sending Solana away won't solve the problem. "Andy, all I need is an improvement in the way they build their evidence," said Sarah.

"Of course not, I'm not sending her away, she requested it," said Andy.

"She requested it after I complained about her performance?" asked Sarah.

"No, she did that long before her performance dropped," Andy confirmed.

Sarah Black queried Solana's decision to request a move to Los Angeles, because having someone to immediately replace Solana could be difficult. "Her mum is sick, and she wants to move closer to her," said Andy.

"Now I know why your unit has suffered some setbacks. Her mum's condition has been affecting her work, and why haven't you brought this up before now?" Sarah queried. Though, Andy claimed not to know that Agent Solana's worries would impact on her job this much, he's now ready to let her go, and if not for anything, at least to save his own skin. The impact of Solana's worries is now palpable, and something needs to be done to nip this from spiralling further.

Sad to say, it might be difficult for the head of criminal justice getting a replacement for Solana, but she has promised to shop around to see if there is anyone who wants to come over to New York, then the swap will happen. After thinking through all previous requests for a transfer and funnily, Agent Donald Whitley came to mind, then Sarah Black called Eddie Taylor the head of the FBI unit in Los Angeles.

She immediately reminded him he once told her that someone in his unit wants to make a move to New York.

"Err, yes. I told you and you said that won't be possible and I don't think I'll want the transfer to go on," replied Eddie.

She interjected and asked why he wouldn't want the transfer to go on, then proceeded to ask if the staff in question has changed his mind. This is one transfer Eddie had wished never happens, he'd prayed secretly in his heart that the matter remain closed, but sadly for Eddie the matter is back on the table. Eddie's position on this transfer isn't out of prejudice against the detective concerned, he just wasn't willing to let go of the pride of his unit.

"No, he's my best hand and no unit head will easily give away their best performing employee," said Eddie.

"An agent in New York needs to come over to Los Angeles because her mum needs her while your agent will move to New York to replace her," said Sarah.

"Did you say, her?" asked Eddie. "Yes, her, she's a lady and what's the problem with that, or are you a sexist?" replied Sarah.

Eddie Taylor coiled away after being accused of sexism, Eddie didn't hesitate to let Sarah know he has no problem with having a lady transferred to his unit, just that she'll be working with

Pauline fisher who's also a lady. But Eddie believes in pairing a male detective with a female detective.

"Is there no other male in your team?" asked Sarah.

Eddy Taylor opened up to Sarah that he has male detectives but giving up a staff as experienced as Donald is a big ask, and other of his male detectives aren't as experienced as Donald.

"I understand, though the swap will still go ahead but in a little while I'll get you an experienced male replacement," Sarah promised.

Eddie Taylor's effort to explain to his boss that in certain situation, a man handles the suspects better and in others a woman handles the suspects better during an investigation, failed to stop the swap, because the swap will proceed.

"I understand there is strength in diversity; I'll get you a male detective soonest, and an experienced one" said Sarah.

Moments after his phone call with Sarah Black, Eddie Taylor looked like a child who just lost his priced toy as he walked grumpily into the central office where Donald and Pauline were discussing the new Federal policy on body cam.

"Donald, what do you think of the new policy requiring cops to wear body cameras?" asked Agent Pauline.

"Really, I don't know which side of the debate to give my support, because it's a give and take policy," said Agent Donald. Pauline continues to pester him suggesting he at least should know whether he's in support of it or not. He then proceeded to tell one of his stories, in his usual way of adding flesh to his conversation.

"When I was a little boy I use to remember that each time my dad buys me and my brother toys, marketing starts immediately. I'll start telling my brother mine is better, and he'll equally tell me reason why his own is better and before you know it, each person begins to be jealous of the other person's toy.

My dad will come to me and say don't mind your brother yours is better, don't you see your toy has these features which his doesn't have. Minutes later my dad will go to my brother as well and tell him yours is better, I only told Donald his is better just to deceive him. Finally, we'll begin to tell each other dad said mine is better, and each person will suddenly fall in love with their toy and that settles it," said Agent Donald.

Agent Pauline burst into laughter. "Did you just answer my question?" asked Agent Pauline. Agent Donald gave Pauline a cheeky grin, even as she continued in her laughter over his illusory story in response to her question.

"Ooh, I think I just did," Agent Donald said with a smile. He then said wearing body camera can help the police prove to the authorities that he has done everything by the book, and it can also put a negligent cop into trouble, but…

Eddie Taylor walked into the central office. "Donald, see me in my office now," said Eddie.

Agent Donald followed Eddie to his office. "I just got a call from the head of criminal justice that your transfer to New York has been approved," said Eddie.

Donald was quite elated as the news of his transfer was relayed to him, he didn't hide his feelings at all, and his disposition said it all.

"Ooh perfect, this is coming at a good time!" exclaimed Agent Donald.

"What do you mean, perfect! Have you been itching to leave us?" asked Eddie.

"No, my wife just got a new job offer in New York and we were in the process of turning it down, but with this news it's all perfect," Donald explained further, as he tried not to stir up ill feelings in his boss.

"You're my best detective, letting you go is a very hard decision for me," said Eddie.

"The feeling is mutual. Everyone here is like a family to me and I'll miss this unit," said Agent Donald.

A week after concluding the swap with the Los Angeles unit, Sarah Black gave Andy Grey of the New York unit the update, but she couldn't communicate properly, as she told Andy his background is noisy and she couldn't' hear him clearly..

"No Sarah, the noise you're hearing is from a suspect that was brought in for questioning," said Andy.

"Can we talk now or later?" asked Sarah.

"We should talk now; I'm already walking to my office," replied Andy Grey.

The noise can wait, but what the head of criminal justice had to say is important to Andy who's trying hard to return to his boss's good books, so he walked away from the noise.

"I've found a replacement for Solana in Los Angeles," she said. "That's good news, when is the transfer happening?" he asked.

Sarah promised to get everything concerning this transfer ready in two weeks. She assured him that the transfer letters will be prepared and sent out to enable this transfer take effect as soon as possible, but Andy is curious, and his inner curiosity couldn't be kept quiet.

"Sarah, which of the agents are you bringing here?" Andy asked curiously. "I'm bringing you Donald Whitley," she replied.

"Ooh, Donald Whitley! I've read a lot about him in the FBI journal. I guess, I'm lucky to have him here in my unit," Andy exclaimed.

Sarah pointed out to Andy that he's giving him a highly prized detective in the person of Donald Whitley whom she considered a firebrand detective with luminous star qualities, and assured Andy that this detective will light up his unit with enough fire, and in a manner he least expected.

"The manner in which Donald Whitley was being talked about in the FBI journals made Andy to inquire of his length of service with the FBI.

"Donald is a senior detective; he has about seventeen years of service in the FBI," said Sarah.

Andy didn't hesitate to break the news of the transfer to Agent Solana the moment the phone conversation with the head of criminal justice ended. "Thank you, let me inform Solana about this," said Andy.

Immediately Andy dropped the phone, he strolled to the Central office and turned to Agent Solana who seemed consumed with her work. "Solana, meet me in my office," said Andy. Agent Solana followed Andy from behind as he returned to his office. She immediately left everything and followed Andy.

"Andy, you want to see me?" she asked.

"I just got a call from the head of criminal justice; your transfer request has been granted," said Andy. "Hmm, good, and when'll it be!" Agent Solana exclaimed.

Andy told Solana he's expecting her letter possibly in two weeks' time, so as soon as he gets the letter, the transfer will take effect, but as Agent Solana turns to leave, she realised there's unfinished business she needed to address, and she then turned back again facing Andy.

"Sorry, do you've idea of who my replacement would be?" she asked.

Err, that'll be, Agent Donald Whitley. I believe you know about him," said Andy.

Hmm, Solana wasn't too happy to hear this, because she was looking forward to being in the same team with Agent Donald Whitley. She actually hoped to use her alliance with Donald Whitely to further her career.

"Yes, I've heard a lot about him, and I've looked forward to working with him in Los Angeles. Unfortunately, I'll miss that opportunity" she said.

"Sorry about that, you know you can't have your cake and eat it," said Andy.

Despite not having her cake and eat it, Solana realised she can't win them all, yet remain grateful to Andy for his understanding during her difficult moments on the job. Then, Solana left and walked into the central office, arguably she was all smiles when she sauntered back into the central office "Guys, my transfer has been approved," she said.

Agent Barry who has been her partner on the job struggled with how to handle the news of Solana's transfer.

"What? Don't tell me it's true!" he said. Solana didn't hesitate to wish her partner of six years good bye. "Yes it is, in two weeks' time my letter of transfer will be ready," said Solana.

Agent Barry responded crankily without ruminating over his thoughts, as his disposition was that of a man lost for words.

"What about me?" Barry asked.

Funnily, Agent Solana's parting comment didn't seem to sooth Barry's anxiety.

"You'll continue your job, while I go and start a new life in Los Angeles and also take care of my mum," she replied.

"No, that isn't what I meant; I mean what about you and me, us?" asked Barry.

"I don't understand, there has never been anything between us and you never said anything to me, so why now?" Agent Solana queried.

"But the way I look at you and even compliment you, should've let you know I like you," said Agent Barry.

Agent Barry's attempt to explain himself further didn't really help to steady the icing on the cake, because his blabbing didn't convey any message to Solana. It's obvious that Agent Solana understands what Barry was getting at, but finds this conversation with Barry sort of stifling, she perceived his charm seems exaggerated and that kind of put her off.

"Sorry Barry, a lot of people complement me and I don't see that as initiating a relationship," she said.

Romantic relationships with team members do not usually work out, and it's usually considered a red line for many, and Barry knows this. More so, making passes at one's superior is another red line for a sensible person. While Agent Barry sounded illusory, Solana didn't think it necessary to goad him, after all she wants to leave on a friendly term.

"You're my team leader and my superior on the job; you shouldn't have expected me to come out direct about my feelings for you. I wouldn't want to get caught up by these 'feminist' movements," said Agent Barry.

"Barry, whatever your feelings are, we'll talk about them when I get to Los Angeles, but for now, let me start making arrangements about my new accommodation," said Agent Solana.

Agent Murphy allowed Barry to finish pouring out his heart to Solana, before congratulating her. "I'm happy for you Solana, though Barry will miss working with you," said Agent Murphy.

Two weeks later the transfer letters are out, and Eddie Taylor wanted to hand Agent Donald's transfer letter to him, but Donald wasn't around. So, moments later he walked into the central office from outside.

"Donald, I've looked around for you before I left the office, where were you?" asked Eddie.

"There's this Sushi I ate two weeks ago in a Japanese restaurant, and I felt I should have a taste of it again," replied Donald.

Eddie laughed knowing that this idea of having a taste of almost every meal out there is one unique quality of Agent Donald. Call it character flaw, or curiosity, that's Donald for you. "I hope you enjoyed it?" asked Eddie.

"Of course, it was quite lovely," said Agent Donald.

Eddie asked Agent Donald to follow him to his office and handed him the letter "That's your transfer letter, it's out," said Eddie.

"Thank you," replied Agent Donald.

"This unit will miss you, because you've helped this unit make a lot of progress," said Eddie.

"Why're you sounding like this, Eddie?" asked Agent Donald.

Eddie was already missing Donald even as he stood right in front of him, but truth be told, the transfer letter meant Donald is no longer one his staff.

"You're a successful agent, and I'll say your career success is a consequence of your intuitiveness, coupled with your charismatic nature," said Eddie.

"I'm only doing my job, Eddie," replied Agent Donald.

Moments later, Donald returned to the central office, and informed Pauline his transfer letter is out. Years of partnership have just been severed by this transfer, and life goes on, but the memories of cases they've solved together meant, they share certain memories together.

"Oh, Donald that's great but we'll all miss you," said Pauline.

"I'll equally miss you, Pauline. You know that don't you?" asked Donald.

"Working with you has improved my experience on this job, and I'll be forever grateful to you," said Pauline.

A week later, it's time for this detective whose ubiquitous presence was quite felt in the FBI headquarters to go, and it's time for Los Angeles FBI unit to send Agent Donald Whitley off to New York, so a send-off party was organised for Agent Donald.

Eddie Taylor and every staff of the unit sing "he's a jolly good fellow, he's a jolly good fellow, and he's a jolly good fellow that nobody can deny."

Eddie Taylor lifted a glass of wine and proposed a toast to Donald Whitley. "Today we're all gathered here to show appreciation to one of our own, who has brought this unit into the limelight in the whole of the United States. Let's make a toast to Donald Whitley," said Eddie.

"To Donald Whitley," said Agent Lane. "To Donald Whitley," said Agent Pauline. Eddie Taylor added his voice to the pack. "To the future and to Donald," said Eddie.

After the toast to Donald, there was a moment of merriment among the staff in the unit. "Those of you that have one thing or the other to say to Donald, it's time to do so," said Eddie.

"Err, Donald, I'll miss you, and it's like I shouldn't let you go, but you've to. I'm proud of you, thanks for sharing your experience with me," said Agent Lane.

"Hmm, one thing I'll also miss about you is the subtle nuance of your facial expression when you tell some of your stories during investigations," said Agent Pauline.

"They say good people don't last, though in this circumstance you're alive but your stay in our unit is like a candle in the wind and I hope life treats you well," said Mark Cleverly.

"Donald, we all love you, and we wish you well wherever you go. On behalf of this FBI unit, we present this gift as a show of appreciation," Eddie Taylor handed him a wrapped gift.

Agent Donald gave a vote of thanks expressing his heart felt appreciation. "I want to thank you all for your love and this surprise send-off party. Eddie, thank you, Pauline thank you, Lane thank you, Mark, thanks, you've all made my working in Los Angeles an enjoyable experience, and I'll miss you all," said Agent Donald.

A week later, Agent Donald reports for Duty in New York City, and funnily stumbled into Andy Grey at the entrance of the building. Agent Donald introduced himself with a handshake, even though Andy didn't hesitate in recognising him.

"Donald, you're welcome to the FBI unit in New York City," said Andy. "It's a pleasure meeting you, Andy, I've looked forward to working with you, and now I'm here," he said with a smile.

"We've heard a lot about you and we hope to benefit from some of your exploits," replied Andy.

The flattered Agent Donald realised he's highly rated, and this laid bare the expectations of the unit before him. "I pray I meet your expectations," said Agent Donald.

"Follow me, let me introduce you to the other agents," said Andy. They walked into the central office, with Andy in the front and Donald following him from behind. "This is Agent Barry," said Andy.

"Nice to meet you, Agent Barry," said Agent Donald.

"Meet agent Murphy, other agents will be introduced to you when they return from the field," and turning around, "that's Gilbert Rivers, he's our IT guru," said Andy.

"It's a pleasure meeting you all, and I hope to enjoy working with you," said Agent Donald.

"You're welcome, Donald," replied Agent Murphy.

"We look for forward to the new energy and dynamism you're bringing into our unit," said Andy.

Days later, Agent Solana is in Los Angeles where she's meant to resume her job after her transfer from New York City, but first she had to put up with her mum who's the reason for her transfer. She stood in front of her mum's apartment and took a deep breath, then a sigh of relief, before pressing the doorbell.

"Hello mum, is anybody home?" said Agent Solana.

"Who is at the door? Oh, that's you". Carol walked to the door and opened the door laughing, and they hugged each other tightly. "Oh, my baby girl, welcome to Los Angeles," said Carol.

After giving the bear hug, Solana entered her mum's apartment. "Good to see you, mum. How're you doing?" asked Agent Solana.

"Oh, I'm fine my baby. I've always told you I'm strong, and I'm holding it together," said Carol.

Not long after settling in her mum's place, Solana's craving seems to have gotten the best of her. She then stood up and walked to the refrigerator, opened it, and was looking but couldn't find her favourite. "Mum, what about your apple pie. Do you still have it?" she asked.

"You know I always have it, and it's right there in the refrigerator, in front of you," replied Carol.

Solana smiled. "Ooh, mum. I've always longed to have a taste of your apple pie," she said.

"You grew up having a taste of it daily, why wouldn't you miss it? And you look pale," Carole said as she examines her daughter with her critical look.

"How do you mean, mum? I'm never hungry and I'm well paid, so I feed well," asked Solana. "You look skinnier than I used to know you, and that look doesn't justify your being well fed," Carol replied. Carol's critical assessment of her daughter's size is one that makes Solana uncomfortable, because she feel her mum is knowingly refusing to separate being thin from looking fit.

"Mum, I'm a Cop, and I'm supposed to keep fit at all time," said Solana.

"Ok, whatever you say, but I'm going to feed you and make you a bit bigger, because my apple pie will do the magic," said Carol.

Moments earlier, while Solana waited by the door before being allowed in by her mum, she noticed a distinct sticker posted on her mum's door.

"Mum, what's the meaning of the sticker pasted on the door of your house?" asked Agent Solana.

Carol interjected and asked her daughter what sticker she's referring to because there are three stickers pasted on that door.

"The one that states 'I love my gun and I hate gun control,' I know you don't have a gun, mum. Why did you put that there?" asked Agent Solana.

"Ooh," Carol laughed. "Just to keep the hawks out," said Carol and laughed again. "You mean, to keep the bad guys out?" asked Agent Solana.

"Of course, yes, you know I'm vulnerable and I want the world to consider me strong and keep off," said Carol.

Carol's wisdom isn't anything but survival, and the benignity of her wisdom is crafted in her desire to offer the hawks in the streets of Los Angeles an olive branch as opposed to guns blazing. Solana looked at her mum in amusement and it's now glaringly obvious to her that her mum's uncanny move to use decoys to stave off the bad guys is something they've in common.

"You never cease to amaze me, mum, I spent so much time worrying about you, but here you're looking strong and displaying so much wisdom," said Solana.

Carol's eye was all over her daughter, as she looks out for indications of a relationship, since her curiosity didn't provide her with the answer she seeks, she decided to voice out her concerns for answers.

"You never mentioned him in all your conversations," said Carol.

"Him? I don't get you," replied Agent Solana.

"Your man, please tell me about him," said Carol.

"Oh mum, it's complicated," said Solana.

This has always been her response to her mum's ubiquitous curiosity about her social life.

"Why is it always complicated? There's a lot of life out there, the world is beautiful, just get a man and have some fun," said Carol.

"Mum, let's change the topic, we'll talk about this later," Agent Solana replied. She tried to quieten her mum to at least enjoy her apple pie. But Carol doesn't seem to be giving up so fast, particularly now that her daughter is within her sphere of influence.

"Slipping into your pyjamas and retiring into your sofa at the end of your shift isn't life," said Carol.

Solana couldn't concentrate on her job over concerns for her mum which she now finds to be illusory. Funnily, Carol's deluge of messages kept her worrying about her mum, but here is Carol attempting to manage her daughter's social life.

"Wear some make up and go out. Socialise, your natural charm will bring the right man your way," said Carol. Carol reminded her daughter that life is a precious gift and it's obvious to all that she has a spring in her step but then made it plain to Solana that she is no spring chicken. Carols' perception of her daughter as some kind of a hopeless romantic, prompted her attempt to turn her daughter into some sort of finely beautified Rubicon that should suddenly become irresistible to the eyes.

"Mum, don't get carried away by platitudes," said Agent Solana.

Carol who was busy netting a sweater for her to-be grandchild left what she was doing, walked towards her daughter and stood in front of her. "Oh, you call this a cliché?" asked Carol.

"Of course, yes!" she replied.

The paradox here is that Carol suddenly thinks it's her daughter that needs the help, but this subtle and unsolicited advice might piss her daughter off. This isn't some kind of girly gossip between this mum and daughter, it's quite thorny, more like waves crashing on the sea shore.

"Hmm, honey, it won't cost an arm and a leg to spice up your life, perhaps you should take time off work," said Carol.

"Ooh, mum, why! You dragged me down to Los Angeles to manage my life or what? Let's drop this conversation," said Agent Solana. Carol realises it's too early to provoke her guest to anger, and decides to lay this matter to rest for the moment.

CHAPTER

THREE

The Sheriff

Agent Donald and Agent Barry were at a crime scene, and interestingly, this is their first time together on a case, as they walked into the scene of a possible homicide.

Sadly, this isn't just any homicide, a Big Gun in Capitol Hill has just died in what looks like an unexplained death. The death in question is that of Alexander Bishop, a Senator of the United States.

Agent Donald couldn't help as Agent Barry got petty with the NYPD officer on the scene, he isn't used to having a partner being jumpy but this one arguably, is quite jumpy. Lieutenant Dempsey was at the scene when the detectives walked in.

"Lieutenant, I suppose the NYPD is waiting for us to solve this case as well," said Agent Barry. Lieutenant Dempsey was quite annoyed with Agent Barry's poorly chosen words and immediately sounded a note of caution, and even though he finds Agent Barry insufferable as always, he still took exception to his remark.

"Know your place, detective," said Lieutenant Dempsey. Agent Barry's public demeanour is far from being described as calm and collected because his boundless arrogance means he wants to have the last say so. The lieutenant then turned to Agent Donald whose hand is already stretched out for a hand shake.

"Agent Donald, I suppose?" asked the lieutenant.

"Yeah, hello lieutenant," he replied.

Agent Donald smiled and asked Lieutenant Dempsey if they've met because he doesn't recollect telling the lieutenant his name. Interestingly, Lieutenant Dempsey is a friend of Agent Solana, who already informed the lieutenant that she's swapping with Agent Donald Whitely. While this pair formally introduced themselves, Agent Barry became quite uncomfortable with the warm ambience between them, he immediately interjected as he tries scuttled this friendly familiarization between this two.

"Hey, Donald, don't let them suck you in," said Agent Barry.

Agent Donald had to tap Agent Barry on the shoulder, asking him to tone down the negativity and take things calmly.

Agent Donald then spoke softly to Barry, and reminded him of the saying "you are my friend does not necessarily mean your enemies must be my enemies, and your friends must be my friends. This is because friendship is subjective, and defined by the parties in the friendship."

"No, Donald, you don't know these guys, I know them, and they're just lazy," said Agent Barry.

"Let me draw that conclusion myself as I acquaint myself with the system," said Agent Donald.

After the brief conversation with the NYPD officers in the scene, the detectives scanned through the dead senator's house for clues that could make this death a possible homicide.

Agent Donald walked back to the Lieutenant and asked if they were able to find anything, but they seem to have the same set of clues and nothing out of the blue concerning the dead senator.

Donald kept racking his brain and thinking out loud, as he assured himself that he hasn't been able to conclude whether the victim's pupil dilated to suggest poison, whether his lungs shows he died of suffocation to prove he was he strangled, and so far his death is unexplained. With nothing concrete to go by, the detectives had to wait for the forensic report to answer the question, too many questions running through his mind.

"Lieutenant, we're leaving, and I think we'll have to wait for the forensic report," said Agent Donald.

"Ok, detective, I'll let you know if anything comes up," said Lieutenant Dempsey.

Like him or loath him, Agent Barry isn't the half-and-half regular kind of guy, he organically hates those who hate him and likes those who like him. His personality is more of a contraption that leaves many bewildered, because he likes only what he chooses to like and hates what he loves to hate. He's always upfront and never shy about his feelings.

Sadly, it's now blindingly obvious to Agent Donald that aside the case at hand, he now has to assume the additional responsibility of helping Agent Barry snap out of his illusory character flaw. His brief assessment of Agent Barry is that Barry sees people as telling fables, and his perceptions are more illusions than palpable.

Hours later, the detectives are back to their office and now reviewing the case, even as they await the forensic report. Gilbert Rivers pulled out an online rant against Senator Alexander Bishop, where a member of the public accused the senator of being bought-over by the mining firm accused of being behind the pollution of their drinking water in South Dakota.

The detectives watched and listened to John Carter's online rants.

"Senator Alexander Bishop, this message is for you, I'll get you. I thought you're different from them but you've just disappointed us," said John Carter.

"Did he just publicly threaten a decorated military chief, and a serving Senator of the United States?" asked Agent Barry.

"Yeah, I think he just did. Gilbert, I want you to check him out, this guy, John Carter or whatever he calls himself," said Andy.

Moments later, Gilbert's search placed John Carter in the same vicinity as the late senator. He was in the Playville Hotel where the senator was a guest, hours before his death.

"How come this guy was allowed to roam the streets freely after promising to deal with the senator, I think we've found the culprit in this case," said Agent Barry.

Agent Donald interjected and turned to Agent Barry, and suggested to him to take a deep breath, saying this John Carter is arguably a person of interest but there's no need jumping into premature conclusions.

Agent Barry interjected and laughed at Agent Donald's naivety as he began lining is ducks in a row, before putting forward his analysis, saying, the guy has a motive and he obviously was in the same hotel at the same time with the senator, and these incidents aren't mere serendipity.

After watching John Carter's online rant, Andy asked his detectives to go and bring John Carter in for questioning. An hour later, the detectives brought John Carter in, and Agent Barry went in immediately to start questioning John Carter while the other detectives watched the interrogation from the watching room.

"Yes John, we saw your rants and your promises to kill Senator Alexander Bishop, so you've the guts to kill a beloved senator of the United States," said Agent Barry.

"Hey, what gives you the gut to accuse me of a crime I didn't commit?" said John.

"You must be a joke to think I'll let you out through that door, without charging you for this crime," said Agent Barry.

"Sorry, I won't say a word, except my lawyer is here," said John.

Efforts to make John speak seem futile as he insisted on having his lawyer present, and the interrogation stalled because John finds Agent Barry's direct accusation to be quite spooky. Andy's patience grew thin, he then turned immediately to Agent Donald, and asked him to go into the interrogation room and find out what this guy has under his sleeve that he's hiding. Immediately Agent Donald went in, John Cater coiled in further.

"Hmm, John, I'm detective Donald," said Agent Donald.

"Hey, detective, I've said I'm not saying a word without my lawyer," John protested.

"Sorry, you will get your lawyer, and I understand your concerns about the water pollution because you felt the senator betrayed you?" asked Agent Donald.

"Ok, I'll talk to you because you seem to understand how betrayed we felt about Senator Alexander Bishop," said John.

"But you were in the hotel where Alexander Bishop was a guest in the night before his death," said Agent Donald.

"Sorry, but I went there to protest, just to let him know he won't have any peace until he speaks up for us," said John.

"I suppose, you're aware the senator is dead," said Agent Donald.

"Look, I've no hand in the senator's death, and I wouldn't be foolish enough to openly protest against a man and then go ahead and kill him, knowing full well that fingers will be pointed at me," said John.

The forensic report came in while John Carter was being interrogated, and sadly, the report ruled the senator's death as unexplained. Andy immediately tapped the glass window from where he was watching the interrogation, and signalled Agent Donald to come over, so they could all look at the forensic report.

"Is it now a crime to protest against your senator's ineptitude? This is the United States for God's sake, and it's my right to protest," said John.

Agent Donald turned around and stood up, then told John Carter he'll be back. "Hey, look I didn't kill this senator, I went to his hotel to protest his silence over our plight, and you can't keep me here because I've done nothing wrong," John protested.

"Do we still need this forensic report, we already have our killer," said Agent Barry. Agent Donald interjected saying he doesn't think John is behind the senator's death because he thinks this guy won't be that daft enough to pull such a brazen stunt. Yet, Agent Barry urged Agent Donald to wake up from his dreams, reminding him that if John Carter is daft enough to post his rants and threats online, and pays the senator a visit to his hotel even after such rants, then he sure should be daft enough to act on the threats.

While the detectives were busy reviewing the case, a phone call from the Head of Main Justice came in. Andy then stepped aside to attend to the phone call, and sadly, time is of the essence for Sarah.

Sarah Black's phone call wasn't one of pleasantries as she asked Andy to get cracking immediately, because the Big Guns in Capitol Hill want answers, and she's the one to give them the answers they seek. She once gave Andy the dressing down, for the poor performance of his unit, and this time she wants so much from him because her job is on the line, and will take no excuses from Andy. The Speaker of House of Congress and even the Senate Majority Leader want to know why this death is classed as unexplained and they want answers fast. Immediately after his phone conversation with Sarah Black, Andy walked back to the central office and asked his men to pay a second visit to the Senator's house and the Playville Hotel where the Senator was a guest the night before his death. Interestingly, Agent Donald serendipitously finds himself dealing with two cases within a short timeframe that has the interest of the Big Guns at the helm of government. The other time it was the Attorney General Nephew's son, and this time it's a beloved Senator of the United States, and this hasn't always been the case anyway, but he'd have to produce the needed result to keep these Big Guns happy.

Interestingly, while Andy was speaking with his men, another phone call came into his mobile, he picked up the phone, and funnily, it was the pathologist on the phone, informing him they found traces of radioactive substance in the late senator's system. This new lead is now a new twist that makes this death not to be deemed unexplained, as presumed earlier.

"What about John Carter, what do we do with him?" asked Agent Donald.

Andy immediately sent his detectives alongside the forensic team to John Crater's house for traces of radioactive substance. Sadly, there was none, and even the CCTV in the hotel reveal there wasn't any contact between John Carter and the senator. Yet, Andy isn't letting this guy off, after all he's so far, the prime suspect in the senator's murder. He'd to keep him locked up while the investigation lingers.

Andy is now sucked in by this new turn of event, as more revelations about the senator's death come to the open. He immediately sent his men to the senator's house instructing them to review all the cameras within and around the Senator's home. "We need to know how he came in contact with a radioactive material," said Andy. He then urged his men to turn the hotel inside-out for traces of radioactive material.

The detectives went with their forensic team and rummaged through the late Senator's apartment and found no trace of radioactive material, except for his pyjamas and the bed he slept in, and they then proceeded to the hotel where the Senator was a guest a night before his death and found nothing after turning the place inside out.

All those working with the senator including his body guards had their lives turned inside out, in this investigation and yet there's nothing linking them to this senator's unexplained death. While the detectives were out and about, they visited the pathologist for more clues.

"Hello detectives, I suppose you're here for more answers about the Senator," said the pathologist.

"Yes, we're still piecing things together, and maybe you might give us a few more clues," said Agent Donald.

The pathologist then said the radioactive material wasn't inhaled, and neither was it ingested. The fact that the clothes the senator wore during the day didn't show traces of radioactive material shows he didn't come into contact with it while he was up and about and even while he was in the hotel. So far it's only his sleeping garment and the bed where he slept and died are the only places where there are traces of the radioactive material. His sleeping garment had traces of radioactive material, but further examination revealed his sweat contaminated his clothes.

"Are you implying someone broke into his house and injected the radioactive material in his system while he was asleep?" asked Agent Barry.

"From your forensic report, there wasn't a break in, or an intruder of any sort, which implies he came into contact with the radioactive material hours earlier," said the pathologist. There are indications of a secondary poison by Nicotine, the pathologist report revealed the presence of Nicotine and said Nicotine metabolises slowly in the body that is why it isn't always noticeable but the quantity was so small that the cigarette shouldn't have killed him. Andy then asked if the Senator was a heavy smoker but Agent Donald interjected and said, yes, but the report emphasised that it was the radioactive material that killed the Senator.

Agent Donald went further to explain that the pathologist findings revealed that the radioactive material in question isn't one that kills immediately to alert suspicion. This substance allowed the senator to finish is daily activities and retired to bed before he suffered from the radiation, and this implied military grade radioactive equipment was in play here, making this a targeted attack at the senator. Possibly, his head and not his body, forehead sort of, was hit in a sniper-style attack.

"Andy, I think we are looking for a trained sniper with ability to deploy a military grade radioactive attack," said Agent Donald.

Sadly, Barry had feared being invisible with a more experience hand in the team, and one thing he hates most is the feeling of being small or non-existent in the room. Yet, this is an opportunity to learn from a more experienced agent Donald if his ego won't get in the way.

"Are you quite sure about this, and I hope this isn't one of those goose chases?" asked Agent Barry.

Immediately the forensic report ruled the senator's death as unexplained, and the use of radioactive substance now thrown in the mix, Agent Donald decided to give some thought to the case, using a new pair of eyes by looking at the case differently. At least, to see if there's anyone who could have a motive to kill the beloved senator of the United States.

Interestingly, Agent Donald was able to narrow this death to the only person who had a motive and able to carry out the murder of a highly protected senator leaving a clean slate.

Two days later, Agent Donald walked to Andy's office and said this senator's death is the handwork of the Sheriff.

"The Sheriff, you said, and who's he?" asked Andy.

This new line of conversation is one that interests Andy, which he seeks to pursue logically, and after all, pursuing any plausible lead at this point is innocuous without any implication lapse. He then stood up and immediately followed Agent Donald to the central office, then asked Gilbert to put Agent Donald's findings on the screen for analysis.

Agent Donald informed his colleagues that the Sheriff is a debt collector, who helps give justice to people seeking vengeance, and when vengeance is served then the debt is collected. He's Sean Cameron, a former CIA agent, Special Forces, sort of, and he's trained to kill because he's bred for war, and sadly, asymmetrical war is his thing. Agent Donald elucidated further that Sean Cameron thought he was working for the government and serving his country diligently, only to realise some Big Guns in the Pentagon are using him to settle personal political scores in other nations. He went AWOL, then resurfaced a year later before being court marshalled, then discharged dishonourably.

Instead of full contrition he chose restitution, at least to provide justice to those wronged by the system, and sadly, that's his own way of giving back to society and righting every one of his wrongs.

"How did you know about him?" asked Andy.

Agent Donald narrated how the Sheriff escaped the FBI years back, they then chased him to Dusseldorf, Germany, he left the city immediately he sensed the FBI followed him there, he moved to Rostock a much quieter city in Germany, the FBI intelligence followed him there. He then ran off to Columbia to seek refuge with the FARC rebels, that was when they had to back-off.

The moment he stepped into Columbia, the stares they got was a killer, and funnily, if stares could kill then he and his partner would be deceased.

He then proceeded to explain that embarrassingly, while in Columbia, they wore their badge around with shoulders high as people proud of having a slice of American history. The situation at this point became tricky and fishing this guy out was more like the proverbial needle, and there's no need surmising prematurely at that point how far the FARC Rebels are willing to go to protect this guy.

"Why didn't you follow him there?" asked Agent Barry.

Agent Donald didn't want to go into further details but said they needed more fire power to engage the FARC rebels in fire fight and since the back-up wasn't forthcoming they had to back down.

Eventually the FBI tracked the Sheriff down when he sneaked back in to the country but one of his hands took the blame for the murder, and the guy is serving a life sentence as they speak.

Agent Donald had to open up to his colleagues that chasing this guy was almost costing the department an arm and a leg. He then narrated when he requested to make a second visit to Columbia and realised the flight cost tripled, he'd to back down after his then boss exclaimed saying he's only booking a few seats in the plane to move his staff from one place to the other and not buying the whole damn plane because of the flight cost that seem hugely exorbitant. More so, the hotel cost wasn't spared the sudden price hike, which also caught his boss's attention resulting in him muttering that he isn't paying that amount because he isn't buying a whole village either.

"One of his hands took the blame, what do you mean by that?" asked Andy.

The sheriff has so many followers that do his bidding and his followership extends beyond the shores of the United States, it's global. Many a time, what we call death from a robbery gone wrong, petty crime, political assassination, and even the death of businessman by business partners could actually be the sheriff collecting a debt. You see a dead drug dealer in the street of Acapulco in Mexico, Rio de Janeiro in Brazil, or you stumble into the corpse of what you supposed to be the victim of a terrorist act in Mogadishu in Somalia, or FARC rebels in Colombia, and in many cases these deaths happen here in the United States.

Agent Donald proceeded to say that many deaths occurring globally are actually the handiwork of the Sheriff, and the last estimate they've was about five thousand annual deaths globally, and justice for the Sheriff is a life for a life, and when life is taken, it means the debt is collected.

Agent Barry turned to Agent Donald and asked if he's implying this guy, the sheriff or whatever he calls himself has such a global reach.

"People seeking justice reach out to him via the dark web, particularly when they think the system have failed in giving them the justice they seek," said Agent Donald.

Kids playing in the field and stumbling into an amputated limb of an unidentified man, like what was reported in the news just a month ago in LA could be the sheriff calling in some favours to collect debt. And DNA later proved the limb belongs to Melvin Ross who was accused of murdering an old pensioner but the Cops didn't take the case further because they don't have enough to charge him.

"So, the Sheriff decided to take Melvin's life for the life of the pensioner?" Agent Barry queried further.

Agent Donald put it more nicely that the Sheriff didn't, but the family of the pensioner did request the Sheriff to collect the debt on their behalf. A life for a life, the brutal murder of the pensioner was mirrored in how Melvin Ross was killed, this got people pointing fingers of accusations at the old pensioner's family but they have got alibi of where they are and what they were doing as at the time Melvin was killed. This implies that that a third hand was involved in Melvin's death.

What they don't know is that this is the work of the Sheriff collecting debt on behalf of the victimised. He speaks for the dead, he speaks for the victimised, and those who felt the system didn't give them the justice they seek loves the Sheriff's idea of justice. They love him for sticking up for them.

Andy wants to know the Sheriff's motive in the senator's murder, and yet, understands that motive alone isn't enough, but evidence is what does the trick, and needed to make sure his team isn't arresting some guy with a water-tight alibi. Agent Donald had to make it plain and simple that this guy is a killer who always has an alibi to help him evade justice, and that's the key reason why he's used for international assassinations without fingers of accusations pointing back to his government. Agent Donald turned to Andy and suggested that at this point, it will be a more realistic approach to delve into the person of the late senator, to be able to have a firm grasp of whom the killer might be, and what the possible killer might share in common with the senator.

"Why the senator, why would this guy want this senator dead?" asked Andy.

Agent Donald went further with his analysis of the case saying, Senator Alexander Bishop was a former General in the Army. He's among those in the Pentagon that used Sean Cameron to do their bidding. Funnily, Sean quipped the first time he realised his bosses were lining their pockets with cash at his behest. When he eventually understood what's going on, he went AWOL but Alexander Bishop smoked him out and court marshalled him before discharging him dishonourably.

His life started with cheers, then jeers but now it has escalated to what's best described as a bad omen. "Is this all you've got for a solid motive?" asked Agent Barry.

But Agent Donald assured Barry that this guy is good at what he does, and most deaths in his hands are usually classed as unexplained. "If we look deeper then we'll find something to tie this to him," said Agent Donald.

Recently, most deaths recorded in Washington DC are purported to be the work of copy cats who claim to be the Sheriff. These copycats have tried mimicking his acts but his unique insignia makes it undeniably difficult for copy cats.

Unfortunately, the Sheriff has a unique insignia that makes death by his hand unexplained. For all it's worth, hardly does Sean Cameron do the collection of debt by himself, he leaves debt collection to his fans worldwide, just those ones that he has personal interest that he collects himself, like this one.

The job of being a part of the Special Forces turned out not to be as gratifying as much a he'd expected, which is the reason he considered his superiors to be nothing but snakes in the grass.

Sean Cameron knows the workings of shadowy government figures, and since there isn't anyone to blame for his betrayal and subsequent court martial, he decided to take out the few people he considered to be bad eggs in the crate.

Andy interjected and asked "How do we catch this guy? And firstly, we need to dislodge his activities in the dark web."

Andy then tuned to Gilbert and asked him to produce a CCTV trail that will give them a minute-by-minute detail of Sean Cameron's movement to see if he'd any close contact with the senator. Andy then turned again to Agent Donald and asked him and Barry to go and see what they could dig up about Sean Cameron without spooking or alerting him for now. By the time Agent Donald and Agent Barry returned to their office, Gilbert Rivers had already pulled out Sean Cameron's movement on CCTV up until the time of the senator's death.

"Andy, did Gilbert find anything" asked Agent Donald.

Sean Cameron isn't the man we are looking for, because he didn't come anywhere close to the senator, on the day or days before the senator's death.

"Andy, maybe we're looking at this the wrong way," said Agent Donald.

"How then are we supposed to look at it?" asked Andy.

Agent Donald then asked Andy if Sean Cameron was anywhere irrespective of distance that gives him unrestricted view of the senator, like a sniper who needed a good position and view without any obstruction to aim at a target.

"I supposed you're aware of the death of the President of the Republic of Trykinsgstan 15 years ago, and if you all remember the death was ruled as unexplained, more so, there were indications that traces of radioactive material were found in his system the next morning when he didn't wake from his sleep," said Agent Donald.

Agent Donald continued the pep talk to remove every supposition in this case and asked his colleagues to take a look at this, as he pulled up a CCTV image of Sean Cameron arriving the country and travel information that showed he returned from the Republic of Trykinsgstan a day after the death of their president.

Andy Immediately called homeland security immigration to verify if Sean Cameron did travel to the Republic of Trykinsgstan, but sadly, the information relating to his trip to the Republic of Trykinsgstan was classified, and he got nothing other than the bureaucracy of the government. He then put a phone call across to the Head of Main Justice, and lucky for Andy, Sarah Black was able to pull some strings, and confirmed Sean Cameron was in the Republic of Trykinsgstan about the same time their president died in a similar circumstance.

"Well researched, but how does that tie Sean Cameron to this murder since he didn't come into contact with the senator?" asked Agent Barry. This is no longer a fishing trip; Sean Cameron is now officially in the middle of this investigation. Now that this investigation began narrowing, Andy isn't ready for Agent Barry's pessimism to get in the way, he immediately instructed his men to bring Sean Cameron in for questioning.

Funnily, Agent Barry obviously came to work looking like a man suffering shortage of sleep, but he'd already assured Donald he had it all under control after taking his triple expresso, and hoping that the hot drink will do the trick.

Immediately Agent Donald and Agent Barry got to the Sheriff's apartment, and knocked, it didn't take long before he came to the door to know who it was that's at the door. He couldn't hold back his bewilderment to see Agent Donald whom he beat in Los Angeles, coming after him again, but this time in New York City.

"You again! You should be in Los Angeles, what are you doing in New York?" asked Sean Cameron.

"You were smart to allow Philip Cruise take the fall the other time, but this time your alibi won't be generous enough to cover you," said Agent Donald. I don't know what it is you're going on and on about, just tell me why you're by my door," replied Sean.

Agent Barry didn't hesitate to cut to the chase as told Sean Cameron he's under arrest for the murder of Senator Alexander Bishop, and he read out his rights to him immediately the cuffs are out.

"You're arresting me, over what offence?" asked Sean.

"Your rights have been read to you, I suggest you get moving, and when you get to our black site, then you'll have to tell us everything you know," said Agent Barry. Be it in the middle of the night or in the middle of the Nile it doesn't matter, what matters is that the word 'middle' appeared in both phrases, and this time it's Sean Cameron in the middle.

Agent Donald immediately gave Barry the long side-glance because he considers Barry's mention of black site to be unwittingly flippant, because a black site is a surprise place suspects find themselves, and he isn't supposed to make mention of black site at the time of making arrest. It didn't take long before Sean Cameron was brought into the interrogation room.

Andy is now saddled with the task of finding the murder weapon, if this evasive character who calls himself the Sheriff will be made to face justice for his crimes. Sadly, the detectives knew they were looking for a weapon that emits powerful fatal radiation through electromagnetic waves, but had no idea of what the weapon looks like. Retired General Bill Compston who was Sean Cameron's direct handler while he was in service and whenever he goes on foreign undercover mission was upfront with this investigation.

The retired General had to give the detectives a detailed description of what the weapon looks like. Now that Sean Cameron, the Sheriff, has touched one of their own, the Big Guns sensed he might be unto their tail also, so they'd to give him up, by assisting the FBI smoke this guy out, at least to cover their backs. The truth is that when giants fall, they fall very hard, this top brass needed to avoid a repeat of one of their own biting the dust. Interestingly, knowing full well that Sean Cameron could be their nemesis, this is the General's moment of schadenfreude, and it's now time to keep this ex-employee-gone rogue canned forever. Yet Andy's concern is why such high-grade military weapon will be allowed in the hands of veterans who are no longer in the service of the United States military.

"General, why was Sean Cameron allowed to keep such a deadly weapon?" asked Andy.

"We didn't ask him to keep it, actually, we were made to believe he lost it in his last mission when things got tricky," said General Compston.

Andy proceeded to ask the General how such a deadly weapon was lost, insisting he needs to find the weapon immediately because this weapon could get to the hands of terrorists, or even the enemies of the United States. The General had to make it clear to absolve themselves of any form of negligence, as he said the last of Sean Cameron's official assignment got tricky at some point, and he was ordered to abort, and on his return, he informed his superior he ditched the weapon in the river to maintain his cover.

"This attack on home soil using the same military grade weapon that was meant for special mission meant he still had the weapon with him all this while," said General Compston. This information is classified and if this gets to the wrong hands it could be a risk to national security.

The information coming from MOD is on a need-to-know basis, even Andy is a bit handicapped with how much from his conversation with this Army General that he could divulge to his team.

After the Sheriff's arrest, a thorough search of his property didn't yield any result, because the murder weapon wasn't found. Sean uses phones with monologue signals so authorities won't be able to track him, this is predicated upon his believe that the telephone is the devil's instrument and arguably, he has now suddenly become a lone wolf detached from the pack.

After their return to the office, Agent Donald then turned to Gilbert and asked him to give them a minute-by-minute analysis of Sean Cameron's movement from days before the Senator's death, and after his death.

Four hundred and twenty-two hours of CCTV review was put in, as the various places where Sean Cameron visited were all searched and nothing came up, yet there's one last place Sean Cameron visited that hasn't been searched, and that's the New York River. He was by the river bank, but there wasn't any visual of him throwing things in the river, yet there's a possibility that the bag he'd with him when he visited the river contained the murder weapon. Andy isn't willing to let this guy walk this time, and he needed to do everything, by going above and beyond to get this murder weapon. He immediately requested the help of the Navy to use their Manned submersibles, ROVs and AUVs sonar and magnetometer detection equipment, to search for the murder weapon underneath the river.

It was quite an arduous task but after a week of combing the river bed, the Navy was able to recover the murder weapon, and there were cheers in the FBI office. Sean Cameron, the Sheriff, is now tied in nuts and wriggling himself out of this will be quite a tall order. Andy immediately released John Carter on bail because there wasn't anything linking him to the senator's death, other than the fact that he was in the wrong place at the wrong time, which is merely providence.

Agent Donald walked into the interrogation room and sat opposite Sean Cameron.

"Sean Cameron, we're about to begin this interrogation, and for all it's worth, as before, we know you're the Sheriff, the bogeyman in the dark alley," said Agent Donald.

"Excuse me! Does it mean you brought me here just to tell me about that?" asked Sean.

Agent Donald looked straight into San Cameron's eyes, and asked him to tell him about his relationship with the late Senator Alexander Bishop. "He was my superior, and I was just a pawn in his hands," said Sean. "Why! You enlisted into the Special Forces, and that's an honourable profession," said Agent Donald.

"What do you do, when you realised you're being used for an assignment that has no business with the state, when your life is being put at risk to satisfy those at the top?" asked Sean. Agent Donald subtly reminded Sean, he should've requested to be redeployed, instead of going rogue on his superiors. Unfortunately, the advice wasn't timely, as Sean sighed, and said he tried to speak up but his words came across as mere sound because his threats to redeploy lacked bite. Giving excuses like the one from a school boy who didn't do his homework just proved damn wrong, and this has nothing to do with the doctrine of turning the other cheek, it's just plain stupidity.

Agent Donald then steered the conversation into Sean's activities as the Sheriff, but that's not an area he's willing to divulge any information, because he's keen to protect his fans. "You might choose to remain silent, but I want you to know the FBI have shut down your activities on the dark web," said Agent Donald. "Closing down my page on the dark web, or the silk road won't stop debt collection, everyone wants peace, but what about justice?" asked Sean.

"Leave justice to those saddled with that responsibility," replied Agent Donald. Sean Cameron, couldn't remain illusory, as the murder weapon was presented before him, after all, it was the same weapon assigned to him for his foreign missions. The river may have destroyed you finger prints on the exterior, but the interior of that weapon, still has your finger prints and DNA on them," said Agent Donald.

"We knew you used this weapon to kill the senator, you targeted him when he came to the window of his hotel room, and you did that from the Cornish tower where you lodged some distance away.

You waited for him to come to the window, because you seemed to have known he organically likes the window view of the city, and you targeted him in sniper styled attack just as the President of Republic of Trykinsgstan 15 years ago," said Agent Donald.

"The death of the President of Republic of Trykinsgstan is classified, and has got nothing to do with this case," said Sean.

"I understand, and I'm only lining my ducks in a row, just to let you know, the FBI knows your style," said Agent Donald.

"They both loved the window view of the city, their appetite for standing by the window was their undoing, and that weapon is mine. I killed the senator, and I don't mind going down for it," said Sean.

Agent Donald pointed out to Sean that the country of the attack might be different but the MO is the same, as he pointed out to Sean that his time is up.

Sean looked at Donald Whitley and said "I understand your little happy life and the good little school boy reputation you try to maintain."

Agent Donald tried to refute Sean's claim of him being a school boy and reminded Sean that he has equally been around the block a few times even though the nature of their assignments differs.

To make light of Donald's understanding of Special OPS, Sean narrated one of his skin-crawling special ops' experiences to Donald and how it came about that he has had enough of these big guns.

"Carson and I went on a special operation in Somalia, we are already in and deep into enemy territory, and too late to get out when the operation was aborted.

We are in Al shabaab's territory and the enemy knew of our presence after Pentagon aborted and refused to send us helicopters to ferry us to safety.

We are surrounded and captured by those terrorists until Carson used the smallest size of a stapler pin to secure our safety.

They left us in a dark cell and this 6 ft 7-inch huge guy that was meant to guard the cell screamed at our faces all through the night, and that's another form of torture to keep us worked up. Al shabaab had planned to execute us the next morning and this execution was meant to be captured on camera to make a mockery of America.

We were in cuffs, our hands and feet were bound, and I was already losing hope until Carson asked me cheer up. I looked around and I just didn't see what hope there is in that situation, I had no idea of how Carson managed to pick a leaflet on the floor and removed the staple pin in it and said to me, Sean, this is hope, and with this I can get us out of here. In a matter of minutes, the guard was on the floor taking his last breath, and I don't know how Carson pulled that off because he was in hand cuffs.

We'd to fight our way in the thick dark of dawn until we arrived Mombasa where our contacts had to provide us with cover. Unfortunately, Carson suffered gunshot injuries and didn't make it out alive despite effort to help him stay alive in Mombasa. While Carson was dying in the hospital in Mombasa, he made it a point of duty to get to the bottom of why we weren't rescued, that was when our contacts in DOD told us the helicopters couldn't come because our mission wasn't official, they sent us here just to help them eliminate competition.

You see, Carson was the man I wanted to be, the kind of hero I wanted to become, someone who will ensure your safety when hope is lost. He died for what, to help those hawks line up their pockets with defence contracts or what?"

It's blindingly obvious to Donald Whitley that relationship between these big guns and the men in their care aren't symbiotic in anyway. This isn't some kind of quid pro quo arrangement, these service men get nothing out of this, just loyalty to their country. It's now common knowledge that these big guns use these guys and dispose of them like tissue, and that was what got Sean kicking off.

"There's time and season for everything in life, you were once a hero by virtue of your job, you were once in love, with someone's heart in your hands, cupid sort of, but this time you're the villain," said Agent Donald. Everyone around this suspect knows for sure that ignorance is bliss but this isn't one of such cases. This time his action is nothing but martyrdom, self-destruction sort of, and his days as a twinkling halo is gone. This isn't news to Sean who has seen better days, and now angered by his poor treatment as a spent force.

Sean narrated how he had a sleepless night gazing at a fake painting of this Senator hanging on the wall of his house. Agent Donald was shock to realise that the painting was fake, and this image has been hanging impressively on the walls of many homes in America for the last decade. The Senator knew who had the original yet allowed the fake of this painting to be out there. After all, it costs him nothing, but rather earned him more popularity in America.

"That's life! What choice do I have?" asked Sean.

"We all have choices and the path we choose is in our hands because life isn't always about serendipity," said Agent Donald.

Sean smiled and muttered, saying the devil is in the detail because life isn't always back and white, Donald decided to wrap this interrogation as he urged Sean to keep the devil out of the detail and face the consequence of his actions.

"Sean Cameron, you'll need an attorney because I'm charging you with the murder of Alexander Bishop," said Agent Donald.

Immediately Sean Cameron was charged for the murder of the Senator, Andy called Sarah Black and informed her the investigation has been concluded and Sean Cameron have been charged for the senator's death.

CHAPTER

FOUR

The assassin

It's Christmas Eve, and it's going to be a white Christmas in New York City. Funnily, this isn't just about the snow flurries falling, but the buzz of Christmas could be felt even inside the office, as Christmas cards and gifts wrapped in brightly coloured wrappers changed hands. Agent Donald stepped out of Andy's office after saying goodbye, he then looked at his watch before putting on his jacket and getting ready to return home to his family, Andy Grey rushed to the central office. "Donald, sorry, we've got job to do," said Andy. Agent Donald turned around and asked if anything came up, because he just finished speaking to Andy minutes ago and there wasn't anything untoward. Andy muttered as he replied saying death doesn't give notice, and that the news of a possible homicide just came in.

Agent Donald arrives at the murder scene stretching his hand for a handshake and introduced himself to the NYPD officer in the scene. "Hello, I'm Agent Donald Whitley," he said.

But Agent Donald is still a bit new to the scene and needs to do more than just a mere handshake when he arrives at a crime scene.

"Erm, I'm Lieutenant Bennett, you're welcome," the Lieutenant said.

"What happened here?" asked Agent Donald.

"It looked like an assassination because the killer didn't take anything. But I've never seen your face before in New York, are you a new agent?" asked Lieutenant Bennett.

"Not really, I'm an old agent but newly posted to New York City. I'm Agent Donald Whitley from the Los Angeles unit of the FBI," he replied. The name strikes a chord in the Lieutenant, who's is a regular reader of FBI monthly journal.

"Oh, Donald Whitley! I've heard a lot about you, though I haven't met you in person, nice to meet you," said Lieutenant Bennett.

"Thank you. You mean everything belonging to the victim is intact?" asked agent Donald.

"Yeah, he wasn't searched after the shooting, meaning they only wanted him dead," said Lieutenant Bennett.

Agent Donald removed his glasses and squatted down beside the corpse as he gave a critical look at the body of the victim. He then stood up and walked around the crime scene scanning the scene for clues. "What direction was the shot fired from?" asked Agent Donald.

"The shot was fired from behind those flowers. The shooter seems to be someone with experience, firing just one shot from such a distance with precision, using a silencer," said Lieutenant Bennett.

"Is there any CCTV camera around?" asked Agent Donald.

"Yes, but the killer successfully avoided the camera; he must have spent time scanning the area and gathering intelligence," said Lieutenant Bennett.

"Were you able to get the bullet casing?" asked Agent Donald.

"Yes, we found them just behind the flowers, strange enough the shooter did not leave even shoe prints" replied Lieutenant Bennett.

Agent Barry who was at the crime scene but somewhere else, joined the conversation while Agent Donald and the Lieutenant were still talking and assessing the crime scene. It's obvious that handshake with Agent Barry are always guarded because the guy is haughty, and arguably, he isn't haemorrhaging friends because he has got none.

"Lieutenant Bennett, I know the cops will never find anything until the FBI does," said Agent Barry.

"You've a very bad demeanour and I must confess nobody meets you the first time and wishes to meet you again," replied Lieutenant Bennett.

There's always a big hullaballoo whenever Agent Barry shows up at a crime scene and most NYPD officers consider Agent Barry to be an irritant. Sadly, that's his character flaw because he's known for throwing tantrums, and this isn't an exception. Agent Donald who's working with Barry for the second time on a crime scene could see a pattern emerging, and didn't hesitate to tone the heat down. He then tapped Agent Barry on the shoulder as a way telling him to put a sock in it, and sadly, making him to stop his organic sarcasm will be more like attempting squeezing blood out of stone.

He then advised Agent Barry, that it's best they concentrate on the job, because that's what matters.

"Donald, did you hear that? These guys are lazy and they leave the entire job for the FBI to do," Agent Barry insists.

"I'm sorry, Agent! You've a foul presence, and you've to excuse me," said Lieutenant Bennett.

Bennett moved away and joined his colleagues waiting for him in the car, leaving the detectives to deal with the homicide. Immediately the Lieutenant stepped away, Agent Donald admonished Barry, saying he's being too impulsive and it doesn't help in an investigation. This new partnership might mean Donald will have to keep Barry on a tight leash if they would have to make progress.

A day later, FBI agents were in their office profiling the assassination and Agent Murphy walked into the central office with the ballistics report. "Andy, the ballistics report from the assassination is here," said Agent Murphy.

"What does the ballistics report say about the weapon used to commit the murder?" asked Andy. Agent Barry then collected the report from agent Murphy to read out the content of the report.

"This is the same weapon used in seven assassinations within the last five years in New York alone," said Agent Barry.

"What about the shooter, who's he and what do we know about him?" asked Agent Donald.

Gilbert Rivers, the unit's IT guru, profiled the killer further based on existing information from previous murders. "He's a killer for hire called 'One Strike,' he has no location, and he never meets the contractor before or after the assassination, with that he can protect his identity, said Gilbert.

"How does he get his payment?" asked Andy.

"The contractor pays into his account in the Cayman Islands and once payment is made the contract is in place," said Gilbert.

"How does the contractor know the assassin's account number?" Andy queried further. Gilbert explained further that the assassin's account details is there in the dark web, and his bullets has a unique inscription, "for your sins" is inscribed into the bullet, which helps the contractor to know when the assassin has executed his assignment. With the inscription in the bullet, the contractor will know for sure who did the killing. This signature bullet isn't anything but to send a message to potential contractors that he's the best.

This distinct killer has a signature bullet that signifies to the contractor that the contract has been executed.

"How does he know his target and how does the contractor contact him?" asked Andy.

"The contractor sends a photograph and itinerary of the target to the assassin via the dark web. Now that it's glaringly obvious that this assassin does most of his dealings in the dark web, Agent Barry then suggested the FBI should use the dark web to lure him out since that's his domain of operation. But most significantly is the shocker concerning this assassin that makes it impossible to catch him over the years.

"One more thing," said Gilbert, and then chuckled.

"What!" exclaimed Agent Barry.

"This guy teleports, based on recent CCTV evidence, coupled with information available in the dark web," said Gilbert.

"How, what do you mean he teleports! Is he an alien or what?" asked Andy.

Stop, Gilbert, stop messing with our heads, be serious for once, are you serious about this, you mean he's a freak?" asked Agent Barry. "Of course, yes, and this is no joke, the cold files are there, study them," said Gilbert.

Barry was rattled by the new information concerning this killer, and catching him terrifies Barry.

"Is this guy into voodoo, or witchcraft, or.....?" asked Agent Barry.

Agent Donald interjects "What's his trigger?" he asked.

"Donald, I don't get you, how does the trigger affect his job? This guy teleports!" asked Agent Murphy.

Agent Donald explained further. "Some people take cocaine, some cigarette, some drink, and others take nothing, however those who take nothing are usually very cruel," said Agent Donald.

Barry remained unconvinced about how the trigger will help this case. "Will his trigger help in this investigation?" asked Agent Barry.

Agent Donald decides to put things into perspective. It'll help you define a behavioural pattern to help you catch this guy. You and I know that the profession of killing people isn't an easy thing to do.

"Do you know of any assassin who needs a trigger to be able to kill?" asked Gilbert.

"I knew an assassin in Havana Cuba, quite an eccentric guy, and all he needs for his trigger is just a tot of tequila. Nothing moves him to kill except a tort of tequila, an entire bottle of brandy, marijuana, hemp, cocaine or cigarette, none of all these moves Esteban. One day Esteban was having a naming for his new-born baby boy, unfortunately one of the guests came with tequila and he inadvertently drank a tot. He was playing with the baby when the trigger was activated and he suddenly became wild as his disposition changed immediately. His guests thought he was merely disinhibited but they soon realised his killer instinct has kicked in and he immediately wanted to kill his own baby who was then rescued from him by the guests. One of the guests sustained knife injuries on his wrist." said Agent Donald.

Andy Grey laughed hysterically. "Donald, that's overly, I suppose," said Andy.

"Yes Andy, it is, but after that incident Esteban only drinks red wine, to avoid the trigger when he doesn't need it," said Agent Donald, then urged his colleagues to search for the tabloids of 20th July 1975, that the story made headlines.

"Why tequila?" asked Agent Murphy.

"Maybe there's a particular aroma in the tequila that causes the trigger and not the alcoholic content," said Agent Donald.

Moments later the detectives returned their focus to the case under review. "Ok, let's find out more about this killer, so we can catch him before he strikes again," said Andy.

It's right there in the dark web," said Gilbert. They all drew closer to the screen as Gilbert began reading out some of the information displayed on the screen about this killer on the dark web.

Brad Washington's dad was based in Israel in 1967 during the Arab wars, he used to do plumbing work for one of the famous Jewish Rabbis in Jerusalem after one of the synagogues was bombed out of shape. During one of the plumbing works, the Rabbi was moving things around and a coin suddenly dropped out of a metal safe that was affected by the war, but as Eddie Washington, who is Brad's dad bent down to pick up the coin for the Rabbi, the Rabbi anxiously rushed to stop him from laying a finger on the coin. "I wouldn't touch that coin even with a 10 feet barge pole if I were you," said the Rabbi.

Eddie was shocked at the Rabbi brash reaction about something that looks like a harmless silver coin.

The Rabbi immediately hinted Eddie that the coin he's looking at is one of the thirty silver coins used to pay Judas Iscariot when he betrayed Jesus, and there is an omen of death around the coin. Eddie immediately stepped away from the coin yet was quite fascinated to have come face to face with history as he gazed at one of the thirty coins paid to Judas Iscariot to buy the life of Jesus Christ.

The Rabbi immediately used a tong-like object to pick the coin from the ground and put it back safely into a box and then locked it up. After safely securing the coin, the Rabbi then gave Eddie a little history of this one coin in his possession. The last ten people in possession of this particular coin died mysteriously, and some committed grave murders even before they eventually committed suicide. The latest was in a ship to Jericho, he suddenly got mad halfway through the journey and jumped in to the river and drowned.

Eddie became weary about the damage done by this one particular coin and inquired of safety of the rest twenty-nine pieces and what harm they might be doing right now.

Immediately after the war ended, the Rabbi went on with the Israeli government officials on a visit to cities affected by the war, to at least assess the level of damage to cities closer to the front-lines and to as well assure victims that the government shares in their pains. It was during this period while the Rabbi was away that Eddie decided to return home to his family in the United States. Funny enough in Eddie's wisdom, of all he could get from

Israel as souvenir, Eddie thought it wise to steal the Judas coin from where it was safely secured because he thinks the coin is the most appropriate souvenir to take home. Life is about trade-offs but Eddie's decision to go for this coin in place of his pay wasn't quite thoughtful.

When Eddie returned to the United States from Israel, he made sure he tucked the coin away from reach by burying the coin in a box in his garage. The Rabbi returned from his official assignment and immediately realised the unthinkable has happened. He tried locating and getting in touch with Eddie but failed. After successfully keeping the coin away from reach, years later Eddie got drunk on his wife's birthday, went into his garage and serendipitously exhumed the box and began taking a closer look at the coin. Strangely not long after he brought the coin out of the box, Eddie became overwhelmed with the thought that his wife may have been cheating on him even when no such thing had happened. He briskly walked into his bedroom, while still holding the coin in his hand, he brought out his gun and shot himself in the head.

His wife and a couple of friends still around and celebrating with them heard the noise of the gunshot, and rushed into his bedroom to find Eddie dead on the floor of their bedroom, in the pool of his blood. The ambulance was called, and Eddie was pronounced dead, and while his wife, Ruth, was weeping over her loss, Little Brad was only two years old walking about, unbeknownst to him that daddy has just passed away.

Years passed after Eddie's death, his son, Brad, had now turned eighteen, and in his preparation for his eighteenth birthday, Brad was moving things around to accommodate his friends coming to celebrate with him. In his attempt to source his childhood photos for his birthday party, he serendipitously stepped on a strange looking silver coin, he then picked the coin up and spent minutes looking at the coin. He then decided to continue with picking up the photo album but needed his hands to do the job, he then placed the coin between his lips so he could use his hands to grab the photo album, and somehow the coin slipped into his mouth and he serendipitously swallowed the coin. He was rushed to the hospital and after undergoing x-ray and scans, coupled with intense diagnosis, the doctor decided that surgery will put the Brad's life at risk, and strangely the coin suddenly fits into Brad's system and wasn't ready to be cut out. There's no one stacking the deck here, this isn't some kind of soviet style mural being paraded as something of interest that people now gravitate towards, it's a coin that does real damage.

They then concluded it's best for the coin to remain until it becomes a concern. Brad was in the company of his friend, Max, on his return from the hospital. To Max's amazement, young Brad suddenly began acting strange and out of the blue was quite mad at his beloved Dog, Jacky, that he used a hammer on Jacky and the poor thing died on the spot.

Max shuddered following Brads' barbaric act, he couldn't hold his anger, he got up and left, Brad was now left with his mum who remained hopping mad at her son as he remained remorselessly unperturbed by his grime act. Brad suddenly couldn't stand his mum, he then decided to move out of the house that night. So far, the coin chose not to be of any concern as it now finds a safe home in Brad who has now decided that taking the lives of other will be a worthy career for him, as dictated by the grim object inside him.

Before he became a gun for hire, he crossed the border to Mexico and spent some time in Tijuana, where he committed another murder. This time he killed his Mexican girlfriend who seemed to have had enough of him and wanted him out of her home.

He didn't shoot her, because he thinks he's rewarding her with a painless death. He used a medieval relic to brutalise her and watched as she stumbled from one point of the living room to another until she stumbled helplessly and bled to her death.

"How did you know about the relics?" asked Agent Barry.

The pathologist dug out one of the jewels on the signet ring of the relic from her skull. The killing looked more like a ritual killing, and that marked the beginning of his reign of terror. This artifact represents retribution, and that's what these two severed fingers represents.

Brad's brutal act brought about a national manhunt in Mexico, in which a good number of Mexican secret service, the CNI, converged in Tijuana but they were unable to arrest him because he bolted.

Agent Barry has no qualms about how the results might come about provided he gets a result, he immediately suggested they drag this killer to the hospital and force the doctors to cut the coin out of him. Gilbert cringed and said cutting the coin out of this guy might not only be a breach of his human rights, it will be quite a painful process, but Barry insisted the guy has killed a lot of people before now, so why feel for him. "Let's cut the coin out of him, to stop this guy teleporting and jumping around like a yoyo, this doesn't make sense because people don't teleport," said Agent Barry.

Agent Donald interjected and said cutting the evil coin out of this guy will require a court order, then suggested that talk about getting the coin out of Brand should be reserved for later when they have the guy in custody.

While Andy was still speaking a phone call came from Lieutenant Bennett and Andy Grey stepped aside to take his call.

"Andy, how're you?" asked Lieutenant Bennett.

"I'm fine Lieutenant, we just found out it's the same assassin that's responsible for this murder as well," said Andy.

"I just got a copy of the ballistics report, it's surprising," said Lieutenant Bennett.

"We're on this assassination case, and we are trying hard to see how quick we can take him off our streets," said Andy.

Lieutenant Bennett has bones to pick with Agent Barry over the kerfuffle at the crime scene. "One of the men in your unit needs to be cautioned about his public demeanour because his attitude does not assist an investigation," said Lieutenant Bennett. "Err, Lieutenant, I know the cops and the FBI hardly agree whenever they're at the scene of an investigation, I hope this isn't one of those cases?" asked Andy.

The Lieutenant interjected in his bid to stop Andy from playing the fraternal fast one on him, he immediately pointed out to Andy that they both know the setbacks the FBI unit suffered in recent past because of Agent Barry's attitude during investigations. He had to spell it out to Andy in no uncertain terms that if he chooses to talk to Barry about it then good, but if he didn't and

Barry continues his foul mouthing, then he wouldn't be talking to Andy about it when this occurs again because he will take it to those on top.

"I've heard you, when we're done with the case at hand, I'll find time to speak to him about it," said Andy.

After about thirty minutes of speaking with Lieutenant Bennett Andy Grey returned to the central office where his detectives are reviewing the case.

"Let's profile the victim of this assassination," said Andy.

"He's Bobby Hall," said Gilbert.

"Who is Bobby Hall, and what do we know about him?" asked Andy.

Bobby Hall was the owner of the Tick Top Towing Company, he made his fortunes in the late nineties but went bankrupt in 2003 and his company was liquidated. Though, a lot of innocent people who have done no wrong lost their cars and some got their cars crushed before their eyes due to the greed of Bobby's firm," said Agent Barry.

"However, Bobby Hall turned his life around, started a charity in 2007, and somehow his new firm went bust last year.

"This man has suffered too many strokes of bad luck; maybe, the law of retributive justice visited him," said Agent Donald.

Andy stood for while then asked who'll want a man with these strokes of unfortunate life situation dead. After spending time and effort chasing other leads without any luck the detectives decided to take a closer look at a limousine owner.

"There was one limousine he crushed two weeks before he was declared bankrupt, the owner never took it likely with him, so he promised him death," said Gilbert.

"The owner of a limousine is rich enough to pay this assassin to do a job like this, because it's only rich people who can afford this particular assassin. But that's long ago, his anger must have subsided, I suppose," said Agent Donald.

"Hmm, yeah, 2003 is quite a long time, isn't it possible that his anger has burn off after all these years?" asked. Gilbert. "Hmm, Gilbert, zero in on this Reginald, let's see if he has any dealings with this assassin," said Andy.

"Hmm, Rivers, zero in on this Reginald, let's see if he has any dealings with this assassin," said Andy.

Gilbert Rivers ran some searches and moments later. "Yeah, there's a connection," said Gilbert.

Hours later, Reginald Rock was brought in for questioning, and agent Donald was in the interrogation room with him while others watched.

"Tell us, did Bobby Hall deserve to die?" asked Agent Donald. Funnily Reginald played dumb for a while, but with repeated pestering he'd to open up.

"Yeah, that fool crushed my car, he deserved death," said Reginald Rock.

"I don't get it, why do you want him dead?" asked Agent Donald. "That fool crushed my Limo," said Reginald Rock.

"And you've to kill him for that?" Agent Donald queried further.

Of course not, I didn't kill him, go find his killer if you can find him," said Reginald Rock.

"But you paid money into the account of the man called "One Strike" to help you kill Bobby Hall," said Agent Donald.

Reginald was naive to think the prying eyes of the FBI doesn't see those little secret transactions that happen on the silk road, as he continued denying he reached out to the assassin to help him do his bidding. He remained full of himself as he proudly told the detective to his face to go find Bobby Hall's killer.

We knew you visited the dark web for this man they call the 'One Strike', copied his bank details and transferred money into his account," said Agent Donald.

"Oh, yeah, I did, but the payment into his account was for other services and not to kill Bobby Hall," said Reginald Rock. This suspect continued his assumed tease-and-fun mindset of a philanderer and he's doing everything to deflect the questions put to him.

"What other service does this 'One Strike' render that you've paid him for?" asked Agent Donald.

"I paid him to help locate my long-lost cousin," said Agent Donald.

You expect us to hand you a pack of chocolates and give you a pat on the back for that response? From his website, he doesn't offer the services of finding a lost cousin," said Agent Donald.

"My cousin, Jaden Spike, has been missing and I needed to find him," he replied.

"You've the opportunity of getting a deal now, or you go down for the murder of Bobby Hall," said Agent Donald.

"But I'm not responsible for his death, why should I make a deal for a lesser sentence?" asked Reginald Rock.

"Look I promise you, we'll catch this guy and when we do, he'll take our deal and you'll never see the face of the Sun again.

This interrogation is beginning to break Reginald's resolve and fears his partner in crime could take the deal and sell him out, yet he's dawdling over making up his mind.

"How can I accept a deal to go to prison?" said Reginald Rock.

Agent Donald stood up, and about to leave to show his seriousness. "I'm about to leave but when I leave, I'll take my deal with me and you'll never get it again," said Agent Donald.

"Ok, ok, I paid him to take Bobby Hall out for crushing my car," said Reginald Rock.

Agent Donald returned to his seat, and then probed further. "How do we find him? We're fully aware this guy teleports, so tell us all you know about him," asked Agent Donald.

"We don't find him, he finds us," said Reginald Rock.

"Then how does he find you?" asked Agent Donald.

"Actually, we only get his message and that's the death of the target using a bullet with a special inscription," said Reginald Rock.

"We know about the special inscription, but how does he look?" Agent Donald queried further.

"Nobody sees his face; from my knowledge, no contractor ever meets him.

"You'll need to help us catch this guy," said Agent Donald.

"He pays an initial visit to the target for proper identification of his target before the actual assassination. For the first visit, he teleports and that's where the mystery lies, but the second visit will be in the street or anywhere, this time no mystery and that's death," said Reginald Rock.

Agent Donald stood up and left the interrogation room to join his colleagues who are watching the interrogation.

"Now, we've a clear direction on this 'One Strike' guy," said Andy.

"But how do we catch this guy? This teleporting thing makes it difficult, but I think a diviner can help us catch this guy," said Agent Barry.

"Er.., diviner? I don't think that's a good idea," said Agent Donald.

Donald Whitley is a devout Christian who doesn't believe in using unchristian methods in his work as a detective, now that a man who teleports is now in the mix, Donald is still bound on sticking to his faith but Andy has to press Donald to allow a diviner's help.

"Donald, I know this is about your faith but Barry is right; we need a diviner at this point, because this investigation has gone beyond the physical," said Andy.

"Andy, you remember the diviner in Albany that was part of the Sony Gerald investigation five years ago?" asked Barry.

"Put a call across to her; let's see if she can be of help," said Andy. Donald remained unconvinced about getting a diviner involved, yet convinced that a catholic exorcist will be more appropriate than employing other spiritual means. With majority of his colleagues in support of the move he'd to give in to the idea.

"I would've suggested we get an exorcist, because I don't like diviners. Hmm, ok, let's do this," said Agent Donald.

"Exorcist are only good with exorcising vampires, and not for a guy hopping from place to place like a yoyo," Agent Barry retorted.

Minutes later, Gilbert Rivers puts a call across to the diviner and hands the phone to Andy Grey.

"How're you, Mrs Solise? This is Andy Grey, FBI unit head in New York City. Do you remember me?" asked Andy.

"Andy, Andy, Andy, the Sony Gerald's case, I suppose?" asked Mrs Solise.

"Of course, yes, glad you still remember me," said Andy.

"Andy, I might be old, but my memory doesn't play pranks on me yet. Of course, I remember you," said Mrs Solise.

"We need your assistance, please speak with my agent," said Andy. "Ok, send them over; let's see if I can be of help," said Mrs Solise.

Moments later, Agent Donald and Agent Barry meets Mrs Solise to seek help with catching the assassin.

"Hello Mrs Solise, I'm agent Donald Whitley, my colleague here is agent Barry, thanks for your help," said Agent Donald.

Mrs Solise knew Agent Barry but vaguely remembered the past and spurned by her apparent loss of memory, she realised she has never met Agent Donald who's new in the scene, maybe a mere passive introduction won't be enough.

"Donald Whitley! Have we met before? I know Barry and other agents, but I don't think I've met you," said Mrs Solise.

"I'm a new agent, from Los Angeles, to be precise," said Agent Donald.

"Andy never told me he has a new staff, but you're welcome to New York. So how can I be of help?" asked Mrs Solise.

"We want to catch an assassin, but he teleports," said Agent Donald.

"You mean, he teleports? Then he's a freak!" Mrs Solise exclaimed.

"Of course, yes, and I've never dealt with a freak before," said Agent Donald. Mrs Solise stayed silent for a while as she tried to process how to deal with this strange case, and after a momentary silence.

"Hmm, Necromancy! Mrs Solise muttered. She then urged Donald not to worry as she assured them of her help, and promising she will help them catch this killer as she expressed her hatred for people who teleport because they make her skin crawl. Agent Barry interjected as he attempts to point out to Mrs Solise that this guy doesn't just teleport but there are rumours swirling around that he has a coin inside him, the Judas coin. But the old lady smiled and urged Agent Barry not to be in a haste, saying she knew about the coin. Agent Barry wasn't having it as he insists, he wants the coin out to stop this guy from teleporting, but while Agent Barry was still kicking off, Agent Donald gave him a nudge as a way of asking him to stop talking. The moment Barry stopped talking, Mrs Solise hinted them she's already aware of the coin and that the coin was gifted to Brad Washington by nature, but this gift is a bad gift and a self-destructive one for that matter.

"Ok, where do we start?" asked Agent Donald.

"I sense you never wanted to come to my place," said Mrs Solise.

Agent Donald owned up to the truth, that this case is a leash that's dragging him into places he wouldn't have originally visited.

"You guessed right, but how do you know?" said Agent Donald.

"Don't worry, Donald, I know. From your investigation, how does this assassin operate?" asked Mrs Solise.

"He pays his target a first visit to identify him or her, but this time he teleports, the second time he doesn't teleport but assassinates with his signature bullet," said Agent Donald.

The diviner advised the agents to get a room and cover the entire wall with mirrors and keep the next target inside the room. The moment the assassin teleports in for his first visit, where he attempts to identify his target the mirror will freeze him, she insists that the detectives should make sure they catch him immediately. Unfortunately, teleporting to check out targets in an enclosure isn't Brad's style, he always allow distance between himself and potential targets when he comes visiting, and does this mostly in a crowded street.

"Just a few mirrors or everything fully covered with mirrors?" Agent Donald queried further.

"All the walls fully padded with mirror, don't leave any space, and you need to catch this man. All my life as a diviner, I've never been confronted about someone who teleports." said Mrs Solise.

Agent Barry muttered in response and said Mrs Solise hasn't been confronted with a case of someone who teleports because humans don't actually teleport and if only the FBI will be brave enough to cut the coin out of this killer, then the evil inside him will leave and the guy will be free and will eventually stop teleporting. Mrs Solise subtly reminded Agent Barry that it wouldn't be a bad idea to be the adult in the room for once as she took a swipe at Agent Barry who have proved to be too feisty for her liking. She then cautioned him that she sees him getting into trouble if he cuts the guy open, and urged him to pursue the path of the cool heads.

"Ok, Mrs Solise, thank you for your help," said Agent Donald.

Agent Donald and Agent Barry left Mrs Solise, and returned to the FBI office and began putting plans in motion to catch this assassin. But it's now important to choose the right target who wouldn't tip the assassin off.

"We need to set Gilbert up as his next target," said Agent Donald. "Why Gilbert?" asked Andy.

"Gilbert isn't a field agent, and this guy won't know he's an FBI agent," said Agent Donald.

"I'll get funds available, so we can make the transfer to his account immediately, alongside Gilbert's phony details and photograph. I want this concluded as soon as possible," said Agent Donald.

Now that the FBI have played into Brad's greed, it's likely that this killer will take the bait.

"We'll use a neutral address in the Brooklyn neighbourhood," Agent Donald proposed.

Days later, the FBI agents put Gilbert Rivers inside a room fully padded with mirrors for a week while other detectives hung around, they also set off a trojan unit to help as they await the assassin's first visit, who never showed up. The detectives became weary, feeling this guy didn't take the bait, but the assassin eventually showed up on the 6th day.

Agent Barry was speaking through the ear piece. "Donald, this guy is a freak, why don't we just shoot this killer the moment he arrives and then go home for a beer?" Agent Barry proposed.

"I know its creepy dealing with a criminal who teleports, I've no experience of dealing with creepy creatures like this, but I suggest you don't lose your moral code because of the ugliness of the sins of others," Agent Donald advised.

Agent Barry isn't known to negotiate his way out with suspects, especially when he already convicts them in his mind. They are as good as convicted by the court once he convicts them in his mind, and this time Barry is getting too chatty.

"Donald, this guy is a gun for hire, he teleports and shouldn't be in the midst of humans, letting him die by the gun is justice," said Agent Barry.

"I suggest you leave justice to the court, let me remind you, that crossing from morality to the other side of immorality, means you can't just cross back," said Agent Donald.

"I understand that crossing my moral code will haunt me forever, but between shooting first to defending myself from a gun for hire and a sorcerer who teleports, is a thin line," said Agent Barry.

"Lurching further towards being a killer cop will be bad news for you" Even as they had their conversation, and yet connected to other members of his team through an ear piece. Agent Donald noticed Agent Barry was walking away from his position.

"Barry, where are you going?" he asked.

"I just need a cup of coffee, at least to keep myself busy," he said.

"Please stay alert, this guy could show up at any time," said Agent Donald.

Not long after Barry's conversation with Donald, Agent Murphy alerted them. "Donald, Gilbert is calling, it's like the guy is here," said Agent Murphy.

"Barry where are you? The guy is here," said Agent Donald.

Agent Barry hurriedly dropped his coffee, and positioned himself immediately while still taking cover. "I'm here, I'm here. What if he's armed?" asked Agent Barry.

"He wouldn't shoot in the midst of confusion, and he's only here to identify his target," said Agent Donald.

"All the agents converged immediately in the room where Gilbert was kept. Funnily, the mirrors did the magic and kept the assassin still, and while "One Strike" struggles to extricate himself from Gilbert, whose hands were wrapped around him, all the other agents surrounded him. "FBI, keep your hands where I can see them," said Agent Barry.

With Gilbert still wrapped around the assassin "Get the cuffs," said Gilbert.

"You're under arrest for the murder of Bobby Hall," said Agent Donald.

The FBI cuffed the suspect and kept him locked up in the mirror walled room and a day later, the FBI decided it's better to interrogate the suspect inside this room as opposed to the regular FBI interrogation room. Agent Donald is in the interrogation room with Brad Washington, the assassin. It's glaringly obvious that this teleporting killer got the shock of his life when held in a room fully padded with mirrors, it was as if he was sucker punched in the gut and he didn't hide his disapproval about it.

"Why're you holding me here since yesterday, and why am I held in a room with mirrors? Take me out of here please, I beg you," said Brad.

"You know why! We're interrogating you over the murder of Bobby Hall and that's the latest of other six murders you've committed here in New York alone," said Agent Donald.

"Did you see me committing these murders; did your cameras catch me killing anyone?" asked Brad.

This suspect waved his right to an attorney, and continued pursuing his defence, hoping his tight alibi will help him out.

"We know you're an expert in what you do, and so you've expertly avoided our cameras," said Agent Donald.

"But you can't link any of these murders to me," Brad insists.

"Yes, we can, because of the gun in your apartment.

If we can stop you from teleporting, trust me, we'll link you to these deaths," said Agent Donald.

Brad Washington laughed, displaying a sense of invisibility, and then sobered up. "If that's all you've got, then sorry, this is a gun country, I've the right to a gun, am I wrong?" asked Brad.

"I know you've the right to a gun, but it's the same gun we found with you that killed six other people in New York alone. You didn't come through the door, you teleported, so tell me a little about it," asked Agent Donald.

"What about teleporting? you can't prove it! For the record, teleporting is an inherited gift, and has nothing to do with this investigation," he replied. Agent Donald smiled and prodded Brad with further revelations as he reminded him the FBI isn't just aware of the teleporting thing but the FBI is also aware of what makes him teleport, the Judas coin. He proceeded to tell Brad that teleporting isn't a gift, it's sorcery, and his gun has proved it, but he's willing to give him another proof if he remains in denial.

"You're only pulling my legs, you've got nothing on me," said Agent Donald.

While Brad Washington continued to play the hard nut to crack, and calling Agent Donald's bluff, Agent Donald then signalled for Reginald who has accepted to play ball to be brought into the interrogation room. Unfortunately, Brad never meets his contractors in person, and had no clue about the person before him.

"Do you know this man?" asked Agent Donald.

"Who's this man, and does he say he knows me? Because I don't know him!" Brad exclaimed.

"Strangely enough he knows you, and he might be your nemesis," said Agent Donald.

"How, tell me?" asked Brad.

"This is the man that contracted you to kill Bobby Hall," said Agent Donald.

"Oh, great, then hold him and let me go," Brad replied.

"Why? You've killed seven people and if I let you go, you'll continue to kill more people," Agent Donald retorted.

"I'm just an agent who helps people achieve their desires, it doesn't matter how dark their desires are, I just bring them to pass. But how can you prove this man contracted me?" asked Agent Donald.

"Your agency job has taken so many lives and this man here transferred money from his bank account to yours in the Cayman Islands," said Agent Donald.

Brad's delusion is beginning to get the best of him as he suddenly become apathetic, particularly now that his cage is rattled by this contractor who's willing to play ball and expose all their dealings on the dark web.

"But those who contracted me are the people you should arrest, not me," he retorted.

"Brad Washington you'll need an attorney because I'm charging you with the murder of seven people," said Agent Donald, as he read out the names of his seven victims.

After concluding the interrogation, Agent Donald left the interrogation room and joined his boss who's observing the interrogation. "Thank goodness, this teleporting killer is off our streets," said Andy.

Agent Murphy interjected. "When are we charging them?"

Andy's response was as expected and he insisted they aren't here for theatrical show, as he told his men the interrogation has been concluded so they should charge the suspect immediately.

"Ok, let me start getting the paper work ready to facilitate prosecution," said Agent Barry.

While the detectives were busy with the interrogation, Gilbert Rivers was consumed surfing through Brad Washington's seized laptop and dark web activities. He combed through all payments, contacts and solicitations and suddenly things began to click.

"Donald, come and take a look at this," said Gilbert.

Agent Donald went through Gilbert's findings and was able to uncover the details of the contractors for the other six murders committed by Brad Washington in New York City.

"Wait a minute, Barry, let's pay the rest of the contractors a visit," said Agent Donald.

"Have you been able to identify them?" Andy asked curiously as he drew closer to take a look at Gilbert's findings.

"Gilbert just did," Agent Donald replied.

Andy Grey curiously drew closer to take a look at Gilbert's findings. "Ok, that's nice, so we can charge them all together," said Andy.

Sadly, two of these contractors are drug lords who can't be taken in without a fight, and while Andy was returning to his office he suddenly turned to Agent Barry. "Meet me in my office," said Andy.

"You want me in your office now?" asked Agent Barry.

"Yes, now," Andy replied.

Immediately Barry entered Andy's office, Andy hinted to him that he had received a complaint from Lieutenant Bennett about his conduct in the field.

"Andy, what I said was the truth but I don't know why they find it difficult accepting the truth," said Agent Barry.

"What's the truth, Barry?" asked Andy.

Agent Barry laughed as he remained apathetic to the realities of his insulting tantrums at NYPD officers. "The truth is that they're lazy," said Barry.

"How did you come about the idea of them being lazy?" Andy asked.

"They're hardly able to resolve any murder case until we do," said Agent Barry.

"Homicide is the responsibility of the FBI, and the cops are there to assist, so why're you antagonising them?" Andy asked, even as he's hopping mad at Barry for always creating a scene at crime scenes.

"I expected them to do more, that's all," said Agent Barry.

Andy reminds Barry that it's glaringly obvious that he has been unable to manage his demons, and that those at the top aren't ignorant of the negative energy around him. Andy is keen to turn the fortune of his unit around for good, and reminded Barry there's a possibility that things might get beyond his realm of influence and the cover he enjoyed over the years from his boss might be lost.

"You know people at the top don't like you, and I've been covering for you; I might soon get tired of doing that," said Andy.

"You know I actually don't like those who hate me as well, the feeling is mutual," replied Agent Barry who remained unperturbed.

"Your divisive rhetoric is dangerous and corrosive, and I want you to know that the FBI is a respected institution and maintaining its sanctity is sacrosanct," said Andy.

Agent Barry shifted his position from being apathetic to becoming defensive. "But I don't see my opinion as divisive," said Agent Barry.

"You're reaching beyond your depth, and the way you're going, do you think you'll ever head a unit? Be warned, and I don't want you stalling my investigations," said Andy as he told Barry off.

Moments after giving Agent Barry the dressing down, Andy Grey returned to the central office putting on his bullet proof vest.

"Donald, let's be prepared for a real fire fight, since two of these contractors are confirmed to be drug lords," said Andy.

"That's to be expected, Antonio and Alejandro go about with armed body guards," said Agent Donald.

"Go with Agent Murphy, and get more hands in case things get gritty. I'm coming with you; we need to bring them in," said Andy.

They all dressed in their bullet proof vest and other protective equipment. Drug lords are known to use their hitmen to take down their enemies, but Antonio and Alejandro aren't just the regular drug lords, they're snakes who play safe and wouldn't stain their hands just to keep the authorities off their backs. It's sad to say that when they actually choose to get rough, things could get really, really, ugly and dirty.

The FBI agents went with some NYPD officers to take down these drug lords, and after an intense fire fight, their arrests were made. By the time the detectives arrived, and stepped into the premises of these drug peddlers, Agent Barry stopped and looked around in shock at how these rooms are ridiculously sized and vast, and the expanse scenery gracing his view was nothing short of exotic. Debauchery and vintage explain the naughtiness and absurdity of their choice of lifestyle. These guys are rich from the proceeds of their drug peddling, and the more money they make the bigger the size of the chip on their shoulders and this morale boosting chip makes them more brutal. It didn't take long before the guns started blazing.

Three NYPD Officers lost their lives, two died from gunshot injuries from the fire fight with Alejandro, and one died from gunshot injuries from fire fight with Antonio.

Five of Alejandro's body guards were killed and three of Antonio's body guards were killed in the fire fight with NYPD officers.

Through Brad Washington, other contractors who paid money into his accounts were discovered and charged with murder.

Brad Washington was sentenced to three hundred- and fifty-years imprisonment, fifty years for each murder he committed and was held in a customised room fitted with mirrors. Alejandro and Antonio were sentenced to life without the possibility of parole. The other four contractors were arrested and sentenced to life imprisonment while Reginald Rock was sentenced to twenty-five years imprisonment because of the deal he was offered.

CHAPTER

FIVE

The Quad killer

Agent Donald, Agent Murphy and Agent Barry were all at a new crime scene. Each detective looking around and scanning the crime scene, but agent Barry inched closer to one of the NYPD officers in the scene.

"Hello detective," said Sergeant Dexter. Agent Barry didn't even hesitate to dispense with the pleasantries before dismissing the

NYPD officer he met at the crime scene. He then took a dig at him in a rather brash tone but sarcastic a sense.

"Sergeant, we're taking over from here," said Agent Barry.

"Do you have to cut us off? You are a bit abrupt," said Sergeant Dexter.

Agent Donald walked into the scene as the conversation between Agent Barry and the NYPD officer became heated, he quickly toned the heat to change the ambience to an amiable working environment.

"Sergeant, this requires a joint effort, please stay and assist us," said Agent Donald.

Agent Murphy uncovers the corpse of the victim to take a look, it didn't take long before Agent Donald joined agent Murphy to look at the corpse as they assess the crime scene.

"How did this happen?" asked Agent Donald.

"I don't know for now, but we knew he was in the bar last night with a lady and we're still gathering information about the lady in question," said Sergeant Dexter.

Agent Donald turned to a member of the Forensic team at the scene of the crime. "When will we have a forensic report on this, because this killer is still on the loose?" asked Agent Donald.

"It'll be ready by tomorrow," said the forensic person.

After scanning the crime scene for a while and reviewing the available evidence, Agent Donald felt it was time to go.

"Barry, let's go and wait for the forensic report," said Agent Donald.

"I'll fill you in as soon as we discover something new," said Sergeant Dexter. He exchanged phone numbers with the detectives. Later that evening Agent Donald got a call from Sergeant Dexter.

"Hello, is that Agent Donald?" asked Sergeant Dexter.

"Of course, yes. Sergeant, how're you?" asked Agent Donald.

"I'm fine, Donald, we just got some more information from people who saw her yesterday," said Sergeant Dexter.

The Sergeant then gave the detective a vivid eye witness description of the possible suspect in this case, and interestingly, this feature calls the detective into remembrance because there was a flicker of recognition.

"What does she look like and who's she?" asked Agent Donald.

"According to those who saw her, she has a tattoo of a black mamba on her upper arm," said Sergeant Dexter.

"Ah, that looks strikingly strange, any other addition?" asked Agent Donald. Just as more details about this murder unravelled Donald began piecing information together and it didn't take long before he made sense out of it.

"Yeah, she fits the description of a killer in another death that occurred five days earlier," said Sergeant Dexter.

"In what part of New York did the first death occur?" asked Agent Donald.

Agent Donald was beginning to piece this evidence together to make some sense out of it, this isn't just any suspect, this one is evasive, and sadly, her killing ritual isn't over.

"That would be in the eastern part of New York; detectives attached to the police unit in the east of New York are handling the case," Sergeant Dexter replied.

"Ah, that's why I've no knowledge of it," said Agent Donald.

Following the information gathered from Sergeant Dexter the night before, Agent Donald was able understand the profile of this killer better. The next morning, detectives were in the central office reviewing the forensic report from the murder scene of the previous day.

"Andy, from the information I just received, I can tell you the Quad killer is in town," said Agent Donald.

"How do you know, and who is this Quad killer?" asked Andy. "She kills four men in whatever city she enters, she was in Los Angeles and I missed her," he replied.

"Who's she?" Andy asked curiously.

"She's single, dangerous, lethal, fluid, not showing mercy when she's about to take a life, and has no specific location," said Agent Donald. Sensing that this isn't a killer who applies the broad brush, she's mysterious and her target must be within certain demographics, but Andy wants to know who she's after and what she wants.

"Who's her target?" asked Andy.

"Just one target, men, and all she does is observe her ritual of killing four men in whichever town she visits and once that's done, she leaves," said Agent Donald.

"What's her passion?" Andy asked further. "Her passion is just to watch a man die," replied Agent Donald.

Andy Grey find's this killer very creepy and the gory details about this person makes his skin crawl. This isn't the regular killer who kills in error in a robbery gone wrong, or someone taken by jealousy and killing over a love affair gone wrong. This is a killer, who satisfies the requirements of her yearly rituals, and Andy can't wait to catch this cruel killer, and he wants to know what could be her trigger that leaves her unforgiving.

You talked about trigger the other time, what's her trigger? We need to catch this person," Agent Barry muttered.

"There's no specific trigger, she has this burning anger in her underbelly, this anger doesn't burn out and this keeps the trigger going," said Agent Donald.

"What does she use to endear victims to herself?" asked Agent Barry.

"Her looks, then sex, she's very attractive but cruel," said Agent Donald.

The description of this killer makes Agent Barry's skin crawl the more and leaves him open mouthed. He's rattled and just can't get his head around this killer's motives.

"How do we know her? This person is treacherous and I'm afraid for my life as well," said Agent Barry.

"Those who have seen her, says she carries a tattoo of a black mamba on her right arm," replied Agent Donald.

Catching this killer might not need an arm and a leg, but requires tact. This isn't about stopping darkness from falling on the streets of New York when its night time, it's more about stopping a killer lacking of mercy. Andy's determination to catch this killer is because she's everything but benign.

"Where do we find her?" asked Andy.

"A bar of course, wherever it'll be possible for men to take a woman for a one-night stand after meeting her for the first time," said Agent Donald.

"Can we lay an ambush in the bar to see if she will return?" asked Agent Barry.

"No, she wouldn't, she divides the city into four, north, east, south, west, one victim from each of the regions and the killings are in a space of five days each, a strange ritual, I suppose," said Agent Donald.

Andy wants to know why the killings must be about the four cardinal points of the city, and why she isn't just killing her victims in one go, but Donald reminded his fellow detectives that this killer doesn't just kill, the ritual is important to her and the days apart must be observed, so also are the four cardinal points.

"Ok, now that she has killed in the north and east, the next point of call will be south of New York," said Andy.

It's now obvious that she will strike next in the south of New York, and the concern of the detectives is knowing the exact bar she will take her next victim. There's need to extrapolate and pinpoint the very bar she will be visiting, and time is running out.

"Gilbert should use the system to draw a pattern to enable us pick out the possible bar where the next man will be picked up," said Agent Donald.

After moments of extrapolation Gilbert was able to come up with something. "I've been able to come up with two bars that'll be her possible target in the southern part of the city," said Gilbert.

With such beauty and power, she's more like a honey trap luring people to their death. It's undeniably hard to resist her charm and the death that follows, but Agent Donald's water-tight pursuit seems to have this under control. He's undoubtedly the man who gets the job done, and undeniably the go-to person when solving the case at hand because he knows the taste of success when the job gets done.

"I want this killer off our streets today and I want this done before she kills another man," said Andy.

"Not today, she wouldn't be in the southern part of the city now; her next target will be three days from now," said Agent Donald.

"Andy, what's the strategy?" asked Barry.

"You should all be combat ready because, if need be, you'll have to take her out. Though, as a plan B, you'll possibly bug her so we can trace her with it.

"What bars have you picked out to be her next point of call?" asked Agent Donald.

Andy isn't too keen on taking this suspect out, he wants her alive in case she has an accomplice in these murders.

"The Blue Cannon Bar and the Water Garden Bar, both in the southern part of New York City," said Gilbert.

"Ok, we should all get ready; three days from now we'll be in these bars to catch this killer," said Andy.

Three days later, the detectives decided to divide themselves into two groups. Agent Barry was in the Blue Cannon bar while Agent Donald and Agent Murphy were in the Water Garden bar. But after spending about an hour in the Blue Cannon bar, Agent Barry spotted a lady that fits the description of the killer, and drew closer for proper identification. The tattoo of the black mamba was quite visible on her upper arm, and he quickly alerted Agent Donald.

"Donald, she's here. Please you guys should come over," said Agent Barry.

"Are you sure, how did you identify her?" asked Agent Donald.

Barry interjected and said she just walked in now and he isn't blind, because the black mamba on her upper arm is quite visible.

"Ok, we're coming," Agent Donald quickly turned to Agent Murphy, who stood at the far end of the bar, and signalled him to come over.

"Let's go, Barry just spotted her," said Agent Donald.

"Oh, that's good, then we have to be fast," said Agent Murphy.

Agent Barry called Donald for the second time and said he wants to approach her to keep her dawdling until they both get there. Now that Agent Barry has come face to face with this killer, it's very important not to push her to the edge too quickly to avoid setting off a panic that could make her lash out in a bar full of people.

"Barry, be careful, she's dangerous and could be armed. If need be, bring the NYPD officers in to help out," said Agent Donald.

"Yes, I know," said Agent Barry.

Agent Barry walked up to her as she was being attended to, he then quickly put on a cheeky grin that makes him fit the description of a lush.

"Hey, I'll pay for that," said Agent Barry.

Oh, you look like an admirer," she said to Agent Barry, then turned to the bar man, smiling. "Make it two," said the Quad Killer. The barman then served two glasses of brandy, and gave one to her, and then handed the other to Agent Barry who collected one of the glasses containing two shots of brandy and proposed a toast. "To the future," said Agent Barry.

"Erm, to my new admirer, don't worry, tonight will be a night you'll never forget," she replied. Agent Barry warmed up to her, to avoid the possibility of awkward moments that could leave room for suspicion.

She was disinhibited and that caused some concern in him even as he played along. "Oh, I like surprises, and I look forward to me and you together," said agent Barry.

The Quad Killer gobbled her drink and stood up, indicating to Agent Barry that it's time to go for a possible nice time together. "Let's go, let's go, come on," she said, in an enthusiastic tone.

"Why are you in a hurry? Fun isn't meant to be rushed," said Agent Barry, in a whisper into her ear. Agent Barry continued to hesitate as he dawdled around pretending to be socialising with her and buying time. Sad to say, she isn't having it, she wants Barry to gobble his drink, so they could get going.

"Forget about your drink, I'll get you drink when we get to where we're going," she retorted.

Moments after her continuous pestering, Agent Barry stood up trying to bring cash out of his wallet. "Ok then, let me pay for our drinks, and where are you taking me?" asked Agent Barry.

She immediately interjected, and in quite a chillingly dramatic move she held Agent Barry's hand preventing him from collecting his change, and urging him to leave the change for the bar man as his tip, saying he wouldn't be in need of the cash ever again.

Agent Barry turned and saw Donald and Murphy walk in to the bar, and then he brought out his gun immediately. "Stop, FBI," said Agent Barry.

"Who are you?" she screamed. Funnily, she wanted to run in the mist of the confusion only to discover she had been surrounded.

"You're under arrest for murder," said Agent Donald.

"Why're you arresting me, and what have I done?" asked the Quad killer.

"You're under arrest for murder," said Agent Donald.

The Quad Killer turned to Barry as she's being put in cuffs. "You're wicked, you deceived me," she said.

It was a big sigh of relive for Andy, to have succeeded in taking this killer off the streets of New York and in cuffs, and by morning of the next day, the Quad killer was processed, and then brought into the interrogation room, before Agent Donald joined her minutes later. While being processed, the FBI detectives verified the identity of the Quad killer, as Josephine Alexi. Just as the interrogation commences. "Hello, Josephine Alexi," said Agent Donald.

"Why are you keeping me here and pretending to be nice at the same time?" she asked.

"I'm not pretending to be nice, it's called courtesy," said Agent Donald.

"But I don't like your kind of courtesy. That's what your friend used to trick me," she replied.

"No one deceived you; we arrested you to prevent you from killing more people," said Agent Donald.

She became irate as she was being accused of killing people and requested a lawyer. The interrogation was paused and a lawyer was provided for her. Even as her lawyer was speaking up in her defence and asking her to be mute, she's still not having it. The lawyer soon realised this juice isn't worth the squeeze, when she got more upset and lashed out at her lawyer who was forced to step aside while Josephine Alexi does her bidding herself. After all, this is about her taking back control.

"Will you prevent me from killing whoever I want?" she asked. There's so much anger in this lady, and the ferocity of her anger was reflected in her voice, this left her lawyer open-mouthed.

"Ok, you admit committing these murders," said Agent Donald.

"I didn't commit any murder. I'm only returning favours," she said, in an apathetic tone.

"You killed innocent people, and you called that returning favours?" asked Agent Donald. The person sitting opposite Agent Donald is quite different from the friendly soft spoken but a little bit brash personality flirting with Agent Barry in the club the previous night. Agent Barry who was watching the interrogation from the other room saw the contrast between the suspect's charming personality and her frank personality which is now laid bare.

"What makes you think they're innocent, they all deserved to burn in hell," she exploded. Agent Donald was taken aback because he rarely find suspects admitting their crimes in such an explosive manner, even Andy and other detectives observing the interrogation were rattled.

"Why should they burn in hell, what have they done to deserve death?" asked Agent Donald.

She opened up and said twenty-two years ago, she was just six years old, and her mum was in the kitchen while she was in the back garden of their house playing with her dad. Four men walked into their house, took all her dad's money from him, then pointed a gun at her mum and shot her. "I cried and one of them said to me, let me help your dad end his misery, then he shot him," said Josephine Alexi.

"Are you sure of this story, or you're telling a lie?" asked Agent Donald. "Go online it's there; it was a story that made headlines twenty-two years ago," she replied.

"What did the government do to those that did this to your parents?" Agent Donald queried further.

"They were caught and sentenced to life in prison, they're all still in prison, doing life without the possibility of parole," she replied. "How did you get to this point of killing people?" asked Agent Donald.

"After the death of my parents, coping with life was difficult for me, as I was moved from one foster care to another until I was eighteen. Though, by then I was already a troubled and damaged child. When I was twenty-two, I made up my mind to return the favours to men who were responsible for my present circumstance by killing four men every year in the month of July in memory of my parents," said Josephine Alexi.

"But justice has been served on those who killed your parents' and therefore, nothing gives you the right to go on a killing spree," Agent Donald retorted.

"No, that justice didn't go far enough," she insists.

"Hmm, the devil makes work for idle hands, I guess." Agent Donald stood up and charged her for her crimes.

"Josephine Alexi, you'll need an attorney, I'm charging you with murder of Rudi Gomez," said Agent Donald.

Agent Donald left the interrogation room and joined his colleagues who were observing the interrogation. "Her story was pathetic, but it doesn't give her the right to go on a killing spree," said Agent Donald.

"Which means for the past six years she has been killing four men each year," said Andy.

The four men who killed her parents thought they have just killed a couple but they've inadvertently killed over twenty men. Alas, the innocent six-year-old girl, to whom they claimed to have done favours, never forgot and never forgave. The detectives were empathic with Josephine's circumstance but didn't sympathize with her decision to take the law into her own hands, and miscarrying justice.

"Her anger is deep seated and it's still burning," said agent Donald. Agent Barry interjected and rhetorically said she'd wanted to add him to her list of trophies. "I know, but that's sad and it's rather unfortunate that the action of four men has resulted in the death of over twenty men," said Agent Murphy.

"I want her charged immediately," said Andy Grey.

The interrogation was over and Josephine Alexi was charged with the murder of twelve people they could verify, but she's considered for diminished responsibility and sentenced to thirty-five years imprisonment.

CHAPTER

SIX

The Leach

Abigail Sims has been declared missing after her failure to return home on Friday from her regular Friday happy hour with her friends.

It's been eight days since her last sighting and the police are doing everything to find her alive and safe, press statements from the police and even pleas through word of mouth from family and friends have gone out yet no news of her whereabouts.

The police have interviewed Abigail's boyfriend who told them all he knew but the focus is not him because he had a strong alibi that ruled him out as a person of interest in this case. They also interviewed every member of Abigail's family and none of them so far is a person of interest in this case.

Two days later another press statement was issued to keep the search for Abigail Sims in the minds of people, and interestingly someone who sighted her close to a petrol station came forward with a helpful info about what he saw. The Police immediately followed this lead to see if it will help them unravel the whereabouts of Abigail, and went for the CCTV around the said petrol station.

CCTV captured a hooded figure who seems to engage Abigail in what doesn't really look like a cordial conversation, but they seem to move outside the CCTV coverage as they strayed further into a footpath that leads to an alleyway.

The Police traced their steps to a wooded area, and observed that two sets of feet walked that footpath to the river, and of these two people, one of the shoe prints is supposedly from Abigail's stiletto. The investigation had a breakthrough when the Police found Abigail's green jacket by the river. Suspicion concerning Abigail's safety became a concern, when only one set of feet returned from the river bank where her item of clothing stained in her blood was found.

The police based their premise on the fact that since two people walked to the river where Abigail's dress was found and only one set of feet returned from the river, meaning only one person returned, then the criminal must have killed her and dumped her body in the river around the spot where her green jacket was found.

Now that the police concluded that Abigail may have been killed even without seeing her body to authenticate such an assertion; the investigation quickly morphed from a case of a missing person to a murder investigation.

The case is now a homicide investigation and the FBI was informed, it didn't take long before the FBI arrived at the scene and began their investigation of the case.

Convinced that Abigail's body was dumped in the river, the police pulled all available resources together as they began searching the river, in a search and recovery operation. When the FBI eventually arrived at the scene, they allowed the police to continue searching the river for Abigail's body while they gathered their own evidence as well as preserving what's left of the crime scene.

The police had to abandon their search after three days because they've been unable to find Abigail's body, they then concluded that the river current may have transported her body miles away from the spot where her body was dumped, hence continued pleading with members of the public to be on the lookout for her body floating along the length and breadth of the river.

The next day after the police abandoned their search, the FBI forensic report was out and the dress was confirmed to be Abigail's, the blood stain on the jacket is hers' as well. Also, the forensic team was able to verify the prints on the ground to come from the stiletto Abigail was wearing. The FBI had to shop for the very type of stiletto Abigail was wearing on CCTV on her last night out, and then compared the markings on the sole of the shoe with the prints on the ground and it was a perfect match.

Agents are now discussing and analysing this supposed murder investigation, Agent Donald interjected and said this is the hand-work of the leach.

"The leach, what do you mean?" Asked Andy.

"You seem to know him, have you investigated him before?" Asked Agent Barry.

"No, I haven't, I called him the leach because of the manner in which he does his thing," said Agent Donald. Now that Agent Donald has opened a new line of conversation Andy Grey then asked Agent Donald to throw more light on his assertion.

Agent Donald then asked Gilbert to put up some of the photographs taken from the crime scene, and immediately, after Gilbert put up the pictures on the screen, the detectives continued their analysis of the case.

If they take a good look at these set of feet, they'll realise the two sets of feet that walked to the river made an impression that is even and regular on the ground but the one set of feet that returned from the river, the footsteps didn't include Abigail's stiletto as they already know. He then pointed out that the foot prints are irregular and made a bigger impression on the ground.

Agent Barry interjected and asked Donald why he's introducing hyperbole and making this simple matter look like there's a puzzle to solve. After all, two people walked to the river and only one returned and evidence on ground proved that the shoes of the person that walked out of that place was the other person and not Abigail's. Agent Barry continued as he said, it's possible that Abigail's killer is hurrying out of the crime scene just as any killer would, and said that could be the reason for the irregular impression on the ground. So, he killed her and dumped her in the river. "Abigail is dead, Donald, and she's in the river," said agent Barry.

Agent Donald smiled and said the two people that walked to the river returned from the river, and that Abigail wasn't dumped in to the river.

"Donald, only the killer returned from the river, and how come Abigail's footsteps are missing?" asked agent Barry.

'Abigail's footsteps are missing on the way back from the river because the guy carried her on his shoulder," said Agent Donald.

Agent Barry shook his head in disagreement with this bizarrely twisted assertion put forward by Agent Donald, saying this is merely a supposition, and urged agent Donald to stop putting forward theories that are improvable. Andy Grey interjected and asked Agent Barry to stop for a minute, and he then turned to Agent Donald and asked him to shed more light in his assertion.

Agent Donald then walked closer to the screen and began using his fingers to point, these footsteps that walked back from the river alone are quite irregular and look like the guy is staggering which is the result of the weight he's carrying. This also explains why the footsteps that returned from the river made deeper impression in the ground. "He's carrying her at this point, dead or alive," said agent Donald.

He proceeded to say that he isn't putting too fine a point in this investigation but the police won't find Abigail's body because it isn't in the river.

Agent Barry queried Agent Donald further and asked why he didn't hint the police of his supposition that Abigail's body isn't in the river and urge them to abort the search. Being too forward isn't Donald Whitley's thing, as he subtly reminded agent Barry that he wouldn't want to do a thing like that, making the police abort their search inconclusively will mean bursting their bubble, and it's not nice.

Andy Grey nodded his head in affirmation and said Donald is making sense then asked why he called Abigail's killer the leach.

Agent Donald then went on describe the suspect as someone with obsessive attachment syndrome (OAS), he's someone who fancied Abigail Sims, and likes her so much, to the point that he now forms a bond with Abigail, without her knowledge.

He creates role play and social interplay between himself and Abigail in his head. He's a fan of Abigail. Agent Barry interjected and said Abigail Sims is just a regular girl, who isn't a celebrity, he then queried how she will have a fan.

"Barry, everyone has a fan, anyone who fancies you is your fan,' said agent Donald.

Andy interjected and asked Agent Donald why this killer would carry Abigail's body back instead of disposing off her body and making a run for it, as any their killer would normally do to avoid being caught by the authorities. Agent Donald continued and said the conventional criminal will be quick to get rid of any evidence that could link them to a crime, but the Leach isn't. The guy likes Abigail so much and can't bear to see her body dumped in the river, or just leaving her body by the roadside uncared for.

Except that she's unconscious as at when he carried her back, but if she's dead, then he has taken her home to clean her up, and possibly wear her the best makeup to make her look pretty, while he stands around and just continues to fancy her.

"I suppose, he now regrets his action, he must be blaming her for making him do this to her," said agent Donald.

"Who romanticize a corpse, this guy must be sick, really sick," said agent Barry.

"The guy is truly sick in the head as you just said, and he may have been trying reach to out to Abigail before her death, maybe not directly, and I don't think she got the message that he likes her," said Agent Donald.

"I need to catch this guy and take him of our streets," said Andy Grey.

Agent Donald then suggested that the killer could be anyone from Abigail's past, primary school, high school, university or some friend she made as she goes out going about her life. Agent Donald stopped speaking for a while, and then said his hunch tells him the killer is someone hanging around the fringes of Abigail's social life, and there's a possibility she might not even know him because she hasn't taken notice of him.

Agent Donald then suggested that it's either he knocked her flat-out unconscious and carried her or he killed by the river and carried her body.

Agent Barry on the other hand took exception to Agent Donald's statement and asked if he's suggesting she's possibly unconscious and not dead as at the time the guy carried her back.

He then took a swipe at Donald as he stopped speaking and muttered saying if Abigail isn't dead, then why are they involved in the case because this isn't homicide. Andy listened as Agent Barry made his point and after a while, he then interjected and said he's pursuing the case with the mindset that Abigail is dead, and said this case is now officially homicide until proven otherwise.

Agent Donald cautioned Barry saying there's no need playing the devil's advocate in this investigation and said this killer is still obsessed with Abigail, he's attached to her and it arguably turned into a sickness of the mind, and even in death she still controls his emotions.

After about a week of pursuing the investigation without any breakthrough, Andy then decided to focus on Agent Donald's Assertion that if Abigail is dead and the guy has her corpse in his home, the corpse must have started stinking by now, and it's possible he must be purchasing some type of strong fragrance with which to regularly spray the corpse to prevent the smell from going out. Agent Barry cuts in again and suggests they open themselves to all possibilities, and asked what if the killer dumped Abigail's corpse in his refrigerator, he proceeded to say that the possibility of buying certain fragrance to keep her body from smelling into the neighbourhood won't be necessary.

The FBI detectives visited most of the supermarkets around to see if they could track down any purchase of Myrrh, which is the fragrant resin of a tree, that helps to seal the body, in addition to warding off the stench of decay. Unfortunately, they didn't succeed, yet they continued going through CCTV cameras with a fine-tooth comb to see if they could find any reoccurring face that could represent this stalker. Funnily, catching this guy isn't just a walk in the park, as this guy proved to be more than a handful for these detectives.

The public outcry over the fate of Abigail Sims was quite overbearing for the FBI detectives handling this investigation, and a deep national dialogue on the safety of Americans in the street of New York has now taken over the headlines. Some have resorted to scaremongering, which the detectives find absolutely stunning. Agent Donald is now up to the challenge, particularly now that he has decided to throw his hat in the ring.

The FBI detectives continue to pursue this investigation by throwing every resource at it, they didn't relent either. Even the cadava dogs didn't do enough to fish out Abigail Sims location. In one of their repeat visits to Abigail's friend whose information they find to be helpful and relevant to this investigation.

Merlin told the detectives about Connor Oblondy, a homeless man who's overly fond of Abigail. Merlin told the detectives that Connor has been serendipitously scarce since Abigail went missing. Connor has a base under the bridge, and the alley is close to the bar visited by Abigail regularly.

The detectives find this clue interesting and immediately decided to search for Connor Oblondy in his mum's home to interview him, because he could possibly be the person they are looking for. His scarcity might be because he has her and might be engrossed with looking after her, dead or alive.

With the understanding that this is a homeless man who could be volatile, the detectives went in the company of some armed police officers.

Immediately they knocked the door and Connor came to the door to open the door, agent Donald went through Connor's back garden to station at his back door in case he wants to make a run from the detectives through the back door.

Interestingly, he opened his front door and Agent Barry was there in the front door to attend to him. Things took a rather interesting turn when agent Donald decided to conduct a cursory search of Connor's premises and found a fresh grave.

The situation was quite tense and heighted as the detectives immediately put Connor in handcuffs and forced him into the back seat. Though, while this new twist got the best of the detectives' attention, Connor continued speaking up and saying he'd no hand in Abigail's disappearance. At this point he'd no choice but open a new can of worms that might give neighbours the creeps, stressing that it was Billy that's in the grave.

The detectives immediately obtained a warrant and began digging the grave so as exhume the contents. Meanwhile, James Tod have been canvassing with neighbours and speaking to everyone in his neighbourhood in search of his dog, Billy. Corner was among the concerned neighbours helping out with the search, but now that he has opened up a can of worms by telling the detectives that it was Billy in the grave, James Tod who was among the neighbours watching the happenings from afar, overheard Connor's claim, and got hopping mad to learn Connor had already killed his beloved pet and buried the poor thing.

James Tod rushed closer to the scene wanting to cross the police cordon, he was quite enraged and kicking off, but was stopped by the cops who are still digging to uncover the content of the grave.

The FBI on the other hand insisted that it was Abigail in the grave, arguing that Connor's claim was a mere lie, and that he's claiming it was Billy in an attempt to pursue a lesser sentence.

The police informed Tod that this is now a police business and asked him to step aside, insisting that they can't tell for sure that it is Billy in the grave, they held unto the assertion that it was Abigail that's in that grave.

James Tod, understood that his dog, Billy, is notorious for harassing Connor for always looking poorly kept, and he's convinced that it was actually Billy in that grave and Connor may have killed his beloved pet as a comeuppance for the sustained harassment he received from the dog.

It didn't take long, the FBI exhumed the content of the grave, and realised it was a dog, and that Connor was telling the truth all along, it didn't take long the news of the FBI find filtered into Tod's ears and got him kicking off. Tod's inability to exact his fist on Connor for the dastardly act got Tod hopping mad, because the police didn't allow him go physical on Billy's killer. Connor was however arrested for animal cruelty, even as he continued to claim that Billy' death wasn't intentional. Andy Grey immediately asked Gilbert Rivers to review Connor's movement from the day Abigail Sims went missing, and after interrogating Connor, coupled with the CCTV review the detectives concluded there's nothing linking Connor to Abigail Sims disappearance. The detectives were left disappointed, as this lead turned out not to be viable, even though they got Connor on animal cruelty and charged him for that specific offence.

While Abigail's friends and work colleagues set up a web page meant to help with the search, or any information about Abigail's whereabouts. So many of the posts expressed sympathy for Abigail's family, and her boyfriend, while other posts commented on the hooded guy that was seen on CCTV with her. Some of the post about this hooded guy who may have kidnapped Abigail weren't kind as they described the hooded guy as a creep, as evil and as a monster who should burn in hell. From the moment the web page was setup, Alec Rylan visited the web page hourly to see comments, but the comment about the hooded guy who should burn in hell touched him, at some point he couldn't help but post a comment and said the hooded guy might be a nice person, and he might not have intentionally killed Abigail.

For all it's worth, Alec Rylan is just some drifter.

He began fantasising about Abigail from the very day Abigail danced with a stranger in the club, and laughed without reservation as she danced with this stranger, after the dance she said goodbye to this stranger who mistook the dance for mutual expression of love.

The stranger in question is Alec Rylan, he's a loner who isn't willing to stay celibate because from the day Alec Rylan danced with Abigail, he began fantasising about her, he lurks in the shadows around her circle of friends, and occasionally shows up and says hello and takes a seat like a few customers who had just come to enjoy a happy hour alone by themselves.

Funnily, Abigail never pieced one and one together to sense that this guy is stalking her. Interestingly, the post by Alec Rylan suggesting the killer might be a nice guy who might not have intended to kill Abigail, touched nerves and attracted some attention and concern, and someone contacted the FBI with their concern.

It's obvious that public sympathy for Abigail was unwavering and the suspicious post by this unsuspecting member of pubic came across as insidious because it touched the raw nerves of many New Yorkers.

Andy Grey asked Gilbert to trace where the post came from, and it didn't take long, the FBI was able to uncover who made the post using the ip address. Serendipitously, a further search about this guy puts him in close proximity around Abigail, and shows was practically stalking her.

"Andy, come and see this," said Gilbert.

Gilbert Rivers displayed his findings on the screen, he then showed so much CCTV footage where Alec was seen lurking around Abigail, which confirmed he was stalking her long before her sudden disappearance. "We need to pay him a visit," said Agent Donald.

It didn't take long before FBI agents are in front of Alec's house and knocking the door. Alec Rylan peeped through the curtain and decided to escape through the back door, unbeknownst to him Agent Barry was by his back door and trigger ready.

"If you move, I will shoot, Alec Rylan, you're under arrest for the murder of Abigail Sims," said Agent Barry. Sadly, the detectives got more than they bargained for when they searched the home of Alec Rylan. They found Abigail's decomposing body, and a trove of makeup items and fragrance. They immediately put Alec Rylan in cuffs, and got the authorities to move Abigail's already decomposing corpse for an autopsy and identification. Agent Donald was in the interrogation room, interrogating Alec Rylan over the death of Abigail Sims, while Agent Barry and Andy Grey watched the progress of the interrogation from the watching room.

"Alec Rylan, tell us your role in the death of Abigail Sim," said Agent Donald.

"Why did you take Abi away? I was taking good care of her," said Alec.

"You needed an opportunity to be with her, to smell her hair, her fragrance, and enjoy her company, I suppose, and you can only do this if she's alive," said Agent Donald.

"Of course," replied Alec.

"She's dead now and already stinking, except you want a pandemic for people living in your neighbourhood," replied Agent Donald.

"I have been reaching out to her to let her know her friends don't really love her, and I'm the only one who truly loves her," said Alec.

"How, what makes you think her friends don't love her, after all, it's you that killed her," asked Agent Donald.

"She's my Abi, and I didn't kill her, it's a mistake," said Alec.

Agent Donald continued focusing the interrogation with the intention of understanding this suspect's personality, to help put the possible criminal charge into the right perspective. He then steered the conversation into the specifics in this case. Alec looked away in guilt, just as Agent Donald reminded him his action could not have been a mere mistake because he deliberately walked Abigail to the riverside and killed her before carrying her body home.

"It wasn't deliberate I only marched her to the river bank for us to talk, just the two of us, like adults, but she kept saying I should leave her alone and let her go," said Alec.

"Then you killed her," asked Agent Donald.

Alec became teary as he said, he only shook Abi so hard, just to make her come to her senses and see how much he loves her, but she slipped out of his hand and hit her head on the rock. He immediately picked her up but she suddenly went limp.

"So, you carried her corpse home, instead of calling for the ambulance to see if they could resuscitate her," replied Agent Donald.

Now that Alec Rylan has accepted, he murdered Abigail Sims, Agent Donald immediately wrapped up the interrogation and charged Alec with murder.

"Alec Rylan you will need an attorney because I am charging you for the murder of Abigail Sims".

CHAPTER

SEVEN

The Scroll

FBI detectives were at the crime scene of a double murder, where two naked murder victims were found inside a car, in what looks like they're supposedly making out before being killed.

Agent Donald arrived at the new crime scene where two people have been murdered but met some NYPD officers already at the scene "Hello Lieutenant," said Agent Donald.

"Oh, Donald, good to see you," said Lieutenant Bennett.

When Agent Barry arrived at the murder scene, he went on and uncovered the corpse of the victims and realised they were both naked. "Oh my God! Why're they both naked?" asked Agent Barry.

"How did this happen? Did you find them naked this way?" asked Agent Donald.

"Yeah, I guess they were making out before they were shot at close range," said Lieutenant Bennett.

"Is that all you could tell us?" asked Agent Barry in his usual tantrum throwing fit. Sad to say, that the lieutenant believes in reciprocity, particularly for snubs like Barry.

"I don't think I'm answerable to you, if you want evidence, seek it yourself," said Lieutenant Bennett.

"This is a double homicide, Lieutenant. This is my jurisdiction and I suggest you take note," said Agent Barry.

Agent Donald interjected to keep the conversation focused on the assignment at hand, and asked Lieutenant Bennett what time these murders occurred.

"I've got no idea, but they were discovered at dawn," said Lieutenant Bennett.

"Is this a robbery gone wrong or a possible assassination?" asked Agent Donald. The detectives continued reviewing the scene and the victims of this murder even as they had their conversation. Lieutenant Bennett turned to the detectives and said this can't be called a robbery, because the victims have their cash, jewellery and bank cards intact, and he doesn't think anything is missing.

"What about the identities of the victims?" asked Agent Donald. This is Ben Cousins, and that is Lana Pen," said Lieutenant

Bennett. It didn't take long before the forensic team arrived at the scene, and the detectives decided to step aside.

"Forensic team is here, let's wait for their report, and take it from there," said Agent Barry.

Agent Donald walked some distance away and then walked back to the Lieutenant and asked if there's any eyewitness to this crime, but Lieutenant replied to him saying, he doesn't think so, but then suggested to Agent Donald that they haven't spoken to the person that made the 911 call. "I Learnt the lady that made the 911 call is an African American," said Lieutenant Bennett.

After scanning the crime scene and gathering as much information as they could, the forensic team is now moving in, and Agent Donald turned to the Lieutenant. "The forensic team is moving in, Lieutenant. Please give me a call if anything comes up," said Agent Donald.

Immediately Agent Donald turned to leave, he realised Agent Barry is still consumed with the gruesomeness of the crime scene, he took off his glasses and stood for a while waiting for Agent Barry, who joined him moments later.

"This is the handwork of a disgruntled anti-gay bigot," said Agent Barry.

"Let's not rush into a premature conclusion, Barry," said Agent Donald, who always insists on working with the facts.

This investigation is still in its early stages, but there is nothing much left to do at the crime scene, the detectives then decided it is best if they visit the caller to see if she witnessed the crime, or if saw anything that could be of help.

Unfortunately, their visit didn't yield much fruit because the lady that made the 911 call was in a hurry to leave the house, but spent some time attending to the detectives. She narrated to them that she didn't witness the murders being committed, but then explained to the detectives that she spotted blood splatters on the ground next to the car, and decided to take closer look, that was when she saw the dead bodies in the car, then thought it wise to alert the authorities immediately.

Later that same day, Agent Donald and Agent Barry pay Mrs Cousins a visit, as they investigate these two murders.

Mrs Cousins opens her door to the FBI agents, after she had earlier refused to speak to the detectives on the phone as she mourns her loss. "Why won't you allow us to mourn in peace?" asked Mrs Cousins.

"I thought catching your husband's killer should be a priority and we would need you to answer some questions," says Agent Barry. Regrettably, Agent Barry's fiery remark makes no distinction between a suspect, and a person mourning her loss, because his apathetic comments lack empathy.

"Why don't you allow us to grieve over our loss?" Mrs Cousins retorted.

"We'll be on our way soon, just help us piece some information together that would help us find those behind this," said Agent Donald, in a calm and reassuring manner.

"Did you come to question me about my husband's sexuality? For the records, my husband isn't gay," Mrs Cousins insists.

But Agent Barry couldn't keep his cool as he jumped into conclusion, even before the facts are laid bare. "How then can you explain the circumstances surrounding his death?" said Agent Barry.

The already frustrated and embarrassed Mrs Cousins became infuriated over Agent Barry's remark. "You're a detective, why don't you tell me?" she asked.

"Your husband was found dead, with the body of a male escort by his side, both of them naked, and you say you aren't aware he's gay?" Agent Barry queried.

"Read my lips! My husband isn't gay; he's a devoted Christian and hates the idea of a man sleeping with a fellow man," she retorted.

"How is your husband's sex life, is there anything that indicates he isn't into women?" asked Agent Donald.

"I'm Ben's wife for God's sake! My husband isn't gay, there is more about his death and I suggest you look beyond what the crime scene tells you," she replied.

Sad to say, God cursed Agent Barry with not being nice to people and in a manner of speaking, and that's his character flaw. Agent Barry never leaves any thought running through his mind unspoken.

"The crime scene already tells us all we needed to know, meaning your husband is gay, you've to get used to that fact," said Agent Barry.

Agent Donald pulled Agent Barry aside and urged him to show some regards for this bereaved family, saying everyone need someone they can rely on, a friend or something like that. "If you continue like this, on the day of your funeral it might just be you and the undertakers only in attendance and no one else," Agent Donald retorted. He then proceeded to urge Barry not to draw premature conclusions, because the investigation is still in an early stage.

"But she doesn't seem to be making it easy for us," Agent Barry retorted. Agent Donald turned to Mrs Cousins and asked if there's anything she can tell them about Ben's schedule, his circle of friends or anything that'll help us with this investigation.

"There's nothing I know of, but if anything comes up, I'll let you know," she promised.

"You mean you aren't telling us anything? You must tell us something to help with this investigation," Agent Barry insists.

The investigation seems to be at a dead end, as there isn't any lead to help the investigation, so it's time for the detectives to take their leave. Agent Donald then turned to Mrs Cousins and thanked her for her time, and said they'll be back if the need arises.

"Thank you, detective, I'm counting on you," she replied.

The next morning, Agent Murphy was scanning through the content of a file, as he walked into Andy's office.

"Andy, the forensic report from the crime scene is out," he said.

"Which of the crime scenes?" asked Andy.

"The naked men crime scene," he replied. .

"Ok, what does it say? Put it up on the screen," said Andy. They both walked into the central office and began reviewing the murder case.

"There wasn't any sexual act between Ben Cousins and the male escort," said Agent Murphy.

"Meaning?" asked Andy.

Agent Barry interjected. "Maybe Ben Cousins and the escort were killed before they began the act," he said.

But Agent Murphy went further to clarify the content of this forensic report, that has the pathologist report also attached to it.

"The forensic report states that the male escort died two hours after Ben died, and that the escort's death occurred in a separate location," said Agent Murphy. The report also stated that the male escort was strangled before his death because of the accumulation of blood in his airway. Agent Donald immediately analysed the report further as he put the content into perspective, saying the male escort and Ben were killed at different times, and in different locations before being dumped in Ben's car to make it look like they were making out. The killer went through a lot of trouble to stage the crime scene, he suffocated the male escort, then shot him after his death.

The killer tried to mislead the authorities by disguising the time of death of Ben Cousins. The killer deceptively adjusted the time in Mr Cousins wrist watch two hours ahead before smashing the watch to make it look like the death happened two hours later, particularly as at the time both bodies were dumped. Lana Pen died at about 11pm, but CCTV showed he was snatched off the street by 7pm, on his way from a night out but Mr Cousins died at about 9pm, just thirty minutes after he left church on his way home. The killers already had Lana Pen, so they adjusted the time on Mr Cousins watch two hours ahead to 11pm before smashing it.

What Agent Murphy has disclosed so far from the forensic report was helpful but not enough to assist this investigation, and Andy wants more.

"Is that all you've got in that forensic report?"

"No, the DNA of Warner Talbot is found on Ben Cousins, and one more thing!" Agent Murphy exclaimed.

"What?" asked Agent Barry.

"This DNA is linked to the death of Morris Doyle, and Morris Doyle is gay, he died last week," said Agent Murphy.

"Donald, I want you to bring this Warner Talbot in for questioning, we've a killer on the loose," said Andy. Instead of rushing to bring this Talbot in, Agent Donald felt it's better to gather more information before bringing Talbot in.

"What do these two victims have in common? I mean Morris Doyle and Ben Cousins," asked Agent Donald.

"Nothing, except they're both gay?" said Agent Murphy.

Agent Donald felt Ben Cousins' wife's insistence about her husband's sexuality might have some truth to it, and deserves more digging. "Morris Doyle is gay but nothing suggests Ben Cousins is gay?" he said.

"The killer knows his victims, he's after gay men, and the fact that Ben Cousins and the male escort didn't engage in the act didn't mean they weren't about to," said Agent Barry.

"What's it with you Barry? I just told you they were killed two hours apart and in different locations," said Andy.

Agent Donald is still needled by the possible connection between these deaths, after all there are several gay men, why these two, he then insisted that apart from the fact that these men were assumed to be gay, there should be something they have in common that makes them a target.

"Bring Warner Talbot in for questioning; we need to know everything there's to know," said Andy.

Not long afterwards, the detectives descended on Warner Talbot's residence. Agent Donald stood by the front door, which was open and knocks the door. "Is anybody home?" he asked.

"The door is open, let's go in," said Agent Barry.

"I don't think that's a good idea, Barry. We're plain clothes FBI agents, he could mistake us for robbers," said Agent Donald.

Agent Barry isn't having it. As far as Barry is concerned, being a detective means you've every right and others have none. Caution and civility is now thrown to the wind.

"We're here to arrest this guy, not to romance him, and it won't be necessary displaying false modesty," Agent Barry retorted.

While Agent Donald stood by the door waiting for someone to attend to the door, Barry walked into the apartment, and Donald had no choice but follow suit, at least to provide cover for his partner.

Sadly, Warner Talbot's apartment isn't one that accommodates intruders, particularly when he has a knife nearby that could come handy, and didn't take long before Talbot came charging at Agent Barry with a knife. "Who are you and what are you doing in my house?" he exploded.

Agent Donald was at hand to save the day, as he quickly points his gun at Talbot. "FBI, stop, I say stop, or I'll shoot you," said Agent Donald.

Talbot raised his hands up. "Ok, ok," said Talbot.

"Apart from the reason why we're here, I'll also be charging you with assaulting an FBI agent," said Agent Barry.

"Who did I assault?" asked Talbot.

"You assaulted me, and you'll go down for that," Agent Barry exploded.

"How would I know you're FBI agents, when you walk into my apartment in plain clothes without identifying yourselves?" asked Talbot.

While Agent Barry continued his hissy fit Agent Donald whispered into Agent Barry's ear. "He has got a point, he has the right to protect his home from intruders and we walked in without identifying ourselves," said Agent Donald.

"What are you doing in my apartment, I haven't committed any crime?" Talbot asked without flinching or batting an eyelid.

"You're under arrest for the murder of Ben Cousins, Morris Doyle and Lana Pen" said Agent Barry, as he puts the cuffs on Talbot. Agent Barry immediately read Talbot his rights, even as he insisted, he didn't kill anyone.

"You'll have to explain yourself better, when we get to the office," said Agent Barry. Talbot continued to protest his arrest as the detectives walked him to the car.

"Why're you doing this? You don't have to arrest me," he protested.

Three hours later, Warner Talbot is being questioned in the interrogation room.

"Why're you keeping me here? I've done nothing wrong," said Talbot.

"Maybe you should start by telling us how you got mixed up in the death of Ben Cousins, Morris Doyle and Lana Pen," asked Agent Donald.

"I didn't kill anyone, and I need a lawyer," he replied.

Agent Donald urged him not to waste his time telling lies, because they found evidence on his laptop linking him to these crimes, and telling lies at this point when his hand was already in the cookie jar will make his evidence further sloppy.

"The evidence never told you I killed them," said Talbot.

"You'll have to explain the coincidence to the judge, your DNA on these victims and the evidence on your laptop is enough to send you to the electric chair," said Agent Donald.

"They're gay, what do you care?" asked Talbot.

Talbot remained apathetic, because his defence sounds vaguely like an insult but in this circumstance, he continues to believe he just did the world a favour.

"You can't take the law into your own hands, I guess you know that?" said Agent Donald.

"Many years ago, when I was young, I enjoyed watching horror movies. This urge makes me romanticised being a part of something horror, like something big, with the devil himself, I fantasized being in a cult, working for the devil and being in a meeting with the devil.

"Why the devil, and why not God?" asked Agent Donald, in surprise at the dark desires in the heart of the man sitting opposite him, but Talbot scoffs at Donald's question in quite an ingenious manner.

"Unlike God who's patient and merciful, the devil is swift, quick to action and unforgiving, features I cherish," said Talbot.

"Hmm, do we now say your fantasy has come true, you've realised your dream haven't you?" asked Agent Donald.

"No, I haven't. How would I have done that when you bumped into me?" asked Talbot.

"With your hands dipped in so many cookie jars at the same time, and considering the number of people you've killed in the service of the devil, you must have had your fill of blood, I guess?" said Agent Donald.

"No, there shouldn't be an end to this war, when sinners are still out there protected by the same society that should be hunting them down," said Talbot.

"That phrase "hunting them down" sounds brutish, doesn't it? The world has moved away from that. We no longer live in the state of nature, where humans take the law into their own hands," said Agent Donald.

"It depends on your definition of the state of nature, there's evil out there and you need evil to match evil, why don't you let us do our job?" asked Talbot.

"What evidence do you have in your possession that gives you the conviction that your victims are actually guilty?" asked Agent Donald.

"We're serving a higher cause; our evidence comes from true revelations and victims' narratives," said Talbot.

"And you think killing of gay men is the best way out?" asked Agent Donald.

"That's the only way we can keep evil out of our land," said Talbot.

"I don't think so," said Agent Donald.

Agent Barry was observing the interrogation with Andy Grey and felt the FBI has gotten all they needed to pursue a prosecution. These guys are trained to kill and not to feel, and it's a shame they are now preserved from oblivion. Andy needed more, as he wants to be sure that this suspect will play the role of a reliable snout.

"Let's wrap this interrogation up, he has confessed to the crimes and I think we've gotten all we wanted," said Agent Barry.

"Give him a little time; we don't know if he acted alone or not," said Andy.

While the interrogation lasted, Gilbert rushed to Agent Barry and Andy Grey as they watch the interrogation from watching room.

"What's it, Gilbert, did anything come up?" asked Andy.

"That tattoo in Talbot's arm is a logo of a cult group," said Gilbert.

"What! Cult group, you said?" Andy asked curiously.

"Yes, the logo has a leopard, an eagle and two swords inscribed in it," said Andy.

"You mean these murders could be linked to a much bigger conspiracy?" asked Agent Barry.

"Sort of, get Donald. He needs to hear of this," said Andy.

Agent Barry tapped the glass screen from which they were observing the interrogation, and signalled. "Hey Donald, we've got something for you," said Agent Barry.

Agent Donald immediately left Talbot and joined Barry and Andy. "Did something come up?" asked Agent Donald.

"The tattoo in Talbot's arm signifies his involvement in a cult," said Agent Barry. Surprised at the new revelations concerning

Talbot, Agent Donald became inquisitive as to the nature of the cult and the level of Talbot's involvement in the organisation.

"What cult, did you get the name of the cult?" asked Agent Donald.

"I could only get the logo online, but couldn't get the name of the cult," said Gilbert.

"Put the logo up on the screen let me have a look at it," said Agent Donald.

Gilbert quickly put the logo on screen for analysis. "Here is it, I think this could be beyond a disgruntled murderer," said Gilbert.

"Oh my God! Hmm, I know this logo, the Scroll," said Agent Donald.

"The Scroll, what do you mean by that?" asked Andy.

Agent Donald chuckled.

"The Scroll has been activated," he said.

"What do you mean by that, was the scroll in a sleep mode before now?" asked Andy.

"The scroll is an ancient cult group; it originated during the Roman Empire and spread across Europe," said Agent Donald.

Agent Barry was rattled that a cult of this nature has been in existence and active all this while and the FBI have no knowledge of it.

"You mean this cult has been in existence this long and we knew nothing of it?" asked Agent Barry.

"No, the cult ceased to exist two centuries ago, a Roman Prince founded it to eliminate his political enemies, he did this with the help of a priest," said Agent Donald. Andy Grey wants to know what the motivation of the resurrected Scroll is, who activated it, and what its mission is this time.

"What's the motivation of this prince?" asked Andy.

"His motivation is nothing but silencing his rivals and exerting his authority," replied Agent Donald.

"How did the prince carry out his political agenda?" asked agent Barry.

"The prince accused these men of being gay, and women of sorcery, even when some of these allegations aren't true, then the dogs are sent in for the kill," said Agent Donald.

"The dogs you said, who are they?" asked Andy.

"The dogs are the hands of the cult, those that carry out the decision of the priest, which in most cases, is the death sentence," said Agent Donald.

"And you think a priest is most likely a part of these killings, I mean these recent killings?" asked Andy.

"I don't know, but most certainly, yes," said Agent Donald.

"If this cult affair is associated with the scroll, then this is a bigger problem," Agent Barry retorted.

Agent Donald muttered saying this threat is big, and this cult could be behind many other deaths, and said he's going in there to see how Talbot corroborates this evidence.

"Ok, rattle his cage, and let's see how Talbot reacts to this new discovery," said Andy.

Agent Donald returns to the interrogation room, and tried to rile Talbot over his occult involvement.

"That tattoo in your arm, what's it about?" he asked.

"It's just a tattoo, nothing more," said Talbot.

"You belong to the scroll, meaning you work alongside a priest, killing those who are rivals to your client," said Agent Donald.

"If that's what it means, then I did it out of ignorance, I saw the tattoo in a magazine and liked it, nothing more," said Talbot.

Agent Donald asked Talbot if he's insisting, he isn't in a cult when they go about killing gay men in line with the activities of the ancient scroll.

"We'd to do this to return the society to the right path," said Talbot.

"The other time you said why don't you let 'us' do our job, and now you used 'we,' what do you mean, we?" asked Agent Donald.

"Sorry, I mean I'd to do this," Talbot said, as he tried to retract his statement.

"You don't have to cover for others; don't take the fall alone, we need to know other members of this cult," said Agent Donald as he presses Talbot.

Talbot realised he has slipped in his utterances, and as he tried to retract his comments, he replied in an emphatic tone. "I acted alone, I'm on my own," said Talbot.

"The lethal injection is waiting for you I suppose, for a person who committed triple murder," said Agent Donald as he tried trip Talbot into opening up.

"Oh, you've convicted me already, even without coming before a jury, and you don't have to put all of it on me," said Talbot.

"I'm ready to help you get a lesser sentence, if you tell me all you know, but if I leave, my deal leaves with me," said Agent Donald. It has now dawned on Talbot that his activities are now in the open, and the idea of a deal for a lesser sentence seems to be enticing for a man going down for triple murder.

"I'll talk, only if I won't get a sentence for these crimes," said Talbot.

"Sorry, you can't walk free after committing triple murder, but I can help you secure a lesser sentence," said agent Donald. Agent Donald stood up and was about to leave, but Talbot quickly interjected.

"Wait, wait, one day I went for devotion, but as I stood to leave after my devotion, the Priest called me back and told me God has a need of me," said Talbot.

"Priest, as in Catholic Priest or what?" asked Agent Donald.

"No, a Catholic Priest isn't involved this time, we work with a Hermetic priest," said Talbot. The detectives are glad to hear this confession from Talbot as his story corroborates the activities of ancient Scroll.

"Ooh, you practice Hermetism! That's some form of cult you know?" said Agent Donald.

"At least we're serving a higher cause, and your thought about it being a cult is a wrong opinion," said Talbot.

"I know you practice magic and spiritism, but how did you come to be in his service?" asked Agent Donald.

"Of course, I was glad actually. I needed an opportunity to let off some steam for God and I got it," said Talbot. The detective watched in shock as Talbot said he's letting off some steam in service for God, as they considered it doubly foolish for Talbot to expect complements for his atrocities. As far as Talbot is concerned it is utterly fantastic and wonderful to be a part of something, with the potential to become part of the thriving new world order.

"What sort of service did the priest ask of you?" asked Agent Donald.

"At first, I thought it was a religious thing, but one day the priest introduced me to other members of the Scroll, and you're right about the Scroll," said Talbot.

"And you've no idea of what the group does?" asked Agent Donald.

"Of course, yes, he told me of the history of the Scroll, how they help clean the society of filth, and how he intends to achieve that in our present-day society," said Talbot.

"Meaning, he gave you the names of your targets?" asked Agent Donald.

"Yes, he told us God hates homosexuality, and we're the hands of God, and our duty is to execute God's judgement here on earth," said Talbot.

The priest could see through the dark desires of Talbot's heart and was able to discern that if this guy would be a killer, he'll be a killer lacking in sympathy. The Priest was damn right, Talbot's darkest desires meets the exact qualification needed to be enlisted in this cult.

"Now let's talk about these victims. Did you catch them in the act, and how come you know they're gay?" asked Agent Donald.

"At least you know the escort is gay, Morris Doyle is also gay but to eliminate Ben Cousins whom we suspect to be gay, we had to incriminate him," said Talbot.

"Oh, you aren't certain about Ben Cousins, but you're certain about the others," Agent Donald queried.

"Yes, the priest told us Ben Cousins and Morris Doyle are both gay, but my findings on Ben Cousins suggested otherwise, so we'd to bring Lana Pen in," said Talbot.

"Meaning, the targets are Ben Cousins and Morris Doyle," Asked Agent.

"Yes, everyone knows Morris Doyle to be gay but for Ben Cousins, we'd to get an escort by his side to make Ben Cousins look gay," said Talbot.

"When your findings concerning Ben Cousins proved otherwise, why then did you go ahead to portray him as being gay?" Agent Donald queried further.

Talbot responded saying he tried to speak up but the priest insisted Ben Cousins is gay, and other members of the group believed him, and suggested they use a male escort to indict him as being gay.

"Who's this priest, and what's his name?" asked Agent Donald.

"Reverend McQueen, the priest of the Onyx Cathedral," said Talbot.

"You mean that cathedral is for Hermetism?" asked Agent Donald.

While the interrogation continues, Gilbert Rivers rushed to Andy Grey for the second time.

"We've got new evidence, Donald needs to see this," he said.

Andy Grey tapped the glass screen from where he's observing the interrogation and signalled Agent Donald. "We've got something new," said Andy.

Agent Donald turns to Talbot immediately. "I'll be back," he said. He leaves the interrogation room to see what the new information was. The moment he stood up to leave Talbot insisted he has told him everything he knows, and asked why he isn't letting him off the hook, and his patience is beginning to grow thin with the length of the interrogation.

"Put your findings on the screen, Gilbert," said Agent Donald.

Gilbert Rivers displayed the findings on the screen. "Ok, Morris Doyle and Ben Cousins have something in common, they're both lead scientists in GMO," said Gilbert.

"You mean genetically modified food?" asked Andy.

"Yes, of course, Ben Cousins is the lead scientist in Bright Grains INC, while Morris Doyle is the lead scientist in New World Grains INC.," said Gilberts.

This latest revelation means there's more water passing under the bridge, Agent Murphy exclaimed and said Donald was right all along, that there must be something these victims have in common that makes them a target.

"Meaning, they were killed for who they are, scientists. That gay thing is just a cover up, a front and a lie," said Agent Donald.

With this new revelation, Agent Barry wants to know what these guys knew that's making them a target. Agent Donald interjected saying this is beyond what they knew, if these two victims are from the same organisation, then they can worry about what they know, but these killings cuts across organisations.

Agent Barry then asked "What's it about these companies and these scientists that made them targets?"

Agent Donald nods his head, as things begin to make more sense to him. "Oh, this now makes some sense," said Agent Donald.

"What do you mean?" Andy asked curiously, as pattern begins to emerge.

Agent Donald quickly pointed out that this is about eliminating competition, he then explained further that Bright Grains INC and New World Grains INC are leading the development of drought resistant grain, to cushion the effect of famine in North Africa.

"Ok, but what has that got to do with these deaths?" asked Andy.

"Killing these lead scientists will definitely stall the possibility of a breakthrough in producing drought resistant products," replied Agent Donald.

"Meaning, a GMO firm must have contracted the priest to take these scientists out, using his cult?" Andy queried further.

Agent Donald nodded in affirmation and said eliminating every possible competition will leave the contractor alone to have monopoly of the North African market. With these new revelations the faceless contractors lurking in the dark are about to be uncovered and brought to the open. This investigation has now moved away from dogs of this cult to the contractors at the top of the food chain.

"We need to find the priest and also uncover this contractor," said Andy.

"Gilbert, please give me a list of GMO firms involved in research to develop drought resistant grain to combat food shortage in North Africa," said Andy.

"You would get that in a moment," said Gilbert.

"Barry, go with Donald, I want that priest brought here for questioning," Andy ordered.

As Agent Donald and Agent Barry prepare to leave the office Gilbert came up with new information relevant to this investigation. "Wait, wait I found something," said Gilbert.

"Ok, go ahead," said Andy.

"There are six GMO firms in the United States, but only three of these firms are involved in the development of drought resistant grains to combat drought in North Africa," said Gilbert.

"Please give us the list of these companies leading the development of drought resistant grains," said Agent Donald.

"We've Bright Grains INC, New World Grains INC, and Durister INC," said Agent Donald.

"Meaning, Durister must be the contractor behind these killings," said Agent Barry.

"Durister INC must have used the Scroll to eliminate competition," said Agent Donald.

Agent Murphy interjected and said this implies that the contractor now has monopoly of the market, now that the lead scientists of rival companies have been eliminated. He then proceeded to say they now know this isn't about killing gay men or sorcerers, killing people based on their sexuality was used as a front to achieve other objectives, of which the dogs themselves have no knowledge.

"Woefully, these young men were used by the priest to achieve other objectives they knew nothing about," said Agent Barry.

"Bring this priest in for questioning, before another murder is committed," said Andy.

Moments later, Agent Donald and Agent Barry arrived at the Onyx Cathedral and proceeded to Rev. McQueen's office. Funnily, the priest was right behind Agent Donald and Barry as they walked into his office. "Hey, can I help you?" the priest asked curiously.

The two detectives stopped to allow the priest take the lead, and followed him into his office, but just as the priest sat down, Agent Donald began his story.

"I've a son, each time he goes to church, he tells me he's going to see God. Meaning, he sees God through the priest and he believes the priest even more than me his dad. That makes me place the priest on a high pedestal and see him as the epitome of righteousness; but you aren't the kind of priest my son is talking about, are you? Your priesthood is one of magic and spiritism, quite different from the kind of church Christ prescribed," asked Agent Donald.

Rev. McQueen looked at Agent Donald with some disdain, and said he'd no idea of what he is getting at with his stories, but then asked who they are. "This is agent Donald Whitley, and I'm Barry, we're FBI agents," said Agent Barry.

"Ok detectives, how can I be of help?" asked Rev. McQueen.

"You're under arrest for the murder of Ben Cousins, Morris Doyle, and Lana Pen," said Agent Donald.

"What! He chuckles, and stared straight at the detectives without batting an eyelid. "Have you forgotten I'm a priest, and how dare you accuse me of such heinous crimes?" asked Rev. McQueen.

"I guess we should be going, Mr Priest. You'll have the opportunity to defend yourself if you consider these accusations frivolous," said Agent Donald.

Agent Donald immediately pointed him to the cuffs and said the choice is his, that they could put him in handcuffs in the presence of his members or he can walk quietly to the car, and asked him "what's your pleasure?" The priest stood up, and began tidying his desk as he gets ready to follow the detectives to their office, yet continued to protest his innocence. The detectives came prepared, they handed the priest a search warrant and conducted a search of the priest's office.

"Give me a minute, I'll go with you since you've failed to realise this is a place of worship," said Rev. McQueen.

An hour later, Agent Donald joined Reverend McQueen in the interrogation room while other detectives observe the interrogation.

"Reverend, you've been implicated in a triple murder," said Agent Donald.

"I won't say a word without my lawyer, I'm invoking my right to counsel and for the record; do you know I'm a priest?" asked Rev. McQueen.

"Your lawyer won't help you, the evidence we found in your office is enough to nail you, and being a priest doesn't protect you from prosecution," said Agent Donald.

"What evidence did you find in my office that could possibly link me to a murder?" asked Rev. McQueen.

Since the priest continues to play 'catch me if can' with the detectives, Agent Donald felt it's best to shut the priest up with all the evidence gathered. Agent Donald then signalled Andy to bring Talbot in.

"Do you know this man, reverend?" asked Agent Donald.

"Why would this man know me? We've got nothing connecting us," the priest retorted.

"But he knows you, evidence of your relationship with him was found in his possession and even in your office," said Agent Donald.

The priest became furious with Talbot and held onto his claimed of not knowing him, but Talbot is the link between the priest and these murders, and this link can't be shirked.

"Do you know me, because I don't know you from Adam?" asked Rev. McQueen.

"I know you, reverend. You sanctioned our actions," said Talbot.

Rattled by Talbot's betrayal, Reverend McQueen charged at Talbot, asking him to keep quiet. It's now arguably obvious that this priest has been blighted by these sticky revelations.

"You idiot, I said I don't know you, and you keep insisting you know me," said Rev. McQueen.

"Reverend, you would have to comport yourself, charging at Talbot won't get you off the hook," said Agent Donald.

Ok, I'm sorry but this man isn't telling the truth about knowing me," the Priest insisted.

"We've conclusive evidence that you were hired to take out the lead scientists of Bright Grains INC and New World Grains INC," said Agent Donald.

"You mean I was hired to kill scientists, what sort of monster do you take me for?" asked Rev. McQueen.

"You were hired by Durister INC to kill the lead scientists of these two companies just to eliminate competition, to enable Durister INC gain monopoly of the North African market," said Agent Donald.

"If Talbot killed men in the street because of their sexuality, why don't you prosecute him for his crimes, and leave me alone?" asked Rev. McQueen. Agent Donald quickly used the priest's comments to tie him in a knot, and asked him how he knew Talbot killed men over the sexuality, because he hasn't mentioned that aspect of their findings to him, except he knew about the actions of Talbot and the basis for his committing these murders.

"You'll explain your part in these crimes to the judge during your trial," said Agent Donald.

"Wait, I have service to celebrate, and people are waiting for me for counselling, you can't keep me here!" the priest exclaimed.

"Reverend McQueen you've the right to an Attorney and I'm charging you with the murder of Ben Cousins, Morris Doyle and Lana Pen," said Agent Donald.

Moments later, Andy Grey asked Agent Donald, and Agent Barry to bring the contractor in, which is the chief executive of Durister INC to answer for these crimes. "Hmm, good, let's bring them in immediately," said Agent Donald.

Reverend McQueen was tried and sentenced to life imprisonment, Warner Talbot was sentenced to thirty-five years imprisonment, while other members of the cult involved in these deaths were sentenced to life imprisonment each, and the CEO of Durister INC was sentenced to fifty years imprisonment.

CHAPTER

EIGHT

The Ripper

Agents Donald, Agent Barry and Agent Murphy walked into a crime scene, and Agent Donald immediately walked towards the NYPD officer at the scene.

"Good morning, Lieutenant, I'm detective Donald Whitley," said Agent Donald. The NYPD officer who squatted as he inspected the crime scene stood up and stretched his hand forth for a hand shake. "Oh, good morning detective, Lieutenant Wolfe Marcus," he said.

"What happened here, this victim looked like he was butchered or something?" asked Agent Donald.

Agent Barry walked over to the body of the victim and uncovered the corpse. "What! His heart was ripped out; did that happen while he was still alive or dead?" Agent Barry queried.

"We're waiting for forensics to give us further details about the victim," said Lieutenant Wolfe.

Agent Donald took a critical look at the corpse, to understand the circumstances surrounding the murder.

"The killer is left handed and the victim didn't show signs of struggle before his death, even though he was tied up," said Agent Donald.

"From what we know there was a similar death like this last month," said Lieutenant Wolfe.

Agent Murphy stopped passing cars, and cars parked near the crime scene, asking the drivers if they witnessed the incident. this time Murphy seemed to be spending so much time with a lady in what seemed to be beyond the police work at hand until Agent Donald beckoned on him.

Agent Donald walked around, scanning the crime scene, then points at prints on the ground from a dog's foot. "Barry, see these prints, the killer had a dog with him as at the time of dumping this victim's body here," said Agent Donald.

"Yeah, a dog was with him," said Barry.

"These are crimes perpetrated by savages, and this is the height of wickedness," said agent Murphy.

Agent Donald then urged his colleagues to join him in search of anything that will help the case, a dog collar or anything. Moments after gathering as much information as they could, the detectives left the crime scene to allow the forensic team do their job.

"Lieutenant, we're leaving, let's wait for the forensic report but if anything comes up please give me a call," said Agent Donald.

A day later, the FBI detectives were profiling the killer in their office. "From what I can say, the Ripper has moved to New York," said Agent Donald.

"What do you mean the Ripper has moved to New York, is he some kind of Jack the ripper or what?" asked Andy.

"They call him the Ripper," said Agent Donald.

"Why does he go about killing people and ripping their hearts out of their body?" asked Agent Barry.

"He's a heart collector, and I believe he must have the training of a surgeon," said Agent Donald.

"What's his passion, and why does he do this?" asked Andy.

"His passion is money, he sells to the highest bidder and the human heart is his trophy," said Agent Donald.

"Who buys the heart and what do they do with it?" Andy queried further.

"He sells them to people needing a heart transplant?" said Agent Donald.

"Is that why you said the killer most likely will be a surgeon of some sort?" asked Andy.

"It's only a person with such experience that'll be able to surgically remove a heart in such a manner that it'll be good enough to be transplanted," said Agent Donald.

"Whichever way you want to do it; I want this savage off our streets," Andy ordered.

Agent Donald turned to Gilbert. "Give us a list and details of all heart patients in New York, awaiting a transplant now," said Agent Donald. Minutes later, Gilbert was able to come with a list of potential heart patients awaiting transplant. "Donald, I've been able to find about three hundred and two people in various hospitals," said Gilbert.

"Ok, let's narrow our search to those who desperately need it," said Agent Donald.

Andy finds Agent Donald's assertion to be quite hysterical and asked Agent Donald if he's having a laugh, for asking Gilbert to search for those who desperately needed a heart transplant, because he thinks that all these heart patients desperately need a transplant.

Agent Donald interjected and said that isn't what he's implying, he then said he meant those whose situation has deteriorated, those who want a transplant badly and are willing to go above and beyond to get it.

Minutes later, Gilbert was able to narrow the search. "Ok, from what I can see here, only about fifty-one of these people are in a desperate situation for a heart transplant," said Gilbert.

"I want the fifty-one patients visited in their various hospital beds, with that we'll know who received a heart transplant, because the heart removed last night must have been given to someone," said Andy.

Agent Donald and Agent Barry left the office immediately, to pay visit to every heart patient in the various hospitals and to confirm if any of these patients received a heart transplant, as well as identify who the donor was. They arrived Bon Angelo hospital which was their third point of call.

"Good morning, how may I help you?" asked the receptionist.

"We're FBI agents, and we're here to see one of your heart patients awaiting a transplant," said Agent Barry.

"Which of them?" she asked.

"Ok, now I remember you've about four patients in your hospital," said Agent Barry.

"We'll like to speak to all of the patients," said Agent Donald.

"You can only see three of them, one is in the intensive care unit, and he's being monitored," the receptionist replied.

"Why's he being monitored?" asked Agent Barry.

"He just came out of surgery late last night, after a heart transplant," she replied.

Agent Donald and Agent Barry signalled each other using eye contacts, like 'here you go'.

"The director of this hospital is a surgeon, isn't he?" asked Agent Donald.

"Of course, yes, he's a surgeon," said the receptionist.

"The director of this hospital is Chad Mitchell, I suppose?" Agent Donald queried further.

"Yes, he's, and what about it?" she asked.

Agent Donald requested a meeting with Chad Mitchell, and the hospital receptionist reluctantly puts a call to the director. "The FBI is here, they want to see you," she said.

"Ok, bring them in," said Chad.

"Ok follow me," she said. They followed the receptionist from behind as she led them into the director's office.

As they approached the doctor's office, they walked past an African American who was leafing through a medical journal and seemed to be waiting to see the doctor. Agent Barry couldn't keep his sarcasm to himself as he turned to this man. "Hello, are you here to donate your heart or something," asked agent Barry.

The man stopped reading and fixed his gaze at Agent Barry, thinking he's just having a laugh before asking him "Where does that question come from and who donates a heart and live?"

"I don't know what your intentions are but be careful with the doctor in there," replied agent Barry.

"Chad is my friend, and he's my professional colleague," replied the visitor, who proceeded to inform the detectives that he and Chad just arrived from a conference and they are returning to the conference soon. Barry cheekily replied to Chad's visitor and said that his response isn't enough justification to hang around this doctor.

"I suppose, you guys are cops, but don't let your mind play tricks on you, because being a detective doesn't give you the permission to go about rabbiting into people's personal space," the visitor retorted.

The receptionist who seemed already irked by these detectives' arrogance was about to climb the steps leading to her boss's office but stopped as these detectives question Chad's friend. Despite her fits of tantrum, she watched and waited for the detectives to do their thing. She then muttered and asked them if they're coming or what, and then urged them to stop acting as if they own the hospital. "Do you know Napoleon was almost assassinated on Christmas eve, but that doesn't necessarily mean he was assassinated," said the receptionist in a manner of chastising the detectives. The disposition of this receptionist looks like someone who would prefer to make her arch enemy her bridesmaid just to punish her. Despite her fits of tantrum, she watched and waited for the detectives to do their thing.

They both turned around and proceeded to the doctor's office, but Agent Donald then whispered and asked Barry to be careful about being too quick with his sarcasm of making unverified allegations and drawing premature conclusions.

They then walked into the director's office and took their seat before the receptionist excused herself and left.

"You're welcome, what can I do for you?" asked Chad.

"Which of your patients had a heart transplant last night?" asked Agent Donald.

"He's Murray Chaplain, and he's being monitored in the intensive unit," said Chad.

"Who donated the heart for the surgery?" asked Agent Donald.

"Sorry, we can't divulge such information, this is part of patient's confidentiality," said Chad.

"There's a murder investigation going on, and we'll need to know," said Agent Donald. Immediately the detectives stepped into Chad Mitchell's office their attention went straight to what hand he's using to write, and realised Mitchell is right-handed. Mitchell on the other hand, informed the detectives he will be returning to a conference in Manhattan and his friend is waiting for him to finish so they could leave. He seems to have forgotten that without satisfying these detectives his conference will definitely be kicked into the long grass.

"I'm sorry, detectives. I can't help you," Chad retorted.

"Then you'll have to come with us gently to avoid attracting attention, or we can do it by force," said Agent Barry.

Chad hesitated and said he's busy, and he doesn't think he will go with them for now until he finishes the work he has at hand. Agent Barry was quick to inform Chad that they can't wait for him, when he goes about ripping people's hearts out. He then suggested to Chad to stand up quietly and go with them if he doesn't want them to take him in by force.

Chad Mitchell stopped what he's doing and raised his hands up as a gesture of surrender, and decided to follow the detectives to their office, even as he continues to protest his arrest.

"Ok, ok, let's go, you guys will pay for this," said Chad.

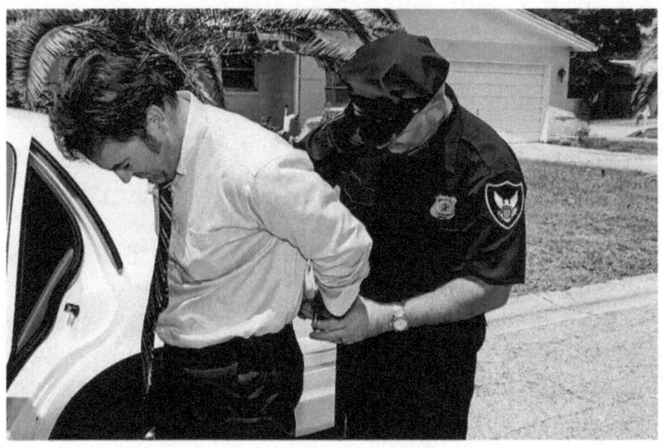

The detectives walked Chad to their car and allowed the NYPD officer put him in cuffs before leaving for the FBI office, and moments after his arrest Chad Mitchell was brought into the interrogation room for questioning.

"Why are you doing this? You know you're putting my patients at risk," Chad retorted.

"Because you've refused to give the answer to a simple question, we'll have to question you further," said Agent Donald.

"Donating an organ like the heart is a very emotional thing for the family of the donor, the recipient of the organ and his family, and even we the hospital. It isn't something for the press to dramatize on," Chad said, as his disposition changed.

Chad Evans considers the heart to be much more than a mere organ, and as far as he's concerned, the human heart is the seat of a person's conscience where decisions of life emanate and the heart determines who's good or bad.

"I understand what you said about the feelings of all the parties involved, but we must have this information to assist us in a murder investigation," said Agent Donald.

"I'm sorry I can't, I don't think I'll be able to help you with the information you want," Chad insists.

"Eugenics or heart surgery, whatever it is you do, you're possibly looking at a life sentence in prison," replied Agent Donald.

"Life sentence in prison over what offence? I think I need my lawyer at this point," said Chad.

"Do you know we can keep you here then go into your hospital, raid all the files and bring them here to get what we want, so the choice is yours," said Agent Donald.

Despite allowing him access to his lawyer, Chad is now in a bit of a pickle, because he's now torn between revealing the heart donor and maintaining his oath of keeping patient's confidentiality. More so, he's riled by the thought of detectives messing his office about and surfing through his patients' files, as they spent so much time attempting to impugn his integrity.

"You know what a misplaced document will mean to a patient's life?" said Chad.

"Then answer me, to prevent me from doing this the hard way," said Agent Donald.

"If you insist, the heart donor is Palmer Braga, who has been in intensive care in my hospital, if you noticed from your record, he died last night and his corpse is still available," said Chad.

"Are you sure about this, because someone's heart was ripped out yesterday for transplant?" asked Agent Donald.

"And you think I'll commit such a heinous crime? That's sickening, and I wouldn't do a thing like that!" Chad exclaimed.

"You think if we investigate further, we'll find out you're telling the truth?" asked Agent Donald.

"Yes, you can come with an independent agent to take a DNA sample from Palmer Braga and compare with the tissue sample from Murray Chaplin, and you'll find out I've told you all the truth," Chad insists.

Now that Chad Mitchell had decided to divulge the details of the heart donor to save his skin, Agent Donald stood up, excused himself from the interrogation and joined other agents observing the interrogation.

"What do you think?" asked Andy.

Even as they pursued the possibility that Mitchell is the man they are looking for, agent Donald remained sceptical following his cursory assessment of Chad Mitchell, because he's right-handed and the man they're looking for is left-handed. Yet, he didn't rule out the possibility that Mitchell used an accomplice who is lefthanded to knock his victim over before stepping in, to surgically remove his heart.

Agent Barry on the other hand continued with his ideology of the wild card as he insisted that anything is possible, and that when people get agitated, they knock things over and it doesn't matter what hand they use to do the knocking.

"My hunch tells me he isn't the ripper we're looking for," said Agent Donald.

"Let's call the Donor's family to confirm," said Agent Barry.

"The donor's family will be in an emotional state and I don't think it's a good idea," said Agent Donald.

The FBI conducted a medical examination to verify the credibility of Chad Mitchell's testimony, and confirmed he has been telling the truth all along, just that he was bound by patient's confidentiality.

Agent Donald then suggested they allow Chad to go, and if peradventure they need him, then they would go for him, but for now it's best to let him off the hook because there are patients under his care who may need his attention.

"Ok, let him go for now," said Andy. Agent Donald returned to the interrogation room.

"Chad Mitchell, we're sorry, you can go but if we need you, we'll have to come back for you," said Agent Donald.

But mere apology from these FBI detectives wasn't enough to calm Chad's frayed nerves, not just because they wasted his time but because he considered himself as someone who shouldn't be some sort of collateral damage in a failed investigation. He then muttered, saying, he saves life, and that he isn't some bogeyman who goes about snatching hearts and killing people, and he didn't just leave the interrogation without expressing his displeasure over his unfair treatment.

"What you just did, is robbing Peter to pay Paul, you just arrested me to prove to the world you're working, isn't it?" asked Chad.

"Why do people complain about robbing Peter to pay Paul? What's Peter doing putting himself in a position where he's always being robbed?" Agent Donald replied.

Moments after the surgeon left, the detectives decided to shift their focus away from the killer to the victim, and decided to profile the victim as opposed to profiling the killer.

"Details of the victim are beginning to emerge; we'll need a full profile of the victim," said Agent Donald.

"The victim is Calhan Boyd; he's a white male with brown eyes, and worked as an event organiser," said Agent Murphy.

"Where does he live?" asked Andy.

"He lived in the Brooklyn neighbourhood of New York City," replied Barry.

"What about his love life?" asked Andy.

"He had a girlfriend three years ago, but they broke up last year," said Agent Murphy.

Relationships these days are like gold dust, they don't last and every attempt to give a relationship a break meant someone like Luke Morgan will creep in to become an unlikely companion.

"Any recent acquaintances?" asked Andy.

"He recently made friend with a surgeon, they usually spend time drinking together and Calhan Boyd use to be a patient in the hospital where Luke Morgan works as a Surgeon," said Agent Murphy.

"Who's this surgeon?" asked Andy.

The detectives decided to profile Luke Morgan, but this requires piecing his history together.

"Luke Morgan is a surgeon, the owner of the Blessed Samaritan hospital, he stabbed his teacher with a pen when he was four years old, was a member of the frat brothers as a sophomore. Twice married twice divorced, two arrests for domestic violence, one drink and drive arrest and was dismissed in the past for violence in the work place," said Agent Murphy.

"Hmm, this guy is a bombshell," said Andy.

Agent Barry then suggested that this guy couldn't get a job because of his record of violence, so he decided to open his own hospital. Agent Donald interjected and said a pattern is beginning to emerge from this profile, insisting that Luke Morgan is most likely the man they're looking for.

"How certain are you? Analyse the pattern," replied Andy.

"Calhan Boyd was a patient in the hospital Luke Morgan owned, based on his record Calhan Boyd could be a perfect donor for a patient that needs a heart transplant. Luke Morgan decided to make friend with Calhan Boyd to be able to lure him for a time like this when he'll rip his heart out for his patient," said Agent Donald.

"Oh my God, robbing Peter to pay Paul, I suppose. Does he have a heart patient seeking a donor?" asked Andy.

"This guy had a long rap sheet, yet managed to avoid long prison sentences. Yes, he has two patients from the records before me," said Gilbert.

"Go and bring him in now for questioning. Remember, this man has long rap sheet, and has been used to the cops so he'll want to evade arrest," said Andy.

FBI agents paid the director of the Blessed Samaritan Hospital a visit, and the receptionist showed them the way to the medical director's office but they interestingly met him attending to one of his staff. After introducing themselves, they followed him to his office to have words with him, and funnily he asked them who they are again, the moment they entered his office.

"Luke Morgan, we're from the FBI," said Agent Barry.

In his usual display of invincibility, Luke Morgan focused on his computer, acting as if the detectives aren't there. He fixed his gaze on his work, ignoring the detectives. "What can we do for you?" he asked passively.

"We want to speak to your heart patients," said Agent Donald.

"I'm sorry, detectives, that wouldn't be possible, they're in intensive care," he replied passively.

"Being in intensive care doesn't stop us from seeing the patients," said Agent Donald.

"The heart transplant you did yesterday, where did you get the donor?" asked Agent Barry.

"Oh! He chuckles. "Is that why you're here?" asked Luke.

"The family of the donor will not allow that," said Luke.

Agent Donald looked on as Luke Morgan continued being evasive and playing catch me if you can, but he must be having a laugh if he's expecting a tummy rub from these detectives after inflicting savagery on an innocent man. After all, he's used to having running in with the Cops. Agent Donald realised it's better to move Luke Morgan out of the comfort of his office, to help him realise the seriousness of the situation.

"Luke Morgan, you have to come with us for questioning," said Agent Donald.

"I can't, I've patients in intensive unit that are being attended to. What if there's an emergency and I'm needed?" asked Luke.

"You're under arrest for the murder of Calhan Boyd, whatever you say or do will be used against you in the court of law," said Agent Donald.

"You want it bumpy, or we stroll to the car, what's your pleasure?" asked Agent Barry.

Immediately after Luke's arrest, the FBI sent in their medical expert to test tissues samples collected from the heart transplant patient and compare with Calhan Boyd's DNA.

Immediately after his arrest, Luke Morgan was left in the interrogation room, while the detectives put their facts concerning their investigation together.

Agent Donald urged Gilbert to run further searches on Luke Morgan because his hunch tells him that this guy must be doing more than harvesting organs by himself, as he tried to understand what his usual trips to the Middle East were all about. Agent Donald thinks there's more to this guy because this person has a fascination with money and that appeal pushes him into being an outlaw, crime fascinates him, and he sort of fetishizes on it. This guy plays around with human tissue, and the human life is very cheap for some of these guys, and taking one means nothing to them.

Gilbert ran further searches and realised that most kidney transplants happen in Blessed Samaritan hospital immediately after Luke Morgan returns from his so-called trip to the Middle East made in the guise of charity work. This guy has made several trips to Yamen, Afghanistan, and a lot of war-torn Middle East countries where the business of organ sale is on the increase. Agent Barry became quite upset, as he seems to have taken this guys' sin more personal, considering how Luke buys these organs for peanuts and makes a fortune out of them, by selling to the highest bidder in the United Sates. With these new revelations concerning this suspect, Andy is eager to get a conviction, as he asked Agent Donald to get in there and confront Luke with the evidence against him.

Four hours after Luke Morgan was brought into the Interrogation room, Agent Donald returned and sat opposite him.

"Do you know Calhan Boyd?"

"Who's Calhan Boyd? I don't know him," said Luke.

"You mean you don't know your friend that works as an event organiser?" asked Agent Donald.

"I don't have any such friend, I'm a surgeon for God's sake," Luke replied.

"This friend of yours used to be a patient in your hospital," said Agent Donald.

"I repeat, I don't know what you're talking about," Luke insists.

Luke continues to vehemently deny knowing Calhan Boyd, not to talk of killing him. But Agent Donald would've to put his ducks in a row, as he now attempts to box Luke in a corner with his trove of evidence.

"We know all about your human organ trafficking business from war-torn countries in the Middle East," said Agent Donald.

He quipped then adjusted himself before muttering about Donald's comments and said he has no idea about what he's getting at. But to push him fast and hard, agent Donald had to give him a print out of the record of kidney transplants that happened in his hospital. "Take a look at this," he handed him a copy of the record "each time you return from your so-called charity work in the Middle East a lot of Kidney transplants happen in your hospital," said Agent Donald.

"Where does this startling conclusion come from?" Asked Luke.

Agent Donald then said this can't be a coincidence, except Luke exists in a different planet were everything happens only by coincidence. He then pointed out to him that each time he returns from his so-called charity work, as many as ten kidney transplants happen in his hospital without any record of who donated those kidneys.

But to pin on him the most obvious crime, Agent Donald had to put his focus on the case at hand, at least if he's charged with the murder of Calhan Boyd then the FBI can have time to dig into his organ trafficking business and then charge him for other crimes committed.

"Let me refresh your memory." Agent Donald showed him CCTV footage of both of them drinking. That's Calhan Boyd, do you remember him now?" said Agent Donald.

"I only met him once and we drank beer together, and that's all," said Luke.

"Should I refresh your memory, there is more footage of the two of you together on different occasions," said Agent Donald. "Ok, he's my friend, what about him?" Luke asked.

The detectives went as far as getting Luke's dog as part of this investigation, they compared the forensic image of a dog foot print recovered from the crime scene, with the feet of Luke's dog, and confirmed it was Luke's dog that was on the scene.

While the interrogation persists, Andy Grey signalled Agent Donald to show him the test results that just came in, and after taking a look at the test results, Agent Donald returned to the interrogation room.

"Luke Morgan, tests results are out so I think there's nothing you can deny anymore," said agent Donald.

"What results are you talking about?" asked Luke.

"Our specialist just performed tests which confirm that Nicky Houston is the recipient of Calhan Boyd's organ that was ripped out of him three nights ago," said Agent Donald.

Luke Morgan flew into fits of rage after learning of the FBI tests on his patient. "You mean you arrested me and started tampering with a patient that just left surgery after a difficult heart transplant?" said Luke.

Agent Donald pointed out that forensic results also confirmed it was Luke's dog that was on the crime scene, where Calhan Boyd's body was found. More so, he also insisted that test on the recipient of the heart transplant is necessary, so they don't go beating about the bush.

"So, what are you saying, are you accusing me of murder?" asked Luke.

"I'm saying, you realised Calhan Boyd would be a perfect donor for your patient, which made you to make friends with him just to rip his heart out for your selfish desire," said Agent Donald.

"How will I know he's a perfect donor, and make him a friend, is it that easy to know who a perfect donor is?" Luke queried.

"Of course, yes, Calhan Boyd was a patient in your hospital and you've all his medical records so it's easy for you," said Agent Donald. Luke's disposition softens as the trove of evidence against him was laid bare before him, it's now obvious that the detective has Luke's feet to the fire, as he maintained the pressure.

At this point Luke couldn't look Donald straight in the face.

"But his heart wasn't wasted, it was given to a younger person who finds it more useful," said Luke.

"So, you consider your action a generous act, do you?" said Agent Donald.

"Yes of course, giving a younger person an opportunity in life is a generous act," he said.

"So, you're the proverbial mouse that bites its victim and fans him at the same time," said Agent Donald.

"I think I'm much better than the mouse in your story," replied Luke.

"It's unfortunate that the fire service is now the arsonist. Luke Morgan you'll need an attorney, I'm charging you with the murder of Calhan Boyd," said Agent Donald.

Luke Morgan was tried and sentenced to one hundred- and six-ty-years imprisonment for the two murders connected to him.

Moments after the successful prosecution of Luke Morgan, Andy Grey gets commendation from the head of criminal division of main justice, as he leaves the court after the sentencing of Luke Morgan.

"Hello Andy, how're you?" asked Sarah.

"I'm fine Sarah, your tone sounds encouraging today," said Andy.

"Of course, yes, after watching the sentencing of Luck Morgan, my tone should sound encouraging because you're doing a good job. Lots of criminals have been taken off our streets," she said.

"Thank you, it's good to hear you're happy with my unit. Though, I'll attribute some of this breakthrough to Donald Whitley for bringing in new energy and dynamism into my unit," said Andy.

"I'm already aware of that, but as the head of the unit the com-mendation will pass through you to them," said Sarah.

"Thank you, Sarah," Andy replied.

"I want you to know that the American public is aware of your good work, keep it up," Sarah said with a smile.

"I'll pass the commendation to the team, thank you, Sarah," Andy replied.

Moments after returning to the office, Andy Grey brought out two bottles of Champaign and walks to the central office.

"Sarah just called me to show her appreciation for the exceptional performance of this unit. I want to equally thank you all for the successful prosecution of Luke Morgan. I must confess, I was happy with myself as I watch the Judge pronounce Luke's sentence earlier today," said Andy.

CHAPTER

NINE

The Artefacts

Isaac Keanu was in a bar with his friend, Ian, drinking and enjoying their happy hour. Isaac thought Ian was blabbing gibberish when he asked Isaac if he likes his present job.

"Erm.., where does this question come from?" asked Ian.

Ian wasn't illusory, it's just that this line of conversation seems overly crooked, even as Isaac insisted it's just a question and nothing more, and reminded Ian that they're friends.

He then insisted that if Ian considers him a friend, then a yes or no will be okay.

Ian George was lost as to what Isaac was driving at, and in an awkward reminder, he quickly reminded Isaac he's a guard at the embassy while himself is a security personnel in a retail outlet, and asked how come he's asking if they both like the job they do. But Isaac wasn't illusory in his bid to end his dystopian lifestyle, but he has to do much more than make passive remarks.

"Following your confirmation of the fact that we both do not like the job we do, I've a proposal which might interest you," said Isaac.

Ian George became critical of Isaac's proposal as he listened with keen interest, and asking him what sort of proposal he's talking about.

"Though, this proposal is capable of changing our fortune if you care to give it a thought," said Isaac.

"You've said nothing, so what proposal am I expected to think about?" Ian queried.

"Ok, now that you've shown interest, there's this artefact that the government of Greece is sending to Spain as a gift to the royal family, but it was erroneously sent to New York last week," Isaac said.

"Yeah, what about it?" asked Ian.

"From my findings, there's a buyer who will be willing to pay a fortune for it, half a million dollars to be precise, and I want us to steal it," said Isaac. Ian was rattled by the nature of the assignment before him, and this isn't just any heist, but one with great consequence if things go south. He's more concerned that Isaac is out to make them loose the little peace currently at their disposal.

"Are you out of your mind! What gives you the courage to think you can steal such a prized possession, from such a well secured embassy?" asked Ian.

"This artefact will be moved to Spain by next week, and then we lose our chance of turning our fortunes around," said Isaac.

"Why're you bringing this proposal to me, even when you know I don't have the capability of stealing this Artefact?" Ian queried.

"I want you to put together a team that'll execute this heist," said Isaac.

"Ok, but I'm not promising you anything, though I'll get back to you," said Ian.

Time is of the essence because this operation is time bound; hence the artefact will make its way to its original destination, and the chances of Isaac turning his fortunes around will be lost.

"Whatever you do should be within four days," said Isaac.

The ball is now in Ian George's court, and all he now thinks about is how to successfully execute this heist. By the evening of same day, Ian's colleague, Aeron, was late to work.

"Aeron, you're just coming to work?" asked Ian.

"Yeah, sorry about that, though I called the supervisor to inform him I'll be fifteen minutes late to work," said Aeron.

"Have you conducted the necessary routine checks, to make sure the doors are locked and electrical appliances switched off?" asked Aeron. Ian is now a man on a mission, his heart is set on the heist and putting together a team that will do the job is the only thing on his mind.

"Yes, I've done that, but that Damien, that guy who usually comes here to steal, where was his information documented?" asked Ian.

"You mean the guy that was barred from entering this retail store, after being caught for the third time for stealing?" asked Aeron.

"Yeah," said Ian.

"His information was documented in the usual log book, for such a crime, what's up about him?" Aeron queried.

"Nothing, it's like I sighted someone like him on my way to work," said Ian.

That night Ian copied Damian's house address from the log book, at least this known thief might be handy in times like this.

The next morning, Ian George traced Damian to his house at the end of his shift, and met Damian mowing the lawn of their front garden. Funnily, Damian wasn't quite a hospitable host to one of the guys that caught him and got him barred from the retail store.

"Hi Damian, my name is Ian," he said.

"You, what are you doing in my house?" Damian asked.

Ian wasn't surprised at Damian's reaction because he shouldn't expect a hug and a pack of chocolates from the man he embarrassed for stealing. Domain threw his tools to the ground and became irate as he charged at Ian who seems to use his smile to calm Damian's nerves.

"Aren't you offering me a seat?" Ian asked with a smile.

"What are you doing in my house and how did you know where I live? I've been barred from entering your store, what then do you want from me?" asked Damian, without any smiles in his face.

"Damian, I've come to you as a friend," Ian assured him.

But Damian isn't having it, as he turned around and screamed on top of his lungs. "Mum, this guy from the retail store traced me to my house, and I'm asking him to leave quietly but he's refusing to leave," Damian retorted.

Damian's Mum walked out to the door, to see what the problem was. "You just woke me up from my sleep, what guy are you talking about?" she asked.

"This guy is from the retail store where I was barred, but what's he doing in my house?" said Damian.

No one wants to be punched in the face on a cold Saturday morning, but Ian is itching closer to being punched in the face, particularly when his irate host considers him a trespasser.

"Ask him why he's here, and stop shouting," she replied. She then turned to Ian. "My son will not come anywhere near your store, I want you to stop bothering him," she said.

"I just want some information from him and there won't be any trouble," said Ian.

"Since he said, all he wants is some information then let me handle him," Damian replied.

"I hope there won't be problem?" she asked Ian and went back in, leaving Damian and Ian to sort themselves out.

Ian insisted he isn't a man with a warped mind and assured Damian he isn't here to spin a tale. "Damian, you know it wasn't me that arrested you when you stole from the store; it was my colleague, Aeron, who did," said Ian.

"But you were there, and you supported him," Damian insists.

"No, I didn't. I was on your side, and it's just that you didn't see it," said Damian.

"That's now in the past, but why're you here?" asked Damian.

"There's an artefact in one of the embassies, we want to move it out but we needed help with someone who can do the job," said Ian. Damian was riled by Ian's request, this isn't just any request, it's a request from the saint who played an active part to forbid him from the store where he was caught stealing.

"Now I know your visit is a sneaky one, and you're here to set me up, aren't you?" said Damian.

"No, I'm not here to set you up, I'm a part of the deal, but I'll need your help with a good hand that'll do the job," said Ian.

"If what you need is a good hand for the job, then why come to me and not Jimmy Thompson?" asked Damian.

Ian interjected and urged Damian to stop being cheeky, saying everyone knows Jimmy Thompson doesn't exist, and that the name Jimmy Thompson is just used to qualify anyone who's a good thief.

"Jimmy Thompson exists, and it's only a few of us that know about it," said Damian.

"Then what are we waiting for? And if you know Jimmy is real why don't we get him on board?" asked Ian.

Now that Ian is consumed by this heist, there's no going back, because he's now willing to lift every carpet, and possibly move the moon and the sun, just to assemble the best team for his assignment.

"Meet me by 7.pm tonight; I'll hook you up with Jimmy," said Damian.

"I'll be at work by then, because I'm on night shift," said Ian.

"Ok meet me by 3.pm, I'll reach Jimmy before then," said Damian.

"Erm.., that'll be fine. I'll have to go straight to work after our meeting with Jimmy," said Ian.

Damian entered the house the moment Ian left his place, and his mum didn't hesitate to inquire of his conversation with Ian.

"Has he gone, and what does he want?" she asked.

"The guy is a good guy; I thought he was one of the bad guys," said Damian.

"What information does he want from you?" she queried further.

"He came to tell me the store was reviewing the ban," said Damian.

As Damian attempts to walk back to the garden, his mum sensed he didn't tell her the whole truth and reiterated her concern as she reminded her son that "the other time, you told me Terry was a good guy, you ended up in handcuffs minutes later," she said.

Jimmy Thompson is the best Thief in the city of New York, who made stealing a career, and have successfully avoided being caught because of his extra sense, call it the sixth sense. Most Americans thought he's a myth, and doesn't really exist but he does, and later that morning Damian contacted Jimmy Thompson.

"Hello Jimmy," said Damian.

"Damian, where are you? I suppose you aren't in the midst of people," asked Jimmy.

"I'm in the mist of all my friends, there are about ten of them here with me," Damian replied.

"Damian, I told you never to call me whenever you've someone with you," Jimmy retorted.

"Of course, I'm alone Jimmy, what do you take me for, a snitch or what? You know I'll never do that to you," said Damian.

"Good to hear that, what's up, Damian?" asked Jimmy.

Damian immediately arranged to catch up with Jimmy which he did an hour later, because Jimmy had earlier cautioned him about holding sensitive conversation on the phone, which is part of his self-censoring approach to remain evasive.

"There's an artefact in one of the embassies that requires being moved out, I was approached but I realised the perfect man for the job is you," said Damian.

"Who's the guy in question, is he genuine?" Jimmy queried.

"He's genuine as much as I can tell, but you'll decide that when you see him later today," said Damian.

"What's the meeting spot and time?" asked Jimmy.

"Its 3.pm, at the usual spot close to where I live," said Damian.

It's 3pm, and Ian George was already at the meeting spot waiting to meet with Jimmy Thompson, unbeknownst to him the man sat by his side was Jimmy, and after personal assessment of Ian George, Jimmy revealed himself to Ian.

"Ian, that guy by your side is Jimmy Thompson," said Damian.

"Hello Ian, sorry for making things a bit awkward for you," said Jimmy.

"Oh, it's you, nice to finally meet you, today must be my lucky day," said Ian.

Jimmy is a man of few words, who likes going straight to the point, and the fact surrounding his invincibility sometimes makes him a drifter of some sort. He then interjected and asked Ian about the embassy and where the artefact in question was located.

"It's in the Greek embassy in New York, and we've an inside man who will give you the low down of everything you need to know.

"When do you expect this operation to take place?" asked Jimmy.

"It must happen within the next four days," said Ian.

"Why the rush? Do you know if I've other things planned out within the week?" asked Jimmy.

"The artefact came in two days ago, it was sent from Greece to Spain, but was erroneously sent to New York and will be redirected to Spain by next week," said Ian.

"Ok, I'll like to meet with your inside man, to get a better picture of the embassy security," said Jimmy.

While the conversation continues, Isaac Keanu walked in, apologising for coming late to the party, where Jimmy is expected to be briefed but Ian doesn't like it when Isaac creates a bad first impression.

"Isaac, you're late, what have you been doing?" asked Ian.

Isaac apologised saying he has an appointment with his wife, and it's something he finds quite of interest.

"What a silly guy! You kept us waiting for about an hour over an appointment with your wife? You're making a bad first impression on our new friends here," said Ian.

"I'm sorry guys, just that I've looked forward to the favour from my wife and I didn't want this opportunity to pass me bye," said Isaac.

"Ian, your friend is funny, I like him," said Jimmy.

"Ok, that's by the way, Isaac, meet Damian, and his friend Jimmy Thompson," said Ian.

"You must be joking, this can't be Jimmy Thompson?" said Isaac.

"Isaac, lower your voice, don't attract attention to me," said Jimmy.

"Isaac, you know I can't be telling you lies, that's Jimmy, and at least I've assembled a perfect team for the job," said Ian.

Jimmy then interjected and said there's no need furthering this hysteria, he then asked Isaac to tell him all he needed to know about this job. They all got into the business of the day, and Isaac began to brief Jimmy who's keener with the nitty-gritty of the heist, as opposed to flattery over the myth surrounding his personality.

"The value of the artefact is about half a million dollars and that's if we're selling at a giveaway price," said Isaac.

"How and where is the artefact secured?" asked Jimmy.

"The artefact is kept in a six-foot tall giant safe. Will you be able to move it out?" asked Isaac.

"Of course, yes, you work there, don't you?" said Jimmy.

Funnily, Isaac has set the ball rolling, yet he's worried about how things might go down because he feared his hands could get badly burnt if this heist goes south.

"Yes, but I want the operation to be such that no one will suspect me," said Isaac.

Jimmy scared the hell out of Isaac when he hinted him that the heist will take place during the day when even the ambassador will be in the office, and not at night, and daring acts like this one is more like what Isaac see in movies not to imagine being a part of it.

Carrying out a heist to steal a prized item from the ambassador's office during working hours, even while he's in his office is quite brazen and something that terrified Isaac Keanu to make him begin questioning why he initiated this heist in the first place. He just couldn't get his head around how this will go down, without raising alarm that will make NYPD officers to come blazing.

"Day time, wouldn't that be too brazen?" asked Isaac.

"From the rumours I've heard about you, I heard you're never armed, and I hope there won't be any casualty since it's going to be a day time operation?" asked Isaac.

"There wouldn't be casualties because I hate every form of violence. I'll need the location of the fire alarms, are there security cameras within and outside the building?" asked Jimmy.

These guys are born thieves capable of stealing your eyes out of their sockets if you aren't looking, and while Isaac feared that this assignment might not be plain sailing, Jimmy sees nothing but a hitch-free operation.

"Of course, yes, and I'll give you a sketch of the camera locations and the position of the fire alarm," said Isaac.

"Ok, I'll also need a uniform worn by the security personnel," said Jimmy.

"You'll have it," said Isaac.

"Give me all I need by tomorrow and by Monday I'll be on it," said Jimmy. Worried that the focus is now on Jimmy Thompson and his voice is hardly heard, Damian needs some assurance that he's still a part of the deal. Interestingly, Jimmy's rules of engagement don't involve betrayal of the middle man.

"Jimmy, I hope you haven't kept me out of this deal?" asked Damian.

"You know I wouldn't do that, you initiated the whole deal, so your cut is assured," said Jimmy.

The next day, Jimmy Thompson gets the final briefing from Isaac Keanu, as he handed Jimmy a schematic of the embassy building as well as security routines within the embassy.

Jimmy gave a thorough look at the sketch presented to him, and gave a nod to the detailed nature of the sketch. "Ok, I've seen what I wanted, this diagram tells it all," said Jimmy.

"How long will it take you to execute this?" asked Isaac.

Jimmy doesn't just get at things, his sixth sense plays a key role on how he approaches every single heist. He's never in haste, and no operation is a must, particularly where his sixth sense senses trouble.

"I don't know, it depends on circumstance on the ground and the position of the guards," said Jimmy.

"I'll be on duty, but I'll be downstairs, how will you handle the CCTV camera, because I don't want to be implicated when things go wrong?" scared Isaac asked.

"I know how to prevent the camera from getting a good view of my face; I'll also wear a bigger shoe size that'll confuse the authorities while trying to use the shoe length to assess my height," said Jimmy.

"Is there anything else you'll like to know?" asked Isaac.

"What's the size of the artefact? Can I hide it inside my uniform comfortably?" asked Jimmy.

"It isn't big; but it's beautiful. It'll fit inside your clothes," said Isaac.

"Then that's all," said Jimmy.

"Where will we meet after the artefact has been moved?" asked Isaac.

"I'll call you; don't worry about the safety of the artefact," said Jimmy.

"What about that guy, Damian. Is he going with you?" asked Isaac.

"No, he isn't, I don't jeopardise a sensitive operation like this, and everything will be fine with just me alone handling this," said Jimmy. As far as the thieves in New York are concerned, it will be an overkill placing Jimmy at par with Damian, who isn't anywhere near the top of the heap, Damian is a petty thief, pretty much about snatch and grab, and finds himself obviously at the bottom of the food chain, though, he remained relevant because he's always around the corridors of power, the top dogs like Jimmy. Arguably, the fact that Damian is at the bottom of the food chain makes him a possible low hanging fruit, and a careful observation of Damian by security agencies will lead anyone observing him with keen interest to those at the top of the food chain. Serendipitously, Damian might be a bit of a loose cannon, but he has proved to be more than a handful for security agents because he isn't some clingy nutter who rides along in Jimmy's apron. He's a street-wise thief who runs most of his parole personally.

"I hope you've seen the names and photographs of every guard on duty and their duty posts," said Isaac.

"I've seen them, at least that won't be a problem," said Jimmy.

A day after getting the final briefing from Isaac Keanu, Jimmy Thompson penetrates the embassy to execute the heist.

Jimmy made his moves as he walked into the embassy during working hours and sat down as a guest who has serious business within the embassy, he then walked up to a guard. "Please can I use the toilet?" asked Jimmy.

"Take the stairs down, you'll find the toilet," said guard one.

Jimmy entered the toilet changed into the guard uniform that was inside his bag, came out immediately and pressed the fire alarm that was nearby and there was confusion as people were running out of the building to the assembly point.

Guard two saw Jimmy who's a new face in uniform. "Who are you?" guard two asked.

"I'm a new guard, aren't you Josh? I just resumed work, and didn't our supervisor tell you anything about it?" said Jimmy.

"Of course, I'm Josh, and I wasn't told anything about you, but we'll talk about that after evacuating the building," said guard two.

Immediately, guard two left Jimmy and rushed in to ensure everyone in the building safely leaves the building to the assembly point.

Within two minutes, Jimmy walked straight into the ambassador's office, splashed the fine sand he came with on the buttons of the safe and was able to identify the pin, he opened the safe, took the artefact and tucked it neatly inside his clothes, then closed the safe. He immediately left the ambassador's office and went back to the toilet, removed the guard's uniform and changed into his normal dress.

Guard one stumbled into Jimmy in the toilet while ensuring the building was completely evacuated, but Jimmy was already back in his plain clothes. "What are you still doing here, didn't you hear the fire alarm?" asked guard one.

"I heard the alarm, but I was really pressed and I can't help it, I'm sorry," said Jimmy.

"Ok, you've to leave now and join others at the assembly point," said guard one.

"Ok, thank you," said Jimmy.

Within minutes Jimmy was at the assembly point and moments later, he left with other guests of the embassy who have other businesses to attend to and couldn't wait to return to the embassy building. Funnily, Isaac Keanu who initiated the heist, didn't know when Jimmy came and left, but was itching to hear from Jimmy, and later that evening he put a call across to him.

"Hello Jimmy, it's me Isaac," he said.

Jimmy is known for his anonymity, and his invincibility meant conversations concerning heists don't happen on phone, and this mustn't happen on the internet as well.

"I can't talk, I can't talk, Isaac, meet me later," Jimmy said and cuts the phone call.

Although, Isaac and Ian expected the heist to happen that day, but they've no idea if it did or not, because aside the fire alarm which sometimes happen in building there's nothing outside the blue to indicate a heist took place. After all, Isaac didn't see Jimmy Thompson come and leave, but they have to meet with him to know if this mythical man did what he's good at.

"How did it go?" asked Isaac.

"It went well; did you hear of any trouble?" asked Jimmy.

"No, there wasn't any complaint about a missing artefact, and did you succeed in taking it?" asked Isaac.

"I took it and closed the safe neatly, so it's only when the safe is searched that they'll discover something is missing," said Jimmy.

Unsurprisingly, Jimmy didn't cower after all, because betrayal isn't his thing, and as a man whose reputation precedes him, he has lived up to his name.

"Is it you who triggered the fire alarm?" asked Isaac.

"Yeah, that's me, and it was part of my strategy," said Jimmy.

Jimmy's astuteness means his tricks must always remain in his sleeve and he never pulls his tricks in the open. Jimmy's 'catch me if you can,' anecdotally implies that his tricks and strategy concerning executing heists must remain shrouded in secrecy.

"How did you do it, did you break the safe to take the artefact?" asked Isaac.

"No, I didn't, the rest of the story is personal," said Jimmy, who doesn't like telling people everything about everything.

"Where's it, where did you keep it?" asked Ian.

"It's with me, it's safe and I'll give it to you tonight," Jimmy promised.

"Why not now?" asked Ian.

"Let's discuss the most important aspect of this deal, and that's the sharing formula," said Jimmy.

"Ok, what do you've in mind, Jimmy?" asked Isaac.

"I wouldn't want to be greedy, I take forty percent, the two of you will take twenty five percent each, and Damian will take ten percent," said Jimmy.

Ian didn't hesitate to voice out as he said he expected Jimmy to give Damian something from his forty percent and allow him and Isaac share sixty percent.

"Ian, let it go, if Jimmy hadn't gone inside, we wouldn't have been talking about percentages," Isaac advised.

Aside the sharing formula, who keeps the artefact until it's disposed of is another matter of concern as this team knows little of each other, and the fear of betrayal is heightened. Jimmy had to insist he's keeping the artefact until a price was agreed with the buyer. However, Jimmy has a personal advice for Isaac who could find himself in the middle of the storm, peradventure suspicion begins to fly and the embassy takes a real look at its staff.

"Isaac, make sure you don't spend a cent out of your cut until the dust about this artefact settles," Jimmy advised.

"Ok, I get you," Isaac concurred.

"Don't leave the money in your account either, and your lifestyle mustn't change for now," said Jimmy.

Days later, Agent Barry walked into the office looking his best in his tailor-made tuxedo, he just returned from witnessing the execution of Klint Willits who raped and shot his sister, and murdered her in cold blood.

Agent Barry promised his dying sister, Emma Briggis, that he will find the perpetrator of this crime and make sure they pay the highest price for their crimes. He eventually used all the available resources of the FBI at his disposal to smoke out and charge his sister's killer to court, and this is thanks to Williams Clay.

Williams Clay is the son of a conservative Republican political activist, Bobby Clay. William is a Church boy and it's now embarrassingly obvious to him that he's quite naive and oblivious with the happenings in street life of New York City. William was smart as a kid but he's not street-wise, and as someone who newly joined the NYPD, Williams was confronted with culture shock as he tries to navigate life as someone who has spent most of his time within the four walls of the church to someone thrown into the streets of New York City. It's more like throwing a lamb into a pack of wolves. Funnily, he'd to face the criminals weaved into activities of the night life of New York City, the deep end sort of, and a culture shock for that matter.

With cars sputtering up and down the street and blaring their horns during the late-night rush hour, the streets finally woke up to its historic legacy of night life and people are loving it. Unfortunately for Williams, identifying what drug he finds in people's possession happens not to be a walk in the park. Williams' perception of night life is solely focused on understanding the criminal mind, in a manner that will help him interpret cause and effect surrounding criminal minds, and how that will help him catch the bad guys. It didn't take long before Williams realised that the activities associated with street life and night life are well beyond his grasp and more than a handful for him despite months spent in training as a new recruit.

Williams is an intelligent chap with an IQ far beyond the average man, and this gift of nature made him occasionally beat his chest before his contemporaries in the Police Academy that carrying out his task as an NYPD officer will be a walk in the park for him, unbeknownst to him the skills required to be effective as a Cop is a bit of a mixed bag. A good IQ, discipline, physical strength when the need to go physical and some street experience. Arguably, Williams has the first three but quite lacking in the fourth. He somehow should have preferred to ride a horse in the old wild west but this isn't the case.

Faced with the realities of the job, Williams now grapples with differentiating between cut cocaine and crack cocaine, and he has often been unable to differentiate between marihuana and Indian hemp. He knows for sure what drugs are classed as, class A, class B or even class C, but when confronted with these drugs particularly when they're outside their wrappers Williams struggles to identify what they are.

Now that the job has proved to be more than a handful, Williams is now embarrassed to expose his naivety to his colleagues, some of whom have held him in high regards. He then began masking his shortcomings by avoiding tasks that will expose his weaknesses. Williams had no idea that his effort to mask his inadequacies in the job didn't escape the keen eyes of Lieutenant Rose who takes her time to observe those under her command.

Despite Williams' inadequacies, his intuitiveness and his under-standing of the criminal mind was quite instrumental in Agent Barry's' quest for justice for his beloved late sister. Catching Klint Willits was more like finding a needle from a haystack because it involves proper analysis of those involved in this crime by separating those that were merely accessories to murder from the main culprit. This isn't anything like a dog with a bone for Williams, as he skilfully picked Klint Willits out of the horde of suspects hustling in the streets of New York being investigated for perpetrating this grisly act.

Agent Barry has always assured himself that he will only find peace if his sister's killer is charged and sentenced. Unfortunately, immediately the court gave the perpetrator of this crime the death penalty, Agent Barry smiled because that's what he was seeking all along for himself and for his dead sister to find peace. Sadly, the peace was short-lived as the hollow feeling seemed to return and take hold of his heart. He then moved the goal posts further saying he will only find peace for himself and his dead sister only when he's there present during the execution of Klint Willits and watch as this killer takes his last breath, interestingly he has just achieved that. Agent Donald just saw him walk into the office looking droopy despite having his best dress on and having achieved his heart's desire.

"Barry, how did the execution go?" asked Agent Donald.

"The bastard is dead" replied Agent Barry.

Agent Donald fixed his gaze at Barry, and reminded him he has achieved his heart's desire, and asked why his face is lacking of joy, but Barry insisted that all he could say, is that the bastard that murdered his sister is dead.

"Your face didn't show you're happy with the outcome of today's execution, at least this is what you desire all along to find peace and closure over your sister's death.

"Donald, I didn't feel any different, I still feel the same way I have always felt since Emma's death. I thought witnessing this guy's death would give me closure but the hollow feeling is still there, and sadly, it seems to have just gotten worse because there's nothing else, an event perhaps, I can look forward to, to bring closure particularly now that the bastard is dead," said Agent Barry.

Agent Donald reminded Barry that instead of finding a way of dealing with a loss of a loved one, people always make the mistake of thinking that punishing the perpetrators of a crime is what brings peace, the truth is that the death or punishment of a perpetrator will not replace the feeling of loss. The feeling of loss never goes away, we just learn to live with it and don't attribute finding closure to a particular event because you might end up feeling hurt and disappointed when that closure doesn't happen.

CHAPTER

TEN

The courier

Freddie deals in crack cocaine and has a cocaine shipment coming from Puerto Rico to the United States and was worried about how to go about making the shipment. Andrea is Freddie's business partner on the other end in Puerto Rico but wants Freddie to hasten up with moving his shipment bound for the United States as he couldn't risk holding it for too long for fear of being nabbed.

"Hello Freddie," said Andrea.

"I'm fine Andrea, but I told you not to call me this time of day," said Freddie.

"Freddie, I don't understand, what's it with you?" asked Andrea.

"I'm at home, and my baby mama is home with me," Freddie retorted.

"What has baby mama got to do with a shipment that's ready?" asked Andrea.

"I'm planning on getting married, and I'm trying to be good by her," said Freddie. Andrea is getting more exasperated by the hour, because holding onto Freddie's shipment for longer than necessary could spell doom for him, and funnily, Freddie is busy with this baby mama gibberish.

"But your shipment is ready, when are you moving it?" Andrea queried. Sadly, while Freddie tried explaining himself to Andrea, the entrance door squawks and that's Sherry, Freddie's baby mama stepping in, and this phone conversation must end abruptly.

"Sherry is coming, Andrea. I have to go," said Freddie.

Sherry on the other hand was in no mood for a clunky joke, she realised Freddie abruptly ended his phone conversation the very moment she drew closer, and she isn't having it. Sad to say, that Freddie's shoddiness could rattle Sherry's quiescent prejudice towards him, and it's now glaringly obvious that Freddie would need a lot of luck to wriggle out of Sherry's keen eyes of scrutiny.

"Who's it, Freddie who're you speaking with on the phone?" she asked.

"No one," he replied.

"What do you mean, no one?" asked Sherry.

"Ok, its Billy," he retorted.

"And you had to cut the call the moment I drew closer to you?" she queried further. For all it was worth even when Freddie isn't in cuffs, Sherry seems to have taken him prisoner.

"The conversation was already over as at when you walked in," Freddie retorted. Sherry isn't ready to accommodate any act of ineptitude from Freddie, and he knows for sure that she's definitely throwing him out if anything shoddy comes up.

"Let me remind you, Freddie. If you remain a bad influence, I wouldn't want you around my kids," Sherry threatened.

Freddie quickly reminded Sherry that the kids she's going on and on about belong to both of them, and asked to be excused because he has an emergency to attend to. Sadly, his attempt to quickly wrap his conversation with Sherry isn't working out.

"This is family time, Freddie, you're going nowhere," said Sherry.

"Sherry, I've to go, this emergency has to be addressed to keep the family going," said Freddie.

"You aren't going anywhere, and if you leave, then don't come back," Sherry threatened. Freddie decided to stay put, and after all, his mission is a dodgy one, and he wouldn't want to spook Sherry any further.

The next morning Freddie called Andrea on phone and immediately apologised for the mess of the previous day.

"I didn't know you live a double life," Andrea retorted.

"Andrea, can you get a courier for me?" Freddie pleaded.

Sadly, Andrea is now in a bind, as his regular courier that moves shipment from Puerto Rico to the United States has just been nabbed by the Puerto Rican authorities and Andrea is now desperate to free himself from all the shipment in his possession. "I just got a call yesterday morning that my courier was nabbed the night before," said Andrea.

"How come, how did this happen?" asked Freddie.

"I really don't know, I just tried getting in touch with him to see if he can deliver to you only to hear the news of his arrest," said Andrea.

"Why're you pretending you've no idea he's in custody, isn't he your courier?" Freddie asked angrily.

"He pulled this job for a different person, so I'd no knowledge of it," said Andrea.

Andrea, you've to get me somebody to deliver the shipment, all my money is tied down in this merchandise," said Freddie.

"That's not part of the contract, you should look for a courier yourself," said Andrea.

"New York police are good; they'll definitely nab me if I move it myself," said Freddie. Sadly, Freddie paced back and forth as he spoke with Andrea, he's now in a bind and must make haste to wriggle himself out of this muddied water. Unsurprisingly, even as he seeks a way of escape, Freddie had to walk a fine line between being nabbed by the authorities and being caught with his hands in the cookie jar by Sherry.

Andrea seems to suddenly conclude that Freddie is lily-livered and that, he's now a man who has lost his mojo. He then asked Freddie what he's afraid of, and reminding him if he don't want to do the time, he shouldn't have done the crime.

"I want to marry Sherry and I need to get away from living on the edge," said Freddie.

"Then get a good hand to help you out," said Andrea.

Freddie's despair has taken over him, and his sudden loss of appetite isn't just because of his anxiety to marry the woman of his dreams, but sad to say, that his investment is about to go down the drain. This restlessness has gone suffuse and it has gotten the best of him, and this means whoever is able to save Freddie's shipment is welcomed, and days later Freddy meets Raymond for help. Raymond was dressed for work and was about to leave the house when Freddy came calling.

"What are you doing in my house this early? You never told me you were coming," said Raymond.

He was looking quite agitated as he hinted his friend, Raymond, that he couldn't sleep, and he just needed someone to help rescue his investment. Sadly, this fine man who never misses his routine of shaving daily to maintain his fine looks, is now looking like a man in a hostage situation, with his beards looking more like a scruffy grassland.

"You look unkept, what's the problem? asked Raymond.

"I need a courier," he said.

"Who moved your shipment before now?" Raymond queried further.

"The guy is in Prison," said Freddie.

"And why don't you move it yourself?" asked Raymond.

"I'm getting married to Sherry, so I can't take the risk," said Freddie.

"Ok, I'll introduce you to someone. Though, he doesn't do drugs, so I don't know if he'll love to help you," said Raymond.

"What a weakling! Then what does he do?" asked Freddie. "He's a thief, just that he doesn't do drugs or carry arms," said Raymond.

Being a courier isn't just any routine assignment for any Tom Dick and Harry, rather it's only those regimented to be an outlaw, and mustn't only talk the talk but walk the walk, and this includes engaging in a fire fight when things get rough.

"Then I don't need him, what sort of man is that?" asked Freddie.

"I don't know of others, but I know he doesn't fail, because he has never failed," said Raymond.

"You're making him sound like a God," said Freddie.

"Maybe his gift is from God then, but you may know him," said Raymond.

"You said I might know him, who's he?" Freddie asked.

"Ok, I'm talking of Jimmy Thompson," said Raymond.

"Did you say Jimmy Thompson, the New York thief?" Freddie asked ingenuously and then burst into laughter.

"Yes, and good you already know about him," said Raymond.

"Jimmy Thompson doesn't exist, he's just a myth and people use him to describe a good thief, like some kind of figure of speech," said Freddie, who thought he knew all that happens in the city of New York.

"Jimmy Thompson is in New York, we met two days ago," said Raymond.

"You're sure this guy exists in flesh and blood?" asked Freddie.

"Jimmy Thompson is now over fifty years old and the only thief that steals almost every day in New York City since he was twenty-five and has never been caught," said Raymond.

Freddie was rattled to learn that Jimmy is a real person, doing his thing on a daily basis, fooling people into believing he's a myth who don't exist in flesh and blood. The paradoxical personality created by Jimmy, has helped to keep his cat-like personality shrouded in doubt.

"How does this Jimmy Thompson do that?" asked Freddie.

"Because he leaves no trail that'll help the police catch him," said Raymond.

"But you say he doesn't do drugs, of what help is he?" asked Freddie.

"People consult him for advice before embarking on operations, because of his perfect senses," said Raymond.

"Ok Raymond, you'll take me to him," said Freddie.

By evening of the next day, Freddie is on hand to meet with Jimmy, not only to find a way around his shipment but to meet this man whose personality is thought to be a myth. Raymond took Freddie to the usual spot to see Jimmy Thompson, but those in Jimmy sphere knew well to vet whoever they bring to him, and that's the secret behind his mythical personality.

"Jimmy, meet my friend, Freddie," said Raymond. Freddie couldn't wait but ask the questions bugging his heart concerning the man sitting right opposite him.

"Are you Jimmy?" asked Freddie.

"Yes, that's me, and who wants to know?" he asked.

"Sorry, I just needed to get this off my chest, but are you truly the much talked about Jimmy Thompson?" Freddie queried further.

What is it? You're freaking me out," Jimmy retorted and turned to Raymond who brought Freddie. "I hope your friend won't out me?" Jimmy asked further.

Freddie apologised, saying he's sorry, and said his ecstatic reaction was because he thought Jimmy was a myth, and that he didn't actually exist.

"Erm.., a lot of people think that way," said Jimmy.

"I think I've seen you before, though I didn't know you're Jimmy Thompson," said Freddie.

"I call it being invisible; a lot of people seeing me and not knowing I'm Jimmy Thompson has helped me stay this long without getting caught," said Jimmy.

"Jimmy, I need your help," said Freddie.

"Raymond gave me a hint but what help in particular?" asked Jimmy.

"I need a courier," said Freddie.

"Go straight to the point, what are you moving?" Jimmy asked.

"I need a courier to move my cocaine shipment from Puerto Rico to New York," said Freddie.

"I'm sorry, I don't do drugs, and I can't help you," said Jimmy.

"Why Jimmy, why can't you help me?" said Freddie.

"Freddie, I'm just a thief and I'm ok with being just that," said Jimmy. The proposal to move a shipment of crack cocaine won't fly off the ground with Jimmy, who's just a thief and forbids every heist and operations that accommodates violence.

"Then what advice do you've for me not to get caught?" asked Freddie.

Jimmy spent about five minutes in deep thought and after a while. "Hmm, tell me about the security at the airport, do they use sniffer dogs to check luggage?" asked Jimmy.

"Yes, they use dogs only," said Freddie.

"Can you get the skin of a Lion, a Tiger, or a Leopard; there must be a place you can find that in Puerto Rico," said Jimmy.

Jimmy's suggestion riled Freddie because it freaked him out, and he couldn't hold back as turned to Raymond and burst into laughter which quickly tuned into hysteria. "Is this guy into some form of voodoo or what? What does he want to do with a lion skin or a leopard skin?" Freddie asked hysterically.

"Freddie, let's hear him out," said Raymond.

Despite the hysteria precipitated by Jimmy's proposal, nonetheless Raymond is all ears to what Jimmy had to say about this novel idea.

"Ok Jimmy, what do I do with that stuff you just mentioned?" asked Freddie.

Jimmy suggested to Freddie that he doesn't need much quantity of whatever skin he will be using, and said all Freddie needed to do is just to sew it as padding for his bag, and that is all.

"What has that got to do with helping me not get caught?" asked Freddie.

"Lion, Tigers and Leopards are superior predators to a dog, when a sniffing dog gets close to your bag, the dog will have no choice but to discontinue," said Jimmy.

"Hmm, this is a novel idea, but are you sure this will work?" asked Jimmy.

"How much is my consultation fee Freddie? When you succeed, which you surely will, make sure you bring my money," said Jimmy.

"Thank you, Jimmy, we'll get back to you," said Freddie.

After spending quality time tapping from Jimmy's wealth of cruel wisdom, Freddie and Raymond left, yet Freddie isn't still convinced this novel idea will keep him from the clutches of NYPD officers, but Raymond was quite reassuring.

"If Jimmy says it'll work, then it will," said Raymond. Now that Freddie has taken Jimmy's idea on board, he needs to get things going, but Andrea's exasperation has gotten the best of him. "Freddie, I've been expecting your call, and when are you coming?" asked Andrea who's anxious to get rid of the shipment in his care.

"Why the hurry? I'm trying to work things out," said Freddie.

"You know your shipment wasn't meant to stay more than forty-eight hours with me, and it's now four days," he said.

"Andrea, please can you get me the skin of any of the big cats?" asked Andrea.

Andrea burst into laughter, and it seems the hysteria from this Jimmy's novelty was quite infectious. "Big cats, what for, you know I don't do poaching, and are you into something I don't know about?" asked Andrea.

"I mean just a little piece of a lion, leopard or a tiger's skin; I know there are specialised people who sell it," said Freddie.

"I'm not a hunter, what do you want to use that for?" asked Andrea.

This conversation didn't gather traction because the thorny subject reflects something fiendish and vicious, and had to wait until Freddie arrived in Puerto Rico. Funnily, as the saying goes, 'knowing how to make scramble eggs doesn't necessarily mean you make breakfast' and trying out Jimmy's idea is now the only one thing in Freddie's heart.

While in Puerto Rico, Freddie and Andrea searched for the skin of these big cats and couldn't find any but were only able to find the skin of a hyena, which they eventually used to pad the bag containing the drugs.

At the airport Freddie was the number twenty-one in the queue, each time the sniffer dog gets to the number twentieth person in the queue she goes back to start from the beginning, moreover an attempt to force the dog to continue made the dog quit sniffing completely until Freddie was through with his airport checks in Puerto Rico.

Freddie then boarded his flight from Puerto Rico to New York City, and on arrival, at the airport in New York City, the sniffer dog avoided Freddie at all cost and Freddie was able to move his merchandise unhindered to his desired location.

Freddie's excitement was beyond measure, he opened his eyes as wide as saucers, as he couldn't believe he just beat the airport security at their own game. Even as he tried to manage his excitement, Freddie remained quite ecstatic as a child on a sugar rush, not just because he's able to move his shipment without being nabbed, but how Jimmy came about this novel idea, was what rattled him the most.

The moment he stepped into his apartment, and waited for Sherry to step out of the house, Freddie put a call across to Raymond as he couldn't wait to tell the world of the extraordinariness of Jimmy who doesn't sell ruse to people.

"Raymond, I'm back," said Freddie.

"Good to hear you're back, how did it go?" asked Raymond.

"It worked perfectly, this guy Jimmy, is a genius. Now, I've got my means of transporting my shipment.

"Which means you need to appreciate Jimmy for his counsel," said Raymond.

"Of course, I'm coming over so we can hook up with Jimmy," said Freddie.

Later that evening, Freddie was promptly on hand to show his gratitude to Jimmy, a new acquaintance, whose company he now cherishes so dearly.

"Oh, Freddie, you're back," said Jimmy.

"Yeah, I'm back and decided to come and see you," said Jimmy. Freddie was quite upfront, and all smiles this time, because a big burden has just been lifted off his shoulders.

"The fact that you're here suggests you weren't caught, which means it all went well," said Jimmy.

"It went perfectly well, Jimmy. I don't know where you got that thought from, but hey man, you're a genius," Freddie said as he couldn't stop buttering Jimmy up.

"It's just a gift, where's Raymond?" asked Jimmy.

"You've given me the best means of transporting my goods. That's Raymond over there, he'll join me soon," said Freddie.

Sadly, Jimmy is about to burst Freddie's bubble with a single pinprick but Freddie is having none of it, and even if he'd trusted Jimmy's sixth sense in the past, he might not this time.

"Don't use this method again," said Jimmy.

Freddie's laughter suddenly disappeared and the smiles quickly turned into a stern look. "Why! I've just gotten the answer I have been seeking all these years and you're asking me to ditch it?" Freddie queried.

"The cops will catch you if you do," said Jimmy.

"How! Jimmy, how? This method is spotless and without trails," said Freddie.

"No, Freddie, it leaves a trail," said Jimmy.

"What trail does it leave?" asked Freddie.

"Later, the cops will review their surveillance cameras and carefully observe what went on there and why the dog was avoiding you, and then they'll place you on a watch list," said Jimmy.

Freddie couldn't bear to hear what Jimmy had to say on this matter, he'd rather appreciate Jimmy for the past and move on. "Take this," said Freddie as he hands Jimmy some cash.

"Oh, you're true to your word, but I must emphasize don't use this method again; you might be treated as a person encouraging the killings of wildlife," said Jimmy.

Freddie went quiet throughout, he had this thought inside of his head that no one knew about, but the thought of ditching this padded bag method kind of scared the hell out of him, yet he remained defiant until he left Jimmy's circle that evening.

Days later, while seated at his desk and flipping through the pages of a cold file, Agent Donald gets a phone call from Lieutenant Mark Russell concerning Teddy Bush, a fugitive.

"Hello Donald, this is Lieutenant Mark Russell of the Green Field Unit of the NYPD," Lieutenant Mark.

"Hello Lieutenant, how're you?" asked Agent Donald.

"Detective, I suppose you still remember me?" Lieutenant Mark.

"Don't be funny, Mark, of course I still remember you. The wine we drank together after the successful prosecution of the killer of Miss Riley Parker is still in my memory, and I'm still looking forward to drinking in that same bar, on the same table and possibly with you again.

"You never cease to amuse me, and you just made my morning start on a brighter note," said Lieutenant Mark.

"What's up, Mark?" asked Agent Donald.

"We've just got tip-off about Teddy bush," said Lieutenant Mark.

"Teddy Bush, the murder suspect?" he asked.

Teddy Bush fired the stray bullet that hit and killed Royce Benson, during a rivalry drive-by shooting between gangs, and NYPD officers have since pinpointed Teddy Bush as the person that fired the fatal shot.

"Yes, he came in through the JFK international airport," said Lieutenant Mark.

"When did he come into New York?" asked Agent Donald.

"That would be last week Thursday," said Lieutenant Mark.

"Ok thank you, I hope we'll catch this guy and bring this case to a reasonable conclusion," said Agent Donald.

It's not long after his phone conversation with Lieutenant Mark, that Agent Donald went with Agent Barry to the Jake Owen, the man in charge of the JFK Airport to request access to their CCTV cameras.

Minutes after permission was granted by Jake Owen, the detectives entered the CCTV room in the JKF International airport to do a follow-up on Teddy Bush's movement after his return to New York City. Unsurprisingly, the detectives were met with a smile and a frown by the two CCTV staff on duty. "Hello Jason, how're you?" asked Agent Donald.

"I'm fine, detective," replied Jason.

Sammy's ineptitude was in full display as he pretended not to have time for the detectives that just walked into the CCTV room as he was in his own world drinking a cup of tea with his eyes fixed on the CCTV screen. "Detectives, I think whatever you're here for should wait," said Sammy.

"Sammy, have you bothered to know why we're here?" asked Agent Donald. Sammy's response was everything but benign and it got the highly irritable Agent Barry all riled up. Funnily, Sammy has just met his nemesis in Barry who doesn't let people displaying ineptitude off the hook easily, without foul mouthing them.

"Stop pretending to be busy Sammy, all you do all day is drink a cup of tea and look at the screen, isn't it?" said Agent Barry. Sammy seems to have found his nemesis in Agent Barry, who walks around, shoulder high with a chip the size of New York on his shoulder like a frustrated life guard.

"Are you telling me, looking at the screen isn't work? You know I hate it when you make me feel so small?" replied Sammy.

"No, it isn't work enough compared to chasing down the bad guys," said Agent Barry. Sammy has been irked by Barry's punchy banter, and sadly, he has to coil back to his shell, as his nemesis won't give in until he sours his day.

"To be frank with you, detective, each time I set my eyes on you my warm disposition melts away," said Sammy.

"What about your appetite, I hope you lost that too?" said Agent Barry.

Sadly, Sammy abruptly, stopped drinking his tea. "I've just lost my appetite as well," said Sammy.

"Guys enough of the tackling," said Agent Donald.

While these two were busy getting under each other's skin, Jason saw it as an opportunity to add his banter to the mix.

"You guys are perfect match for each other," said Jason.

"Jason, please I need to review your CCTV for last week Thursday," said Agent Donald.

"What's up about last week's Thursday?" asked Jason.

"There's a murder case we were handling about a year ago, the suspect left the country, but intelligence reaching us is that the guy just entered through this airport," said Agent Donald.

"What's his name?" asked Jason.

"His name is Teddy Bush. A bad guy who wants to be invisible, he might come in using a different name," said Agent Donald.

"Last week Thursday, you said?" said Jason.

But while Jason's focus remained glued to screen, watching what goes on in the airport, he called out to Sammy to give the detectives the help they seek.

"Ok Sammy, let's go to work, get me everything that relates to last week Thursday," said Jason.

Sammy isn't moving, particularly now that his appetite has been scarred by Agent Barry. "Jason, you know I'm busy," said Sammy.

"Sammy, you seem to be stalling, the guy we're after is a suspected killer, what if he comes in unnoticed and kills again?" asked Agent Donald.

"You're right, I guess, but provided he isn't killing me?" said Sammy.

"Stop guessing, just give us what we need," said Agent Barry.

Sammy turned around and looked at Barry with disgust, but sadly, Agent Barry's eyes kept speaking subtly to Sammy telling him 'the lame will walk'. "Enough of your insolence!" said Sammy, as he handed the tapes to Jason.

It isn't long before Jason began reviewing the CCTV camera tapes. I hope you'll recognise him if you see the guy?" asked Jason.

Agent Barry immediately interjected "Yeah, we'll," he said.

Agent Donald watched keenly as Jason reviewed the camera, searching for Teddy Bush. Funnily, the search hasn't gone that far when Agent Donald suddenly saw the drama between Freddie and the sniffer dog. "Wow, wow, what's that? Go back please," said Agent Donald.

"What's it, you're saying I should go back to?" asked Jason.

"That dog drama, we just passed," Donald said.

Jason went back to the drama between the sniffer dog and Freddie. "Is that the Teddy Bush you're looking for?" asked Jason.

"No, that isn't Teddy Bush, but haven't you wondered why the sniffer dog isn't sniffing that guy," said Agent Donald as he tried calling the attention of others to this dog drama.

"You're right, Donald, each time the dog gets close to him, she backs off," said Barry.

"We saw it, but we never attached any meaning to it," said Jason.

"Now you know, even the man handling the sniffer dog seems not to notice it," said Agent Donald.

"Is this guy using some voodoo or something?" asked Agent Barry.

Agent Donald was rattled by what he just saw, and his interest isn't just about what crime he has committed but what he did to keep the sniffer dog at bay. "I don't know but we'll need to catch this guy. Maybe we'll get a breakthrough in solving a new kind of crime," said Agent Donald.

"Ok, we'll be on the lookout for him, I'm certain he'll come around again," said Jason.

"Ok, let's continue with our search for Teddy bush," said Agent Donald. They continued reviewing the CCTV camera for Teddy Bush, and moments later.

"That's him," said Agent Barry, as he spotted the fugitive on camera.

"You're right, Barry," said Agent Donald.

"Teddy Bush is in town, Jason, please give us a call whenever he steps into this airport," said Agent Donald.

Agent Donald took down the details of the cab Teddy Bush boarded as he left the airport, maybe the cab man will help to furnish the detectives with a little more information concerning the itinerary of this man on the run.

Three months later after Freddie's successful heist, Jimmy Thompson was at the Criss Crescent bar, his usual spot where he enjoys the happy hour. "Hey Raymond, what's up?" asked.

"I'm good, Jimmy, good to see you. Can I fix you up with some bottles?" asked Raymond.

"That's what the happy hour is for! Go ahead Raymond, and how's your friend, Freddie? It's been long I saw him," Jimmy asked.

"Freddie is good, but he just left for Puerto-Rico this morning," said Raymond.

"What for?" Jimmy inquisitively asked.

"To move his merchandise, of course," said Raymond.

Jimmy listened keenly and prayed to God in his heart and hoping to hear something that isn't going to rile him all up. "Ah, is it through the same method, I showed him?" Jimmy queried further.

"Yeah, the skin bag, he's using the skin bag," said Raymond.

"I told him not to do it again, now they'll catch him, and he'll expose me," said Jimmy. Sad to say, that Jimmy's unholy association with Freddie has unwittingly gone belly up, but even if Freddie's trip goes south, Jimmy isn't certain his neck will be spared.

"Freddie won't expose you, and he won't do a thing like that, but how do know they'll catch him?" asked Raymond.

"Because I know, why don't you ask me how I managed to stay away from prison all these years?" asked Jimmy. Sadly, Raymond didn't do a good job in vetting Freddie before linking him with Jimmy, despite placing so much faith that his crack cocaine dealing friend will remain tongue-tied if things go south. Jimmy sensed an undercurrent that this Freddie will end up being his nemesis.

"I advised Freddie, but he didn't listen. Hmm, what are you going to do about this?" asked Raymond.

"I have to leave town, and I'll be travelling tonight or first thing tomorrow morning, until this dust settles," said Jimmy.

Raymond seems not to understand that things have already gone south, but realising the fact that Jimmy's sixth sense is at work, he queried further. "Is it this serious?" he asked.

"It's to me, you brought the wrong person for consultation, and this might come back to bite me," said Jimmy.

CHAPTER

ELEVEN

The Escape to the Cayman Islands

Jimmy decided to flee to the Cayman Islands, as a way of escaping the wrath of the law enforcement agents because he's convinced that Freddie will eventually be caught, and the squawky consequence might reverberate outside his control.

While on the plane to the Cayman Islands he was privileged to sit next to Alicia who had just divorced her husband.

Jimmy sat motionless beside Alicia reminiscing the life he left behind, even as he watched as Alicia entertained herself with a trendy feminine magazine. After a while he summoned courage to initiate a conversation with Alicia. "Please can I have one of those?" he said.

Alicia immediately turned to Jimmy. "Sorry, what did you say?" she asked.

Jimmy smiled as he pointed to one of the magazines on Alicia's laps. "Please, can I have one of those?" asked Jimmy.

"Oh, why not, sure you can, and which of them do you want?" she asked politely.

"Any of them, they all seem to be trendy magazines," said Jimmy.

"Yeah, that's usually every woman's first choice, when it comes to the papers," she said and handed Jimmy one of the magazines.

"Ah, thank you, I'm Jimmy by the way," he said as he introduces himself formally. Interestingly, one thing led to the other, and mere exchanges extended into formal introduction and they got chatting.

"I'm Alicia, is this your first time of travelling to the Cayman Islands?" asked Alicia.

"Yes, this is my first time, what about you?" he asked.

"No, this is my third time, but my reason for travelling this time is different," she said.

Funnily, the conversation between Alicia and Jimmy seems to be coming on smoothly and didn't come across as awkward as the pair seemed to click with each other, and suddenly they steered the conversation away from mere pleasantries into more personal stuff.

"We both seem to have special reason for travelling to the Cayman Islands this time, what's your reason?" asked Jimmy.

"You go first, tell me your reason and then, I'll tell you mine," said Alicia, with a smile.

"I guess you haven't forgotten the saying, 'ladies first,' said Jimmy.

Alicia laughed, as she pushed Jimmy's proposal back to him. "Sorry, not on this occasion," said Alicia.

"I'm just trying to keep away from some friends who are trying to bug me to death," said Jimmy.

The pair shifted their focus and attention away from their magazines and focused on each other, because their conversation has a taken a friendly turn.

"Oh, yours is understandable, I just divorced my husband, and I needed some space to clear my head," she said.

"You mean your, husband?" he asked.

"Yes, Charlie is beginning to suffer from mid-life crises and his choices are becoming blurred so we have to call it quits," said Alicia. Jimmy burst into laughter following Alicia's remark on Charlie's mid-life crises. "How do you know?" asked Jimmy.

Alicia became quite jocular as she told Jimmy that when a man in his early or mid-fifties begins to suffer indecision, particularly when it comes to romance with his wife, then it's sufficient to say that he's suffering mid-life crises.

Jimmy laughed, even as he reminded Alicia that her assertion is weird, saying she's just being biased against men, but then proceeded to ask how old Charlie is.

"Charlie is fifty-five, and I'm forty-eight, what about you?" she asked.

"I'm the same age as Charlie, I'm fifty-five," said Jimmy. Alicia suddenly turned to Jimmy in surprise and exclaimed.

"Oh, what a coincidence! Are you sure you aren't going through your own mid-life crisis?" she asked.

"Ah, no, not at all, and why the question?" Jimmy queried.

"Maybe running off to the Cayman Islands might be your own way of dealing with yours," she said.

Funnily, the drifter has found company in Alicia, another beautiful soul who just turned her back on her marriage and might be needing company, and while the conversation persists, the air hostess interrupts.

"Excuse me, what do you care for, white wine, red wine?" asked the hostess.

"Hmm, give me white wine," said Jimmy.

The hostess turned to Alicia. "I want the red wine, give me that and that as well," said Alicia as points to a piece of chicken and vegetables. After the Hostess finished with them and moved to the passengers in front of them, they continued their conversation. Alicia's body language tells that she has found a liking in Jimmy, while Jimmy on his part constrained himself from making the wrong move and preferred to wait it out for Alicia to do the bidding.

"Are you married, Jimmy?" asked Alicia.

"No, I'm not," said Jimmy.

"Any kids?" she asked further.

"Yeah, my boy, Jerry, he's twenty-eight now," said Jimmy.

"Then you'll be my plus one," replied Alicia.

Jimmy's waiting game seemed to pay-off as their conversation seemed to move away from a mere hello, and this is now becoming steamy and the puzzle is coming together, with Alicia pulling the strings. "How do you mean! Your plus one, you said?" asked Jimmy.

"If you don't mind, we can keep each other company, and help each other forget about what needs to be forgotten," she said to Jimmy and winked her eyes at him.

"Erm.., ok, that'll be nice," said Jimmy.

"You don't seem to look like someone who will bore me," said Alicia.

"In what part of New York City do you live?" asked Jimmy.

Now that the Cat is out of the bag, the courtesy of avoiding making the wrong move seem not too necessary, as they chatted forever.

"I don't live in New York, I live in Los Angles," said Alicia.

"You mean, Hollywood? But how come you're flying from New York?" asked Jimmy.

Alicia hinted Jimmy that she has a big boutique that caters for the needs of people in Hollywood, and that she only stopped over in New York for some business, and to also see her son who's based in New York. Jimmy and Alicia arrived in George Town in Grand Cayman and checked in into the Ostricagreen Hotel. The hotel reception welcomed the pair as they arrive through the lobby of the hotel.

"We need a double room," said Alicia.

Jimmy looked through the list of rooms, and after reviewing the cost of the rooms. "Give us that," said Jimmy said as he points to one of the moderately priced rooms.

"Why're you choosing the cheapest of all the rooms?" asked Alicia.

"We're spending about four weeks here. That's a considerable amount of time, so we need something affordable," said Jimmy.

Alicia reminded Jimmy that she knows he doesn't have money, and told him not to worry, that she's footing the bill, because she's here to clear her head and she needed the best room to achieve that.

"Ok, the woman from Hollywood," he said looking right into her eyes.

Alicia laughed and pointed to the most expensive room on the list, this lady isn't ready to add to her stress, she's moving onto a new chapter of her life, and that means fun. "Give us that," said Alicia.

Moments later, the receptionist handed Alicia the keys to her room. "It's all done for you," she said.

They left the reception then meandered through the lobby before entering the elevator to the third floor. Immediately they entered their room Alicia rushed to the bathroom and spent some time in the bath enjoying a bubble bath with a soft music at the background, while Jimmy sat on the bed watching the television.

It took a while by the time Alicia stepped out of the bathroom into the room, after an hour and half in the bath. "Jimmy, go and have a shower," said Alicia. Funnily, Jimmy couldn't get his eyes off Alicia as she dried the water on her body with a towel, and his eyes remain glued to Alicia. "You look wonderful," he said.

Alicia felt it's too early for Jimmy to allow his emotions take over the best of him, and that if his emotion start running riot by now, then how can he handle her if they're finally in each other's arm.

"You said you're forty-eight; it's surprising because you don't look it," said Jimmy.

"How do you mean? I told you I'm forty-eight and that's true," said Alicia.

"I must confess, I'm taken aback, because you're a woman in her late forties arguably retaining the firm body of a teenager," Jimmy said with a smile.

"I suppose, I eat well, I live healthy and lots of workouts. Maybe through romance or physical exercise," she ingeniously said and then burst into laughter.

Jimmy rushed off to the shower, before he lost his mind looking at Alicia. It didn't take too long before he dashed out of the shower and went straight to wrap his hands around Alicia. They then spent the rest of the night in each other's arms. The next day, Jimmy and Alicia had their breakfast served in their hotel room, but Jimmy didn't fancy being cooped indoors all day without stepping out of their hotel room, even if it's just for an opportunity to enjoy the stunning tranquillity of the hotel's outdoor terrace.

"Why don't we go out? We've been cooped up indoors since morning," asked Jimmy.

"You never asked why, I also want to enjoy all the fun this island has to offer me," said Alicia.

"Ok, then why've we been indoors since morning?" asked Jimmy.

"Because I've reserved the outing for this evening," said Alicia. Jimmy and Alicia both stood by the window looking at the adjoining street. He curiously turned to her, but then subtly asked her if there's a live band tonight or something of interest happening in the hotel that they're meant to enjoy, that made her reserve the outing for that evening.

"We're going far away from here, we going to enjoy the fun of the seaside boulevard," said Alicia.

"Oh, that sounds nice," Jimmy said.

Alicia's plan for the evening was meant to kick off when its 4.pm. "we'll leave the hotel by 4.pm, and go have some fun," she said.

"Ok, I never knew you've it all planned out," he replied and wraps his arm around her.

That evening they spent time in one of the restaurants located in the seaside boulevard on the Grand Cayman. As they eat dinner at a seaside grill, they chatted all night as though they've known each other forever. Jimmy confessed to Alicia he liked her choice of spot for the evening outing.

"I told you this is my third time of coming to the Cayman Islands, so I know how to catch the fun this Island offers.

"I love it, because it's all like a paradise experience, and the ambience is perfect," said Jimmy.

"This is what the Seaside Boulevard offers, and it's good you like it, because I'll be sharing these experiences with you," said Alicia.

Jimmy stood up and stretched his hand to Alicia, excusing her to come on to the dance floor. "Come on, let's dance. I don't want this music wasting away," said Jimmy.

Alicia stood up, as Jimmy took her hand and walked her to the dance floor. "You sure know how to keep a lady entertained," said Alicia. "Yeah, let's enjoy the live band," said Jimmy.

"My guess was right; you weren't suffering from mid-life crisis like Charlie, even though you're both of the same age," said Alicia.

As they danced in this seaside boulevard Jimmy immediately left Alicia and excused one of guitarists for a minute as he collected the guitar and played with the band for ten minutes and then returned to Alicia.

"I don't know you know how to do that!" Exclaimed Alicia.

Yeah, I am good with the guitar. I remember one ukulele I bought for my little boy, vintage, he used to cherish it. Each time I play the guitar with him his friends always gather around us.

Jimmy didn't really buy Alicia's story that Charlie is suffering from mid-life crisis; he perceives Alicia's prejudice as being overstated. "Charlie's problem isn't mid-life crisis, Charlie has money, and his problem is choice from the varieties of options available to him," said Jimmy. They danced, giggled, laughed, and enjoyed the beauty of the outdoor experience by the seaside and retired to their hotel room at about 11.pm.

Freddie is back from Puerto Rico, he was able to beat the airport security in Puerto Rico and this time, he must have to beat the New York City Airport security to make it home. Just as before, the sniffer dogs are still refusing to sniff him.

It isn't long before Jason Blake spotted similar reaction from the sniffer dog as before on his CCTV camera, and realising that this guy is a person of interest, Jason didn't hesitate alerting the security on ground. "Sammy, take a look at this," said Jason.

Sammy looked into the CCTV and watched the sniffer dog going back and forth but not getting to Freddie, he immediately called Phil on radio but sadly, Phil wasn't picking up. "Wow, Jason, it's the same guy," said Sammy.

"Then let's find out what he has in that bag," said Jason.

Sammy hastily stepped out of the CCTV room to alert the security on the ground, but firstly, he'd to alert Phil who walks the sniffer dog. Funnily, when Phil saw Sammy rushing towards him, he thought Sammy' needed a quick wee away from the usual urinal allocated for that purpose, but not this time.

"What's up, Sammy, and why're you in a rush?" asked Phil.

"Why wouldn't I be when you aren't picking up your radio? Your dog is acting strange each time she comes close to that guy, and you've failed to notice it," said Sammy.

"I think the dog is just tired, that's all, but if you noticed anything from the CCTV, then let's take him in for questioning," said Phil. Moments later, Phil and Sam approached Freddie and excused him from the queue. Sadly, Freddie's world is about to unravel before his eyes, and his planned marriage to Sherry about to go up in smoke.

"Officer, why're you taking me out from the queue?" asked Freddie.

Ronny, one of the officers conducting searches in the airport, quickly interjected. "Sorry, it's just for a quick search," she said.

"I'm clean, and it's almost my turn," Freddie insists.

"Don't worry, in a few minutes, it'll all be sorted," she said, then opened the bag, started the search and immediately found bags of Cocaine.

Freddie's absurdity was on display and his mockery got the best of him as he screamed in pretence. "How did that get there?" asked Freddie.

"It's your bag, and your drugs, but you'll have to answer to that," said Ronny.

Freddie was arrested immediately and put in cuffs. "Stop, stop, it's not mine, and I don't know whose it is," said Freddie.

Moments later, Sammy returned to the CCTV room. "Jason, our hunch wasn't wrong, that guy has eight kilograms of cocaine with him," said Sammy.

"That's good, thanks to agent Donald who noticed it," said Jason. Moments later, Jason brought out his phone and immediately dialled Agent Donald.

"What are you doing?" asked Sammy.

"I'm calling Agent Donald. He said, if and whenever we catch this guy, I should let him know," said Jason. But the self-indulgent and highly irritable Sammy seemed not to think getting Donald involved is a good idea, he finds Jason to be overly patronising. "Why! Is he the only FBI detective in New York? Moreover, I don't think this matter is for the FBI," said Sammy.

"He just wants to know what this guy did, that made him able to beat our sniffer dog," said Jason.

"Ok, that won't be a bad idea," said Sammy.

"Hello Jason, how're you doing?" asked Agent Donald.

Jason didn't hesitate before hitting the nail on the head. "Detective, we have the guy," he said, but the agent has a lot going and seems not to remember he'd a pending conversation with these CCTV security personnel.

"Jason what are you talking about? I seem to be lost here," said Agent Donald.

"Do you remember three months ago when you're reviewing the CCTV for Teddy Bush, you spotted our sniffer dog not being able to sniff a particular guy?" asked Jason.

"Erm.., now I remember, did you find anything with him?" asked Agent Donald.

"We searched his bag and found eight kilograms of cocaine," he said.

The detective's keen interest in this particular case isn't about what was found on Freddie, but what he did to keep the dog at bay. "Did you search him, and did you find out how he was able to beat the dog?" asked Agent Donald.

"They didn't find anything on him, but he has been taken in for interrogation," Jason replied.

The next morning Agent Donald needed to come face to face with Freddie in the interrogation room even though this wasn't his case and he'd to come with Agent Barry.

"Barry, there's this guy we'll have to interrogate; maybe our findings will help us be more proactive," said Agent Donald.

"What's it about, and what did he do?" he asked.

"That guy the surveillance camera showed at the airport, the guy the sniffer dog was avoiding," said Agent Donald.

"Oh, if he's in custody, then it'll be good to make him pay for beating our security," said Agent Barry.

"Barry, this isn't about beating security or making him pay, he definitely will pay, but my interest is what he did to beat the security," said Agent Donald.

"Where's he being held?" asked Agent Barry.

"South Bridge station, we've to get going, so we can be part of the interrogation," said Agent Donald.

Moments later, the two detectives left the office but as they attempt to get into the car, Barry rushed back towards the office. "Barry, why're you going back?" asked Agent Donald.

"Sorry, I left my badge on my desk," he said. He picked his badge, rushed out and joined Agent Donald and they continued and not long, they arrived at the South Bridge unit of NYPD, while the interrogation was already in progress.

"Hello Lieutenant," said Agent Donald.

Interestingly, Lieutenant Rose is a familiar face, and she was the NYPD officer handling the case. She sensed a mission creep the moment she saw the detectives and didn't hesitate to remind them she doesn't think they have an appointment, before asking what they're doing in her unit.

Agent Donald realised he isn't getting past Lieutenant Rose who wouldn't want to touch Agent Barry with a ten-foot barge pole, without applying a little charm to win her soft side.

"I'm interested in the man caught at the airport with eight kilo-grams of cocaine," said Agent Donald.

"Why? That isn't your jurisdiction, and I don't think I'll allow you interfere with my investigation," said Lieutenant Rose.

Agent Barry immediately interjected in his usual manner, as he gave the Lieutenant his unblinkingly brutal banter. "Why must you look for every opportunity to make yourself important?" he said.

Lieutenant Rose wasn't keen to get dirty with Barry, and her perception of him is that Barry isn't such a good guy, and neither is he the bad guy, he's a bit of a mixed bag really.

"Barry, every Cop in New York knows you're mouthy, so I wouldn't waste valuable time running my mouth with you," Lieutenant Rose retorted.

"Donald, can you hear her call me mouthy? I think we'll have to go," said Agent Barry.

Agent Barry is a man who banters yet he himself can't take the banter, a fitting comparism with an arsonist who hates the sight of fire. He's like a stun grenade, and funnily, he doesn't like the heat yet wants to remain in the kitchen. Agent Donald understands what it means to rattle the Lieutenants' cage, and this kerfuffle could derail Agent Donald's interest in this investigation, unless he intervenes to dial things down.

"Be patient, Barry. Rose, I knew for sure this case isn't within our jurisdiction, that was why I called you this morning to seek your permission to be a part of it," said Agent Donald.

"Did you call me this morning?" she asked.

Of course, I did, but you didn't pick up and this is what I was trying to avoid," he said.

"The truth is, I haven't checked my phone since I resumed work, and sorry I didn't pick up your call," she said.

"All we wanted to know is how this guy was able to beat the sniffer dog? Maybe it'll help us in our jobs," said Agent Donald.

"Then you're welcome to be part of this interrogation," said Lieutenant Rose.

"Thank you, Rose," said Agent Donald.

Now that they've succeeded Agent Barry tried to flip things around with a smile. "Rosie, thank you," he said.

Lieutenant Rose smiled. "I did this for Donald and not you, Barry," she said.

"At least you've done it, and it doesn't matter who you did it for," Agent Barry retorted.

"Your vulgarity could cost you your career and you'd better watch it, Barry," replied the Lieutenant.

Moments later, Agent Donald joined Freddie in the Interrogation room, and sat opposite him as he begins the interrogation.

"Look detective, I've said I wouldn't say a word, except in the presence of my lawyer," Freddie protested.

"I understand you want to enjoy cover from your lawyer. Then who put that thing in your bag?" Agent Donald asked.

Freddie remained stone-faced as he continued to deny knowledge of the content of his bag. He kept a straight face without blinking even as he masked the guilt of being caught. Sadly, Freddie has got no alibi this time, and his marriage to Sherry is about to go down the drain.

"As I said earlier, I don't know how it got there," said Freddie.

"Stop being cheeky, Freddie. We can arrange a deal but that'll be if only you tell me the one thing I want to hear," said Agent Donald.

"Ok, first thing first, what's the deal?" he asked.

"I'll ensure we cut down on your sentence," said Agent Donald.

"To what extent will my sentence be cut down, if you want me to cooperate?" asked Freddie.

"At least between twenty-five and thirty percent, it might be more, but this is the much I can promise you for now," replied Agent Donald as he reassured Freddie.

"Now, what do you want to know?" Freddie asked.

"What did you do that make the sniffer dog stay away from you, are you into some kind of voodoo or are you carrying anything that's kind of putting the dog off?" the detective asked.

"Of course, not, I wasn't carrying anything, at least your guys checked me and didn't find anything," he said.

"Then what did you do?" Agent Donald queried further.

Freddie is now like a man in a crocodile infested water with the option of sink or swim, and would rather think of giving the gator something to get busy with, than attempt swimming. He realised swimming out of this will only be possibly if he gives something away. He read the detective's facial disposition and realised there isn't any need playing 'catch me if you can', as this could imply his deal is off. He quickly decided to give the detective something to keep his deal, and that means throwing Jimmy Thompson in the deep end. Sadly, Freddie's betrayal of throwing Jimmy under the bus is sucker punch, and that means Jimmy's drifter's myth and invincibility is now over.

"Ok, it was Jimmy Thompson who helped me with this idea," said Freddie.

"Which Jimmy Thompson are you talking about, and is it the famous Jimmy Thompson you're referring to?" asked Agent Donald.

"Of course, yes, the famous Jimmy Thompson. I thought the guy was just a myth, until I met him," said Freddie.

"Yeah, I know Jimmy is a real person, but a lot of people think he doesn't exist, and what's the idea he gave you?" asked Agent Donald.

"He asked me to sew and pad my bag with the skin of one of those big cats," said Freddie.

"Big cats! I don't understand you?" asked Agent Donald.

"Yeah, the skin of a lion, leopard, hyena or tiger, which ever," Freddie said.

Agent Donald couldn't get his head around what the skin of a big cat has to do with moving the shipment of cocaine yet continued patiently as he queried further.

"And what has that got to do with this?" asked Agent Donald.

"With a little patch of such skin in my bag, the dog cannot come close because those animals are superior and the dog cannot stand around with the smell that signifies the presence of a superior predator," said Freddie.

Agent Donald Marvelled at the idea behind this trick to beat the airport security. "Oh, now I get it, where the hell did Jimmy get his idea from?" Agent Donald asked curiously.

"I never thought it would work, but it worked," said Freddie.

"Where can I find this Jimmy? I knew he exists but I've never met him," said Agent Donald.

"I've told you what you want to know, what about my deal?" asked Agent Donald.

"The deal is still in place, I keep my word, but one more thing, how do I find Jimmy?" asked Agent Donald.

"I don't know, but I met him at the Criss Crescent Bar, behind the Milky Way Street," said Freddie.

"Ok, thank you, I'll get the paperwork for your deal ready," said Agent Donald.

"I'm looking forward to it, detective," replied Freddie. Agent Donald leaves the interrogation room and joined Lieutenant Rose and agent Barry who were observing the interrogation. Sadly, Agent Barry didn't allow Agent Donald to say a word before debunking all what Freddie has said.

"What that guy said isn't true, how come he knows Jimmy Thomson?" said Agent Donald.

"How can we ever move forward, if we never believe anybody? You must trust someone at some point," said Agent Donald.

"But not to believe a drug trafficker!" Agent Barry exclaimed.

Agent Barry seems not to be familiar with the old saying, there are three sides to every story. "Yours, theirs, and the truth." Maybe Freddie is telling the truth this time.

"Ok, don't believe him, Barry, but believe me," Agent Donald replied, then walked up to Lieutenant Rose. "Please tear his bag open, to see if it's padded with an animal skin," said Agent Donald.

"If he did, then that'll be animal cruelty, his sentence will be doubled and the deal cancelled," said Agent Barry.

Agent Donald was plagued by Barry's continuous nagging and fits of tantrums, then decided to call Barry aside. "Why do you talk with so much paranoia? Do you know you're creating a scene? Look around," said Agent Donald.

Agent Barry turned around and noticed eyes were on him, and suddenly realised there isn't any need rocking the boat, particularly when their host is just doing them a favour of being a part of this case. "Ok I get you, I'm sorry," said Agent Barry.

After twenty minutes of going back and forth Freddie's bag was torn apart and the Hyena skin used to pad the bag was discovered, making his confession true.

Agent Donald pleaded with the Lieutenant, requesting her to allow them take Freddie so he will take them to Jimmy Thompson the next day morning, but the Lieutenant immediately sounded a note of caution, accusing the detectives of creeping into her case.

"This isn't about me; there's something I want to learn from this case, and it's still your case," said Agent Donald.

Nothing irritates Lieutenant Rose like when detectives' creep into her case and take it over, even in the most exceptional circumstance just as the one at hand, she still finds it quite annoying. "What's it you want to learn from my case?" asked Lieutenant Rose.

Agent Donald interjected in a bid to justify his request, suggesting that these are crazy ideas, and he's keen to learn more from it. Maybe one day he could save just a life from whatever he's able to glean from this case.

"Your combative determination to catch this Jimmy Thompson startles me, Donald," the Lieutenant said.

Donald had to remind the lieutenant that the wisdom of a detective isn't always acquired formally and in most cases it's through incidents like this that they grow in knowledge.

"Then by this time tomorrow I'll be expecting you," the Lieutenant said.

By the next evening Freddie took the detectives to the Criss Crescent bar to help them identify Jimmy Thompson, but as they alighted from the car Freddie needed to save face and asked that the cuffs be taken off. Sadly, Agent Barry turned to Freddie and asked if he's having a laugh making a request he would never agree to, and he obviously isn't having it. "I'm not running away, and why don't you take off the handcuffs from my hands?" Freddie asked politely.

"That won't be possible, you've a long sentence ahead of you." said Agent Barry.

Agent Donald thought of taking the cuffs off Freddie, but he then decided not to irk Agent Barry any further. "Ok don't worry, let me use this to cover the handcuffs," Agent Donald said as took off his coat and placed it on the handcuffs, and they alighted from the car and walked into the bar.

"Ok thanks." Freddie replied, and Immediately Freddie entered the bar, he saw Raymond and then he walked up to him. "Is Jimmy here?" asked Freddie.

Dismally, Freddie's pal Raymond was at the bar as the detectives walked Freddie into the bar and Raymond immediately understood that Freddie was in trouble, even though the detectives gave him some space. "Jimmy isn't here," Raymond replied. "When last did you see him?" Freddie asked further. Raymond was careful not to let out too much information as he suddenly became economical with the truth. "I haven't seen him for quite some time," said Raymond.

Freddie walked back to the detectives. "They said they haven't seen him," said Freddie.

"For how long have they not seen him?" Agent Barry queried further.

"A few days back," said Freddie.

"You're sure about this? I hope you aren't letting him escape?" asked Agent Donald.

"I wouldn't do that, because I still want the deal," said Freddie.

"What do you intend to do, Donald?" asked Agent Barry.

On a second thought, Agent Donald decided to think on his feet, and came up with a plan B. He immediately suggested he will review the CCTV footage in the bar and Freddie will identify and pinpoint Jimmy from the footage.

"Yeah, another good idea," said Agent Barry.

Minutes later, Agent Donald approached the Bar manager to request the CCTV footage. Sadly, Paul Grandee, the bar manager who has been Jimmy's childhood friend isn't selling him out so easily. "Hello, I'm detective Donald," said Agent Donald.

"Ok, I'm Paul, Paul Grandee, and what can I do for you?" he asked.

"Do you know Jimmy Thompson?" asked Agent Donald.

Paul Grandee burst into laughter "Why should I know him? People believe he's a myth and doesn't exist, so I think the same way as well," said Paul.

Paul's rhetoric attracted Agent Barry who doesn't hesitate in making difficult people feel small and putting them in their place. Barry sounded like a Rottweiler when he looked at Paul who isn't willing to accede to the detectives' request. "Paul, look at me, you think he doesn't exist because people think he doesn't exist, or you don't know him?" asked Agent Barry.

"I said I don't know him," he responded.

"Your face doesn't look like you're telling the truth," said Agent Barry.

"I've told you the truth, except you already have a different truth you're expecting from me," said Paul.

"Ok Paul, we'll need to review the CCTV since you said you don't know him, maybe Freddie will help us identify him," said Agent Donald. Sad to say, that Paul isn't giving these detectives a free pass to his friend. He immediately asked if they have a warrant because they haven't a cat in hell's chance that he would allow them scrutinize his CCTV images.

"Will that be necessary?" asked Agent Donald.

"Considering the circumstance, yes, it'll be necessary," said Paul.

"What circumstance are you talking about? I hope you aren't thinking of wiping stuff from the CCTV?" asked Agent Barry.

"If that's what you're thinking, I'm not into that," said Paul.

"You'll go to jail if you do that," Agent Barry retorted.

The detectives spared Paul the third degree and left the Criss Crescent Bar taking Freddie with them, and promised to return with a warrant to access the CTTV so as to uncover the personality of Jimmy Thompson.

Meanwhile, Jimmy was busy frolicking with the newly divorced Alicia, not knowing he has been outed by Freddie, though his sixth sense tells him this might happen but he has no knowledge of the degree of his trouble. A week later in the Cayman Island, Alicia asked Jimmy to get dressed because a cab was enroute, and will soon be at the hotel's car park waiting for them. He inquisitively asked what the destination was.

"It's just 10.am, and we're used to going out in the evenings, why're we going out this morning?" he asked.

Alicia kept the destination up her sleeve and didn't divulge too much about her plans for the day, as she didn't want to spoil the surprises she has lined up for Jimmy.

She interjected and reminded him that she has been taking him out since they arrived the Cayman Islands and it has all been perfect. "Why don't you continue to trust my judgement," said Alicia.

Since the cab man is still enroute Jimmy felt he still had some time to play around with Alicia who's already putting on her make-up. He pulled her into the bed. "Come here, let's have some fun, the taxi can wait," he said.

"We'll continue when we come back, but for now get up and get dressed," she said.

He got up from the bed, dressed up, and minutes later the cab came to pick them up and they drove to the Devil's Grotto.

"Where are we?" he asked.

"This place is called the Devil's Grotto," said Alicia.

"The Devil's what!" exclaimed Jimmy.

"The Devil's Grotto," Alicia echoed and pointed to a signpost "read that," she said.

"The name sounds weird, it's like the Devil himself lives here," said Jimmy.

Alicia went further to dispel Jimmy's fears by letting the cat out of the bag, as she made the expectation known to Jimmy, even before they drove into the swimming park.

"No, it's a diving spot, and you'll love it. Each time I come to the Cayman Islands, I don't fail to come here, and the experience is second to none," she said.

"But I can't swim," said Jimmy.

"Erm.., you can't swim! What a shame?" Alicia surprisingly asked, because she's among the few Americans that think all American men can swim.

"Yeah, I can't, so why should I go diving into this Devil's Grotto as they call it?" Jimmy retorted.

She became quite jocular as she made jest of Jimmy, and said it's sad to say, that he's the first American man she has seen that can't swim, but urged him not to worry, because the interesting thing is, this place is both for beginners and experts alike.

The cab dropped them off and they walked straight and bought swimwear and costumes, then they went on walking around enjoying the sight of this nature's wonder.

"Where do I start then? At least I want to enjoy the experience with you," said Jimmy.

Alicia crossed her arm around Jimmy's shoulder pointing out the beginners' corner to Jimmy. "Start over there, maybe this experience will spur you into learning how to swim," said Alicia.

Having a spot for beginners didn't dissuade Jimmy over his fears, as the confidence to deal with this waterfall is still lacking. "Join me here, to encourage me into doing this," he pleads. Moments after changing into their swimming wears, Alicia jumped into the pool but soon realised Jimmy is still afraid of stepping in, so she left her corner and joined Jimmy. "Ok, let's do it together," she said.

Jimmy held her by the hand and chuckled. "Who should go first? I suggest you take the lead," he said.

"Ok, let me go first, and then you join me," she said and dived into the water.

Jimmy continued to drag his feet, as he yelled from outside the water "How is it?" he asked.

"It's all fun, come on," she said to Jimmy.

Jimmy braced himself and jumped into the water even though he's still afraid, but enjoyed it after landing in the water. "Oh, this is fun and I like it," he said.

Alicia burst into laughter. "I'm glad you like it," she said.

"Yeah, let's do this again," he said.

They went back and continued jumping and splashing into the pool together for a while, and not long Jimmy is able to continue alone. After about an hour frolicking around in the pool, Alicia drew closer to Jimmy, as she thinks it's time to take some recess. "Jimmy, let's have something to drink," Alicia said.

They left the water and went to the poolside bar, and moments later Alicia was holding her glass of Champaign. "When we return to the pool you'll continue where you were, while I'll go to the top and dive right from there," she said.

"You mean that height?" Jimmy asked, pointing to the highest diving point, "isn't that risky?" he queried further.

"No, it isn't, that's my favourite diving spot," she said.

"Ok then, have your fun," said Jimmy.

After spending quality time enjoying the Devil's Grotto, they returned to the hotel and remained indoors for the rest of the day. Moreover, Agent Donald has obtained a warrant that empowered him to review the CCTV cameras installed in the Criss Crescent Bar, and Paul can't obfuscate his friend any longer.

The moment they arrived at the Criss Crescent bar Agent Donald asked Agent Barry to stay with Freddie in the car, while he gets the Bar manager's attention.

"Ok Donald," Barry immediately became tacky the moment Donald stepped away, he then turned to Freddie. "You must stay put and stop nodding your head," said Agent Barry.

Freddie was already frustrated with the highly irritable nature of Agent Barry and didn't hesitate to register his protest. "What's it with you?" asked Freddie.

While Freddie muttered continually over Agent Barry's disdain for him, Agent Donald walked back and joined them, Donald immediately urged Barry to stop the pettiness, saying they don't need that because this is a public place, and there's no need creating a scene. Agent Barry reluctantly piped down, as he waited in the car for Agent Donald to get Paul to make things ready for the CTV review. "Hey Paul, how're you?" asked Agent Donald. Unsurprisingly, Paul wasn't in any mood for pleasantries, no jokes either.

"Detective, do you have a warrant?" asked Paul without flinching or batting his eyelid.

Of course, I do," said Agent Donald who then handed the warrant over to Paul.

After going through the warrant and realising there isn't a way out. "Ok, give me a minute; let me give this drink to a customer," said Paul.

Minutes later, it's all set and ready, and Agent Donald called Agent Barry to bring Freddie in. They went inside the bar manager's office where the CCTV was being played "Are we all set?" asked Agent Barry.

"Yeah, Freddie, just watch and let me know the moment you spot Jimmy Thompson," said Agent Donald.

Paul Grandee can't do much at this point, yet he can still display some attitude, Paul looked at Freddie with disgust as he nods at Agent Donald's request. "Detectives, I don't want this man spending time in my office," Paul protested.

Funnily, Agent Barry isn't having anyone displaying attitude around him, even Paul's mild attitude irritates Barry. "Paul, do you know I saw that look in your face? Are you hiding anything?" asked Agent Barry.

"Detective, the CCTV is what you came for, that's it playing, and when you're done, I'll need my office to myself, but if you've bones to pick with me, I suggest you spit it out," said Paul.

Agent Barry's organic distemper meant he lacks the wiggle room for creating a warm ambience, and he couldn't help himself but stir up mud with his own feet at the slightest opportunity. Sadly, this detective can't do without the banter, even though he hates being bantered. "I understand your frustration, and as you can see, we're about to discover your Jimmy Thompson who takes shelter in your bar," said Agent Barry.

After reviewing the CCTV for a while, Freddie spotted Jimmy. "That's him, that's Jimmy Thompson," he said.

"Is that him and are you sure?" asked Agent Barry.

"Yeah, that's Jimmy Thompson," said Freddie.

"I've seen this man a couple of times, he knew who I was, but I didn't know he was Jimmy Thompson," said Agent Donald.

"Where did you see him?" asked Agent Barry.

"The first was inside the train, and he asked to take a look at the newspaper in my hand, but the other I can't remember," said Agent Donald.

Agent Barry turned to the bar Manger. "Your friend has been uncovered, no more secrets," Agent Barry said.

Agent Donald thanked Freddie for his assistance and urged him not worry, that his deal is intact. Agent Barry interjected immediately. "But you said you've seen Jimmy Thompson before, so I don't think this deal should stand," he said.

"You're an overzealous detective, and why're you like this?" Freddie retorted.

"Barry, I've given him my word, and I can't go back on it," replied Agent Donald.

Agent Barry turned to Freddie and told him today is his lucky day, but just as the detectives turned to leave, Agent Donald calls Paul's attention and points to Jimmy in the CCTV footage.

"In case this man comes here, call me," he said and gave his card to Paul.

Days later, Alicia called her usual Cab driver to take them out for the night.

"Hello Rafael, will you be available by 8.pm tonight?" asked Alicia.

"Of course, I'll make myself available if you want me to come around," said Rafael.

"Now, I'm convinced you're a real businessman, Rafael," Alicia replied jocularly.

"Anything that brings in the money shouldn't be taken for granted," Rafael replied.

"I'll want you to take us to club tonight, will you be available by 8.pm?" Alicia queried further. After her conversation with Rafael, Alicia turned to Jimmy. "Get dressed, let's go clubbing and burn off some fat," she said. Alicia then begun making jocular gestures with some dance moves, accentuating her waist and punching her fist in the air.

"You don't have to burn off any more fat, you look perfect just the way you're," said Jimmy.

Two hours later, they arrived the Oceans Night Club, a place that's purely for the over 30's. "Oh, this club is for the mature," said Jimmy.

"This club is not meant for boys pretending to be men; it is only for the mature mind," Alicia replied.

After about twenty minutes of dancing and giggling between the pairs, Rafael walked up to Alicia and said he will wait for her and Jimmy in his car, and when they're ready to go, he'll take them back to the hotel.

Alicia was upfront with her jokes with Rafael as she asked him if he's a boy or a man, in her casual display of her humorous side. "Oh Alicia, you know I'm a man," he said and chuckled.

"Then why do you want to chicken out? Come inside and enjoy yourself, I'll foot the bill," she said.

Rafael smiled and walked to the bar to get his choice of brandy. "Thank you, Alicia," said Rafael.

Jimmy was a drifter whose lifestyle of being a thief never gave him the privilege of having a steady relationship since the death of his wife, this few moments with Alicia was one to be remembered as he's now drowned in excitement of what's supposedly a healthy relationship. "Oh, this club isn't about the dance steps; it's about the joining of the minds on the dance floor," said Jimmy.

"Are you now into poetry or what?" asked Alicia.

"Your bringing me to this club has provoked my poetic skills," he said and smiled.

"Are you sure alcohol isn't responsible for this? There's so much fun here, let's enjoy the best of it," she said.

"I'm still within my limit, so this isn't the alcohol," said Jimmy, who's overwhelmed by emotion. Moments later, Alicia tapped Jimmy on the shoulder. "Jimmy, look at that," she said. She pointed to Rafael who was dancing with a lady. "Rafael has found himself a dance partner," said Alicia.

"Tell me Rafael has found himself a woman, from what I'm seeing this will extend beyond the dance floor," Jimmy replied, and they laughed hysterically.

"Rafael is of mature mind, it's just that he's putting business first, which is the right thing to do," said Alicia.

An hour later, it's time to go, but Jimmy's excitement means he will like a repeat of the experience. "I like this, can we do this again?" asked Jimmy.

"Since you like it, then we'll," she replied. Alicia and Jimmy stayed a little longer, and they'd so much fun but about 11.30pm they left the club and Rafael took them back to the hotel after a pulsating night out. The next day, as the pair continues to have their forever fun, and as far as Jimmy is concerned if this is a dream, he'd rather not wake up from it. Things could get sour between this romantic pair, as Alicia discovers the identity of Jimmy Thompson after three weeks into their stay together in the hotel. Alicia lay on the bed while Jimmy's phone rang. "Jimmy, your phone is ringing," she said.

Jimmy couldn't leave the bathroom, as he was in the middle of taking his shower. "Who's it, that's calling?" he asked.

"Hmm, I don't know, but let me see if the name of the caller appeared on your screen," said Alicia.

Jimmy has been so hooked up by his love for Alicia, and he's now beginning to play house with Alicia and funnily, he has inadvertently let his guard down.

"Please do," he replied.

"It's Jerry Tomball," said Jimmy.

"Oh, that's my son Jerry; just tell him I'll call him back," Jimmy said. Alicia took the call. "Hello Jerry," said Alicia.

"Yes, this is Jerry, is my dad there?" he asked.

"Your dad?" she repeated, even though Jimmy mentioned to her that Jerry is his son.

"Yes, my dad, Jimmy Thompson," he replied.

"He said I should tell you he'll call you back," she said, but sadly for Jimmy, the name Jimmy Thompson could not leave Alicia's memory. She just couldn't shirk this feeling off, and her hunch serendipitously tells her there's more to this man she's sharing a room with than meets the eye.

Not long after Jimmy left the bathroom "I promised Jerry I'd see him before travelling but sadly, I couldn't make it," he said. Alicia couldn't hold her peace as she interjected immediately. "Are you the popular Jimmy Thompson people talk about?" she asked in a soft-spoken tone. Jimmy was speechless for a moment yet decided to let the cat out of the bag, with hope that Alicia's interest in him will help, and as they say, love covers multitude of sin. "If you really want to know, yes, and why're you asking?" he asked. "Wait a minute! Is this a joke or what, you mean you're the much talked about Jimmy Thompson?" she asked curiously.

"Yes, that's me, and I'm sorry I never told you about this all along," said Jimmy.

"I can't believe my eyes and ears that you're the Jimmy Thompson I've been hearing about since I was in my twenties," she retorted, with this sense of foreboding reflected in her broken voice.

"Actually, I've lived all my life trying to remain invisible and it has helped me stay hidden," he said trying to explain himself further.

"I always thought you were a myth, that the name Jimmy Thompson was some kind of figure of speech," she said. Jimmy realised the news wasn't well received by Alicia as her facial disposition wasn't expressing amusement but disgust. Jimmy is now faced with the prospects of either tucking his tail between his legs and finding his way or stay around while trying to pacify Alicia.

"Now that you know and fate has brought us together, should I move out?" he asked to know where his fate lies with Alicia.

"It would've been better if we stop seeing each other, but I've already fallen in love with you," said Alicia.

Jimmy realised he'd to tread with caution particularly now that Alicia knows too much "Don't worry; I won't cause you any trouble," he replied.

"Is Jimmy Thompson your real name or an alias?" asked Alicia, as she queried further.

"No, it isn't my real name, it's an alias," said Jimmy.

"Then what's your real name, and why did your son expose you to me?" Alicia asked curiously.

"Jim Tomball is my real name, my son wants me to come out of the shadows and I don't know why he made this move now," said Jimmy.

"No wonder, because if it's your real name, the police would have tracked you through your information in their data base," she retorted.

"I've learnt to live in the background. That's why I haven't been in the police net," Jimmy replied.

Realising she has been frolicking with a renowned thief whose conscience to take from people doesn't prick him. She is now plagued with the thought that Jimmy has intentionally been stringing her along all this while, and she never saw it.

"But how am I sure you haven't stolen from me since we got here?" she asked, her suspicion suddenly takes the best of her. This sudden turn of even rattles Jimmy's cage, making him coil further into his shell, and wriggling out of this quagmire might be an arduous task, yet he'd to stay and deal with. "Why would I do that? It wouldn't be an honourable thing to do," said Jimmy. "I'll have to go through all my stuff to be sure it is all intact. I just can't believe you blindly," replied Alicia.

Jimmy and Alicia have remained cooped in the hotel room for the next two days after Alicia discovers Jimmy's identity. It's now undeniable that the ambience within the room is now a bit moody, yet they kept things courteous and civil.

"What have you planned out for today, and where will the fun be today?" asked Jimmy.

"Let's just spend some time in the bar within the hotel at least that'll be ok," said Alicia.

"Alicia, I noticed since you discovered my true identity, you've stopped going out with me," said Jimmy.

"I like you, Jimmy, but I just don't have to be foolish, you already have a reputation which precedes you, and I wouldn't let you rub it off on me," Alicia replied.

"But no one knows me here, if my son hadn't called and you picked the call you wouldn't have known of my true identity," said Jimmy.

"But I've my reservations and that's human nature, I can't pretend everything is ok, when I don't feel it is," Alicia insists. It's now glaringly obvious that things have gone south and Jimmy is now in a bind, yet trying to hold things together.

"I'm sorry, I ruined your holiday," said Jimmy.

"No, you didn't, you spiced it up for me. It's me that ruined yours," Alicia said, as she tried to keep things civil. But Jimmy felt the best thing to do is take the blame and absolve Alicia of every wrong doing irrespective of how she chooses to react to the situation at hand.

He then comforted her saying after a divorce Alicia travelled to the Cayman Islands to clear her head and be happy, but he just made the whole thing cold for her with all this his Jimmy Thompsons' story.

The pair had a light-hearted tiff, but he avoided being misunderstood even as Alicia felt its best not to fire some cheap shot at him.

"Don't worry, get dressed and let's go to the bar and do things that'll make us laugh. Fortunately, the live band is playing today," she said as she tries to make light of the situation.

It didn't take long before Jimmy and Alicia dressed up, and went to the bar.

The next day Jimmy Thompson got a call from Paul Grandee who's obviously aware that Jimmy's invincibility has come to an end, and it won't be long before this drifter's hands will be in cuffs. Jimmy picked the call and stepped aside as he communicates with Paul.

"Hello Jimmy, are you ok?" asked Paul. "Yeah, I'm fine Paul, what's up?" said Jimmy.

"The FBI was here," he said.

"What did they come to do? I don't seem to get you clearly," Jimmy replied.

"They were here for you, there's this guy, Freddie. Though, I don't know him, he's the one that brought them to me," said Paul.

"I knew it would come to this, and what did you tell them?" asked Jimmy. Paul Grandee is a man known for his unwavering commitment to friendship. It's now obvious that he couldn't obfuscate his friend any longer, particularly now that he needed to avoid being sucked into the wild wind of this FBI investigation.

"I told them nothing, but they later came with a warrant to view the CCTV," said Paul.

"You mean the cops now have my face?" Jimmy curiously asked.

"Yeah, Jimmy, and I'm sorry, I did all I could to keep them away," said Paul.

"I knew it would come to this one day, but what I didn't know was how," said Jimmy.

"What are you going to do now, Jimmy?" asked Paul.

"I don't know what to do yet. I just need some time to figure something out," he said, hoping his sixth sense will come handy.

After four weeks in the Cayman Islands frolicking with recently divorced Alicia, it's now time for Jimmy and Alicia to return to the United States.

Alicia observed that Jimmy was dawdling while she packs her bag, she then asked why he isn't packing his bags, reminding him they are leaving next day, except he isn't leaving yet. She then proceeded to say that as for her, she's leaving by morning of the next day.

"Alicia," said Jimmy. Alicia then stopped what she was doing and focussed on Jimmy. "If the hands of the clock could be turned back, I would be a man who isn't a thief," said Jimmy.

"Why're you sounding like this?" she laughed. "Are you just realising it's a bad thing to be a thief," said Alicia. Funnily Alicia's emotion for Jimmy seems to have waned, and she doesn't have time for something that looks more like bedtime stories.

"The love you've showed me and your reactions from the day you uncovered my true identity, made me realise that being a thief isn't a good thing, and I've missed the true love I just found," said Jimmy.

"It's not too late to turn your life around. Start now before it's late, but why aren't you packing your things?" asked Alicia.

"I've a case to answer in the United States, though it isn't about a crime I committed," said Jimmy.

"Then what's it, a lot of strange things about you are beginning to unfold, now I get why you're reluctant to pack your bags," she said. Alicia is now bored by Jimmy's excuses, and nothing he says now makes sense.

"You already know everything about me Alicia, there isn't anything unfolding," he retorted.

"Is this why you came to the Cayman Islands? I'm ashamed of myself; I was running from my husband because he's suffering from mid-life crises, only to end up with a thief," said Alicia.

"I didn't steal, Alicia!" Jimmy exclaimed.

"Then what did you do, that has made the Cops to be looking for you?" asked Alicia.

"I only advised someone and the advice helped the person to beat the Cops," he said.

Alicia advised Jimmy to go and face the cops and do the time, instead of looking for sympathy from her, because she doesn't have any to give. It's now obvious that whatever Jimmy had to say seem not to make any sense to Alicia whose mind is made up, as she considers Jimmy a negative force who should be kept at bay.

"Ok, you seem to hate me more tonight," said Jimmy.

After moments of going back and forth, Jimmy went to bed, and funnily, Jimmy woke up in the middle of the night and was surprised to find Alicia sitting with her bags. "Alicia, why're you still awake, it's midnight, and why aren't you sleeping?" asked Jimmy.

Alicia is now overwhelmed by suspicion that this thief by her side could undo her and steal her belonging, especially now that it's obvious that this guy by her side has got no address and no permanent location. "I don't want you to steal from me," she said in soft spoken manner.

"How, what do you mean by stealing from you?" he asked curiously.

"You might take something belonging to me and run away to somewhere in the Cayman Islands, because you know I'll be travelling by morning and will not be able to go after you," said Alicia.

Jimmy was rattled by this sudden new twist thrown into the mix of events, yet efforts to make Alicia see him in a good light seem to have fallen on deaf ears. "Is this how bad your thoughts about me have become! Why would I do such a thing after all you've done for me, am I that cold and heartless?" he asked.

"You must be cold and heartless to steal from people. Have you imagined how many people you've made to weep?" asked Alicia.

"Don't worry, for your sake I've stopped stealing, because I don't want to lose you," he said, as he tries to salvage what's left of the relationship.

"You've lost me already. Do you think I'll put myself at risk by going out with you?" she queried further.

"What risk?" Jimmy asked.

Alicia understands that the risk of associating with a known thief will be catastrophic to her reputation and had to severe every tie with Jimmy to avoid any possible drama with the cops that'll make her business suffer. Jimmy sat up and tried to pull her to himself, in his attempt to make her go back to bed, at least to tone the tension down, but she isn't ready to play along and insists on watching over her stuff.

"Please come to bed, Alicia. Stop punishing yourself, I'll do no such thing to you," he insists.

"Stop, stop Jimmy. You're on the run, and don't want to go back to the United States, so I prefer to stay with my luggage," she protested.

"Ok, I'll go back to the United States with you to face the cops. Maybe that'll put your fears to rest," said Jimmy.

"Erm.., that'll be good, but I'm still not taking my eyes off my luggage," she insists.

After much drama Jimmy decided to let Alicia be and went back to sleep. By morning Jimmy and Alicia left the hotel, they said their goodbyes, awkwardly anyway, and Alicia flew straight to Los Angeles, while Jimmy flew back to New York.

On his arrival to New York, Jimmy went straight to the Cris Crescent Bar to see Paul Grandee. He stood outside, in front of the bar for about five minutes, watching as the customers sauntered into the bar one after the other, before walking in.

"Hey man! When did you come back?" asked Paul.

"I returned earlier today, how're you?" said Jimmy.

" You're asking me about how I feel? I feel like crap because you've been exposed by Freddie," Paul retorted.

"What do you advise I do now?" asked Jimmy.

"Go to the cops and sort things out, before they come here and start dragging you around," Paul advised.

"How do I locate the detective that came for me?" asked Jimmy.

Paul Grandee opened one of the drawers, brought out a card and gave it to Jimmy. One of them gave me his card; you can give him a call, and I wish you luck.

"Thanks for being a friend," Jimmy said, and left the bar.

Not long after leaving the bar Jimmy called Agent Donald. After all, there isn't any other option other than facing up to his nemesis.

"Hello, is that Donald Whitley?" asked Jimmy.

"Yes, this is detective Donald Whitley, who's on the line please? He asked.

"This is Jimmy Thompson; I learnt you were looking for me," he said.

Agent Donald smiled on his side of the phone. "Yes, we want you for questioning over your involvement with Freddie," he said.

"What have I done wrong?" Jimmy queried.

"You'll know, only when we establish your level of involvement, and I advise you to come to the office," said Agent Donald.

"I've your card with me, is it the address on the card I should come to?" Jimmy asked.

"Yes, but let's make it tomorrow, because it's already late," said agent Donald.

Jimmy didn't sleep all through the night because he just couldn't get over the thought of his face all over the media and the myth of his invincibility busted. His fate is now hanging on a tiny thread, yet he had to face this head on, and by morning, Jimmy was all dressed up and went to the FBI office to see Agent Donald. A few minutes later, he was with Agent Donald in the interrogation room.

"You're welcome, Jimmy Tomball," said Agent Donald.

"Thank you," Jimmy quipped.

"Tell us about your role in the cocaine peddling business?" asked Agent Donald.

"I don't have any role, he came to me to seek advice on how to get through the airport security and I gave him ideas on how to go about it," he said.

"You think you're smart, but we beat you to your game," said Agent Donald.

"No, you didn't," Jimmy replied.

"Why, but you've been caught. Sorry, the genie is out of the bottle and can't get back in," Agent Donald said jocularly.

"I told him to use the method once; that the cops will catch him if he repeats it, so you guys didn't beat me, you beat him. If he'd listened to me, we wouldn't be here," said Jimmy.

"How did you know we would catch him if he does it again?" asked Agent Donald.

"I know how the cops think, he came back happy saying it was a perfect trip without a trail and I told him no there's a trail," said Jimmy.

"What trail are you talking about?" Agent Donald queried further.

"The CCTV cameras of course, I told him the cops will be marvelled at why the dog wasn't sniffing and they'll be alerted to catch him the next time," said Jimmy.

"You did?" Agent Donald asked curiously.

"Yes of course, I did, you can ask him," Jimmy insists.

"I'm marvelled at your intelligence, if you hadn't been a thief, I would've recommended you for a job with the FBI right away," said Agent Donald.

"Then what's stopping you? I've given up stealing," said Jimmy.

If wishes were horses even the beggars will ride, and wishes aren't fishes either. So, Jimmy can't just wave his mythical magic wand and get recommended for a job with the FBI, not now, and not any time.

"But why did you choose stealing as a career?" asked Agent Donald.

"Ignorance, I suppose, but I've found love. It's just that I'm haunted by my past," he said.

"In life, there are prices to pay for our actions," said Agent Donald.

"So, why're you keeping me here? I've told you all I know," Jimmy retorted, thinking he's just there to tell the cops some fairy tale.

"The court will determine whether you should be freed or punished for the extent of your part in the crime," said Agent Donald.

Jimmy's sixth sense didn't stop his glaring ambivalence in his vague defence. "But it's Freddie you should be taking to court not me," Jimmy protested. Agent Donald wrapped up the interrogation as he charged Jimmy with conspiracy to peddle cocaine, and encouraging the killing of wildlife.

"Hey, I didn't kill any animal, and why're you charging me?" he protested.

The arrest and the exposure of the identity of Jimmy Thompson graced the headlines in the United States.

The news presenter had to interview Lieutenant Rose Greenland who carried out Freddie's arrest that led to Jimmy's prosecution. Lieutenant, America is happy with the arrest of the mythical Jimmy Thompson who a lot of people think is a myth and doesn't exist.

"At least the debate over the years on whether Jimmy Thompson actually exists as a person or not will be laid to rest," said Lieutenant Rose.

"People are eager to know how this genius was arrested," asked News presenter.

"It was his ingenuity that implicated him," said Lieutenant Rose.

"How did this happen? We want to know," said TV Presenter.

"He advised a drug peddler on how to evade arrest and actually the peddler was able to evade the arrest but implicated himself later, consequently implicating Jimmy Thompson," said Lieutenant Rose. "Lieutenant Rose, thank you for your time, at least the famous thief is now in custody," said News Presenter.

Unsurprisingly, Jimmy Thompson rocked his boat himself, and the chickens have eventually come home to roost. He was sentenced to twelve months imprisonment for his part in the crime, while

Freddie Knight was sentenced to four years imprisonment as a result of the deal he was offered by the FBI.

A month after his incarceration, Jimmy remained in prison, and all he does all day is think about Alicia, he has arguably been unable to shake off Alicia's hold on him because his four weeks of frolicking around with Alicia in the Cayman Islands is now a spell that kept him bound. A month later, Jimmy called Alicia from Prison to see the possibility of fanning the flames of their romance. Sadly, Alicia was in the mist of her friends, drinking coffee when Jimmy called. "Hello Alicia," said Jimmy.

Alicia looked at the number and couldn't place who the caller was, as Jimmy was calling using a prison line. "Hello, who am I speaking with?" asked Alicia.

"Alicia, this is Jimmy," he anxiously said.

Realising it was Jimmy on the line, she then stood up and walked some distance away from her friends, as she is more determined to keep this pestering thief canned forever. Unsurprisingly, she didn't even spare Jimmy the luxury of pleasantries before eviscerating the guy with her harsh rebuke for trying to rekindle a relationship she binned and left dead in the water the moment she left Cayman Island. This isn't because Jimmy is being upfront, but for his missteps. "Oh my God, Jimmy, you're in prison! Why're you calling me?" she asked unblinkingly.

"I just can't stop thinking about you; I'm still in love with you," he said as he tries to sweet talk Alicia.

"You can't be in love when you're in prison, stop thinking about me and don't call me again," she insists.

Jimmy pleads with Alicia not to be hard on him, asking her to please tone down her fury, but Alicia isn't having any of it. She insists she isn't putting her reputation on the line for this famous thief. Jimmy got the dressing down from Alicia as she reminded him, he put himself in his present state.

"Alicia, Alicia," said Jimmy.

"Everyone saw you on the television as a thief, so I can't associate with you," said Alicia.

"Why're you sounding like this, Alicia?" asked Jimmy.

Alicia interjected immediately. "Goodbye, Jimmy, don't call me again, or I'll call the cops and tell them you're stalking me," said Alicia.

CHAPTER

TWELVE

The sniffer dog

Months later, there's an attempted robbery in which Mrs Bullock fortunately, called 911 to report a break-in into her house before the robbers succeeded in entering her apartment.

The NYPD officers didn't hesitate to attend to the robbery at Mrs Bullock's address. The receiver of the call remained on the line with Mrs Bullock as the NYPD officers made their way to her address. "They're already inside the house, I can't hide," said Mrs Bullock as the phone dropped from her hand.

It's not long before Lieutenant Jones and his team arrive at Mrs Bullock's apartment in response to her 911 call. Sadly, the NYPD officers heard footsteps as they entered the apartment.

"Officer, what's it?" asked Lieutenant Jones.

"Sir, someone just ran out through the back door," said Officer Wayne.

"Wayne, Bruce and Johnson, you go after them, let Karri and I look around the apartment," replied Lieutenant Jones.

Officer Karri saw a dying Mrs Bullock who have just been shot by the intruders, and rushed to her, she then beckons on her boss to come over. "Lieutenant, over here."

"How's she?" asked Lieutenant Jones.

"Not good, sir. She's dying," said Lieutenant Jones.

Mrs Bullock was speaking in a faint voice, as she bleeds out. "I'm Mrs Bullock, they took my box of jewellery and a bag containing valuables. It belonged to my late husband," she said.

"Is there any other person in the house?" asked Lieutenant Jones.

"No, I'm the only one in the house, my children are all grown up and staying on their own," Mrs Bullock said and coughs.

"Shush, it's ok, stop talking let's get you help," said Officer Karri, as she tries to make the dying woman comfortable. It didn't take long before the paramedics arrived at the scene, and began attending to the injured victim.

After securing the crime scene, the NYPD officer decided to meet Mrs Bullock in the hospital. Sadly, the officers who went after the bad guys lost them as they ran into the nearby bushes after a brief moment of intense chase, and after a while the officers decided to call off the chase.

"Then let's call off the chase, we'll come and search this area when it's daylight," said Officer Wayne.

They called off the chase and left, and while at the Accident and Emergency unit of the Hospital, Doctor Green pronounced Mrs Bullock dead on arrival.

Lieutenant Jones was quite hopeful that he will be able to rescue this robbery victim and save her life.

"Lieutenant she's dead, we all want her back, but it's too late," said Doctor Green. Lieutenant Jones was miffed by the news of his inability to save Mrs Bullock, and this increased his resolve to catch the perpetrators of this crime.

"Ok, we'll contact her family," said Lieutenant Jones. Then they left the hospital after completing some documentation, and by morning the homicide team arrive the scene.

"Hello Lieutenant, you're here?" asked Agent Donald.

"Yes, we attended to the 911 call last night, but unfortunately, she didn't make it," said Lieutenant Jones.

"This is now homicide and it's our case," said Agent Donald.

"Yeah you're right. This is no longer our case it's, it's now for the homicide unit," said Lieutenant Jones.

"Barry, get the forensic team in, the detective then turned to the Lieutenant who just ordered his men to step back for the FBI to take over. "Lieutenant, please I might still need you and your men," said Agent Donald.

"Ok, I'll gladly give you whatever help you need," said Lieutenant Jones.

After hours of scanning the crime scene, the forensic unit didn't find anything that'll help this case, and the detectives were rattled at how this hastily orchestrated robbery could happen without leaving a single trail.

"Lieutenant, this is strange," said Agent Donald.

"What do you mean, I'm not following?" said Lieutenant Jones.

"This is a carefully orchestrated robbery; we can't find a clue that could help in this investigation," said Agent Donald.

"You mean there isn't anything?" asked Lieutenant Jones.

"Nothing, no latent prints, no bullet casing, nothing dropped, no clue whatsoever, even the bullet went through her, and we haven't been able to find it," said Agent Barry.

Sad to say, that the Lieutenant whose presence made the intruders leave the burgled premises hastily expected the forensics to find a trail but was surprised to hear the bad guys were able to leave a clean sheet.

"These are sophisticated criminals who knew exactly what to do before they left their base," said Agent Barry.

"Did they come with a car?" asked Agent Donald.

"No, they didn't, and it's strange," said Lieutenant Jones.

"Which means they came on foot and disappeared into thin air?" asked Agent Barry.

"Lieutenant please we'll need to work with your men who did the chase last night," Agent Donald said.

Lieutenant Jones called his men forward and asked them to work with detective Donald, after he requested for their assistance. They all searched the path of the chase the night before to see if they can get any clue about the guys that committed this crime, but nothing came up that would lead them to the perpetrators of the crime.

The FBI agents and the police team involved in the case didn't stop as they went over and over again through the path of the chase of the previous night, but the whole effort didn't yield the expected result. that would lead them to the perpetrators of the crime.

Months have passed after the death of Mrs Bullock, the FBI tried all they could to crack this Mrs Bullock's murder case but sadly, there wasn't any headway, and this case is now about being filed away in the cold file. Woefully for Agent Donald, he isn't comfortable leaving this case without a break. "The past week, we've been searching the path of the chase and even the bushes where these guys ran into, but can't find even a single clue," said Agent Donald.

"Donald, I think the people never wanted us to catch them," said Agent Barry who has no qualms sending the case to cold file.

"No criminal wants you to catch him or her, but if we do a good job we'll catch them," said Agent Donald. Agent Barry interjected and suggested to his colleagues to send this case to the cold file and move on until such time when new evidence to solve the case comes to light.

"I hate to show signs of mental vulnerability when presented with a complex scenario like this one," said Agent Donald.

Agent Barry used Donald's regular phrase as he asked him to take a deep breath and step backward, while the case remains open. "Another unresolved homicide going into the cold file? Ah, that's not my style," said Agent Donald.

"What will we do about it then?" asked Agent Barry.

Just as the detectives sulked about their helplessness, agent Murphy cuts in with the weirdest of ideas that leaves jaws dropping. He told them his idea may sound crude, but it could yield a positive result if they chose to give it a second thought.

"Say it, Murphy, let's see if it's workable," said Agent Donald.

"Take Jimmy Thompson to the scene, he'll find the answer you seek," said Agent Murphy. This weird suggestion by Agent Murphy got Agent Barry hopping mad because it got him all riled up, and he began kicking off. This time he isn't just kicking the can down the road by standing on the fence, he is putting his foot down as he stands against having a thief in his team.

"Oh, Murphy, I thought you'd something better to say, a prisoner?" Agent Barry asked.

"Hold on Barry." Agent Donald turned to Agent Murphy. What do you mean?" he asked.

"He has extra senses that help him look at things from the perspective of a thief," Agent Murphy said.

"Donald, I hope you aren't giving this talk a thought?" Agent Barry asked. Funnily, Barry's tantrums seem not to deter Agent Donald, into giving this a thought.

"I'm actually giving it a thought; it's just that Jimmy Thompson is in prison at the moment," he said.

"But I don't think that's a good decision either," said Agent Barry.

Agent Donald's idea of solving crime can sometimes pass for weird, because sometimes the worst thought that comes to his mind produces the best decision ever made.

"Donald, this Jimmy guy is in prison, and how will he be of a use to you?" asked Agent Barry.

Interestingly, Agent Murphy didn't only come up with this idea but gave Donald the nudge to take things further to Andy, suggesting that permission from the court will enable the FBI use Jimmy Thompson for his investigation.

"What if after all the trouble Jimmy can't help us get what we want?" asked Agent Barry. Agent Donald insists on giving this idea a try despite the strong opposition from his self-absorbing colleague, who insisted the idea should be tossed into the bin and will stop at nothing to make sure a thief isn't in his team. Agent Barry has a morbid imagination, and his motive isn't purely because Jimmy is a thief, but he can't bear to have someone take his place.

"Donald, why this startling choice?" asked Agent Barry.

"Because this is the only choice," replied Agent Donald.

"No, this isn't a choice, Donald. No choice is better than this bad choice," said Agent Barry.

Even as the pair continued their back forth debate over Jimmy Thompson, Agent Barry insists that people don't change, and Jimmy will continue to be a thief until the cows come home and urged Agent Donald to stop being illusory. This is arguably a more absurd or rather bizarre hypothesis put forward by Agent Barry whom most of his peers considered inept by all standards.

"You're a detective, Barry, sometimes people go out of their way to pursue the only option before them and it's better than no choice," said Agent Donald as he walked into Andy Grey's office.

Agent Donald walked in while Andy was on phone and making notes, and moments later Andy raised his head up to attend to Agent Donald who was standing opposite him. "Donald, any-thing?" he asked.

"Yeah Andy, it's about this Mrs Bullock's case," he replied.

"What about it? I think you told me you couldn't find anything that could lead you to her killer?" said Andy.

"Yeah, but Murphy just gave me an idea and I want to see if you'll see any wisdom in it; though I like it," said Agent Donald.

"Go ahead, what was the suggestion?" asked Andy.

"I'm thinking of taking Jimmy Thompson to the scene of the crime; maybe he could reason out something that'll assist us," said Agent Donald. While Donald was busy trying to get Jimmy to help, he never even considered how the embattled Jimmy Thompson will react to a request for help from the very man who exposed and shamed him.

"It's not a bad idea but Jimmy is in prison, will he agree to assist us after prosecuting and exposing him?" asked Andy.

"Actually, I don't know, and we can't know until we try," replied Agent Donald.

"Then let's give it a try; you'll have to pay him a visit," said Agent Donald.

"We might need permission from the court to be able to take him out of prison," said Agent Donald.

"Don't worry about that, let's finish with Jimmy, if he agrees to assist us in this investigation, I'll help you get the permission you need from the court," said Andy.

The next morning, Agent Donald and Agent Barry visited the City Marsh Prison in New York to discuss the idea with Jimmy Thompson. First thing first, they'd to go through the prison officer before any conversation with Jimmy could happen.

"Hello Donald, why're you here this early?" asked the prison officer.

"We need Jimmy for an investigation," said Agent Donald.

"What has he done this time?" asked the Prison officer.

"It's not about what he has done; we just want to have a word with him," said Agent Donald.

"If you need to take him out for an investigation, the court will have to be involved," said the prison officer. The Prison officer went back in and moments later brought Jimmy Thompson to the detectives who have come to seek his help. Interestingly, Jimmy came out laughing, feeling quite unperturbed as he had made friends inside.

"How're you, Jimmy?" asked Agent Donald.

"I'm fine, detective, and I hope I'm safe?" asked Jimmy.

"Yes, you're, but I need your help to solve a crime," said agent Donald.

"What's in it for me? You now need my help after sending me to prison," replied Jimmy.

"Donald, this guy is a joke, I don't think we'll need him," Barry said.

"You've to allow me do my Job," Donald retorted.

"I'll help you, detective, but there must be something in it for me," Jimmy said jocularly. Surprise, surprise, Agent Donald is a man known for making deals just to catch bigger fish, and extending a deal to catch the killer of Mrs Bullock won't cost him a thing.

"What do you want?" asked Agent Donald.

"I've about a month to leave the prison," said Jimmy.

"You want me to discuss your release with the court so you can help me?" asked Agent Donald.

Agent Barry's rivalry with Jimmy seem to take the best of him as his opposition to Jimmy smells of jealousy than it is of his unwillingness to having a thief around him. He has however steered away from mere tantrums into engaging in tiffs with Jimmy who have no qualms giving the detective the help they seek.

"Donald, this guy is a thief and should remain here," said Agent Barry.

Jimmy interjected and urged Barry who have unwittingly assumed the posture of a spoiler not to worry, saying he doesn't intend to leave prison yet, because he enjoys being here and he sort of considers this a sabbatical leave. Donald seems to be in a bind, particularly now that Jimmy isn't interested in any barter arrangement that will spur him to help these detectives.

"I'll help you, detective, just remember, one good turn deserves another. What's this investigation about?" asked Jimmy.

"There was a robbery and someone was murdered," said Agent Donald.

"Oh, I hate it when someone is killed by robbers," said Jimmy.

Jimmy's comment irked Agent Barry who couldn't stay mute without his usual banter particularly when the opportunity to dish it out comes calling "You steal here and there, and you say you hate it?" said Agent Barry.

"I've never killed and will never take a life, it's not my thing," said Jimmy.

"Jimmy, all we need is any clue that'll lead us to those that committed this murder. I really want to solve this murder, at least for the dead woman," said Agent Donald.

"Don't worry, detective, I'll help you," Jimmy promised.

After having a good conversation with Jimmy, Agent Donald reported back to Andy Grey who later obtained the permission from the court that enabled Agent Donald take Jimmy Thompson out of prison to assist in the investigation.

"We're here for Jimmy," said Agent Donald. The detectives then handed the prison officer the letter from the Court granting permission to take Jimmy out of prison to assist their investigation.

"Ok, let me get Jimmy for you," said the Prison officer. The Prison officer went in to get Jimmy Thompson from his cell, but sadly it's time for breakfast.

"Detective it's time for breakfast; give me some time to have my breakfast," said Jimmy.

"Jimmy, I haven't had my breakfast either, come on let's go," said Agent Barry.

"Do you know, helping you is a choice? I'm not bound by any law to help you," replied Jimmy, who's itching to get back in for his breakfast.

Agent Donald interjected and urged Barry to let Jimmy have his breakfast, so they don't mess things up for themselves. Sadly, Agent Barry couldn't help himself but to plague Jimmy further with his fits of tantrums, but Jimmy isn't deterred by Barry's tiffs either. "You're bound to do it if I charge you under the patriot Act," said Agent Barry.

"Detective, I'll be back in thirty minutes time. I don't want to miss my rations," said Jimmy.

Agent Donald interjected as he attempts to keep the ambience friendly. "Jimmy we're waiting, just don't take too long," he said. Jimmy went back inside to have his breakfast, and moments after sorting himself, he joined the detectives.

"You're just too annoying, Jimmy. You spent thirty minutes eating, while we were waiting for you," Agent Barry retorted.

"I'm ready. Let's go, but no handcuffs," said Jimmy.

"Yes, you're right," said Agent Donald as he removed the handcuffs, but reminded Jimmy to be on his best behaviour.

"Ok, I promise," said Jimmy.

The FBI took Jimmy Thompson to the crime scene and took him through the path of the chase to the point where the criminals entered the bushes, and even to the adjourning street to help sniff out any evidence that could lead them to the criminals. Funny enough, Police sniffer dogs haven't been able to find a thing to help the investigation.

Lieutenant Jones who attended to the 911 call on the day of the robbery was in the company of the detectives as they walk Jimmy through the path of the chase. "Jimmy, this is where they entered the bushes," the Lieutenant said. Jimmy paced back and forth scanning the area for while looking around for about forty-five minutes and suddenly focused on a particular spot and pointed.

"Check there," said Jimmy.

"Where, Jimmy?" asked Agent Donald.

"There, under your feet, Barry. Jimmy rushed to the spot where Barry stood. "Remove this slab," said Jimmy.

"What do you mean, under my feet?" asked Agent Barry.

"Yes, I mean under your feet," Jimmy insists.

Immediately, the detectives and the NYPD officers present worked hard to uproot a slab and discovered a stash of jewellery. "Oh my God, Jimmy, you've done it, you've found where they hid their stash, Agent Donald said and burst into laughter.

Agent Barry didn't hesitate to qualify Jimmy's sixth sense. "Jimmy you're better than a sniffer dog, because we brought those good for nothing dogs here, but they just couldn't find a thing," he said.

"Whatever you may think, we all have our gifts," said Jimmy.

"From what I'm seeing, this guy is a sniffer dog himself," said Lieutenant Jones.

Agent Barry's laughter was momentary as his joy quickly shifted into suspicion, and if Jimmy didn't tread carefully Barry's dramatic banter could suck him in. "Jimmy, how come you knew this is where the items were hidden?" asked Agent Barry.

"I know, because if I'm a thief, this is where I'll possibly hide my trophies," Jimmy replied.

"Are you sure you aren't part of this robbery?" asked Agent Barry.

"Why are you asking?" Jimmy queried further.

Agent Barry had wanted to hold Jimmy's feet to the fire, as he's now accusing him for being spot on. Saying they've been here several times and they couldn't find anything, but Jimmy found out where these items were hidden in less than a hour of his being here.

Funnily, while others watch as these two went back and forth, Barry sustained his accusation of Jimmy, saying he might be running a sniffer programme on the side, and possible Jimmy has some of his friend working as private surveillance contractor. Jimmy tried as much as he could not to get sucked in by Barry as he used a simple analogy to describe Barry's reaction.

Jimmy walked away from Barry but described his action as that of two men who left home to hunt for deer but along the line, while in the forest, one of the men turned to the other and said he looks like a deer. "Meaning?" asked Agent Barry. "You've suddenly left the killers you are searching for and now made me your target," replied Jimmy.

Agent Donald had to step in to stop the squabble, in his bid to stop Agent Barry bungling this sensitive operation at the slightest provocation.

"You know why? It's because you think like a cop while I think like a thief," said Jimmy.

"How does a cop think?" asked Agent Donald, who's always quick to seize every opportunity to learn.

"You're fond of following protocols in your investigations; all you do is follow routine. You go into an investigation with a conviction even before you start work on the case, you're always optimistic about your thoughts and do not leave an open mind," said Jimmy.

Barry is a strange soul who would always say it as it was. "But following protocol is the right thing to do," said Agent Barry.

"Following protocols isn't bad. It's just that you're always too optimistic about your views when doing your investigations," said Jimmy.

Jimmy hasn't spoken to his son since he exposed him to Alicia, he perceived Jerry's move was an affront to his invincibility. Even though that phone call has nothing to do with his going to prison he still had this grievance against his son, over his attempts to expose him.

Jimmy himself knew that it was his entanglement with Freddie that sent him to prison, which is something of his own doing, but he kind of rubbed it on his son.

Jerry has tried to make peace with his dad, he visited Jimmy in prison but Jimmy refused to see him.

CHAPTER

THIRTEEN

The Wood Pecker

Agent Donald and Agent Barry arrive at a new crime scene, and while Barry went about scanning the surroundings, Donald walked straight to the spot where the victim lays dead. Fortunately, Donald's old school mate was at the crime scene.

"Donald, you're here!" Lieutenant Brian exclaimed.

"Brian, you look as if you were expecting me," said Agent Donald.

"This Job doesn't give me enough space to spend time with you, or have you forgotten how we started, and how's Natasha?" asked Lieutenant Brian.

"Natasha is fine and why will I forget how you and I left home to pick up forms for Quantico. Each time I try to assess how I got to where I'm today, you always come into the story," said Agent Donald.

"One of these days you'll join me for a drink, so we'll have time to look into our past and have a laugh," said Lieutenant Brian.

"You know I relish such moments," Agent Donald replied but Agent Barry walked into the conversation between these two old friends. Donald then turned to Barry to formally introduce the Lieutenant to him. "Barry, Brian and I left home together to go to Quantico twenty years ago when we were living in Illinois.

"Oh, good to hear that, Lieutenant. How are you?" asked Agent Barry.

"I'm good, Barry, it's just that this killer is heartless," said Lieutenant Brian.

After exchanging pleasantries, the detectives went straight to work, and immediately Barry uncovered the victim, Donald held the sheet up and assessed the victim's injuries for a while.

"What direction did the shot come from," asked Agent Donald.

"The shot was fired from the third floor of that high-rise building," said Lieutenant Brian.

"What! From a distance of over a kilometre," said Agent Donald.

Lieutenant Brian retorted and said nothing strikes him like the fact that the killer is able to hit the same spot on his victim twice. The splatter shows that the victim was moving, and in motion when the shot was fired, and the direction of the blood splatter indicates the shot was fired from the south.

"Did you find the casing of the bullets?" asked Agent Donald.

Lieutenant Brian nodded saying, they did find the bullet casing, but nothing yet about the killer, though forensics is scanning the area to see if they can find something.

"I don't know much about this shooter, but one thing I know is that he has shooting skills which he acquired through formal or informal training," said Agent Donald.

While stepping aside to make space for the forensic team to move in, Agent Donald spotted an electronic dog collar in the crime scene and quickly picked it up and called in for the details of the dog in question. Gilbert Rivers didn't hesitate in his response. The dog collar is now a lead he intends to pursue, Donald then excused himself from the crime scene to chase after the lead before him.

"Brian, we'll wait for the forensic report, and in case something comes up please let us know," said Agent Donald.

"Donald, when this is all over, we'll make out time for drinks," said Lieutenant Brian.

"I know it isn't the drink that fascinates you, but the catching up is what matters most. Actually, sometimes I kind of reminisce some of those good moments in Quantico," said Agent Donald.

"Of course, yes, and I like to hear more about it," said Lieutenant Brian. Unsurprisingly, after paying a visit to owner of the dog whose collar was found in the scene, Agent Donald concluded it was a false lead, because the dog and its owner has a solid alibi, and also, the collar was reported missing months back and had since been replaced.

Two days later, the ballistics report was ready and the detectives were already at hand to review the report and profile the homicide victim. Agent Murphy collected the ballistics report and walk to Andy Grey. "The ballistic report is here," he said.

Andy Grey collects the file from Agent Murphy "Ok, what does it tell us about the victim?" asked Andy. They both walked into the central office and Murphy displayed the victim's information on the screen for profiling.

"The victim is forty-two years old, Jamie Malcolm, and he's a family Lawyer," said Agent Murphy.

"Is there any other information about him?" asked Agent Barry. "Nothing else except the fact that the gun that killed Jamie Malcolm is responsible for eleven other deaths in the United States of which the last three were in New York City," said Agent Murphy.

Agent Donald who was following keenly, turned to Gilbert. "Who are these other eleven victims and is there anything connecting all these people in one way or other?" asked Agent Donald. "No, nothing suggests these victims have engaged in a business relationship together except that they're all family lawyers," said Agent Murphy.

"Now we know these victims are all family lawyers, at least a pattern has emerged, what about the shooter?" asked Agent Donald.

"We know nothing about the shooter except the fact that he fires only two shots using a silencer and the second shot penetrates the very puncture created by the first shot," said Gilbert.

"How does he aim at the same spot twice? That makes him the most dangerous shooter in the United States," said Agent Barry. Interestingly, as more information emerged from the profiling, Agent Donald is able to piece bits and pieces together to make a sense of who the possibly killer is.

He then moved closer to the screen and said he can now conclude that the Wood Pecker is now in New York.

"What do you mean by that, Wood Pecker, and who's he?" asked Andy.

"He's Otto Allan; they call him the Wood Pecker because of his ability to strike his victim twice on the same spot. He's a former Mossad agent, sacked for pointing his gun at his unit head, and in a fit of anger he turned around and promised a female colleague he'll strangle her with her intestine.

Andy muttered, saying this is the kind of guy who wouldn't want people making a meal out of their errors. He then inquired further about what actually transpired between Otto Allan and his boss. Agent Donald then continued with his narrative that Otto Allan pointed his gun at his boss during a Palestinian intifada. He seemed to be shooting at protesters indiscriminately and when his boss called him to order, he turned his gun on him. He later became a shooting range instructor, after losing his job for his lack of discretion.

"Hitting the same spot twice on a moving target is almost an impossible thing to do, but now I know why he's good at aiming at his target," said Agent Barry.

"What's his passion?" asked Andy.

"His passion is nothing but the death of a family lawyer that succeeds in helping the woman collect everything the man owns during a divorce," said Agent Donald.

"Why family lawyers?" asked Andy.

"Otto Allan made his fortune from his shooting range business, but his twelve million dollars assets were split fifty, fifty, between him and his wife. The lawyer was able to dig out all the assets he tried to hide despite all effort to hide his wealth," said Agent Donald.

"Then what happened to the rest of his fifty percent share of the assets?" asked Agent Barry.

"In an attempt to restore his assets back to the original twelve million dollars value it was before the divorce, he went into gambling and unfortunately, he lost the rest of the fifty percent, packed up his business and went on the rampage," said Agent Donald.

"So, he decided that family lawyers should pay for his misfortune?" asked Agent Barry.

"Yes," said Agent Donald. Among the difficulties faced by the FBI agents' concerning this killer was what he presently looks like. Otto Allan is evil personified, a wicked soul devoid of emotions trapped in a body.

"But there are conflicting pictures of his face," said Andy.

"After killing the lawyer that handled his wife's divorce case, he went for a facial reconstruction to change his looks since he knew the cops were after him," said agent Donald who narrated how they chased this killer in the past.

"How does he choose his target, because there are so many family lawyers in town?" asked Andy.

"He looks for cases where the man losses everything to the woman, but he doesn't go for celebrated cases to avoid being a subject of a national manhunt," said Agent Donald.

"Where does he pick out his target?" asked Agent Murphy.

"Quiet divorce cases in the papers that people don't take notice of," said Agent Donald. This cold killer makes enmity with a divorce lawyer who'd succeeded in helping a woman take most of the family assets in their divorce settlement.

"This leaves the husbands of these women to be prime suspects in the deaths of these lawyers," said Agent Barry.

"Of course, but his signature of two shots on a moving target, where the second bullet penetrates the puncture of the first, exonerates the men in question," said Gilbert.

"How do we catch him? I want him off our streets immediately," Andy retorted. The detectives are now expected to put on their proactive caps, especially when the manhunt is for a killer who's clearly a sharpshooter. Arguably, Andy Grey who couldn't bear to have cold killers like this one prowling the streets of New York, suddenly became concerned that this guy might be going after a fresh target, and he just couldn't wait to take him out.

"Let's work with a family lawyer and make comments in the papers about a successful divorce case in which the woman got eighty two percent of the entire estate of the man as a result of a prenuptial agreement signed by the man," Agent Donald suggested.

"Are you sure he'll take the bait and will that attract him to the Lawyer?" asked Agent Barry.

"Yes, provided the lawyer involved is in New York City. Let's create a business appointment for her around the spot of the previous shooting," said Agent Donald.

"I want that done immediately," replied Andy.

The race to catch Otto Allan is on, and there's no more dawdling about, particularly now that the FBI has arranged with a family lawyer, Montana Trobe. And news about a divorce case in which the man lost eighty two percent of all his estate to his wife were placed in all the papers but not as a front- page news, because Otto Allan doesn't go for the front-page news. Montana Trobe isn't comfortable with the idea of being used as bait to lure a cold killer out of his den, yet Donald's assurance for her safety might mean she will give this a try. "This is risky, Donald. Are you sure this will work and how far can you ensure my safety?" asked Montana.

"Montana, your safety is in the hands of God, and I don't know if you believe in God, but I do," said Agent Donald.

"I do believe in God, but what about the plan you've put in place to ensure my safety?" asked Montana.

"Don't worry, I'm good at what I do, and I promise you, no harm will come to you," Agent Donald Promised. The stunt of using Montana Trobe might seem ingenious, but it's quite a risky move to smoke out a creepy invasive killer, but sadly, this bait might just be as happy to get this over with since this killer is after her kind.

A week-long workshop was quickly put in place, in which Montana Trobe was the guest speaker. The spot selected for this stunt was one that gives the killer a false sense of cover, unbeknownst to him there wasn't any, because FBI agent were sprawling in the midst of the crowd.

"Donald, we need to wrap this up quickly, let her go to the spot where the last victim was shot, at least we knew where the wood pecker stayed to aim at his target," said Agent Barry.

"That's a good idea, and let's hope he's already out to take out his next victim," said Agent Donald.

The FBI and other plain clothes policemen kept watch over Montana Trobe as she walked around, but the Woodpecker didn't show up.

"Donald let's call off the hunt for today, he didn't show up today," said Agent Barry.

Funnily, Agent Donald thinks differently because he was quite convinced that Otto Allan is out there, walking and mingling among the crowd, and possibly scanning the area as he puts his next target under surveillance.

"If he's in the square, why didn't he just shoot her?" asked Agent Barry.

But Agent Donald asked Barry to calm down, suggesting that a wise killer like that doesn't go about carrying a gun, he must want to understand the itinerary of his target before the day he'll carry out the act. "Which means he's watching her as well," said Agent Barry.

"Of course, and we'll have to repeat this about three times or more to catch this creep," said Agent Donald.

"Ok, what do we do now?" asked Agent Barry.

The world isn't as flat as a pizza as they say, and Agent Donald had to call off the stunt for the day, and hoped to repeat the process the day following.

The detectives continued in their effort to catch Otto Allan, and sadly, the Woodpecker didn't show up after four attempts, but he showed up on the fifth attempt. Interestingly, while Montana Trobe was still in the spot where the previous victim was killed Agent Barry spotted the creep heading towards his safe shooting spot. "Donald, he's here," said Agent Barry.

"Barry, are you sure it's him?" asked Agent Donald. Once the confirmation was received, detectives immediately asked Montana Trobe to walk away into safety.

"Yeah, he just went upstairs," said Agent Barry.

"Upstairs, where?" asked Agent Donald.

"The building he used to aim at his previous victim," said Agent Barry. Time is now of the essence, and these detectives must make haste to prevent the wood pecker from taking aim at Montana Trobe because he doesn't miss his target, even if that target is in motion.

"We need to move fast before he kills her, let's follow him upstairs now," said Agent Donald.

Agent Barry rushed as quickly as his feet can carry him and finds the Woodpecker as he tries to position himself for a good aim at Montana who keeps moving clumsily away from his line of sight. "Stop, FBI, put the gun down now," said Agent Barry.

"No!" exclaimed, Otto Allan. This creepy killer was unforgiving and insists on taking the shot at Montana Trobe. Sadly, he immediately decided to take Agent Barry down first, then his planned victim will follow, Otto Allan then pointed his gun at the detective who's now standing in his way, but Barry fired the first shot.

It isn't long before Agent Donald arrived at the scene immediately after Barry took the gunshot. "Oh Barry, thank God you're ok," said Agent Donald.

"I wanted to take him in alive, but he tried to shoot me, so I'd no choice but to take him out," said Agent Barry.

Agent Donald tried calming Barry down. "From his kind of person, I know he would rather die than allow you to take him in alive. You did a good job," said Agent Donald.

CHAPTER
FOURTEEN
The FBI Contractor

Jimmy is done serving his sentence, and has interestingly stopped stealing, yet Alicia whom he hoped will give him a second chance didn't. Funnily, he's now cooped up indoors, day in and day out, particularly now that his invincibility has come to an end.

Jimmy and his son eventually made up a week after Jimmy's release from prison, they talked things over. Strangely the relationship between these two has been cordial even though their lifestyles are worlds apart.

It was Sunday morning and Jerry was at Jimmy's door waiting for someone to answer to the door, and after several minutes of knocking the door. Jimmy got up from bed, feeling sleepy and muttering. "Who's disturbing my sleep?" Jimmy muttered. Interestingly, his son Jerry didn't hesitate to respond to his dad's muttering remark.

"It's me. Dad, its Jerry," said Jerry.

Jimmy opened the door to allow his son into the house. "Where are you going, holding a bible?" Jimmy asked hysterically.

"Aren't you going to let me in before giving me the third degree?" asked Jerry.

"Erm.., my bad, come in, this is your home," said Jimmy.

It's paradoxical that while Jimmy is a notorious thief and belongs to the street, his son Jerry is a church boy who plays by the book, thanks to Trina, Jimmy's daughter in-law. Jerry has for years been trying to pull his dad to church, but church isn't Jimmy's cup of tea, yet Jerry wouldn't give up on his dad.

"I guessed right," said Jimmy.

"Erm.., what was your guess about? We've a music concert in church, get dressed, you'll enjoy it," said Jerry.

"I knew my son would be caught up in this web of religion with the way Trina was going on about church," said Jimmy.

"Dad, Trina is the best thing that has happened to me and my two kids. Now, I've seen the light, and I want you to experience that light," said Jerry.

"What light, Jerry, aren't we both experiencing the same daylight? Is yours any different?" Jimmy asked jocularly.

"You've lived all your life in the dark. Now that America has uncovered your person, this is the best time to allow the light of God to take over," said Jerry. Jimmy can't wait to dispense of his son whom he still begrudges for exposing him to Alicia, and he thinks Jerry has overstayed his welcome, and at least they're done with the pleasantries. Sadly, for Jimmy, his grudge against his son doesn't seem to hold water because it was Freddie that eventually exposed him to the cops, but Jerry came prepared this time, and he isn't leaving unaccompanied by his dad.

"Son, I think you're running late for church and you need to get going," said Jimmy.

"Dad, I'm not leaving, we need a turnaround, you and me. I've just turned my life around what about you?" asked Jerry.

"I'm still feeling sleepy, and I need to go back to bed, maybe next time," said Jimmy, who's itching to get back to bed.

"You aren't going to the electric chair, dad. You're only going to spend time with your maker, and I know you love music. It's just about praise and worship," replied Jerry.

"I know, it's just that I'm not used to this," said Jimmy.

"Its 9am already, dad, get dressed, let's go to church. Trina and the kids are already waiting for us," said Jerry.

Jimmy's disposition suddenly changed, because he reasoned it to be insulting that his daughter in-law would pit his son against him. "Did Trina put you up to this?" asked Jimmy.

"Of course not, I want good for us, you and I. If mum was still alive our lives would've been better, so it's time we do things differently," said Jerry.

Jimmy's defence began to thaw, as he stopped being antagonistic and warms up to his son.

"Ok, but I haven't taken my shower, and I guess you'll be late waiting for me," said Jimmy.

While they continued their conversation, Jerry walked to the refrigerator and took out a can of juice, then looked around for his favourite crackers but found none. "Do you still have my favourite crackers?" asked Jerry. "You are grown now, Jerry, stop troubling about cookie," replied Jimmy.

Not that jerry's question isn't deserving of a response, Jimmy has given the greenlight to visit church with Jerry, he's nonetheless sullen that he's being pressured to attend church.

It didn't take long before Jimmy dawdled to the bathroom, and minutes later, they left the house for church. Jimmy had no idea his visit to church will unravel in quite an unexpected dimension, he got to church and found music, and Jimmy's music interest was like a fairy tale made from heaven.

Despite his calm non-petulant and non-violent disposition, Jimmy is still a deviant of some sort. While the church service was going on, he couldn't bear the urge for a cigarette break, Jimmy originally doesn't smoke, he picked up smoking during his time in prison. He then walked to the back of the church for a stick of cigarette.

The church service continued, and in the middle of the praise and worship the guitarist became poorly, and after taking a sip of water a number of times he still didn't feel any better. He then dropped the guitar while the other instruments were still playing, and the singer continued even without the guitarist.

The guitarist then walked to the back of the church for some fresh air, to see if that could be therapeutic enough. Jerry who is a member of the church ushering team followed Dean, the guitarist to give some comfort. Interestingly, his dad was standing by the corner, at the back of the church, with a fag in his hand.

"Dad, you're meant to be inside the church, and what are you doing here?" Asked Jerry.

"I just needed a fag, that's all," replied Jimmy.

"Dad, this is a church and not some street party where you go for a fag every ten minutes," Jerry retorted.

It's now obvious to Jerry that you can't teach an old dog new tricks. He muttered and left his dad behind and went after Dean who is obviously feeling poorly and would make do with some kind words of encouragement. Jimmy immediately took one long draw of his cigarette before putting out the cigarette and then joined Jerry and Dean as he inquired if Dean is ok.

"I'm not feeling too good, I need to go home," said Dean, who then requested Jerry to please get him a taxi.

"What about your guitar, and the praise and worship?" asked Jimmy.

Dean replied to Jimmy saying his friends will bring the guitar with them, but he just can't continue with the songs' ministration, particularly now that he's very poorly. Jimmy interjected again and asked Dean if he should take his place, as he informed Dean that he's equally good with the guitar.

Dad, I don't think that's a good idea," said Jerry.

"I suppose so," Dean retorted.

Jimmy seemed not to be giving up, even as his son reminded him that this is his first day in church, and the church isn't the best place for people pussyfooting about and not the best place for stunts like this either. After his obvious words of caution to his dad, Jerry then focused his attention on Dean, and without further conversation on the subject, Jimmy walked straight into the church, picked up Dean's guitar and began playing along.

The moment Jimmy got hold of the guitar the sound of the music became exceptionally good and the church audience danced more. Within a minute, it was as if there was a sudden epiphany that dawn on the audience as they suddenly realised it was Jimmy Thompson, the famous thief, on the pulpit and attempting to desecrate the house of God.

Most of the church members stopped dancing, and the question in their head was what this thief that has graced national headlines is doing on the pulpit. The shock wasn't limited to the church members, and even the pastor was quite taken aback.

The only thing left for the church members to do was to boo and chorus, go, go, get down from our pulpit, but they didn't do that as they watched to see how their pastor will react to this awkwardness.

The pastor is damned immediately he knew he will be judged either way, if he asks Jimmy to drop the guitar and return to the audience where he should be in the first place, he will be seen in the bad light as not giving this sinner the opportunity to find God, and if he allows Jimmy to continue, he will equally be perceived as making a mess of the pulpit.

Pastor Bowers knew that everyone has a right to the house of God and no one has the absolute right to chase another out of the church, particularly when the individual came to church looking for God.

The singer knew something was wrong the moment most of the members stopped dancing as they whispered to one another, but couldn't place a finger on what the problem might be because she has no recollection of the new guitarist as Jimmy Thompson, the famous thief.

This pastor has some close ties with Jerry, and knows that he's Jimmy's son, since Jimmy made headlines during his arrest, but they haven' met. Interestingly, Pastor Bowers saw Jerry walking into church earlier with Jimmy, and was able to associate the face with the name.

Pastor Bowers stood up immediately and walked to Jimmy and spoke in quite a low tone as he asked of Dean's whereabouts from Jimmy and was told Dean isn't coming back because he's very poorly. He then asked Jimmy the obvious. "You're Jimmy Thompson, the famous guy, I suppose?"

Jimmy concurred, and he then asked Jimmy if Dean asked him to cover for him, Jimmy opened up and said Dean didn't, he just felt the need to help so the praise songs didn't suffer. "Do you mind if I make this right for you, I mean with Christ?" the pastor asked further.

"I don't mind," replied Jimmy.

The Pastor now left Jimmy and went for the microphone. "Brethren, we want to welcome a special person to church," said Pastor Bowers, who then asked Jimmy to come forward.

Jimmy walked forward with the guitar in his hand. Right there and then he led Jimmy to Christ without much ado, and asked Jimmy to continue playing his guitar, he then asked the singer to continue. The music started again and the audience began dancing, and within minutes the tempo returned.

Jimmy is a self-contained man, and isn't really the church kind of guy, but he kind of loved the experience and henceforth became a regular in church.

Jimmy became more forthcoming, yet hardly went out to socialize with his old friends, and a few weeks after Jerry's visit, Donald is trying to see to it that he turns Jimmy's fortunes around, as he's bent on giving Jimmy a second chance.

It was a new day, Agent Donald Walked into Andy's office. "Andy, are you busy?" he asked.

"If there's anything you want to say, you can go on," said Andy.

"I've a proposal to make. It might sound weird but I think it's a wise idea," said Agent Donald.

"Go on Donald, say it," said Andy.

"I want you to employ Jimmy Thompson," said Agent Donald.

"What!" He chuckles and looked straight into Donald's eyes. "Where on earth did such an idea come from? This isn't just weird, it's over the top," said Andy.

"Jimmy Thompson will make a very good agent, and he'll help you save more lives if you look at it from that angle," said Agent Donald. This novel idea is one that could attract a backlash from New Yorkers known for being upfront with their views, and Andy is more concerned about the political ramification than what Jimmy could possibly offer.

"But how do you think people will react to this suggestion?" asked Andy.

"When it yields fruit, people will enjoy it, particularly when they hear that Jimmy Thompson now assists the FBI in fighting crime. I suggest you make him a contractor and not a direct employee of the FBI," Agent Donald proposed.

"What if he commits crime and taints our reputation?" asked Andy.

"If he commits crime then he'll go down for it," said Agent Donald.

After a momentary silence, Andy seems to make sense of the idea but shifted the responsibility to Donald. "Do you trust him?" asked Andy.

"Don't trust him, trust me," Agent Donald assured.

"This isn't a bad idea, but I'll discuss it with the head of criminal division of main justice.

Immediately Donald stepped out, Andy Grey picked up the phone and dialled Sarah Black to discuss Jimmy Thompson.

"How're you, Andy. Is there anything that needs my attention?" asked Sarah.

"Are you busy?" asked Andy.

"I'm busy but go on, I still have a few minutes to spare," said Sarah.

"Ok, there's a weird proposal that came to my table, but I wish to hear your opinion on it," said Andy.

Interestingly, Sarah doesn't like being surprised with surprises that will irk her. She's the kind of person who thinks if it doesn't make sense then it isn't true, and don't bother telling it to Sarah, if you don't want her to be all riled up. She immediately interjected and reminded Andy that when it's weird, then he should know it won't get her blessing, then ask why bother to discuss it with her.

" Donald Whitley suggested I should employ Jimmy Thompson as a contractor, to assist the FBI in fighting crime," said Andy.

"Is that what you called a weird idea? I've often wished that Jimmy Thompson worked for us," said Sarah.

"You mean you support this idea?" Andy anxiously asked.

"Yes, people like that make wonderful agents, it's just that we'll have to work with him using a long handle, so that he doesn't dent our reputation, said Sarah."

"Which means the idea just got your blessing?" asked Andy.

"Yes, but as a contractor, as you suggested," said Sarah who prefers playing the long game with Jimmy.

"Ok, thank you," said Andy. Using ex-convict as FBI contractors is likened to walking on thin ice, and Sarah's recent experience in her FBI unit in Arkansas means using ex-convicts could cut both ways. They had their run ins with the cops in the past, and using them for the good of all could be a plus if things doesn't go south.

"But you need to keep him on a tight leash. I guess you know the ramifications if he goes haywire," said Sarah.

"Yeah, I'll keep my eyes on him," Andy promised.

Andy couldn't hold back on his excitement as Sarah gave her blessing to his proposal and his facial disposition tells it all as he walked into the central office. Andy Grey then exclaimed as he informed Agent Donald that Sarah Black has given a go ahead with Jimmy Thompson.

"I told you it wasn't a bad idea. That man will be more of a blessing than a curse," said Agent Donald as he hinted his colleagues that Sarah Black just supported Jimmy's employment as an FBI contractor.

This news came as a stinker to Agent Barry who was also at his desk in the central office, and he didn't only respond passively, but gave the news his middle finger. He insisted that there is darkness in Jimmy, and Jimmy's career in stealing is just a shadow of the level of darkness inside Jimmy. He then warned his colleagues that the idea of making the apparatus of the state available to Jimmy will be likened to the FBI losing its moral compass.

"What! That's a sick idea, why would she do such a thing?" asked Agent Barry.

"If he directs his ideas towards doing good, it'll be for the benefit of all," said Agent Donald. Barry was particularly angry at Agent Donald for initiating this idea in the first place, and as he has always been, Barry hates playing the second fiddle. He immediately fixed his gaze at Donald, asking why he acts as if he has some esoteric knowledge that is lacking in others.

"Why're you becoming so emotive about this? I'm just a man that likes having all the facts on the table, and I think Jimmy will help me get that," said Agent Donald. Agent Barry's disputation isn't just tied to jealousy but because he particularly felt slighted by the fact that he wasn't consulted before the suggestion was taken to the top. He isn't just taking this new addition to the team lying down, particularly now that he feels Agent Donald is thinking of Jimmy, as a possible preference for a partner.

"He's a thief and I can't work with a thief. That will not happen," said Agent Barry. While agent Barry was busy throwing his toys out of the pram in a showy display of a hissy fit, his colleagues saw a cautionary tale in his action. After giving him some time to vent, it's now obvious that this showy display seems to be taking forever, Andy Grey had to interject to put stop to this bickering, particularly when a decision has been reached in the matter.

"It's already too late, and that ship has sailed, Barry. Approval has been given from above, and it isn't always about you!" said Andy.

Agent Barry was beginning to feel increasingly isolated as more of his colleagues are lining up behind the idea of having Jimmy in the unit, and it didn't take long before his opposition began to thaw. "This isn't a bad idea, let's use Jimmy's knowledge to our advantage," said Agent Murphy.

Agent Barry insists that he isn't denying the fact that Jimmy is gifted, but he just can't work with him because he was a cunning sleazebag and a thief with a reputation.

"You like his gifts and hate his person. You are like a man who likes the art but hates the artist," said Agent Donald.

"Oh, Picasso! You now liken Jimmy to Picasso," Agent Barry exclaimed.

While the conversation persists, Agent Barry took some steps leaving the central office, to attend to a phone call but Gilbert thinks he could help Barry be more accepting of Jimmy. He then walked up to Barry to see if he can change his perception about Jimmy.

"Barry, if you open your mind, you'll enjoy working with Jimmy, he's a nice guy," said Gilbert.

Agent Barry turned around and replied, "A nice thief, you mean!"

Gilbert had to step back, as Barry remained in his cocoon of me, me, me, and me alone.

Two days later, Andy prepared Jimmy's appointment letter and handed it over to Agent Donald who's ecstatic to be the one delivering the good news to Jimmy. It didn't take long before Agent Donald paid Jimmy a visit, he stood by the door and pressed the bell and moments later Jimmy opened the door. Sadly, Jimmy wasn't in any mood to receive any guest, and the least person he expects to see by his door is the detective that sent him to prison.

"How come you traced me to where I'm living?" Jimmy asked.

"Is it bad for a friend to come around and say hello to another friend?" Agent Donald replied in a soft-spoken manner. People don't just find friendship with Cops to be patronising, many finds it to be a bad omen, and Jimmy isn't an exception. It doesn't matter if Donald walks around in plain clothes, he's still a cop.

"I was nice to you, and I assisted you when you needed help, so stop stalking me, stop looking for something to hang on me," Jimmy said as he frowned at the detective's visit.

"I'm here to also return the favour you did for me last time," said agent Donald.

"What favour are you talking about?" asked Jimmy.

Agent Donald handed him the employment letter. "Open it and read," said Agent Donald.

"Is this a joke or what?" asked Jimmy.

"Of course, it isn't, and I want you to work side by side with me. I appreciate your potential and I want it to benefit many and not just you alone," said Agent Donald.

Jimmy needs to be convinced that this isn't an entrapment, and he suspects this detective is out take away the little sanity he has got left, and if so, then he might have to walk away from this employment scam placed before him.

"What if I say no, will you continue stalking me as you just did?" asked Jimmy.

"Then I'll leave, and I'll take the offer with me, it's just that this would've been an opportunity for you to change your reputation for good," said Agent Donald.

"This is just a contract job and you want me to be stitching people up, don't you?" asked Jimmy.

"Yes, it is, but people will now know you as a good Jimmy Thompson that saves life, and not just as a thief," said Agent Donald. Jimmy's disposition lightens up in a dramatic twist of fate, it was as if scales just fell off his eyes, and he suddenly became soft spoken, when he realised that this is a rare opportunity presented to him on a plate.

"I'll take the offer, when will I start?" asked Jimmy.

"Start next week, if that suits you." He stretched out his hand for a handshake. "Welcome to my team," said Agent Donald.

"Thank you for this offer, it means a lot to me," Jimmy said with a smile.

CHAPTER

FIFTEEN

The Paedophile

Andy Grey received a phone call and it's Sarah Black that was on the other end of the phone.

"Hello Andy, how are you?" said Sarah.

"I'm fine, Sarah," Andy replied.

"There is a case of interest I want your team to take part in," she said.

"What case is that?" asked Andy.

"The South Bridge unit of NYPD is handling the case," said Sarah. Andy knows for sure that nothing infuriates Lieutenant Rose like when FBI agents' get involve in her cases, because it presents to her as if she can't solve her case without the involvement of FBI detectives.

"Is the case within our jurisdiction?" asked Andy.

"Of course not, but I've informed Lieutenant Rose, I want my men to be part of the investigation," she said.

"What's the nature of the case?" Andy queried further.

Sarah had to elucidate further on the case, and said this is a case of child exploitation and child grooming, it's about a teacher pressuring a student for a sexual relationship.

"But why're you particularly interested in this case?" asked Andy.

"The accused is my cousin," she said.

Andy decided to err on the side of caution, and said he hopes it won't be wrongly perceived that they're trying to pervert the course of justice or influence the investigation in anyway. Cases of sexual exploitation can easily gather traction, then snowball into something big and precipitate rapidly turning into a national outcry. This time Andy intends to tread with caution, to avoid the short end of the stick.

"No, no, Andy, I want your team to dig out the truth, and if my cousin is guilty, let him face the consequence of his actions," she said.

"Ok, I'll send my team immediately," said Andy.

Immediately after Andy Grey finished with the phone call, he walked to the central office to send his team out for this investigation.

"Donald, I want you and Barry to visit South Bridge station, there's a case I want you to take part in," said Andy.

"What's the nature of the case?" asked Agent Donald.

"It's the case of a suspected paedophile," replied Andy.

Agent Barry quipped immediately, and he doesn't want Rose embarrassing him because this isn't their kind of case and isn't within their jurisdiction.

"She has been informed already and she knows you're coming, take Jimmy with you," said Andy.

Andy has to quickly address the elephant in the room, as he sensed his men wouldn't want to be used by those at the top to prevent justice taking its course. Andy assured his detectives that all Sarah Black wanted is the truth, and she isn't asking him to turn a blind eye, deaf ear, and silent tongue, if her cousin is found wanting in the matter.

Barry didn't like the idea of giving Jimmy the opportunity of feeling like a detective, and he didn't hesitate to register his protest as he kicks against the idea of having Jimmy come along with them. Sadly, he isn't in a position to say who goes where.

"Why! What does Jimmy know about investigation?" Agent Barry protested.

"Jimmy will be useful, Barry. Let him come with us," said Agent Donald.

Agent Barry reluctantly went along with this popular view, and it didn't take long before the detectives arrived the South Bridge unit, where Lieutenant Rose was already waiting.

"Detectives, you're here. I was told to allow you be a part of this investigation," she said. But Agent Barry didn't hold back his banter as he begins mouthing off all over the place.

"You were told or you were instructed, which of the two?" asked Agent Barry.

"You act like a man suffering from insufficient sleep, Barry," said Lieutenant Rose.

"Lieutenant, please fill us in," said Agent Donald.

"The girl's mother reported the case to us, after a text message from the teacher requesting sex, and other complaints from the girl about the same teacher's attitude towards her," said Lieutenant Rose.

"Then why're we here? This man should go straight to prison, with such mountain of evidence against him," said Agent Barry. Agent Donald interjected by asking Agent Barry to take a deep breath, and reminded him he can't be a cop, and a judge at the same time, ignorance they say, is bliss.

"The girl is in the interview room, you can speak with her," said Lieutenant Rose.

Moments later, the NYPD officer interviewing the victim stepped out and Agent Donald stepped into the interview room and began speaking with Katherine Cooper.

"Hello Katherine, how're you?" asked Agent Donald.

"I'm fine, detective," said Katherine.

"How old are you, Katherine?" asked Agent Donald.

"I'm fourteen," she said.

"Tell me everything," said Agent Donald.

Katherine began to sob, as she informed the detective that her teacher keeps telling her he likes her, and that he wants to have sex with her, and she has continued to resist him.

"Why didn't you tell your mum about it?" asked Agent Donald.

"I told him I'll tell my mum, but he begged me not to," she insists. Katherine began crying out loud, and Agent Donald paused for a moment to give her some respite so she can pull herself together, and then continued with the interview.

"And you did?" he asked.

"Yes," she said.

"Why did you decide to tell your mum about it now?" he queried further.

"Because the pressure has become too much," she insists.

"Let me see the message he sent you," asked Agent Donald.

"Katherine opened the text message and showed it to the detective. "This is it," said Katherine. "This message was about a month ago, why didn't you show this to your mum the moment you received it," asked Agent Donald.

Katherine screamed, as she began showing sign of distress. "He's the one you should be questioning, because he has put me through so much emotional trauma," she retorted.

"Ok, ok, you can go," said Agent Donald.

Agent Donald stood up and left the interview room almost immediately after he gave Katherine permission to leave. Agent Donald joined Lieutenant Rose and other agents observing the interview. Sadly, for this detective, Katherine's mum finds her daughter's interview to be invasive and too intense. Agent Donald's probing questions touched her already frayed nerves and she flared up at Agent Donald and gave him the dressing down.

"Do you've to interrogate my daughter that way? The girl has been emotionally abused and you're adding to her trauma," said Katherine's mum. "I'm sorry, if my interview angered you, this is about justice, and I just have to do my job," Agent Donald replied.

"Then learn to do your job properly and you don't interrogate a victim if you don't know. She then turned to her daughter. "Katherine, let's go," she said.

Just as Katherine and her mum turned to leave, Agent Donald turned to Lieutenant Rose. "What do you think?" he asked.

Lieutenant Rose reminded Agent Donald, that Katherine is already emotional, and he shouldn't have questioned her with embarrassingly prodding questions. She insisted that all she expected from the detective is to take the victim's complaint, after all the evidence against her teacher is so much.

"Of course, yes, and she has overwhelming evidence against the teacher," said Agent Barry.

"Do we bring the accused into the interrogation room?" asked Lieutenant Rose.

"Yes, let's gather all the evidence against him and then you can charge him," said Agent Donald. Moments later Joseph Fowler was brought into the interrogation room, and Agent Donald stepped back in to hear Joseph's side of the story.

"How're you, Joseph?" asked Agent Donald.

"I'm not fine, detective," said Joseph.

"You have a wife, Joseph. Why this little girl?" he asked.

Joseph continued to maintain his innocence, saying he doesn't have anything to do with the girl, he then added a twist to the interrogation, saying it was Katherine that was actually chasing and pestering him, and saying all sorts of things like, she loves him, and can't do without him, and many other things.

"You're saying she's the one chasing you and not you chasing her?" asked Agent Donald.

"Of course, I'm surprise about these allegations," he exclaimed.

"When you noticed she was pestering you and wouldn't let go, why didn't you report the matter?" asked Agent Donald.

Joe as he's popularly known became overwhelmed by this accusation as it now dawned on him that he's on his way behind bars. He began to sob, as the evidence against him piles up, and effort to wriggle himself out failed.

"I never knew it would turn out like this. Moreover, if I'd reported her it would end up being my word against hers, and how many would believe me?" asked Joseph.

Agent Donald shook his head in disapproval of Joseph's assertion saying there's no need telling lies because the message he sent to Katherine's phone requesting sex, is already significant evidence against him.

Joseph retorted, and continued to maintain his innocence, saying he'd no idea of how the message came about and from what he has seen, his phone sent the message but there isn't any record of the message in his phone. With cases like this on the table,

Agent Barry is perhaps too angry to care about what Joseph will lose at this point.

"The evidence of the text message alone is enough to put you away, and I'm certain your wife will divorce you, because no woman will want anything to do with a paedophile," said Agent Donald. Joseph exclaimed saying his wife is gone already, and that the truth remains that he doesn't know how Katherine got the message in her phone because he didn't send that message.

"You may have sent the message and deleted the message from your sent items," said Agent Donald. Joe became silent for a moment and burst into tears, as he sobbed uncontrollably, yet no one sympathised with him, at least not for a confirmed paedophile.

"Why does this girl want to destroy me? I don't know where she coded the message from," he insists.

"So, you mean the message didn't come from your phone?" asked Agent Donald.

"No, why would I send such a message? I'm a decent family man with three kids?" Joseph insists. These allegations seemed to have riled Joseph who suddenly felt the temperature inside the interrogation room is dropping like stone, and it's dropping fast. Agent Donald didn't stop probing Joseph with more damaging evidence despite his being all teary.

"But forensic evidence shows that this message is from your phone, and I don't think your tears will save you," said Agent Donald.

"I didn't send any message, is it possible for your phone to send a sexually explicit message to a particular girl that claims you've been harassing her without your knowledge?" asked Joe, as he continued to maintain his innocence.

It didn't take long before agent Donald wrapped the interrogation up and joined Lieutenant Rose and other detectives watching the interrogation.

"What do you think?" asked Agent Donald.

"He's denying it as usual, just as every guilty person does," said Lieutenant Rose. Agent Barry thinks he'd heard enough and concluded that Joseph was a liar whose words are devoid of any truth and shouldn't be believed. He then suggested they charge Joseph immediately and let him live the rest of his life in jail. It's obvious that this case is now left for the jury to deal with, and Joseph will have to reserve his story for the Jury to decide. With the overwhelming evidence against Joseph, agent Donald turned to Lieutenant Rose and suggested to her to start charging Joseph.

Thirty minutes after the interrogation of Joseph concluded and the detectives' conclusion that he should be charged, Jimmy interjected, saying Joseph didn't do it despite the stack of evidence against him. "I know a guilty person when I see one," said Jimmy.

Sadly, for Jimmy, his comment enraged Agent Barry who isn't ready for a clown like Jimmy to oppose his views on this matter, and he didn't hesitate to give Jimmy a dressing down. "What do you know? And I don't even know why Andy asked us to bring this ex-con here," asked Agent Barry.

It's general knowledge that Agent Barry's canteen culture is his character flaw. Agent Barry's forbearance is one that leaves much to be desired, and his zero skills of scepticism is a thing of general knowledge and this makes him a kind of new joke.

While he sustained his verbal attacks on Jimmy whom he considers way off his antenna, and so far, Agent Barry seems not to have learnt about his singularity before pursuing a career of becoming a detective. All he does, is throw red herrings into the investigation and blow the whole thing out of the water.

Funnily, Jimmy's view in this case seems to have caused a rethink in Agent Donald who reluctantly suggested that Joseph should be charged since there isn't anything exonerating him. He turned to Barry who wouldn't want to hear any different opinion that his proclivity for instant justice astounds him. He then informs Barry that he shares the same view with Jimmy, that the evidence against this man is overwhelming, but his hunch also tells him Joseph is innocent but there isn't anything to prove his innocence.

"Are you suggesting we should let him go or what?" asked Lieutenant Rose. Agent Donald's neutrality during investigation helps him to see things from an altruistic point of view, and he almost missed it this time, but the burden of proof to prove Katherine wrong, lies with Joseph.

"I'm not the judge to decide that, and if we don't find anything further, then we'll charge him immediately," said Agent Donald.

"This guy is guilty, Donald; let's not waste valuable time chasing shadows," said Agent Barry.

While the detectives were busy analysing the different scenarios of this case, they held onto the key evidence that implicated Joseph, but Jimmy's primary focus was on the key evidence against Joseph which is the text message Joseph claimed to have no knowledge of, and the time the text message happened is now his interest.

"The time of the text message shows that it was sent on a school day, and during school hours. I suggest we review the school's CCTV footage to see what Joseph Fowler was doing at that time," said Jimmy. This suggestion by Jimmy seems to make a lot of sense as it'll support the forensic report on the source of the text message.

"That's a good one Jimmy, Barry let's go to her school to review the CCTV footage as Jimmy suggested," said Agent Donald.

Agent Donald, Agent Barry and Jimmy proceeded to The Prima-Trima Schools Brooklyn New York where Joseph works as teacher, but Agent Barry wasn't fine with the stretching of this investigation, yet he dawdled along. The detectives' first point of call was the school principal's office, and the principal wasn't quite pleased with the detectives' continued poking around instead of putting Joseph away for good.

"Hello detective, how're you going with the case?" she asked.

"We're still investigating," said Agent Donald.

"What are you still investigating? With all the evidence available, Joseph should be in court by now and awaiting his sentencing," said the principal.

"Madam Principal, you've to let us do our job, yours is to report, ours is to investigate and the court passes judgement," Agent Donald replied.

"We need the CCTV footage of 9th of August, which was the day the text message was sent," said Agent Barry.

"Ok, you can come with me to the security unit," replied the principal who then stood up from her seat. She took the lead, while the detectives followed her from behind until she entered the security unit. "Arthur, please these detectives need to view some footage," the principal said.

"Ok, that'll be ready in a few minutes," said Arthur.

It didn't take long before Arthur made the tapes for 9th August available to the detectives, and they began reviewing the footage, and while reviewing the footage. "Stop, stop Arthur, Barry can you see that?" said Agent Donald.

Arthur stopped and went backward and played it again. "That's Katherine, taking Joseph's phone and typing a message into Joseph's phone while Joseph wasn't in class and his phone was on his table," said Agent Donald.

"This CCTV footage holds the answer to all our questions," said Agent Donald. This CCTV footage just got Agent Barry all riled up, because of his earlier insistence that Joseph is guilty and should be behind bars. Sadly, in his guilt and shock, Barry turned to Donald. "You mean a fourteen-year-old could do a thing like this?" he asked.

"Jimmy, get the principal let her see this, because we're taking this evidence with us," said Agent Donald.

Moments later, the principal was in the security office as the detectives prepare to lay bare their findings before her. "You sent for me, detective?" the principal asked.

"Yes, please take a look at this," said Agent Donald.

"That's Katherine, what's she doing with her teacher's phone?" asked the principal.

"Katherine realised the class was rowdy, took advantage of it, to take her teacher's phone, typed a sexually explicit message into it, sent it to her own phone and deleted the message from Joseph's phone that was why Joseph had no knowledge of the text message," said Agent Donald. The principal was rattled by what she just saw Katherine did and exclaimed, this new revelation was a kick in the gut for this principal who has stood by Katherine all along.

"You mean Katherine could go this far just to destroy Joseph, why would she do a thing like this?" the distraught principal asked.

"Is she in class? I believe her mum brought her back to school after we finished interviewing her," said Agent Barry.

"Yes, she's in school let me bring her here," said the principal. The principal stepped out of the security office to get Katherine and moments later, Katherine was with the detectives watching her act on the camera.

"Katherine, can you see this?" asked Agent Barry, who has taken Katherine's betrayal more personal than his colleagues. He played the footage again for Katherine to see. "Your game is up," he said.

"Why would a little girl like you want to destroy a teacher? You want to destroy his family, his career, his reputation and even put him away!" Agent Barry exclaimed.

Katherine began sobbing immediately her sin was laid bare before her. "I'm sorry; please don't tell my mum about this," she replied.

Agent Barry was already worked up by the cruelness of Katherine's heart and wasn't buoyed by her tears. "Stop shedding your crocodile tears, you're a horrible person. A man with three children is about to lose his wife, his children, his career and even is freedom for your lies?" said Agent Barry.

"Katherine, I'm calling your mum, so she can see how despicable your actions are," the principal said.

Moments after uncovering this CCTV evidence, the detectives left the school, leaving Katherine behind, and returned to the South Bridge Police unit, and took the CCTV evidence with them.

"Detectives, did you find anything?" asked Lieutenant Rose.

"Yes, please watch this CCTV footage," said Agent Donald.

The detectives handed the tape to Lieutenant Rose, and funnily, the lieutenant didn't hesitate as she immediately began reviewing the content of the CCTV footage.

"Wait, that's Katherine taking her teacher's phone and this, is on the 9th of August, the day and time of the purported sexually explicit text message.

"And that teacher is Joseph," said Agent Barry.

"You mean she typed the message into her teacher's phone herself and sent it to her own phone?" said Lieutenant Rose.

"She then deleted the message from her teacher's phone that was why Joseph had no knowledge of the message," said Agent Barry.

"Then, I'll need to bring Katherine here for further interrogation," said Lieutenant Rose.

"She has already admitted her crime, and she's a minor but it's up to you to decide what action to take against her, at least it's your case," said Agent Barry.

The detectives advised the Lieutenant not to go chasing off after Katherine, typical actress she is, yet destructible by her beauty. The school principal is still gobsmacked by Katherine's indulgence in this craziness, and more troubling is the tact in her approach.

"I'll still have to bring her here to answer for her sin." The Lieutenant muttered then turned to Agent Donald. "I'm sorry, Donald, for telling you not to interrogate her because she was the victim," she said.

"Horses for courses, I suppose," replied Agent Barry.

"I wasn't interrogating her, Rose. I was only interviewing her and sadly, a lot of cops have joined the band wagon by not interviewing the victims and sending an innocent person to prison," said Agent Donald.

Donald stressed that interviewing the victim of assault doesn't mean sex assault victims don't deserve to be believed, he made his position clear that victims deserve to be heard, and they also need empathy and protection during their ordeal.

"But if you interrogate only the accused you will know whether he's telling the truth or not," said Lieutenant Rose.

"Not everyone knows how to defend themselves even when they are innocent. Sometimes a prosecutor will build an ugly scenario around an innocent person, and that evidence whether circumstantial or otherwise will send the person to prison. Therefore, a thorough interrogation of the accused and an empathic interview of the victim will help any investigation," said Agent Donald.

"But what about the slogan "Interrogate the accused only and not the victim," asked Lieutenant Rose.

"That's a slogan coined by deluded advocates, and that has pushed cops into drawing premature conclusions even before the investigation," said Agent Donald.

Just like Joseph here who would've lost his wife, his career, and his children might probably grow up with a stepdad and so many other ugly scenarios," said Agent Barry.

"My slogan is "protect the victim, but find out the truth from the victim so you don't create another victim by sending an innocent person to prison," said agent Donald. He proceeded to say that lots of women are being raped daily and the predators behind this shouldn't be allowed on our streets, but should be behind bars.

Arguably, lies like this one by Katherine sometimes throw spanner in the works and takes the paddle away from people with genuine case of sexual assault. While the legal system is predicated on being blind, those who work in the legal system aren't, they kind of loose objectivity sometimes, particularly when their personal emotion gets in the way.

The detectives returned to their office after their investigation in the South Bridge Unit. Alicia on the other hand, had her Los Angeles home burgled, and she dialled 911.

The cops arrived and met Alicia weeping like a baby. "I'm Alicia Wright, I just got home and discovered that my home has been burgled," said Alicia.

"I'm Sergeant Cooper Perry, of the Los Angeles Police department. We received a 911 call from this address," said Sergeant Cooper. The police officer asked Alicia if she has any idea who might be responsible.

"No, I can't say, because I don't suspect anybody. I just don't know who to suspect," said Alicia.

"Is there anything missing from your house?" asked Sergeant Cooper.

"All my jewellery is gone, everything I've bought over the past twenty-eight years, all gone," she said.

"Is any other thing missing from your house apart from the Jewellery?" asked Sergeant Cooper.

The Sergeant and his team walked around Alicia's property taking down notes as she tells them of her loss.

"Just a little money, about one thousand dollars and an old credit card that has expired, but my Jewellery is worth over half a million dollars, I want it back," she said.

"Were you in the house when it happened?" asked Sergeant Cooper.

"I went for an evening dinner with a friend, then saw this when I got back," said Alicia. The sergeant decided to ask about the other occupants in the apartment, to rule out the possibility of this being an inside job. "Are your kids staying with you?" asked Sergeant Cooper. "Jake doesn't stay here, he lives in New York," said Alicia.

The NYPD officers looked around Alicia's apartment but sadly, the only functioning CCTV camera was turned off by Alicia days before, over faulty electricity cables. More so, CCTV review shows that Jake didn't come to town the day leading to the burglary, but the only evidence left behind by the burglars was a piece of paper. The only word on the paper was "get the Old Bill, or bugger off," and this creates a suspicion that the burglar is British, yet the cops want to know more about Jake.

"Does he have keys to your apartment?" asked Sergeant Cooper.

"Yes, he has a copy, but I just spoke with him, he's in New York City, and Jake doesn't steal so it can't be him," said Alicia.

"We'll get back to you; our forensic team is working to see if we can find something to point us to the perpetrators of this crime.

"Ok, please do everything you can to help me get my jewellery back, I don't mind the money," she said.

The Sergeant and his team left and returned to Alicia two weeks later. "Alicia, we've gone through all the information the forensic team was able to gather and we're not able to link the crime to anyone," said Sergeant Cooper.

"After two weeks, you still can't identify the thieves with my Jewellery?" asked Alicia.

"The people responsible for this crime were wearing gloves and face masks, we couldn't identify them through the street CCTV footage, but we're still on it," said Sergeant Cooper.

"I want you to try harder; I can't lose my jewellery to some scumbags," Alicia retorted.

After her hopes on the NYPD officers were dashed, Alicia thought of giving Jimmy a call after learning he now works with the FBI. Maybe with the apparatus of the FBI now at his disposal, Jimmy might be able to help. She picked up her phone, then paused for a while, but decided go ahead to give Jimmy a call.

"Hello Jimmy, how're you?" said Alicia.

"Er.., Alicia, is that you?" asked Jimmy.

"Yes Jimmy" Alicia said.

"I'm surprised you're calling me now; remember you said you want nothing to do with me?" Jimmy retorted.

"Yes, I did, but I need your help," she said.

"This is quite strange, and won't people know you're seeking help from me, the famous thief?" Jimmy retorted, in quite a jocular manner.

"I learnt you now work with the FBI, that you've turned your life around and that's a good thing," said Alicia. Funnily, Jimmy has bones to pick with Alicia, and must visit the past before going forward into a new chapter, even though he has no idea of Alicia's intentions.

"You turned me down when I needed you most. Though, you were good to me once, what can I do for you?" asked Jimmy.

"My house was burgled and all my Jewellery is gone," said Alicia.

"Oh, that's bad, when did this happen?" asked Jimmy.

"Two weeks ago, are you sure you've no hand in it?" Alicia asked, expressing her suspicion in a subtle manner.

"If you still don't trust me, then why're you troubling me for help? Who else has access to your house?" asked Jimmy.

"Only my son, Jake," said Alicia.

"And he said he didn't take it; I suppose Jake lives in New York City?" asked Jimmy.

"Yes, but Jake doesn't steal," said Alicia. Jimmy's initial suspicion falls on Jake as the main culprit behind the burglary, but he knew his suspicion will put Alicia off, so he decides to begin with Jake's sphere of influence and cunningly made her a part of the investigation.

"Fly down to New York tomorrow to help me identify any piece of your Jewellery, in case we find any," said Jimmy.

"I thought you'll come over to Los Angeles to help me find it?" said Alicia.

"Let's start from New York City, if a piece of your Jewellery enters New York, I'll find it, and I will use it to trace the thieves," said Jimmy. Alicia mumbled and went silent, grimacing slightly; she then took a deep breath. "Ok, but you seem to be suspecting my son, if not, why start from New York? This trip is not a romance trip; I only need your help with this," Alicia retorted.

Jimmy didn't think it wise to further engage Alicia in a turf, especially now that he has cunningly poked his finger at her son. "You're welcome, and I guess we should start from the known to the unknown," said Jimmy.

Alicia's sudden faith in Jimmy means she didn't hesitate to book her flight to New York City for the next day after her conversation with Jimmy. Interestingly, Jimmy was quite early at the airport as he looked forward to seeing Alicia once again even though it's glaringly obvious that Alicia's visit isn't a romantic one. It was quite a sight at the airport as the pairs re-enacted their flings with a bear hug. Moments after dispensing of their pleasantries, Jimmy took Alicia to the possible spots where stolen Jewellery are sold including Pawn shops.

"As we move from place to place, if you find your Jewellery let me know," said Jimmy.

The pair strolled along the busy street of New York City, from Northern Manhattan and all the way down to Lower Manhattan, moving from one store to another, it was quite a long walk for a posh Hollywood lady like Alicia. It's been more than thirty minutes of what Alicia considers aimless trek, tough luck though, and it didn't take long before Alicia protested that this isn't a wise use of her time.

"Ok, but we've been moving from one place to another and we haven't found anything," Alicia retorted.

"Be patient and trust me," said Jimmy.

"I hope I didn't fly to New York for nothing," said Alicia.

Sadly, Jimmy himself soon realised the mission has suddenly become more difficult than he expected. He's now like a man searching for a needle in a haystack because he no longer enjoys the free flow of information from his old circle of friend as was the case when he was a thief. Jimmy then brought out his phone and dialled Damian's number. "Hello Damian, how are you?" asked Jimmy. Sad to say, that Damian isn't particularly excited with this phone call from his old friend who turned into a cop. "Jimmy, what do you want from me? I know you now work with the cops," said Damian.

"Damian, you're still my friend, please I want some information, it's for my fiancée," said Jimmy. The moment Alicia heard Jimmy refer to her as his fiancée, she gave him a sidelong glance in a manner that says don't be silly!

"Ok, what do you want? Provided you aren't stitching me up," said Damian.

"Is there any set of Jewellery stolen from Los Angeles and sold in New York City within the last two weeks?" asked Jimmy.

"I hope you're not going to stitch me up and make my friends to see me as a snitch?" asked Damian.

"You know I wouldn't do such a thing," said Jimmy.

"There's this guy that brought Jewellery from Los Angeles two weeks ago, his name is Jake," said Damian.

"Do you know the places he sold them? I've checked around and haven't found anything," asked Jimmy.

Damian burst into laughter, and his laughter laid bare Jimmy's limitations as a cop, because the running of the underworld has now eluded him. "That's because you're no longer a thief, Jimmy, you can't be a cop and a thief at the same time," said Damian.

"You're right, I now realise information doesn't flow to me as it used to, please fill me in, where will we find the jewellery?" asked Jimmy.

"Go to the Bazooka link in Lower Manhattan, you'll find some of it there," said Damian.

"Thank you," said Jimmy. Alicia has her ears wide open while Jimmy was on phone with Damian, and funnily, she heard Damian mention her son's name as the key person behind the burglary.

"Are you sure we'll find it there?" asked Alicia.

"Your son Jake is behind this," Jimmy retorted.

"Are you sure, and why would he do such a thing? I'll get to the bottom of this before I lay the blame on my son," Alicia retorted.

Forty-five minutes later, Jimmy and Alicia were in the Bazooka link as advised by Damian, he immediately walked into the premises of his former friend who buys stolen items from him. It didn't take long before Alicia pointed at jewellery on display.

"That's my Jewellery," said Alicia.

"Are you sure?" asked Jimmy.

"Of course, of course, it's my jewellery!" Alicia exclaimed.

"There's a possibility your son is involved, so you don't have to scream," Jimmy advised.

"What are you doing here, Jimmy? Are you out to stitch me up like you did to Warren?" asked Derek.

"I'm about to save you only if you listen," said Jimmy.

Most of the bad guys in the area who know Jimmy seem to want to distance themselves from him to avoid being his next casualty and Derek is a hustler who thinks Jimmy's jostling could cause him harm.

"What are you talking about?" asked Derek.

"That's my Jewellery, who sold them to you and where's the rest?" asked Alicia.

"One guy, Jake, brought it here. I only bought these few pieces, and I believe he still has the rest," said Derek.

Jimmy turned to Alicia and asked her to pick out the jewellery that's hers, but Derek isn't quite happy with the visit of his old acquaintance whom he shares some memories with, and he isn't letting this happen without a protest.

"Stop, what are you doing? I paid for those," Derek protested.

"That will be your loss, you'll have to bear it, and at least I'll not take you in on this," Jimmy retorted.

Derek protested further, as he asked Jimmy to stop playing the Saint, he then urged Jimmy to cast his mind back, before reminding him of those times he used to sell things to him in the past. It's now obvious that her son isn't a saint after all, and immediately they left Derek's jewellery shop, Alicia dipped her hand in her bag and brought out her phone and dialled Jake.

"Hello mum, how're you?" asked Jake.

"I'm fine Jake, where are you?" asked Alicia.

Jake retorted, saying he's in New York City, and then asked his mum in quite a rambunctious tone "where else should I be?"

"I'm in New York at the Bazooka Link with the Cops and the FBI," said Alicia.

Jake sensed trouble the moment Alicia mentioned the Bazooka Link which is where he sold his mum's jewellery, he suddenly became worried as his anxiety was reflected in his broken and trembling voice.

"What are you doing there, I mean the Bazooka Link?" asked Jake.

Alicia didn't hesitate to read the riot act to her son, and made sure her subtle threat to her son who has bones to pick with her was clearly received.

"Jake, I give you thirty minutes to bring the rest of my jewellery, and I've already collected the ones you sold" said Alicia.

"Which Jewellery are you talking about?" asked Jake.

Alicia wasn't in any mood for play, as she made it clear and in no uncertain terms to Jake that if he brings the Jewellery to her, she will spare him, but if he wants her to come over to his house with the police and FBI then he knows what that meant. Jake smelt a rat and he's now convinced that if his mum could trace her jewellery from Los-Angeles to New York City, and to the Bazooka Link, then his mum will stop at nothing to get him. "Ok, wait for me I'm coming over," Jake said.

Forty-five minutes later, Jake was at the Bazooka Link where his mum was waiting, and sadly, there wasn't any appetite for pleasantries between this mother and son before Jake handed the bag containing the rest of the jewelleries to his mum.

"Take your Jewellery," said Jake.

"Wait, let me see if it's all in there," said Alicia. She rummaged through the bag and checking out if her jewellery is all complete. "A few are still missing, but I don't mind," said Alicia.

Funnily, it didn't take long before Jake's memory clicked as he realised that the man standing next to his mum is the famous Jimmy Thompson, the thief exposed by the press about a year earlier, and Jake's disposition suddenly changed.

"That's Jimmy Thompson, what are you doing with him?" asked Jake.

"He's my boyfriend, what about it?" asked Alicia.

"Your boyfriend you say, don't you know about him?" asked Jake, with an expression of disgust.

"He's a thief that just helped me recovered what I lost, while you're a thief that wants to destroy me," said Alicia.

"Is this what you left dad for? For the record, I'm not a thief, and don't call me that," Jake retorted.

"You are! Is it because I spared you, and why would you do such a wicked thing to me?" Alicia asked.

"You left dad when he needed you most, and if I see my opportunity to make you pay for that, I'll do it," said Jake.

Alicia stood for a while trying to get her head around why her son would want to wreak havoc on her without any just cause. Jake wasn't just unrepentant; his anger grew particularly now that his mum has been frolicking with a prominent thief.

"The next time, I'll not spare you," said Alicia.

Jake angrily left, leaving Alicia and Jimmy behind, and Jimmy suddenly turned to Alicia. "I'm glad you've found your Jewellery, should I accompany you to the airport now or when are you leaving?" asked Jimmy.

"Are you chasing me away?" asked Alicia, who seems not to be in a hurry any longer.

"I'm not chasing you, but you've found your Jewellery and I don't want to push my luck too far," Jimmy said with a smile.

"What do you mean by pushing your luck?" asked Alicia.

Jimmy knew right from the moment he set his eyes on Alicia at the airport, that she's still into him, considering the manner she hugged him so tightly without letting go.

"You said it, that you aren't coming for a romantic visit and I got the message clearly," said Jimmy.

"I'm spending the night in your place," said Alicia.

Jimmy turned to Alicia and asked what she intends to do about her ticket, reminding her she's meant to fly back today.

"I'll reschedule my flight but I'm spending the night," Alicia insists.

"Ok, you're welcome," said Jimmy.

Now that Alicia has indicated her interest to spend the night with Jimmy Thompson, the pair began chatting and reminiscing the time they spent together in the Cayman Island. Later that evening Alicia and Jimmy were in a Chinese restaurant for their dinner, which is Alicia's choice restaurant in New York City. Funnily, Alicia's choice of menu was frog menu which Jimmy finds to be something untoward and very amusing. "What are you doing with frog meat?" asked Jimmy.

"Frog meat, popularly referred to as field chicken is my favourite, that's the reason why I make this spot my choice restaurant in New York City," said Alicia.

"I wanted guacamole but since they don't have it, I've to settle for either crab or frog," said Alicia.

Moments after placing her order, the waiter returned to inform Alicia that they have run out of frog meat menu, sadly, she'd to go for an alternative menu. It didn't take long before a menu of crab was placed before Alicia.

"Are you sure you like that," asked Jimmy, pointing to the Crab in Alicia's plate.

"Yeah, it's nice and very rich in calcium; you once asked me why I looked younger than my age," asked Alicia.

"Yeah, and are you saying this is part of the reason?" asked Jimmy.

"Sure, I always try to make healthy choices," said Alicia.

Jimmy is now different from the man he was in their previous encounter. He's somewhat a church kind of man, a lifestyle he acquired since after his previous encounter with Alicia. Pastor Bowers led Jimmy to Christ, and has since helped Jimmy to remain in the straight and narrow path. Consequently, even as his heart pants for Alicia, he isn't quite keen about running into her arms, he wants marriage, something permanent. He has been searching for the right person to settle down with, and Alicia seems to have a hold on him but settling down with someone's wife is something he finds quite needling.

"Talking about healthy choices, I think the best choice is living for God," said Jimmy.

"Living for God! How does that relate to you?" asked Alicia.

"I'm a Christian now, and I now look up to God in all things, thanks to my son," said Jimmy. Alicia was taken aback by Jimmy's comments and couldn't get her head around how a known thief would suddenly turn out to be a church person.

"This has taken an interesting turn, and I'm glad you're making efforts to better your life," said Alicia.

"What about you, Alicia! What do you intend to do differently?" asked Jimmy.

"You know I have a thing for you, and frankly, since we parted ways in the Cayman Island, I haven't been able to get over you, and I don't mind doing anything for God, provided I'm with you," said Alicia.

Unsurprisingly, Jimmy's newly found Christian faith held him bound, and he's now troubled with guilt that he's taking a woman away from her husband.

Jimmy tried to slow things down, as he reminded her, he's quite aware she's divorced but he's held back by the feeling that she's still Charlie's wife. Alicia immediately became red-faced as she immediately sounded a note of caution to Jimmy urging him to stop referring to her as Charlie's wife, she immediately informed Jimmy that Charlie his now married and has moved on with his life.

While the conversation continues, he realised Charlie has moved on, and he's now in a new relationship. It's obvious that life isn't always black and white, sometimes we think is white and some other time we think it's black rather, but in reality, we are actually in the grey zone. And funnily, that's a little of black and a little of white, neither here nor there, just grey.

"Are you doing it for me, or for God?" asked Jimmy.

"Erm., I want to do it for God, and to equally prove to you that I want to be better. I like you, Jimmy!" said Alicia.

"What about us? Does it mean you pass the night in my place today and leave tomorrow for Los Angeles, that's it?" asked Jimmy.

"No, I want something more than that with you, except you think differently," said Alicia.

"How can I rely on a relationship with you after the shameful treatment you gave to me?" asked Jimmy.

"You put yourself in that situation, Jimmy, and what should I have done, go around the United States, holding hands with you everywhere you go?" asked Alicia. Jimmy looked on even as Alicia was quite blunt, and as a businesswoman that she is, she doesn't mince her words when stating the facts.

"The state of your relationship with your ex-husband is still fluid and that makes me weary of a relationship with you," said Jimmy.

"What makes me fluid, tell me?" asked Alicia.

"Ok, by the way, now you know I've a job in New York, how'll this relationship work? What about the distance between us? I think it's better to make this relationship official," said Jimmy.

"Like marriage?" asked Alicia.

"Of course, yes. I can't continue anything outside marriage," said Jimmy.

Alicia was forthcoming with answers, as she suggested she will come over to New York during the weekends or Jimmy will have to come over to Los Angeles during the weekends, and with that they can sustain their relationship until they sort things out.

After spending quality time catching up as they ate their meal, the pair talked about the past, as well as planned for the future, and moments later they left for Jimmy's place where they spent the night.

CHAPTER

SIXTEEN

The Amorous Insider

Rob was enjoying the cool of the evening with his friends, Bart and Jensen, in their usual Sunday evening night out in Rob's restaurant. Rob had a jug of Beer in his hand, topping up his friends' glasses and suddenly veered into some apparently vague conversation.

"Jensen, you know I saw you yesterday," said Rob. Jensen smiled without making much meaning out of Rob's assertion. "You see me all the time, what makes your seeing me yesterday any different?" asked Jensen.

"Hmm, let me jog your memory, because this is actually different," said Rob. Jensen and Bart looked on expecting Rob to let out whatever cat it is that's in the bag.

"Why the hype, what makes it different?" asked Bart.

"I saw you in a quiet neighbourhood in Brooklyn; does that mean something to you?" asked Rob. While Jensen seems lost as to what Rob was driving at, he suddenly realised that Rob isn't filling the lines with expletives, but was establishing value. Rob got cheekier with Jensen, even as Jensen tries to play things down, but he soon opened up.

"Oh my God, my cover is blown despite efforts to keep things under wraps," said Jensen.

"She's a very pretty lady, and who is she?" asked Rob.

"The truth is beginning to come out, it's like you've something going, why don't you put me in the picture?" asked Bart.

"She's just somebody who does me favour when I feel honey," said Jensen. Sadly, Jensen might think he still has a sock on it and he's letting only a little out, but Rob funnily seems to know more than Jensen is letting out, even as he jocularly tricks Jensen into telling it as it is.

"Bring this special person to us Jensen, let's meet her," said Rob.

"That won't be possible, she's hooked," said Jenson.

"What do you mean she's hooked? You guys are perfect for each other, and you'll have to unhook her," said Rob.

"She's married, sorry," said Jensen.

Strangely, despite efforts to keep things under wraps, Rob whose eyes are alternative to the CCTV cameras in the Brooklyn neighbourhood sees every of Jensen's moves, as well as those happening under the cover of the night.

This is someone's wife that Jensen is messing with, and Rob is letting him know he's aware of what's going on.

"Isn't that Ava, Louie's wife?" asked Rob.

Jensen was amazed to hear Rob mention Ava's name, and understanding his history with Rob, that automatically puts Jensen in a bind. "How do you know her, and have you met her husband, Louie?" asked Jensen.

"I know things, Jensen!" Rob exclaimed in a jocular manner.

"The thing is, her beauty reached out to my youthfulness, and there was an instant connection," said Jensen. Rob has now steered the light conversation between friends enjoying their happy hours into something more surreal and steamier, and their mutual friend who has been listening as these revelations unfolds has already had his ears full.

"That's low, Jensen, she's someone's wife, you said. Then where are your morals?" asked Bart.

"Why the premature conclusion? Jensen hasn't confessed to having an affair with her," said Rob, as he tries to make light of the whole affair thing.

Rob has wittingly opened a can of worms, and these worms are now sprawling all over the place, Bart knew Rob was trying to obfuscate the worms by steering the conversation away, and refused to be swayed by Rob. Bart then looked right into Jensen's eyes. "It's written all over him, he has committed the act," said Bart.

Jensen muttered, saying the lady in question is his flat mate's wife, and it's just a fling, nothing serious. Sadly, Jensen was overtaken by guilt as a result of Bart's rebuke and tried walking back on his earlier comments. "How'll you feel, if your wife cheats on you? I suggest you end it right now. For God's sake, don't indulge in another person's wife!" exclaimed Bart.

Rob remained unfazed by Bart's rebuke as he seems bent on pumping Jensen, and continues to fuel Jensen's adventure with Ava. Moments later, Rob raised his glass to propose a toast. "To Jensen and his new found love," said Rob.

"Be careful and not let greed poison your soul Jensen," said Bart. Jensen went along with Rob and raised his glass to the toast but Bart didn't, and after a while of chatting and laughing, Jensen and Bart left. A week later, while Louie was getting ready for work and Ava was making breakfast in the kitchen. "Honey, your breakfast is ready," said Ava.

Moments after he finished dressing for work but instead of going straight to have his breakfast, Louie was busy looking around for his mobile phone charger. "Ok thank you, but I can't find my phone charger," he said.

"Erm.., I gave it to Jensen last night, go ahead with your breakfast let me get the charger," Ava said.

Ava rushed upstairs to Jensen's room and stood by his door and then knocked.

"Hey Jensen, are you still asleep?" asked Ava. Jensen opens the door and winked at Ava, as he tried to lure her inside his room. "Hmm, Ava, you want to come in?" asked Jensen.

"I need Louie's mobile phone charger," she said.

"You can come in, I don't bite," he said and smiled.

Ava laughed as she enters Jensen's room "Of course, I know you don't bite, you cheeky man," she replied.

Jensen didn't hesitate to pass his hands around her and kissed her, and funnily, she allowed him some moment of frolicking.

"You know I'm not going to let you off easily," Jensen joked. After a while Ava sensed Louie will be waiting for her, and was itching to leave. "It's ok, I need to go, Louie is waiting for me, don't blow my cover," she said.

"Ok, I look forward to our outing tomorrow," Jensen said, as he reminds her of their rendezvous.

Ava rushed downstairs. "This is it, I'll put it inside your bag," she said.

"Why did it take you so long?" asked Louie. She quickly improvised with a lie, to save her skin from any suspicion from her husband.

"Jensen was searching for the charger," she said.

Ava herself was already prepared to leave the house, but had to finish off with her baking. The moment Louie stepped out of the house for work, Jensen rushed downstairs and joined Ava in the kitchen where she's baking stuff in the oven. The interplay between this two meant each time Louie leaves the house Jensen takes over like the proverbial mouse that runs around the house once the cat is on holiday.

Days later Jensen paid Rob a visit in his restaurant and they both sat on a separate table away from other customers, and Jensen was wondering why Rob wants to see him urgently.

"You said I should see you, and you said it's urgent, is everything ok?" asked Jensen.

"Yeah, but why don't we get something to drink before we get on with our conversation?" said Rob. Jensen's ominous gut feeling of impending trouble tells him something is off. Yet, he kept his cool without obviously doubling his fears, but quickly dispensed of all pleasantries, as well as not willing to go along with any offer of refreshment from Rob.

"I'm on medication; I really do not wish to drink anything," said Jensen.

Rob wants to lighten the mood, realising that his call has inadvertently made Jensen become unnecessarily anxious. Jensen isn't keen for refreshments, as he's eager to know why Rob wants to see him. "Not even a glass of red wine, the healthy choice?" asked Rob.

"I'm ok for now," said Jensen.

"This girl, Ava!" said Rob.

"Ava, what about her?" asked Jensen.

"I've been thinking, why aren't having her to yourself?" said Rob.

"I told you she's married and Louie is a good guy?" Jensen insists.

"Have you told her about it?" asked Rob.

Jensen was taken aback with Rob's line of conversation, and he's rattled by how a man who has no dog in a fight will be neck deep in another man's private affairs. Rob is no longer speaking in vague terms, and he's now making his intentions clearer even as he employed his deadpan humour to keep Jensen calm.

"I know Ava, she won't give in to such a proposition, and I don't want to burn my bridges myself," Jensen protested.

"I feel strongly about this, I think you should tell her, she might like the idea," Rob insists.

Jensen wasn't buying the fib from Rob whom he now thinks is speaking from both side of the mouth, he had to remind Rob that even their friend, Bart, didn't consider this morally right either. More so, suggesting to Ava to leave her husband for him, is quite a brazen request, and will definitely do great harm to his friendship with Louie.

"Presently, I must confess, I'm bogged down with guilt," said Jensen.

"Leave Bart out of this, he's rustic and a total recluse," said Rob.

After much back and forth, Rob impressed on Jensen to make the move on Ava. Funnily Jensen has a history with Rob and he's keen on treading softly, softly with Rob and fears his stern refusal to go along with this Ava scheme could spook Rob and precipitate a temper that isn't palatable.

Jensen is rather convinced that this move will end up being more or less a damp squib. Yet, the next day, Jensen and Ava were in their usual secret rendezvous in the quiet Brooklyn neighbour-hood, and he took the bold step to bring the proposal before Ava.

Jensen was dressing up, after spending time with Ava, he then stopped for a moment and fixed his gaze on Ava to get her atten-tion. "How long will this continue?" he asked.

"As long as we can manage it, and our cover isn't blown," said Ava.

"That isn't what I meant," said Jensen as he tries to make his inten-tions clear. Ava anxiously turned to Jensen, with a keen interest.

"What then do you mean?" she asked.

"I want more than this; I want all of you for myself," said Jensen.

"What! What about Louie?" exclaimed Ava.

"You can leave him, at least you don't have kids with him yet, which makes it much easier," Jensen said to Ava, who looked on open-mouthed. This conversation has entered into a grey area that touched a nerve, and it's now getting quite thorny for Ava as she grapples with this sudden turn of events. Jensen kind of get under her skin with this request.

"We're a newly married couple and we aren't in a hurry to have kids. That decision isn't because I am planning on running off with you," Ava retorted.

"But that makes separation easy and clean," he replied.

"This is all you're getting, Jensen. I'm married and I love Louie," said Ava. Jensen pulled Ava close to himself trying to persuade her to fall for his proposal, Ava resisted at first, but had to let go of her resistance.

"Spending two hours with you weekly, in hiding, isn't enough," said Jensen.

"Not me! I'll not leave my husband. If cheating on my husband with you isn't enough, then we have to call it quits," said Ava.

"Why're you sounding furious, does it mean you don't enjoy the time we spend together?" he asked.

The kitchen is now getting too hot for the pair, and their nice time together has suddenly turned awkward, Ava tried to manage the situation as she began stroking Jensen's hair, and spoke softly to Jensen, telling him she does love and enjoy every bit of their rendezvous.

"You're sweet, Jensen, and I consider time spent with you as therapeutic but I want things to stay that way," she said.

"I intend going the whole hog for you, but I seem to be asking for too much. I rather have two hours of your attention than lose you altogether," said Jensen, as he tries not to burn his bride to Ava's heart.

Rob remained committed to seeing to it that Jensen continues on his conquest for the sole ownership of Ava's heart and affection, and later that same day, Rob gave Jensen a phone call as he's keen for an update on how the audacious move went. This time Rob didn't think it necessary to begin with the usual pleasantries before hitting the nail on the head.

"Hello Jensen, did you speak to Ava about your interest in her," he asked. These constant pestering by Rob is beginning to get on Jensen's nerves and he's now getting all riled up about it. He's now filled with disgust for Rob, but sadly, he owes Rob a favour, one which Jensen knows must be paid, but the terms might by uncanny.

"What's it with you and Ava?" asked Jensen.

"Nothing, I'm just concerned for you, and I don't think this concern of mine is misplaced," said Rob.

"Let me handle my affairs my way. You're creeping into my, my head, into life, and I don't like it," Jensen retorted. Sadly, even when it's glaringly obvious that Rob's moves have a cynical undertone, he still maintains a posture of doing Jensen a favour.

"This is a heavily incentivised assignment; and does it mean my efforts towards giving you a woman as a gift isn't appreciated?" asked Rob.

"What do you want, a hug, a kiss or an extravagant gratitude for a ghastly gift as this?" Jensen asked in an outburst of anger.

"You know you owe me," said Rob.

"Are you grooming me or what? This conversation has taken a surreal twist," asked Jensen. It's obvious to Jensen that he's now in a bind, and sadly for him, his blabbing and bad mouthing didn't in anyway put Rob off, to make him stop. "Nobody is grooming you, you're a paedophile, remember? Just do as you are told," Rob instructed.

"You and I know I'm not a child abuser; you set me up with your child and filmed it," said Jensen.

"This isn't about what the truth is, it's about what I have on you," Rob insists.

"I resigned from your business because of your twisted mind, yet you kept following me after I've moved on," Jensen chuckled. Rob is a man on a mission, of which Jensen have no knowledge about, and he's about being sucked in by this man who's after his tail, and isn't letting go. It's obvious that Rob has taken advantage of Jensen's greed for another man's wife to plague him.

"All I know is that I have you on tape and that video of you could surface anytime of my own choice," said Rob.

"You sent your child to sit on me and told her touch me all over, and you filmed it," said Jensen.

"I instructed you to tell Ava you want her to leave her husband for you," Rob insists. Realising the stakes are high, and Rob determination to scurrilously smear him, made Jensen to soften up, as his tough talking began to thaw. He now has to report back to the man pulling his strings, and this must include his last-ditch attempt to make Ava leave Louie.

"Whatever, I've told her about it already, she didn't bulge," said Jensen.

"Erm.., since this approach didn't work, then we'll initiate plan B," said Rob.

"Plan B, are we fighting a war or what?" Jensen asked ingenuously.

"Yeah, what if we take Louie out of the equation, like bump him off or something?" said Rob. Jensen is beginning to realise that his frolicking with Ava was a mistake that wouldn't have happened. He has now given Rob the bullet he's using against him, and it doesn't matter to Rob any longer if Jensen's head ends up on a Plate.

"What! Bump him off? Sorry I'm not up for this," said Jensen.

"You don't have to be up for this, all you've to do is play along," said Rob.

"This is becoming dangerous, I can't and sorry, I have to go," said Jensen. Rob interjected immediately, as Jensen attempted to end the phone call because he isn't letting him go without the usual subtle threat.

"Wait, I said wait, what do you think will happen to you if Louie hears about you and Ava, plus that tape getting to the cops?" asked Rob.

"There should be other ways of getting around this, and I don't have to kill a man just to have his wife, give me some time," Jensen pleads.

"Maybe you should pay me a visit at home," said Rob.

Even as Rob continued to present himself as a friend and brother to Jensen, paradoxically, Jensen is now realising he's being led down the rabbit hole that will eventually lead him to the slab on the butchers' table. All effort to wriggle out of this seem not to have worked, leaving him in the lurch. Arguably, Jensen shouldn't expect any better mingling with friends like Rob, because if you lay with dogs, you get fleas.

"Now I know your posturing as a brother was a sham," said Jensen. Thinking he could talk some sense into Rob to make him snap out of his madness, Jensen visits Rob at home to conclude on their previous conversation. Moments after letting Jensen into his apartment, Rob walked into his bedroom and came back out of his bedroom with his cat, 'Kittas,' on his shoulder.

"Come here Kittas." Jensen took Kittas from Rob, attempting to play with the cat, but noticed the cat is looking more like a vampire than a cat.

"Oh my God, what did you do to her teeth?" Jensen asked.

"I worked on her teeth; I want my cat to look different," said Rob. Rob left his cat with Jensen and walked into the kitchen as they speak, but Jensen isn't impressed by Kittas's new look. The cat is now less of pet and looked more like some blood thirsty vampire, a semblance of evil.

"Why make your cat look like a vampire? That's scary for what's supposed to be a pet," said Jensen.

Rob walks out of the kitchen holding a kitchen knife, and retrieved Kittas from Jensen. "Let's forget about Kittas, tell me about Ava," said Rob. "I can't hurt a man I call my friend just because I want to have his wife to myself," Jensen said.

"When will you grow up? You've always been witless and faint hearted since you were a kid," said Rob.

"Faint hearted lily livered, or whatever you call it. I just don't want to do this, and I can't hurt Louie," said Jensen.

Rob pressed Jensen further using the cliché that if it's ok for him sleeping and frolicking around with a man's wife behind his back, then it'll equally be ok for him to kill him, and blame it as just another little accident.

Rob's hubristic posturing didn't obfuscate his vituperation in any way, Jensen looked on, and couldn't help but cautioned Rob to stop the semantics, accusing Rob of wanting Louie dead even when it isn't within Rob's gift to decide who lives or die.

"Why're you so interested in hurting Louie, do you know him from before?" asked Jensen as the pair got into a kerfuffle.

Rob's role as a friend has run rampant, and sadly, Jensen felt whacked and didn't see this coming, particularly now that Rob has come through as a precursor to something fatal.

"You want to know the truth?" asked Rob.

"Is there something you aren't telling me? I would like to know," said Jensen.

"Louie broke my heart, he took my girlfriend when we were teens, the girl I would've married," said Rob. Jensen listened keenly as Rob tells his teen tale that set him off on a fatal vengeance.

"When you were teenagers, that should be about twenty years ago, but why didn't I know of this?" asked Jensen, who grew up in the same neighbourhood with Rob.

"That happened when I paid a visit to my granny, that was where I knew Louie," said Rob. This tale left Jensen quite unimpressed, as he's now been used to settle a score that relates to his teenage flame.

"But why now, why do you want your pound of flesh now?" asked Jensen. "Your relationship with his wife opens the door to the opportunity I seek. I knew all along that you share a flat with Louie," asked Rob.

Jensen looked on and remained speechless while Rob narrates the tale of his failed romance but was rattled by how Rob is able to carry this kind of bitterness in his underbelly this long.

"Now you know, take this knife," said Rob.

It's now blindingly obvious to Jensen that Rob's next move will set off a course of negative emotions that might make reversal to common sense impossible. Rob then hands Jensen the knife in his hand, as he tests Jensen's resolve.

"What for?" asked Jensen.

"Kill Kittas, I want you to kill Kittas," said Jensen.

"Kill your cat! What sort of twisted mind is this? This is your beloved pet you have had for three years and you just want me to kill her," said Jensen.

"You know I love my cat, but I need to test your resolve," said Rob. Sadly, Jensen hesitated as Rob pressed on him to act like the tough guy he claims, and funnily, Jensen is a social being with no violence in his bones and wouldn't engage in some cruel act on an innocent animal.

Rob took the knife from Jensen immediately and gruesomely stabbed Kittas to death, and with Kittas blood spattered all over, he then hysterically burst into laughter. "I've just done what a lily-livered man like you wouldn't do," said Rob.

Jensen was quite shaken with the sight of the events unfolding before his eyes, he stepped away leaving a gap of some feet between himself and Rob, fearing he could possibly attack him next.

"Oh my God, why're you so ecstatic, you just spilled your cat's blood all over the place, this is animal cruelty," Jensen retorted. Rob continued in his hubristic posture, saying he isn't just being ecstatic, but he thinks his laughter is hyperventilating.

"Does that make it right? This is lunacy," replied Jensen.

"Now you know I'm serious, the tape I've on you will be handed to the police within the next two weeks and Louie will know you're sleeping with his wife," Rob threatened.

"You have this deep-seated bitterness for Louie all along and you want to use me to even the score," said Jensen.

Rob insists that Jensen will be the one to carry out the vengeance on his behalf, and Jensen's closeness to Ava is Louie's weakness which he intends to exploit. Moments later, Rob walked out of his bedroom, and then brought out a small bottle containing a coloured liquid. Jensen is now an enemy Louie had no knowledge about, and this enemy is well strategically position, because he's an insider with free access to Louie through Louis' wife, Ava.

"What's this for?" asked Jensen who feels so trapped in Rob's web.

"That's aconite, don't let it touch your skin because it's highly toxic. Just make sure the only person making contact with it is Louie," said Jensen.

"Aconite, oh my God! Isn't this the devil's helmet? This is as poisonous as the deadly hemlock," exclaimed Jensen.

Rob pressed on Jensen to take the bottle of aconite, and after much hesitation, he eventually accepted it from Rob.

Jensen looked on and realised he can't sustain his deadpan humour, now that Kittas has just bitten the dust over this cruel display of power and strength.

"How does this work?" asked Jensen.

Rob didn't hesitate to remind Jensen that this aconite is a rare breed, and it is the most poisonous of all species of aconite, quite different from the regular aconite available to the public. He then proceeded to inform Jensen to be careful because contact with the liquid results in asphyxia, suffocation, and then heart attack which brings death.

"Ok, I'll do a search on aconite and I'll see what I can do," said Jensen.

"Don't leave any trace, and let me know when it's done," Rob instructed.

Days later, it was Saturday, the washing machine was playing up as Louie attempts to do his weekend laundry, and he's consumed trying get the machine back and running. It didn't take long before Ava walks in on Louie, and inquired what the problem was with the machine.

"The machine is playing up, though I'll get it up and running soon," replied Louie. Ava didn't hesitate to suggest getting Jensen to help Louie out.

"Oh, let me get Jensen to help you out," said Ava. As she attempted running upstairs, Louie interjected.

"Didn't you hear me say I'll get it up and running, why rush to Jensen?" he retorted.

"You need someone to help you out, should I get him?" asked Ava.

Ava retraced her steps backward, then stood by and watched as Louie battles with the machine. Louie remained silent and didn't respond to Ava's question.

"Hello, hello, why're you giving me the big freeze?" she asked.

"I'm not a snub, Ava," he said.

"I abhor the manner you sneer at me, each time I try to help," she retorted. Sad to say, that even if Ava fails to notice, her bond with Jensen is almost laid bare before her husband as Jensen's name is always at the tip of her tongue. She barely starts or finishes a conversation without mentioning Jensen's name. Arguably, she's inadvertently painting her husband as some sort of fragile tea cup that's about to shatter into tiny pieces, and posturing Jensen the hero who should save the day, is one thing her husband will not acquiesce.

Interestingly, Louie isn't suspicious of anything going on between his wife and Jensen, he's only enraged that his wife has suddenly turned Jensen to this super hero who should come to his rescue at all times.

"Why're you always quick to involve Jensen to help out in our affairs?" asked Louie.

"Nothing, but I don't think there is anything wrong seeking help from Jensen, " said Ava.

"Your actions are always suggesting you prefer his ideas and sug-gestions to mine," said Louie. Ava became upset with Louie's claim that she's undermining him, with her always saying Jensen this, and Jensen that, she turned and walks away angrily.

"You're taking this too far, Louie, I was just trying to help" she said.

By Monday morning, armed with the understanding that Louie is in the bathroom and that Louie normally spends about fifteen minutes taking his shower as he prepares for work, Jensen rushed downstairs to Ava who's in the kitchen making breakfast. Interestingly, Jensen knows full well that Louie has his red line, and wouldn't like it if he knows that Jensen walks in and out of the bedroom he shares with his wife as he pleases.

"Ava, please can I quickly grab a pen from your room?" asked Jensen.

"Ok, I'm busy and my hands are dirty, but be quick about it," she said, knowing that her husband might not like it if he meets Jensen in their bedroom.

"I'll quickly grab the pen; I just want to take down an address," he replied.

She immediately advised Jensen to go into their bedroom and grab one, but then urged him to be fast because she doesn't want Louie to meet him in their bedroom.

"Just a minute, I'll be out," said Jensen.

Jensen had to walk the tightrope, as well as make allowance for plausible deniability, this time he'd to go for an item belonging to Louie that Ava will possibly not touch, so he went for Louie's pair of eye glasses and immersed it in the poison and sneakily returned to his room immediately after the act.

Forty-five minutes later, it's time for Louie to leave for work, he entered his car, turned on the ignition and as he attempts to move his car, he brought out his pair of glasses and realised it was a bit wet. He then wiped it with his fingers as he usually does before putting it on. Moments after Louie arrived at his workplace, the aconite was absorbed into Louie's system through his skin and he slumped.

His colleagues present at the time he slumped rushed to help, and then the paramedics were called in, the paramedics tried to revive him but he remained asystolic after thirty minutes. They then rushed him to the hospital, and sadly, Louie was pronounced dead on arrival. The next morning, Andy Grey receives a phone call from Lieutenant Jones.

"Hello Lieutenant, how're you?" asked Andy.

"I'm fine Andy; we just received a call from the hospital, concerning a dead patient," said Lieutenant Jones.

"What's it about this patient?" asked Andy.

"He slumped at work, it was thought to be a heart attack but the doctor just informed me the death isn't natural," said Lieutenant Jones.

"Meaning, a murder may have been committed?" Andy queried further.

"Yeah, most likely," said Lieutenant Jones.

While still on the phone, Andy's worry is how the crime scene can be preserved, which is key to any investigation, and he needs to act fast before evidence at the crime scene are destroyed.

"Is your team already at the scene of the incident?" Andy asked.

"Not yet, we'll leave soon, I just felt I should inform you since this is now homicide, your jurisdiction," said Lieutenant Jones.

"Thank you, my men will be on the scene. Now concerning the patient, what's his story?" Andy asked.

"He's Louie Ayden, he slumped at work, and confirmed dead on arrival at the hospital," said Lieutenant Jones.

"Ok, we're on our way," said Andy.

Immediately after the phone conversation with the Lieutenant, Andy Grey stood up and walked straight into the central office, and asked his detectives to take up the case immediately, so as to preserve whatever evidence that's left in the crime scene. The detective hurried down to the hospital where Louie's body was deposited, and their first point of call was to the doctor that confirmed Louie's death to be everything but heart failure.

"Hello Doctor, we're FBI agents and we're here for Louie Ayden," said Agent Barry.

"Yeah, welcome, what do you guys want to know?" asked Dr Madison.

"Everything you know about his death, and what does the autopsy say?" asked Agent Donald. Doctor Madison immediately opened one of the draws to the table in his office and handed Louie's autopsy report to the detectives, he then stood up and they continue talking as the detectives followed the doctor from behind.

"His death isn't natural, and his symptoms are consistent with poisoning, I found traces of aconite in his system," said Dr. Madison.

"How did the Aconite get there?" asked Agent Barry.

The doctor replied, saying he'd no idea and reminded the detectives that he supposes that knowing how the aconite got into the victim's system is the reason behind their visit. He proceeded to hint the detectives that one thing is for sure, the victim didn't ingest the poison. The doctor took them to the morgue and pulled out Louie's body, pointing to the features on his body as they speak. This corpse is now a crime scene and Chain of evidence must be maintained.

"Ok, which means it can be absorbed through the skin or..." said Agent Donald. The Doctor interjected immediately.

"Yes, mere contact with a deadly specie of aconite could kill, because it goes into the blood stream through the skin, and there isn't any sign of struggle to make me believe he was forced," said Dr. Madison.

"Then suicide is the only explanation for this," said Agent Barry.

"Hold your breath, Barry. Let's not rush into premature conclusion," said Agent Donald.

"Ok detectives, I'll leave you to it, " said Dr. Madison.

Agent Donald thanked the doctor and said they'll be back if there's any concern, they would want him to clarify. Three days after Louie's death, Ava lay on the couch sobbing ceaselessly all night. Jensen opened the door and walks in after a late night out. "Its 11.pm, Ava, and you've been crying all night?" asked Jensen. She has been crying all day, and has got no more hair to pull out, and all she could do at this point is sob.

"What do you expect me to do, celebrate my husband's death?" Ava retorted.

"Of course not, but you could become unwell if you continue like this," he said.

Ava protested, saying the news of her husband's death is quite a bitter pill to swallow and then asked why the cold hands of death will take her husband from her just at the beginning of their marriage.

Jensen then sat beside Ava, and held her hand. "But you promised to put yourself together, when I spoke with you earlier today," he said.

"The Police just informed me his death isn't natural and that breaks my heart the more, who'll want to kill Louie?" she cried. Jensen has tried as much as he could to keep his guilt under wraps, even though he hasn't reported back to Rob because he isn't proud of what he did, but his folly might mean challenging the doctor's position that a murder has just occurred.

"You mean the Police told you Louie's death isn't natural?" Jensen asked with keen interest.

"Yes, of course, my husband is a good man, and who'll want to kill him?" she cried. The news that Louie's death is suspicious rattled Jensen's cage and puts him on the back foot, as this is the kind of news he isn't prepared to hear, and he's now faced with the choice of deflecting this investigation.

"That's a ruse," said Jensen.

Ava turned to Jensen in anger, and asked why he would say the doctor's finding concerning her husband's death is a ruse. He immediately tried to justify his assertion, saying sometimes the police engage in phony investigations just to keep themselves busy.

"I'll want to know who killed Louie" she said, and then turned to Jensen, looking straight into his eyes. "Wouldn't you want to know who killed your friend?" she asked.

"Yes, yes. Jensen adjusts his tie, speaking in a broken voice. "Erm.., I would want to know who the killer is," said Jensen.

Since Louie died at work, Ava is now convinced that the killer must be in his workplace and her finger of accusation points to his colleagues.

"How come his colleagues at work are so hypocritical? I thought they all liked him," she retorted.

"You can never truly know people, Ava," he replied, then looked way.

"He died at work, meaning someone in his workplace is behind this," Ava insists.

This line of conversation that there's a killer out there, got Jensen all riled up, and it's now discomforting him, he suddenly got up and walks to the fridge. "Let me get you something to eat, and I guess you must be hungry," said Jensen.

"I don't feel like eating, I don't have appetite for food," she replied.

"You would've to eat something, and you can't continue sobbing on an empty stomach," he said.

"Go ahead then, thanks for being a true friend," she said.

After paying a visit to Doctor Madison for insight surrounding the circumstance of Louie's death, the detectives visited Ava the next morning to ask her a few questions, which is usually the norm. "Hello Ava, I'm Agent Donald and this is my colleague, Agent Barry, sorry for your loss, Ava," said Agent Donald.

"Have you found Louie's killer? I just need to see the face of my husband's killer," she asked.

"You'll need to help us do that," said Agent Barry.

"How! I expect you to be interrogating his colleagues, he died at work," she said.

"Help us fill in some blank spaces, to help facilitate this investigation, and make our work easier," he said.

"Yeah, go ahead, provided it'll help you find my husband's killer," she said.

"Does your husband have anything to do with aconite," asked Agent Donald. Sadly, Ava has no knowledge of what Aconite is, and the question sent her into confusion, but with news coming in dribs and drabs, it's now dawning on Ava that there's a grim story behind her husband's demise.

"Aconite, what's aconite?" said Ava.

"Oh, the poison they found in his system," said Agent Donald. "Please allow our forensic team do a search to see if the poison is from your apartment," she said.

"Where and where do they want to search?" asked Ava.

"Give them access to your food area, your cutleries, plates and your bedroom," said Agent Donald.

Interestingly, the forensic team examined Ava's room, and all the ground floor, but didn't go upstairs into Jensen's apartment since he alone occupies the top floor, and he wasn't at home as the time of the search. After the search, the forensic team found no trace of aconite.

"Did you find anything?" she asked.

Funnily, instead of giving an answer to Ava's question, Agent Barry looked straight into Ava's eyes. "Do you know of anyone who'll want your husband dead?" he asked.

"I don't know of anyone who'll want to kill Louie. I thought his colleagues love him, why should they kill him?" she asked and began to sob.

Agent Donald taps her on the shoulder, to calm her down, as he assured her that they'll do their best to bring her husband's killer to book.

"I don't know, but if there's anything I know of, I'll contact you," she promised.

"Ok Ava, we'll get back to you. Agent Donald turned to Barry. "Let's go, Barry," said Agent Donald.

Moments after the detectives finished with Ava, they decided pay a visit to Louie's place of work for a second time to interview his boss and colleagues. This time his boss was on hand to attend to the detectives.

"Hello, I'm detective Donald Whitely and this is my colleague Agent Barry," he said.

"Alton Manson is my name, you're welcome, detectives," said Alton.

"We're looking into the suspicious death of your member of staff," said Agent Donald.

Alton noted that he wasn't around when the detectives visited his office the previous day, but was quick to refute the detective's claim as he stressed that Louie's death could not have been suspicious, that he died of heart attack in the presence of everyone.

"He's a young man full of life, with so much to offer, and why should his heart park up this early?" Alton asked curiously.

Agent Barry interjected immediately. "His heart didn't park up, his life was snuffed out," Agent Barry retorted.

"I don't like talking ill of the dead, but Louie died in our presence and I think he died of natural causes," Alton insists.

"But the doctor thinks otherwise, he thinks Louie was murdered," said Agent Donald.

"Oh my God! Who would want to kill him?" Alton exclaimed.

"Why don't you help us out?" Agent Barry replied.

"Help you out in what way? You sound as if I know Louie's killer," Alton said. All efforts by Alton to make the detectives leave his place of business without giving out much to help their investigation didn't work, because they are determined to dig deep. Agent Donald prodded Alton with more questions, as he asked if there's anything unusual, he observed or any reason why any of his colleagues will want him dead.

"I don't know of anyone who'll want to kill Louie and I haven't observed anything either," he replied.

"No strife or contention with any of his colleagues?" Agent Donald queried further.

Alton went quiet for a while as he thinks through to remember if there was any time Louie was in contention with any of his colleagues. Hmm, he once had a bitter quarrel with Amos, who promised to see him to the grave," Alton said.

"When did this happen?" asked Agent Donald.

"About two months ago in the presence of everyone, after Louie was promoted ahead of Amos," said Alton.

The detectives are keen to hear more about the threat from Amos, they need to ascertain if the threat was credible enough, as something Amos would eventually follow through.

"How did Louie take the threat?" asked Agent Donald.

"He discarded it in the bin and moved on with his life, can Amos be responsible for this?" asked Alton.

"We'll find out if he did, though we'll need to interview every one of your staff," said Agent Barry.

"Oh, go ahead, just be nice to my clients, and a little smile won't hurt," said Alton.

After interviewing every other member of staff, the detectives arrested Amos because his response wasn't quite convincing, and they took him to their office for proper interrogation, but before the interrogation begins, the agent discussed the case as Amos waits in the interrogation room.

"We don't have anything on him," said Andy.

"He promised to kill Louie in the presence of his colleagues, now Louie is dead. What else do we need to send this killer to prison?" asked Agent Barry.

"His comment makes him a suspect, but that doesn't mean he committed the act," said Agent Donald.

Andy is convinced, the District Attorney will not charge based on what Amos said in the heat of a quarrel, unless there's some evidence to prove he went through with his threat.

"Yeah, we still need to get something out of him, even though all his colleagues implicated him," said Andy.

"I'm going in; let's see what we can find," said Agent Donald.

It didn't take long before Agent Donald began the interrogation.

"I don't have anything to say to you," said Amos.

"Ok then let's do this quickly, and why would you want to kill Louie?" asked Agent Donald.

"I didn't kill Louie, but glad he's gone," said Amos.

"Why're you so unfazed by the death of your colleague?" asked Agent Donald.

Amos unblinkingly told the detective that Louie snatched a promotion that was meant to be a launchpad to a glittering career for him. Amos insisted that life isn't just a waiting room, it's there for the taking, and Louie took that which belongs to him.

In such a morbid joke, he hinted the detective that his hamster died just a day ago, he immediately reminded the detectives that he didn't shed a tear over his hamster's death because the hamster has been naughty of late.

"Would you mind to join me so we can cry together, as I mourn my hamster? Because I would rather cry for my dear hamster, than for Louie," Amos unblinkingly retorted.

Amos's woke culture meant he can't do without the concern for social justice and racial justice, yet he's held back by his pacifist philosophy that believes violence are unjustifiable. Funnily, his lack of empathy over the death of his colleague is arguably in contrast with his pacifist philosophy, which makes him a person of interest in this case.

The detectives listened as Amos poured out his venomous anger towards Louie, 'say no ill of the dead', isn't a moral code Amos intends to uphold. Amos isn't backing down, and sadly his anger still burns. Obviously, this Amos of a man wants nothing but to shake the hands of whomever it was that took Louie out of the equation, and he has made no secret of it.

"You promised to kill him because you aren't comfortable with the idea of answering to a younger person," said Agent Donald.

Amos' responses were more like a scatter-gun, as he poured out his heart, and said after giving so much to the company, the thank you he got was the humiliation of making a new member of staff his superior.

"Not being comfortable with Louie being your superior doesn't give you the right to kill him," said Agent Donald.

"What makes you think I killed him, I'm only glad about the fact that he's gone and no longer a threat to my career," said Louie.

Agent Donald reminded Amos of the consequence of committing a murder, and then said the career he intends to save will be lost.

"I didn't kill him," Amos protested.

Even as Agent Donald continued his line, and said Amos promised to kill Louie and now Louie is dead. Amos on the other hand is like a sponge, he absorbs anything and everything thrown at him, as he insisted that he has no hand in Louie's death. He assured the detectives that it was rage speaking, not him, when he promised to kill Louie in the heat of an argument. Realising he could be in for a big trouble with the evidence against him, Amos dropped his hard man's stance, and begins to tone down his fiery utterances.

"From the abundance of the heart the mouth speaks," said Agent Donald.

"Meaning?" asked Amos.

"There's a motive, and you never promised to kill him before he was made your superior, you told him you'll see him to his grave after he was promoted ahead of you," said Agent Donald.

"Your analysis is startling," said Amos.

"Meaning, you've a reason, and a motive to kill him. Whether genuine or not," said Agent Donald.

"Is this all you've on me? You can't charge me on what I said in anger," Amos retorted.

"You'll have to tell that to the judge," said Agent Donald.

"Why don't you let me go if you don't find anything on me? I'm not his killer, and I've no idea who did," said Amos.

"I'll be back," said Agent Donald. Just as Donald stood up to leave, Amos screamed from the top of his voice, requesting he should be left off the hook, so he could go back to work because he had no hand in this. Agent Donald didn't look back, he continued and left the interrogation room, then joined Andy Grey and Agent Barry who were observing the interrogation as it progresses.

"What do you think?" asked Agent Donald.

"I don't know, Donald! Something is amiss," said Andy.

"I didn't get the feeling he did it, yet he remains our best bet," said Agent Donald.

"His defence isn't convincing enough, and his expression of satisfaction over Louie's departure makes him the more dangerous," said Agent Barry. Funnily, Jimmy equally seems to be toeing the same line as Agent Donald, as he insists that Amos is obviously stone-hearted, and possibly a cold fish but his disposition doesn't express guilt.

"We don't have much on him to charge him with, and I may have to let him go," said Agent Donald.

"Yeah, let him go, but dig further you may find something," Andy insists.

While the conversation between the detectives persists Gilbert Rivers interrupted, as his surfing through the CCTV cameras seem to have paid off.

"You guys need to see this," he said.

"What's it, Gilbert?" asked Agent Donald.

"Ava seems to be having an affair leading up to her husband's death," said Gilbert. The detectives turned around and immediately followed Gilbert to the central office as they speak.

Agent Barry interjected immediately.

"With whom? She could be behind this," he said.

Gilbert then plays the CCTV footage which shows Ava visiting a secret spot in the Brooklyn neighbourhood weekly with the same man.

"Oh my God, that woman is a snake!" Agent Barry exclaimed.

Agent Donald isn't quick with drawing conclusions, he quickly toned down the hysteria following these unnerving findings and suggested that visiting the hotel together is one thing; but there's need to verify whether the pair checked into the room together. He emphasised that there's a possibility the pair might be attending a meeting or have other business dealings that have no romantic attachment.

Andy immediately asked Agent Donald and Agent Barry to pay the hotel a visit, and go through their CCTV to verify the affair.

Hours later, Donald and Barry returned from the hotel after confirming the affair, at least it's now confirmed that pair checked into a room together in each of their visit to this secret spot. Arguably, unravelling the personality of this mystery man in the footage becomes the new focus of these detectives.

"The affair between Ava and the unknown man has been con-firmed," said Agent Donald.

"Who's that man?" asked Andy.

"His name is Jensen Brock, he shares a flat with Ava and her late husband," said Gilbert.

"We need to bring this man in, let's see if he has a hand in the crime," said Andy.

Agent Barry immediately suggested that they should take the pair by surprise and conduct a much more through search of their property to see if they'll find anything that makes them culpable.

"Agent Donald turned to Andy, what about Amos?" he asked.

"Let him off for now, tell him we'll invite again if the need arises," said Andy. The detectives paid Ava and Jensen a second visit and this time they went with the forensic team to conduct a more thorough search of the entire property. The search of Ava's apartment and Jensen's apartment were to be carried out concurrently. Ava opened the door, as the detectives stood by the door and knocked.

"Detectives, any news, have you found Louie's killer?" she asked.

"Your amorous relationship has resulted in your husband biting the dust," said Agent Barry.

"What a clunky joke? I take exception to that," said Ava.

Diplomacy isn't one of Agent Barry's strong suit, and he's giving it to Ava as it is, without exception. He kept asking her, why she kept the role she and her boyfriend played in this murder.

"What boyfriend are you talking about?" asked Ava.

"The one you secretly spend time in Brooklyn with," said Agent Barry.

"You mean, Jensen?" asked Ava.

"Oh, you know his name already?" asked Agent Barry.

"You've searched my house and found nothing," she protested.

Sad to say that the detectives aren't friendly and courteous as before, particularly when Agent Barry seems to take Ava's betrayal of her husband more personal which obviously is outside the scope of his work as detective.

"The circumstance is different," he said.

"Hell no, you dare not carry out your audacious raid of my home without a search warrant," said Ava.

Ava isn't quite keen to indulge in this craziness, and sadly, Agent Barry has ruined her appetite for a constructive conversation because she finds his remarks to be nothing but tactless. Agent Barry's debate with Ava didn't abate either, as he pointed out to Ava that the first time he saw her he considered her an enigmatic, and a strong-willed woman but he has just realised she isn't any of that.

"Your remarks are incendiary, and I hate your demeanour. How dare you walk into my home and accuse me of my husband's murder?" she protested.

Agent Donald stepped in, as he attempts to keep the ambience to be a friendlier one. "We aren't accusing you, we're just here to conduct a search to help with the answer you seek," he said.

Agent Barry was beaming with smiles as he hands Ava the search warrant, because he's convinced with the prospect of Ava ending up behind bar. "This is the search warrant, now let us do our job," said Agent Barry.

"As a prime suspect or what?" Ava asked. Interestingly, Agent Barry, never miss any opportunity for banter, and this time he's giving Ava a piece of his own mind as he reminded Ava that going all misty-eyed when she talks about her affection for her husband doesn't bother him because she doesn't truly love him.

"You're a cynic," she retorted, as she stepped aside to allow the detectives in.

"We'll let you know the status of our investigation when the time comes," said Agent Donald.

Ava stood by as the detectives picks her stuff apart piece by piece, the sight kind of irked her and she suddenly became uncomfortable with the manner in which the detectives comb her apartment. "Stop rummaging through my stuff, those are personal stuff," she protested.

After two hours of search, the detectives found nothing linking Ava to the crime in her house, but sadly the detectives who conducted search in Jensen's house found laptop evidence and the tiny bottle containing aconite in his apartment. Serendipitously, he hasn't disposed of the bottle of aconite before this surprise search happened.

The detectives didn't leave without taking Ava, even though Aconite wasn't found in her apartment. Ava was brought into the interrogation room amid her tears and the preposterous accusation. Moments later, Agent Donald walked into the interrogation room, and sat opposite Ava.

"Why're you doing this?" asked Ava.

"Ava, tell us about your mystery lover?" he asked.

"I had an affair with Jensen and I made a mistake, ok. But that doesn't mean I killed my husband," she said.

"You've to stop crying, all we're doing is finding your husband's killer," said Agent Donald.

"What makes you think I would kill my husband! Do you know how this accusation makes me feel?" cried Ava.

"Do you know of anyone who would want to kill your husband?" asked Agent Donald.

"I don't know of anyone," she said.

"What about Jensen did his actions in anyway suggests he might want your husband out of the way?" asked Agent Donald.

"No not at all, he only asked me once," said Ava.

"Hmm, what did he ask of you?" he asked.

Ava went silent for a moment, and Agent Donald looked through her eyes as he waits for her to say what it is, Jensen asked of her. Now that her secret romance is no longer a secret, telling it all seem the only option before Ava, and it doesn't matter whose bubble is burst.

"He asked me to leave Louie, and I told him no," she said.

"And you've no idea he had other plans?" he asked further.

Ava muttered, saying no, not at all, but proceeded to assure the detective that if Jensen has a hand in Louie's death, she's going to kill him herself.

Agent Donald interjected as he admonished Ava, reminding her it's not up to her to decide Jensen's punishment, and that if at all Jensen should punished then it behoves on the judge to decide what his punishment should be. "Let's ascertain your level of involvement for now," he said.

"Though it might seem like a fling, but I truly liked Jensen, and time with Jensen was really exhilarating," she said.

"Love is a fragile flower, and everyone knows that," replied Agent Donald.

"I loved Jensen, even though that could be wrong by other people's standards," she confessed.

"My job isn't to judge what's wrong or right, you can leave, we'll invite you again when the need arises," said Agent Donald.

But Ava's was held bound by guilt of her amorous act, and her unsolicited effort to justify her lasciviousness wasn't well received by the detectives.

Her efforts to justify her actions didn't abate, as she elucidated further that loneliness pushed her into Jensen's arms and insisted, she still consider it spurious that she's a suspect in her husband's murder.

"Engaging in extramarital affairs as a solution to fighting doldrums doesn't help," said Agent Donald.

Agent Donald left the interrogation room after asking Ava to leave, and he immediately requested that Jensen be brought in for interrogation. It didn't take long after Jensen was seated, that Agent Donald walked into the interrogation room. "Hello, I'm detective Donald Whitley and you're Jensen Brock," he said.

"Yes, I'm Jensen Brock, why're you holding me here?" asked Jensen.

"We're about to begin your interrogation and we're recording every bit of what happens here," said Agent Donald.

"Why am I here?" asked Jensen.

"Tell us about you and Ava, your secret is out," said Agent Donald.

"Me and Ava is real, we're rock solid, and has nothing to do with Louie, I didn't commit any crime," said Jensen.

Agent Donald focused on Jensen facial disposition as he denied having anything to do with Louie's death. Jensen kept a straight face and didn't bat an eyelid, yet the detective whose craft it is to read peoples' lips and facial expression smelt a rat the moment he sat opposite Jensen. Sadly, Jensen didn't ask for a lawyer, he thought he could talk himself out of this trouble.

"You said it has nothing to do with Louie, are you aware Ava is Louie's wife?" he asked.

"That doesn't constitute a crime, does it?" Jensen retorted.

"We'll know about that within the next one hour," he said.

Jensen acknowledged to the detective that they live in a dark world, with too many prejudiced people crawling out of the woodworks to do harm to innocent bystanders like Louie, or just to take their pound of flesh in retribution for offence that went unnoticed. He then reminded the detective that he isn't someone the detectives should be concerned about because he is innocent in all of this.

Jensen realised the interrogation is taking a difficult turn and prefers not implicating himself any further.

"I need a lawyer, and I don't think I'm inclined to speak any further," said Jensen.

"A lawyer can't help you, Jensen. We found this bottle containing aconite in your apartment, and searches on the effectiveness of aconite three days before Louie's death was found on your computer," said agent Donald.

Realising his bubble has been punctured, Jensen decided to drop the idea of getting a lawyer, as he tries to wriggle himself out of this muddied water." But that means nothing, it doesn't mean I killed Louie," said Jensen.

"You'll tell that to the judge, your window of opportunity is closing," said Agent Donald.

"What window of opportunity are you talking about? Read my lips, I didn't do it," said Jensen.

Agent Donald was keen on finding out if Ava instigated and orchestrated her husband murder, but now that the murder weapon was found in Jensen's apartment, a confession exposing everyone involved in this murder is now the primary interest of this detective. He immediately hinted Jensen of the opportunity of getting a lesser sentence, and asked him who and who participated in the death of Louie. "Did someone from his work place hire you to do this, or it's just you and Ava, what role did Ava play in this?" asked Agent Donald.

"Ava didn't play any role in this, leave her out of this," said Jensen.

"Then you acted alone," said Agent Donald.

"I was coerced into doing it," Jensen confessed.

"Who coerced you! Ava coerced you, or your emotions did?" asked Agent Donald.

Jensen became all emotional as he narrated to the detective that it was all a set up, and said a friend blackmailed him into doing it.

"Who's this friend, and what's his connection to this?" asked Agent Donald.

"His name is Rob, he used me to settle an old score. Louie coveted his girlfriend when they were teens," said Jensen.

"Hmm, he used you to get back his pound of flesh? You must have displayed some qualities of a cold and heartless killer, which was why he enlisted you to carry out the act," said Agent Donald.

Jensen realised there isn't a need to be evasive any longer, he'd to open up in a tell all kind of story, he immediately narrated that he worked in Robs' restaurant years back, "one day he sent his daughter to sit on my lap and I was playing with her innocently, not knowing he filmed me," said Jensen.

Agent Donald listened keenly to Jensen as he laid bare his sordid past with Rob, yet this extraneous tale might help in solving this puzzle.

"How old was the daughter?" asked Agent Donald.

"She was eight then," said Jensen.

"Did you molest her, and if you didn't why do you let that trouble you?" asked Agent Donald.

"He told his daughter what to say about the incident and he recorded her complaints on tape, and promised to use it against me if I didn't do this," said Jensen.

"That pressure isn't enough to make you take another man's life," said Agent Donald.

"Things took a dangerous turn when he killed Kittas," said Jensen.

Agent Donald leaned backward a bit, and then leaned forward again thinking another murder was committed, as the news of Kittas' death seemed to hit a raw nerve.

"Who is Kittas?" asked Agent Donald.

"Kittas is his cat of three years, just to prove his seriousness to me," said Jensen.

"How did you carry out the act?" asked Agent Donald.

"I sneaked into Louie's room without his knowledge but with the consent of his wife, and I sprayed the aconite on his pair of glasses," said Jensen.

"Why his glasses?" asked Agent Donald.

"Since it's possible for aconite to be absorbed into the bloodstream through the skin, I knew he wipes his glasses with his fingers most times before he puts them on and drives off to work," said Jensen.

"Meaning?" asked Agent Donald.

"Louie won't die at home; he'll either die on his way to work or at work. That will take the attention away from home," said Jensen.

Rob turned a teenage love squabble which should have ended in a mere bare-knuckle brawl between teenagers, into a long-standing bitter bruising ego trip, which resulted in a murder.

"I'll be back in a moment," said Agent Donald, he then stood to leave the interrogation room, but just as Donald walks away Jensen interjected. "I've told you everything I know; my phone conversations with Rob will bear witness to this. You promised me a lesser sentence," said Jensen.

Agent Donald left the interrogation room and joined his colleagues, who were observing the interrogation. "What a gut-wrenching confession," said Agent Donald.

"It's all over, I expect you to charge Ava along with him," said Agent Barry.

"She didn't commit any crime," said Agent Donald.

"She caused her husband's death in a way, and I expect her to go down with him," said Agent Barry.

"Barry, you know the law doesn't work that way, you hate what she did and I do too, her action is utterly, utterly disgusting, but that doesn't make it a crime," said Agent Donald.

"This killer used Ava to get at Louie," said Agent Barry.

"Jensen's closeness with Louie's wife makes Louie vulnerable to Jensen," said Andy.

"No matter how careful a man can be, he's vulnerable once the enemy finds a weak wife," said Jimmy.

"Yeah, that makes her a moral criminal, and funnily, not all immoral acts are unlawful," said Agent Donald.

"Then the law should be changed to accommodate moral crimes like this," said Agent Barry.

Maybe yes, and maybe not, and like him or loathe him, Barry is an independent thinker. It doesn't matter what others think, Barry always has his opinions and he must air them, and it doesn't mean he's as thick as hell.

"She had no knowledge of the crime and she didn't in any way participate or conspire in her husband's death," said Andy.

"Meaning?" asked Agent Barry.

"Meaning, no crime was committed," said Andy.

"The debate never ends when the system pits law against morality," said Agent Donald.

"It's a shame, she trusted him and he killed her husband," said Agent Barry. Agent Donald summarised the whole episode and said betrayal is what a person gets when they befriend a snake.

Agent Barry sees this as an opportunity to get personal with Jimmy as he revives his old animosity with banter, Barry turned to Jimmy with a sarcastic look. "A bite on your back, that's what you guys will get for bringing a snake into this unit," said Agent Barry. Everyone around knew that remark was targeted at Jimmy, and they didn't find it amusing.

Andy Grey was angered by Barry's sustained disdain for Jimmy and felt it's time to address it and put Barry in his place once and for all.

"That's grossly out of place, Barry, the next time you go personal on Jimmy, you'll have to face me," said Andy.

"But I was just stating the obvious," said Agent Barry.

Barry thinks of Jimmy as the elephant in the room, and riding this elephant is his right. Barry's sense of entitlement could rock this boat that thrives on teamwork, and his decision to continue flogging this horse against the advice of his boss might mean his own fingers will soon get burnt.

Agent Donald reminded Barry that they are a team and must learn to work together as one even if they don't like each other. He emphasised the importance of teamwork, stressing that their job is more about trusting your life in the hands of your colleagues who must watch your back at all times, as they go about busting the bad guys.

"Ok boss," Agent Barry said and walks away.

The next Morning Rob Holt was brought in for interrogation, and as he sat in the room, Agent Donald walks into the interrogation room. "Rob Holt, I guess you know why you're here?" he said.

"Am I in trouble? I guess not, because I've done nothing to warrant being kept here," said Rob. "Leave that to the judge to decide, tell us all about Louie?" asked Agent Donald.

Rob kept a straight face and gave Agent Donald a stern look. "Who is Louie?" he asked.

"Oh, you don't know Louie? I guess you know Jensen Brock," said Agent Donald.

"I know Jensen, he used to work for me. What did he say I've done this time?" asked Rob. The mounting evidence against Rob didn't bother him because he's still of the impression that he still had Jensen wrapped around his finger. He remained illusory and he's keen to remain the man on the fence who only watched a romantic domestic squabble unfold.

"Ok, since you know Jensen, I guess you know Louie as well," said Agent Donald.

"I'm not speaking any further without my lawyer," Rob retorted. Agent Donald interjected and reminded Rob, that he's willing to wait for his lawyer to come around but a lawyer won't help him because they have a transcript of his phone conversation with Jensen. "Tell me why you ordered Louie's murder?" asked Agent Donald.

"Jensen is a paedophile whose words were cotton candy, and he should be the one to tell you about his affair with a married woman, and I suggest you don't take him serious," said Rob.

"He isn't a paedophile, you set him up," said Agent Donald.

"But I caught him abusing my daughter, and I have him on tape," said Rob.

"When did this happen?" asked Agent Donald.

"Two years back," said Rob.

After going through the transcript of the phone conversations between Jensen and Rob the detectives are convinced that Rob's allegations lack merit and don't help to tie the loose ends in this particular interrogation.

Also, the detectives decided to verify Jensen's story that Rob's initial intention was to use the tape to pressure Jensen into working against Rob's former business partner, who later quit and allowed Rob to have full ownership of the business.

"If Jensen actually abused your daughter and you've evidence of the act, you should've put him away for good long before now," said Agent Donald.

"But I've just told you about it, and I expect you to put Jensen away for good," Rob retorted.

"The tape you said will only surface if Jensen refuses to kill Louie isn't relevant in this instance, but I'll interview your daughter to ascertain your allegations," said Agent Donald.

But in order to avoid being complicit in covering a sexual assault on a child, the detectives decided to approach the investigation with an open mind, as they switched their attention to the sexual assault claim. If Jensen messed with Rob's daughter, then he will pay dearly for his crime because there's scarcely any sympathy for a paedophile.

The detectives took Rob to his house and called her daughter aside for an interview, and after spending time chatting with her. The poor girl was quite terrified at first, with her eyes bizarrely flickering for minutes, unabated like a troubleshooting fluorescent bulb.

She eventually opened up to the detectives that it's her dad who orchestrated everything, that he asked her to sit on Jensen's laps as well as what she said about Jensen.

Bizarrely, Rob seems to have taken Jensen for canon fodders but he unfortunately realised he's unable to fool the detectives. This is some kind of fifteen minutes of fame that turned out to be mistake on Robs part. It's didn't take long before the detectives retuned Rob to the interrogation room.

"But I didn't kill Louie, Jensen did," said Rob.

"You bullied him into doing it, and the act of killing an innocent cat is an act of cruelty," said Agent Donald.

"Kittas was my cat, that shouldn't bother you," said Rob.

"The judge will decide that, and what did Louie do to you to deserve death?" asked Agent Donald. Interestingly, Rob began to own up to the crime in part after the interview with his daughter busted his bubble. He's now giving it in dribs and drabs, as he opened up that Louie took his girlfriend when they were teens, all he did this time was to deny Louie the luxury of his lovely wife, and helped Jensen to take her over.

"And when you suggested this idea to Jensen, how did he take it?" asked Agent Donald.

"He was wreathed in smiles, and loved the adventure," said Rob.

"But the transcript of your phone conversation shows Jensen took it differently," said Agent Donald.

"My conversation with Jensen didn't implicate me in anyway," said Rob. "Traces of aconite in your apartment and your laptop searches tell it all," said Agent Donald.

"Yeah, I accepted playing a part in Louie's death but I didn't kill him, Jensen did," said Rob.

"You should tell that to the judge, you're both partners in crime," said Agent Donald.

"Louie got what he deserved," Rob insists.

"Rob Holt, you'll need an attorney, I'm charging you with the murder of Louie Ayden and for your cruelty to animals," said Agent Donald.

Jensen Brock was sentenced to forty years in prison while Rob Holt was sentenced to Eighty-three years in prison. Seventy years for the murder of Louie Ayden, and five years for animal cruelty, and eight years for using a minor for conspiracy of a sexual nature.

By evening of the day of court sentencing of Jensen Brock and Rob Holt, Agent Donald walks into Andy Grey's office. Andy stopped what he was doing to attend to Donald but then requested him to open the upper shelves in his office to get a bottle of wine out. Agent Donald opened the shelf and brought out the bottle of wine.

"Oh, Chardonnay," he said.

"Get two glasses." Andy requested. Donald got the glasses and handed one to Andy, who opened the wine and served himself first.

"Help yourself, Donald," said Andy.

"You seem to be working late tonight?" asked Agent Donald.

"Sarah Black will be going before senate tomorrow, and I need to get these documents ready for her," said Andy.

Agent Donald only had a glass of wine, and spent some time chatting about the politics in the work place. "I think I am fine," he said.

"One more glass, Donald, you're going straight home, isn't it?" asked Andy.

"I think this is ok, I'm driving," said Agent Donald.

It didn't take long before the detectives wished each other good night, and Donald left.

CHAPTER

SEVENTEEN

The Worm

Agent Donald and agent Barry arrive at a crime scene near a park where Lieutenant Rose, her officers and forensics are already examining the crime scene.

"Hello Lieutenant," said Agent Donald.

"Oh, Donald, good morning, you guys are late," she said jocularly, but Agent Barry sees the Lieutenant's joke as an opportunity for a banter.

"Rosie, how come you were expecting us? You seem to be enjoying our company," said Agent Barry.

"This is homicide, and this is your jurisdiction, so what are you afraid of?" asked Lieutenant Rose.

"Afraid? We seem to be running into each other more frequently these days," said Agent Barry. The Lieutenant, who's keen on solving this murder, saw Agent Barry's banter as a light tiff that doesn't need to be taken to heart, and for all it's worth, this is among the few occasions she didn't consider Barry's casual banter as vile.

"Any idea of what happened to her?" asked Agent Donald.

"We can't really ascertain the cause of death, one thing we know is that she was killed somewhere else," said Lieutenant Rose.

"Barry, we need clues, please look around for cameras," said agent Donald.

Agent Barry turned to Donald then said he has looked around and there aren't any cameras except the ones over there and there, as he points to two cameras at a distance.

"The cameras you're pointing at have been reviewed by the forensic team and there isn't anything in them," said Lieutenant Rose.

"It means the killer knew where the cameras are and deliberately avoided them," said Agent Donald. After uncovering the corpse and taking keen look at the murder victim, the detectives scanned the area for a while to gather as much information as they could. Agent Donald turned to the Lieutenant as he was about to leave.

"Lieutenant, we'll wait for the forensic report, if there's anything new, please give me a call," he said.

"Ok detective, the forensic report will shed more light on what happened," said Lieutenant Rose.

"Rosie why don't you request that we leave this case for you to solve?" asked Agent Barry.

"Barry, let's go," said Agent Donald.

While out and about, Jimmy stopped to pick a phone call, and it happens to be Alicia on the phone. She has a little gossip to share with Jimmy as he hinted him Charlie just left her place.

"Charlie, you said, and is anything the matter?" asked Jimmy.

Jimmy's reaction was hinged on the fact that Alicia and Charlie's relationship hasn't been cordial, since they parted ways.

"Yes, of course, he was here spouting nonsense about wanting us to get back together," replied Alicia. This new revelation is an indication that Charlie hasn't actually moved on, he was just in a relationship he broke off from and hoping to return to his ex-wife. With Charlie oscillating back and forth like a pendulum, Jimmy is inadvertently considering his position with Alicia. But Alicia's reassuring words to Jimmy that Charlie is now history, did calm Jimmy's sudden anxiety. Jimmy was all ears, with the phone by his ear as he listened to Alicia's story of how she emphatically told Charlie that she has moved on and doesn't intend to return to what she left behind.

Sadly, even as the detectives were still trying their heads around the homicide of the previous day, another death was reported at the East River, and the detectives rushed to the scene as Amelia Benjamin was pulled out of the river, in what looked like a suspected swimming accident which occurred days ago, that resulted in drowning.

"This isn't our case, since it's an accident, maybe she fell into the river from somewhere, and the current moved her body to this point," said Agent Barry.

"Hold your breath, Barry. We can't tell whose case it is until we unravel the circumstance surrounding how she ended up in the river," said Agent Donald.

It didn't take long, the detectives began scanning the area for clues and later ended their review of the scene, before returning to their office, as they await the coroner's report concerning the victim.

Days later, at the FBI office, Agent Murphy walked into Andy's office and informed him the forensic report for the previous day's crime scene is out. Andy stretched out his hand to take the report but as Agent Murphy handed the report to him, he reminded Andy the forensic report came alongside the pathologist report.

"Where's the report? Let me have it, and what does the report say?" asked Andy. They then walked to the central office, even as they talk about the report. Agent Murphy replied and said she was injected with ricin, and the report equally stated she had inhaled nitrous oxide gas before her murder. Agent Barry's confusion is more about the specificity that's lacking in Murphy's comments concerning the report, he then interjected immediately by asking "what actually killed her? Was it the nitrous oxide gas or the ricin?"

It's the ricin that killed her, and this pattern of murder matches five other deaths," said Agent Murphy.

"Tell us about the victim; profile her," said Agent Donald.

"The victim is Lonnie Morris; she's a midwife and a pro abortion activist?" said Agent Murphy.

"Oh my God, this autopsy report linked the murderer to Amelia Benjamin, whom we think drowned in the East River," said Agent Murphy.

Amelia Benjamin drowned, we are only trying to locate how she fell into the river, and or who pushed her into the river," said Andy.

"Sad to say that Amelia Benjamin didn't drown in that river, she was dumped inside the river, because this report said there wasn't any water in her lungs, meaning she died before getting into the river. Interestingly, she's a mid-wife and the report said there was nitrous oxide gas in her lungs," said Agent Murphy.

Agent Donald turned to Gilbert. "Please profile the five other victims who have died in a similar manner, mentioned in this forensic report," he said.

"They're all pro-abortion activists, and are all midwives," said Agent Murphy.

Agent Donald listened keenly, as he takes his time to separate the case at hand from the regular textbook murder mystery story, he then takes away the insanity in the story and replaces it with the pragmatism of the human heart. It didn't take long before he's able to piece the new details coming out of this report together to make some sense out of it.

"From the lurid details we are getting from this report, I can categorically say that 'The Worm' is now in New York," said Agent Donald.

"The Worm, who's he?" asked Andy.

"He's a killer who worms his way into people," said Agent Donald.

"Who are his or her targets?" asked Andy.

"His targets are pro-abortion advocates," said Agent Donald.

"Why pro-abortion advocates, what's his motivation?" asked Andy.

"His motivation is nothing but vengeance," said Agent Donald.

"Vengeance for what?" asked Agent Donald.

Agent Donald profiled the suspect further, saying the suspect in this investigation was a victim of an unsuccessful abortion which affected the sight in his left eye and made him have dyspraxia.

"Did you just say he has dyspraxia?" asked Agent Barry.

The mention of dyspraxia seems to make Agent Barry underestimate this killer, because he thinks a person with dyspraxia lacks the social skills of worming his way into the lives of these intelligent midwives. Agent Donald interjected and reminded Barry that the guy obviously has dyspraxia but he's good at worming his way into the lives of his victims.

"You mean when his mum was pregnant with him, she tried to abort him and it didn't go well?" asked Andy.

This guy isn't some dim-witted guy, and his wit means he's able to pull the wool over the eyes of the wise even without them knowing it. These ladies always seem acquiesce that something is off about this guy, yet they fall for him, but the truth is that this guy isn't likeable when you get beneath the surface.

"So, being a victim of abortion, he resents and hunts down anyone who supports abortion," said Agent Donald.

"How do you know of this?" asked Andy.

Agent Donald had to narrate his experience with this suspect, and said nine years ago, this same suspect used nitrous oxide gas on a victim but wasn't quick enough to kill her before he was caught. He was then sentenced to eight years for his crime, and that his prison years have since elapsed.

"And that victim was a pro-abortion advocate?" asked Andy.

"Of course, yes, he seems to be on the rampage since he left the prison," said Agent Donald.

"Of the entire pro-abortion activists, why does he target midwives?" asked Agent Barry.

"His anger against midwives boils down to the fact that he felt the midwives who are meant to deliver babies, should be on the side of the baby in the womb and shouldn't support their deaths," said Agent Donald.

"How does he lure or access his victims?" asked Andy.

"First he stalks them, then worms his way into their lives," said Agent Donald.

"It means after stalking them and knowing their routines, he now makes friends with his possible victims, that's why they call him the Worm," said Agent Donald.

"But why the use of laughing gas on his victim?" Andy asked curiously.

"He loves to kill his victim while they're laughing," said Agent Murphy. Agent Barry's anger with this killer isn't just the fact that he kills his victim, but his approach startles him, because he meses with people in their most vulnerable state before taking their lives. Even though his excuses for committing murder was tactless, yet his ingenuity of making his victim laugh before taking their lives is cruel, and that requires a bag of tricks.

"Just as the midwives make their patient comfortable before the process of abortion, that's how he makes his victims laugh before killing them," said Agent Donald.

Andy listened keenly and didn't take likely the rationalisation of this killer's murderous acts, as he insisted that this is a menacing parallel, and he want this Worm or whatever his name is, off the streets of New York.

"Then we'll need to draw a pattern on pro-abortion midwives, to identify who could be his next possible target," said Agent Donald.

The next day, Agent Donald picked up his phone and dialled Lieutenant Rose to discuss the investigation further.

"Hello Lieutenant, how is your day?" asked Agent Donald.

"It's still early but my day is fine, and I'm certain this call isn't for a casual discourse?" asked Lieutenant Rose.

"Do you know the hummingbird?" asked Agent Donald.

"Of course, yes, what about it?" said Lieutenant Rose.

"The humming bird was flying and singing just like any other bird, and one day she thought to herself, if I can fly very well, why not be able to flap very well, then she tried flapping and became perfect at flapping. Another day while all the birds were singing, she thought to herself if I can sing very well why not be able to hum very well, then she tried humming and became perfect at it. Then on one fateful day, while all the birds were flying and singing, the hummingbird flew into their midst and began flapping and humming at the same time and suddenly all other birds stopped flying and the ones singing stopped singing and watched the humming bird in amazement as she flapped and hummed. That was how the hummingbird became the centre of attention in the mist of all birds.

"I'm the hummingbird in your story, I suppose?" she asked and chuckled.

"Of course, yes, your relevance can't be over-emphasized," said Agent Donald.

Lieutenant Rose burst into laughter. "Erm.., this isn't a bad way of starting my day," she said.

"Yes, of course, we just finished analysing the forensic report from the two crime scenes of two days back," said Agent Donald.

Lieutenant Rose hasn't stopped laughing but said she also has the report on her table yet said they haven't been able to come up with something concrete concerning the killer.

"I think we've a clue about who the possible killer might be," said Agent Donald.

"Who's the killer, do you've the suspect in your custody?" she asked.

"No, but this is a killer whose anger is against pro-abortion advocates," said Agent Donald.

"Hmm, ok, if his victims are pro-abortion advocates, then why kill a midwife?" asked Lieutenant Rose.

With this killer still at large and the count still on the increase, Agent Donald needed to give as much detail as possible to the police as they partner in their effort to catch this worm. He then furnished the Lieutenant that the suspect is a victim of an unsuccessful abortion, causing him to lose the sight in his left eye at birth, and he also has dyspraxia.

"How can we catch him? We can't leave him roaming our streets and killing midwives," asked Lieutenant Rose.

"His name is Harris McKee, and his next set of possible victims could be any one of Kendal Larson, Piper Goya, and Patricia Torres," said Agent Donald.

The Lieutenant is very aware that this phone call isn't just for a casual exchange of pleasantries but one that'll end up with favours being requested. She immediately interjected and asked the detective if she should deploy the police, but then pause for a while and asked for a second time if there's something in particular, he expects her to do.

"This killer doesn't just attack his victim, he stalks them, then worms his way into their lives," said Agent Donald.

"Then deploying plain clothes police officers will be best," she replied.

Agent Donald then suggested that this guy will probably be wearing dark glasses, because of his bad eyesight and will possibly be showing some signs of unusual behaviour because of his dyspraxia.

A month later, Roseberg Thornton, a man who had a healthy dose of his share of run ins with women, was in a shop when he spotted a lady that he took a liking to. In his usual disposition towards women, he followed Piper Goya, one of the mid-wives under police protection and walked up to her at the car park. "Hello, good morning," he said.

Interestingly, Piper Goya realised this was the same man walking right behind her at the supermarket. "Who are you and why're you stalking me?" she protested.

Roseberg Thornton was shock with Piper's outburst and finds her reaction as cruel. "Stalking you! I don't stalk people," he said.

"You followed me to the supermarket and now you've traced me to my workplace, what do you call that?" she asked.

"Sorry, if you call that stalking, but I saw you at the supermarket and fancied you, then felt I should tell you how I feel about you," he said.

Piper Goya immediately alerted the police. While Roseberg continued to express his love for the woman who finds him suspicious, he had no idea his hands will soon be in cuffs. "Don't worry, the police are already waiting for you," she said.

"Police, why would you do a thing like that?" asked Roseberg.

In a twinkle of an eye, plain clothes policemen showed up, and put Roseberg Thornton in cuffs as he was trying to assuage Piper's fears that he's a good guy. "You think you can kill me, and you want to add me to your list of victims, don't you?" she retorted.

"You're under arrest for stalking and attempted murder of Piper Goya," said Officer Burk.

"Stalking, attempted murder, what do you mean?" Roseberg protested. The NYPD officer immediately read Roseberg Thornton his rights as he took him away.

"You've the right to remain silent, anything you say or do, will be used against you in a court of law," said Officer Burk.

"For what! For telling a lady how I feel about her?" asked Roseberg.

The NYPD officers who arrested Roseberg Thornton handed him to the FBI who wanted him for questioning, but after spending considerable time questioning Roseberg Thornton, Agent Barry finds this crack head to be more difficult to understand than he'd earlier thought, so he gave Agent Donald a ring.

"Donald, where are you?" asked Agent Barry.

"I've an appointment with my doctor," said Agent Donald.

"Are you dying or what! What are you doing with the doctor?" Agent Barry asked jocularly.

Interestingly, Agent Donald revealed to his colleague who wants to know, that checking his blood pressure is his usual routine.

"Is it high or what! What did the doctor say?" Agent Barry asked.

Agent Donald burst into laughter, as he spoke with Agent Barry even as he's being attended to by the nurse.

"Don't be silly, Barry, it's normal. I'm not dying yet, and I advise you to do the same," he said.

"We've Harris McKee in our custody," said Agent Barry.

"The Worm?" asked Agent Donald.

"Yes, the Worm, he's already being questioned," said Agent Barry.

"Ok, I'll be with you within the hour," said Agent Donald.

Forty-five minutes after his conversation with Agent Barry, Agent Donald walked into the unit. "Barry, have you questioned him?" he asked.

The detectives were confused by the silky nature of this suspect, as he hinted Donald that he's convinced that this is the guy, but he seems to be denying all of it, even though he fits the description. He pointed out the salient features that makes this guy the suspect they've been looking for, but Roseberg isn't keeping quiet either as he accused Agent Barry of attempting to railroad an innocent man for a crime he didn't commit.

"This person isn't the person we're looking for, there isn't any-thing to link him to the crime and his body language confirms it," said Jimmy.

Agent Barry turned to Jimmy Thompson with a look of disdain and rage.

"Shut the hell up, what do you know about interrogation?" said Agent Barry.

"Did you search his home. and did you find anything in his phone or laptop that relates to Piper Goya?" asked Agent Donald.

"No, but he fits the description of the killer," said Agent Barry.

Agent Donald turned to Andy Grey. "Andy, what do you think, did you observe the interrogation?" he asked.

"This guy's response puts us in a dilemma, and I don't know what to think," said Andy, he then proceeded to say the MO is the same but this guy's disposition speaks innocence.

"Then let me go in," said Agent Donald.

Agent Donald enters the interrogation room and sat opposite the accused while his colleagues observe the interrogation as it progresses.

"Harris McKee, I'm detective Donald Whitely," he said.

"I've told you guys repeatedly, I'm not Harris McKee," said Roseberg.

"Then who are you?" asked Agent Donald.

"I'm Roseberg Thornton," he replied.

"We know you're Harris McKee, and we know you changed your name to evade arrest and that's an offence on its own," said Agent Donald.

"I didn't change my name, and that's the name I've been known with since I was a child," said Roseberg.

"What happened to your left eye?" asked agent Donald.

"I lost my left eye at birth," said Roseberg.

"Erm.., did your mum tell you how it happened?" Agent Donald queried further.

"She said it was the consequence of a prolong labour," said Roseberg.

"I noticed you behave a little erratic, why?" asked Agent Donald.

"I don't know why, but a lot of people often say the same thing," said Roseberg.

"Why're you stalking Piper Goya?" asked Agent Donald.

"Stalking, that's a spurious allegation, and is her name Piper Goya?" he asked.

"Yes, but your action is called stalking," said Agent Donald.

"Piper Goya is a woman I fancy, and I like her, don't you see she's beautiful?" said Roseberg.

"If you like somebody, I expect you to walk up to them and tell them how you feel about them," said Agent Donald.

"That was exactly what I was about doing when they messed it up," said Roseberg.

"How, and who messed it up?" asked agent Donald.

Roseberg insisted that there isn't a way his action would've been characterised as stalking, saying, he saw Piper once in the supermarket, and decided to follow her to her office to tell her how he felt about her, but was quite surprised that she called the cops on him.

This guy isn't just some kind of nut case, he has seen too many rejections from the society because of his disability and he now takes every banter personal. Agent Donald's attempt to prod him further provoked a backlash from this guy. "Do you know we have people who make jokes with you just to make it look like you get along well with them, isn't it? That's called acting. You are trying to do that to me right now, and I don't appreciate it. There are people like that everywhere, in the workplace, neighbourhood, and even in churches," Roseberg retorted.

"Do you know, following people around and monitoring their movement is called stalking?" said Agent Donald.

"People do crazy things when they're in love, at least I need an opportunity to tell her how I feel, and I'll still do so the moment I leave here," said Roseberg.

Agent Donald left the interrogation room and joined his colleagues who were observing the process. Sad to say that the disposition of this suspect, kept the detectives all guessing what he's presenting with, and funnily, they can't handle it. Candid expression of friendship was bizarrely confused to be an aggressive invasion of Piper's space, and he was misunderstood to be the killer on the loose.

"This isn't the person we're looking for," said Agent Donald.

"No Donald, this guy matches the description of the killer; he lost his left sight from birth and behaves unusually weird," said Agent Barry.

"He behaves erratic not unusual, and he's psychotic but doesn't have dyspraxia," said Agent Donald.

"How do you mean?" asked Andy.

"We're looking for someone who behaves unusual, but this guy behaves erratic and we're looking for someone who's has dyspraxia, but this guy is psychotic," said Agent Donald.

"I've observed his countenance and body language, this is just a man pursuing love strangely," said Agent Donald.

Agent Barry, who believes in the idea that a bird in the hand is worth two in the bush concluded he isn't willing to let this guy off easily, so he interjected immediately. "But we can't just let him off the hook," he said.

"Nothing links this guy to the crime," said Agent Donald.

"I need more proof he isn't the one," said Andy.

"Let's get his biometrics for confirmation," said Agent Donald.

"We can trace his roots, his parents and relatives will prove his identity," said Jimmy.

Agent Donald decided to elaborate further, by putting it so nicely to his colleagues that the suspect's biometrics will do because Harris McKee has been to prison before, which means his biometrics are already in the system, he then insisted that if this is him, then there will be a match.

After conducting a Biometric test, Roseberg Thornton was released because he wasn't a match. Arguably, when asked to go, Roseberg accused the detectives of making him the fall guy, and then said the detectives put cart before the horse, reminding them that the biometric confirmation should have happened before putting him through hours of rigorous interrogation. Agent Donald immediately apologised to Roseberg as he tried to smoothen the bumps caused by this undeserved arrest.

Two weeks later, another death was reported, and by the time the detectives arrived the crime scene, they soon realised they're faced with another death of a midwife. This time, it was Rose Dawes that bit the dust. Unfortunately, what seem like an unfortunate freak accident that took the life of Rose Dawes happens not to be an accident after all, as the keen eyes of the detectives saw beyond what the crime scene was suggesting.

"She wasn't on the sofa, and didn't slump from the sofa," said agent Donald.

"This is an accident, Donald, and are you saying otherwise?" Asked agent Murphy.

"Take a good look at that blood splatter, she was struck from the front and then fell backwards. Unlike what the perpetrator wants us to believe that she lost her balance, fell off from the chair and hit her head on this desk when the chair swerved," said Agent Donald.

This is a killer, posturing as a Good Samaritan, saving unborn children from the menace of pro-abortion advocates, yet couldn't stand anything that might threaten his benignity.

Days later, the pathologist report from the death of Rose Dawes was out, and confirms the presence of laughing gas in her system, as well as ricin in her blood stream. It soon dawned on the detectives that this death is the handwork of the Harris McKee, the Worm.

The latest death, seem to set Andy Grey on the edge, he's convinced he'll soon get a phone call from the head of Criminal Justice over these deaths, particularly now that this killer seems to be escalating.

Arguably, he's convinced that whatever excuse he gives for allowing these deaths to persist will unwittingly come across as a lame excuse. The detectives continued their hunt for Harris McKee, The Worm, who they feared could strike again.

Three months later, Jenny Webber was on a day out with her kids in the park when she noticed a strange character that perfectly fits the description of Harris McKee. Funnily, she felt a bit skittish but held her nerves as this strange character walked to her and sat by her side, as she sat and watched her kids on the rollercoaster.

Harris McKee had two cones of ice cream in his hand. "Hello, lovely day and lovely weather, isn't it?" said Harris McKee.

Jenny Webber turned around to respond to this character sitting by her side and trying to initiate a conversation. "Oh, you're right, what a wonderful summer day," she said.

Harris McKee handed her one of the cones of ice cream, and interestingly, Jenny took it, as she pretended to warm up to him, in a conversation. "I just bought two; because I knew you would need one," he said, in quite showy display of affection. This guy is vacuous, but good at creating a warm and friendly ambience. His idea of murder isn't something done in a rush, he takes his time as he displays an elaborate charade in how he orchestrates his murder.

Jenny Webber realising Harris McKee is actually here for her but fearing he could be armed she decided to play along, and she was quite ingenious about it. She played his game with him, by warming up to him. "Oh, that's thoughtful of you, who wouldn't want a cone of ice cream on a sunny day as this?" she said.

"I'm an hour early," he said.

"You're an hour early for what?" she asked.

"My fiancée will join me in an hour's time, but until she comes, let me keep you company," he said.

Arguably, Jenny Webber is afraid the ice cream might be poisoned and doesn't want to eat this ice cream offered to her by this strange character, but she has to create an excuse to dispose of this ice cream sensibly. It didn't take long before she pretended to stumble and dropped the ice cream on the ground. "Oh shame, my ice cream has fallen," she said.

"What a shame really!" Harris McKee stood up immediately and attempts to leave. "Let me get you another one," he said.

Jenny Webber tried being tactful. "Ooh that's kind of you," she said. Immediately Harris McKee left for the ice cream, Jenny tried not to spook him by attempting to make a phone call, she quickly brought out a piece of paper and scribbled a phone number on it.

Minutes later, Harris returned with a cone of ice cream for Jenny. "Have it, your ice cream looks more decorated this time," said Harris.

"I like your humour, and you must be fun to be with," she said and burst into laughter.

Immediately Harris McKee returned with the ice cream, Jenny stood up and began walking away while Harry is still holding the two cones of ice cream. "Where are you going?" he asked.

"Let me get a bottle of water, that's my jacket near you." Jenny pointed to a jacket. "Hold my ice cream; I'll be back in a minute," said Jenny.

Sadly, this guy doesn't lose sight of his target, and must keep them company even if it's unwanted. Harris McKee then stood up immediately and rushed to catch up with Jenny. Wait for me, I'm coming with you.

"What about my jacket?" she asked.

"Let me grab it for you," he said as he rushed back and grabbed Jenny's jacket.

Jenny walked straight into a nearby stand in the park where she was supposed to get a bottle of water, but this guy seems too close and Jenny needs to keep him at bay. "Wait for me here; let me stay in the queue," she said.

"Ok," he said and then stood some meters away from the counter as he waited for Jenny in the shop.

When it's time for Jenny Webber to be attended to, she quickly slipped the piece of paper into the hand of the shop keeper along with the money for the bottled water. "Call that number please, that's the police," she said.

The shop keeper saw that Jenny was nervous, and convinced she's in distress, he asked her in a whisper. "What do I tell them?" asked the shop keeper.

"Tell them Jenny Webber is in distress and they should come right away," she said.

Harris McKee watched from some distance as Jenny and the shop keeper spoke in whispers, and his desire to gobble Jenny up couldn't stop him from expressing his displeasure about the sudden closeness between this pair.

"Aren't you through, you seem to be speaking in a bedroom voice, are you flirting with him?" Harris retorted.

Jenny Webber burst into laughter, as she tries to make light of Harris comment. "Don't be silly, the weather is too hot to be flirting, and I'm just getting my change," she said.

"Ok, tell him to be fast, your ice cream is melting away," he replied.

The shopkeeper stayed out of sight and dialled the police, and within minutes the police arrived the scene. Interestingly, the police do not know who the suspect was among the customers, but Jenny pointed Harris McKee to them. This guy may have had a pack of punch in the past but there's no more room for manoeuvres for him.

"Harris McKee, this is the police," said the NYPD officer.

"What's the problem? I'm just keeping this wonderful lady company," he said.

"You're under arrest for stalking and attempted murder," said the NYPD officer.

"Stalking who?" Harris turned to Jenny. "Did you call the police?" he asked.

"Yes, I did, go and explain your mission to the police," said Jenny.

"What mission?" asked Harris.

"I'm your target, and I know you aren't waiting for your fiancée, you only lied about that," said Jenny.

The next morning Agent Donald and Harris McKee were in the FBI interrogation room. Harris McKee looked on as the FBI detectives sauntered in and out of the room, giving him the side-long glance, without indulging him in any conversation. Yet the permanent smile of a man having the fun of his life remain in his face, an analogy that leaves the perpetrator a wiggle room for escapism now seem a bit farfetched.

"Hello, I'm detective Donald and you're Harris McKee, aren't you?" he asked.

"Of course, I'm Harris McKee and why're you holding me?" he asked.

"We're holding you for stalking and the attempted murder of Jenny Webber," said Agent Donald.

"Stop being naive, how did you come up with the conclusion I'd wanted to kill her? You didn't find any weapon on me, and neither did I assault her in any way," said Harris.

"But you were stalking her," said Agent Donald.

Interestingly, Agent Donald is beginning to understand the character sitting right opposite him better as sneaky, but astute with his choice of words. This guy isn't limited by his disabilities; he's a worm who understands the intricacies of friendship and how he endears himself to people.

"Stalking, define stalking, did I show up in her house, her place of work and wherever she goes? When does meeting a person for the first time, amount to stalking?" asked Harris.

"You're playing smart aren't you, and by the way, what happened to your left eye?" asked Agent Donald.

"I'm born with it; my mum said it was the result of a complication during pregnancy," said Harris.

"Did your mum tell you how the complication came about?" asked Agent Donald.

"Of course, she did, she tried to have an abortion and I wasn't ready to be flushed," he replied.

"But you have dyspraxia as well, don't you?" asked Agent Donald.

"Oh, is that what you call it? Though, some say I have dyspraxia, but I know I'm smart," said Harris. Sadly, this guy is a worm, and his dyspraxia meant nothing, and mustn't be underestimated, because he remains as fit as a butcher's dog.

"Why do your cohorts call you, the worm?" asked Agent Donald.

"Because they say I'm sometimes sneaky," he replied.

"Are you?" asked Agent Donald.

Harris McKee smiled, and after a momentary silence. "Yes, I could be, if I choose to," said Harris.

"Did you kill Lonnie Morris because she's a pro-abortion advocate?" asked agent Donald.

"Where are all these allegations coming from? First, Jenny Webber, and now Lonnie Morris!" exclaimed Harris.

Agent Donald put it before Harris McKee that he killed Lonnie Morris, Rose Dawes and other five pro-abortion advocates, within the last twelve months as a revenge for being a victim of an unsuccessful abortion. Harris interjected saying he refused to be cooped up in this interrogation room with the detective, insisting that all of these are baseless allegations and he'll only speak in the presence of his lawyer.

"Your lawyer won't help you, because we have evidence of your involvement in their deaths," said Agent Donald. With Harris McKee, what you see is what you get, minutes after the interrogation was stopped to allow his Lawyer come in, he requested he wants to continue with the interrogation even without his Lawyer present.

"You didn't find anything on me and didn't find any weapon in my house either," Harris retorted.

"We found the laughing gas you use on your victims before injecting them with ricin in your house, and we also found a bottle containing ricin in your house," said Agent Donald.

"Finding those things in my house doesn't mean I killed them; anyone can have those things in their home," said Harris.

"Do you want me to remind you it's unlawful to possess ricin? I'm not dwelling on that because you've bigger charges hanging over your neck," said Agent Donald.

Agent Barry seemed tired of listening to the too many twists and turns in this interrogation, and he's now itching to wrap the interrogation quickly. Funnily, Andy who was standing behind the screen and observing the interrogation used his hand as a gesture to ask Barry to be patient to allow the interrogation run its course.

"But you can't link me to those deaths," said Agent Donald.

"Your laptop revealed you did an online search about all these six dead victims before their deaths occurred and Jenny Webber is the most recent pro-abortion advocate you searched online before you reached out to her," said Agent Donald.

"Internet search about people doesn't mean you're responsible for their deaths," said Harris.

"Searching about people before they die is a coincidence you'll have to explain in court," said Agent Donald.

"But why do you care about these people? They're committing murder," he said. Instead of slinging mud at Midwifes for his woe and choosing self-help in addressing what he considers unjust by unwittingly digging himself a hole. Agent Donald thought it wise to give this guy a heads up by pointing him to other ways of going about his views on abortion, and sadly, agent Donald seemed not to be making in-road with this guy.

"Can't you see how abortion has destroyed me? And are you aware there are so many others like me?" asked Harris McKee.

"You should've become an anti-abortion advocate by using yourself as a reference point, instead of taking the law into your own hands and becoming a murderer," said Agent Donald.

"Their dexterity and commitment towards abortion makes me want to see these midwives suffer a little of what the baby in the womb suffers," Harris retorted.

Agent Donald stood up as he wraps up the interrogation. "Harris McKee, you'll need an attorney. I'm charging you for the attempted murder of Jenny Webber, the murder Lonnie Morris, Rose Dawes, Joanne Blunt, Amelia Benjamin, Kim Johnson, Grace Sutton, Anna Gibson and Mary Cummings," said Agent Donald.

"You can't charge me, it's them you should charge for murder," Harris protested.

Agent Donald left the interrogation room and joined his colleagues who were observing the interrogation.

"Thank goodness, this killer is off our streets," said Andy.

"This guy seems to have a genuine anger," said Agent Barry.

"He shouldn't vent his anger by going on a killing spree," replied Agent Donald.

"When is he appearing in court?" asked Agent Barry.

"Immediately, start preparing the papers, let him answer for his crimes," said Andy.

Jimmy Thompson thinks there's a possibility that this killer didn't act alone as he emphasised his suspicion that there are many more people damaged by abortion out there, but Agent Donald thinks otherwise, and he's convinced the FBI isn't looking any further.

"He's a lone killer, a lone wolf, that was why he has successfully evaded arrest all this time," said Agent Donald.

Jimmy Thompson has assisted the FBI in solving so many unsolved and pending cases. Jimmy's role as an FBI detective is now too close to comfort for the bad guys in New York City, who aren't only issuing death threats against him, they are about to act upon their threats particularly now that a bounty has been placed on Jimmy's head. It's now time for Jimmy to do something about his safety, and he needs to act fast, fortunately the open arms of Alicia are waiting for him on the other side of United States. Jimmy sat in his car in front of the FBI office, looking at the road as vehicles ply both ways, while assessing the risk of continuing his job. He concluded in his heart that heaven forbid that he will remain in this job until some bad guy makes a scapegoat out of him. Jimmy's current dilemma coupled with Agent Barry's sustained attacks on his person, now likened Jimmy to a candle burning on both sides.

And after a while, he made up his mind that it's best to cower, he then reached for his phone and dialled Alicia.

"Erm.., Jimmy, why're you sounding like this?" asked Alicia.

He muttered to Alicia, saying the death threats are becoming too many, and he doesn't think he can continue with this job because the thick cloud in the air, isn't anything benign but one with a sense of evil.

"Why're they targeting you? I know for sure you aren't the only FBI contractor," said Alicia.

"They're afraid I'll expose them all," he replied.

"Will you like to join me in Los Angeles so we can stay together?" asked Alicia.

"Do you think that's a good idea, what will I be doing in Los Angeles?" asked Jimmy.

"You'll be working with me in my business, and you obviously won't be idle," said Alicia.

Alicia was quite upfront with her offer and Jimmy was all for it, but his excitement suddenly went cold, as he feared that leaving everything behind and moving in with Alicia is like standing on one leg. He's worried that standing on one leg might mean he could end up in the street over a little domestic squabble, like over a cup of coffee or something, when he least expects it.

Alicia interjected as she assured Jimmy that she isn't as cold hearted as he may have cast her, she then assured him that she wouldn't treat him in such a shabby way knowing that he left everything behind for her, she then promised he won't regret a relationship with her.

"Ok, I'll give it a try, let's do this," he said.

After his conversation with Alicia Jimmy stepped out of his car and walked straight into the central office to discuss his resignation as a FBI contractor. But his first point of call was the man who gave him a second chance to better himself.

"Sorry detective, I'm resigning my job with the FBI," said Jimmy.

"What, why now! Why're you doing this now?" asked Agent Donald. This news is coming as a big surprise to Agent Donald, who's beginning to enjoy his work with Jimmy, as they seem to see things from the same lens in most cases. Jimmy opened up about his fears, saying the threats have become too much, and it's now unbearable, as he narrated to the detective that all the thieves in New York have placed a bounty on his head, and as far as New York thieves are concerned he's now a walking corpse if he remains in the job.

Agent Donald immediately suggested to Jimmy of his willingness to help in prosecuting these bad guys, but said all Jimmy had to do is point out the guys that are after him, since he knows who they are. The underworld isn't an illusory world, it's a palpable world, and works in alliance, Jimmy isn't safe wherever he goes, particularly now that the dark web hosts a bounty placed on his head, and funnily, Jimmy is now a walking target.

"How many of them will I prosecute?" Jimmy asked in frustration.

"I have made arrangements with a church in California, they're willing to help me," said Jimmy."

"How?" Asked agent Donald."

They have employed me to work for them, and be a part of the choir, I suppose," replied Jimmy.

Agent Barry interjected and asked Jimmy if the church in question is aware he's a thief.

"Stop saying I'm a thief, I was a thief," Jimmy retorted.

Agent Barry didn't stop prodding Jimmy from this sedentary position, as this news couldn't have come at a better time than this, and it's now an opportunity to let out his banter. "We've offered you a job, now you want to run off like a chicken, don't you know we face the same threats every day?" said Agent Barry.

Jimmy turned around and admonished Barry as he reminded him, "my threats and yours aren't the same, you don't know all the bad guys, I know them, we ate and drank together so they want me out of the way to keep them invincible," said Jimmy.

"You are resigning for them to remain invincible, isn't it? You know you're encouraging crime," said Agent Barry.

"Your thoughts in this matter don't matter, Barry." Jimmy retorted and then turned to Agent Donald.

"I'm sorry, it has to end this way," he said.

"Jimmy, your safety matters most. Moreover, you've helped us solve so many pending cases and having you in our team wasn't a bad idea," said Agent Donald.

"I'll be relocating to Los Angeles immediately," said Jimmy.

"Erm.., oh, now I get it, you're joining Alicia, I suppose. Are you guys taking things to the next level?" asked Agent Donald. Of course, yes, I found love once and lost it, now fate brought us back and gave us a second chance, so let me give it a try," said Jimmy.

Agent Donald stood up and gave Jimmy a big hand shake.

"I wish you well, Jimmy. Stay safe and don't involve yourself in anything dirty," he said.

"I'm not going back to the gutter; I am moving on, and thank you," said Jimmy.

Agent Barry wasn't that cold and heartless after all, and throwing tantrums and bantering others is just his personality, he immediately stood up and walked up to Jimmy, then stretched forth his hand for a handshake.

"Let's part ways formally, without grudge," he said.

Agent Donald injected as he watched Barry make up with Jimmy. "Good move, Barry," said Agent Donald.

After saying their goodbyes, Jimmy walked into Andy's office to inform him of his next move, but interestingly Andy seems to understand Jimmy's predicament and thanked him for his service to the FBI, and then wished him well in his future endeavour. This news didn't really come to Andy as a surprise, Jimmy seem to have given Andy a hint about his next move.

Andy arranged for Jimmy to be debriefed immediately, to at least to make sure his job didn't unwittingly become the tenterhooks that could put him at risk. Jimmy was then relieved of his duties.

Jimmy walked out of the office and dialled Alicia immediately.

"Hello Jimmy, what's up?" asked Alicia.

"I've just resigned my job, Alicia, and I'll be in Los Angeles tomorrow," he said.

"Oh, great, that'll be lovely, and I'll be waiting for you at the airport," said Alicia.

"Good, thank you," said Jimmy.

While Jimmy was busy packing up his stuff after booking his ticket for New York, his son, Jerry, walked in and seems not to like the idea of his dad running off into the arms of a divorced woman. His Christian view on marriage is now in sharp contrast with his dad's interest in Alicia. After their conversation on the subject, Jerry seemed to have taken the fanfare out of Jimmy's planned trip to Los-Angeles.

All Jerry could see is the banality of an amoral relationship, he then reached for his phone and dialled Pastor Bowers and informed him of his dad's intention to run off to Los-Angeles into the arms of another man's wife. Jerry's conservative Christian views on marriage meant that divorce isn't permitted, consequently he still considers Alicia to be another man's wife. Funnily, Jimmy's intended trip to Los-Angeles has turned out to be a confluence of escapism and adultery as far as Jerry is concerned, and that got Jimmy kicking off. He was stunned by his son's unnecessary involvement in his personal affairs. Jimmy didn't really like the fact that his son is trying very hard to take the wind off his sail, it's like Jerry is trying to micromanage his dad's social life and this has now set them on a collision course.

The Pastor immediately dialled Jimmy's phone just after his conversation with Jerry. Jimmy has already had an earful from his son, yet he'd to reluctantly pick the call as Pastor Bowers went into specifics, and asked Jimmy about the status of his relationship with Alicia.

This stunning reaction from Jerry that left his dad frazzled, was Jimmy's own doing. He seemed to have forgotten so soon, that he recently hinted his son that Charlie still has a thing for Alicia, after Charlie's plea to Alicia to return to him. Jerry isn't just being flippant, even though his action is nothing but unnecessary interference, he's convinced that his dad's involvement with Alicia will put him in Charlie's cross heirs.

He initially requested Jimmy to see him on Sunday in church, but Jimmy made it clear that he doesn't have the luxury of time. While on phone with the Pastor, Jimmy continued packing, as he narrated to the Pastor that Alicia's husband has moved on and now in another relationship, and as such he isn't marrying another man's wife. Jimmy insisted that age isn't on his side, and his son shouldn't expect that he would be going for the under thirties.

The Pastor's effort to dissuade Jimmy from going ahead didn't work, he then moved the conversation to other areas of concern. He then inquired about Alicia's Christian faith, and was sort of satisfied with the answer he got from Jimmy.

The conversation soon became cordial, and after spending some quality time giving Jimmy some words of advice, he'd to reluctantly allow Jimmy to ruminate over the conversation they just had.

The threats to his life that should have transcended into his pursuit for a new life and a fresh relationship with Alicia has now been thrown into a quagmire. This whole conversation did leave Jimmy in a panic mode and left him kicking off like a maniac, but the calm words of Pastor Bowers did do the trick of helping him come to terms quickly.

Jimmy soon realised his marriage to Alicia can't go ahead, and obviously; the Pastor had to do some heavy lifting to get Jimmy to see things from his point of view. After the serious conversations with Pastor Bowers, Jimmy saw sense in the Pastor's view on marriage and immediately decided to put the brakes on this trip, and delayed his trip to Los Angeles. Jimmy decided to inform Alicia of his decision to call it quits right away, and even at that, he didn't intend to return to work for the FBI during this period either.

That night Jimmy didn't sleep as he spent most of the night thinking about how Alicia will receive the message and how it will impact on her. Considering the fact that this news will come across to Alicia as a betrayal, he spent the night considering his choice of words.

The news came to Alicia as if Jimmy wanted to jump-scare her, but it soon dawned on her that Jimmy was dead serious. She immediately ended the conversation to deal with the news but then called Jimmy back. Jimmy couldn't deal with the blow back as he avoided her call, and when she eventually got hold of Jimmy on phone, she insisted that it's not within Jimmy's gift to call off the relationship and that she isn't accepting his decision to break-up with her.

The news was quite devastating for Alicia, but after the back and forth, she had to concede that Jimmy is a lost battle. The news literally broke her, and she didn't go about the break-up kicking down doors in a fit of rage but went about it benignly.

Jimmy himself felt the separation, he was an emotional wreck for a while but he'd to stay focus and stand by his decision.

Pastor Bowers had to throw Jimmy a lifeline, and that's a paid job as the church's solo guitarist. Jimmy soon took a liking in a sister in the church, and months down the line, Jimmy and Penny officially tied the knot.

www.ingramcontent.com/pod-product-compliance
Lightning Source LLC
Chambersburg PA
CBHW060729190726
48285CB00001B/125